DARREN CRASKE began his c... comic books before his pro... of the Cornelius Quaint ... *Principle. The Eleventh Plague* is the second book in the series. Craske has a knack for fast-paced, boisterous adventures and he has many more left in him to tell. He only hopes that they see print before no one wants to read them any more or he goes insane or he dies – whichever comes first. He lives in Hampshire with his wife and two children.

Also by Darren Craske

The Equivoque Principle

THE
ELEVENTH
PLAGUE

Darren Craske

FRIDAY
BOOKS

The Friday Project
An imprint of HarperCollins*Publishers*
77–85 Fulham Palace Road
Hammersmith
London W6 8JB

www.thefridayproject.co.uk
www.harpercollins.co.uk

This edition published by The Friday Project 2010

1

A catalogue record for this book is available from the British Library

ISBN 978-1-906321-85-7

Set in Sabon by Palimpsest Book Production Limited,
Grangemouth, Stirlingshire

Printed and bound in Great Britain by Clays Ltd, St Ives plc

Mixed Sources
Product group from well-managed
forests and other controlled sources
www.fsc.org Cert no. SW-COC-1806
© 1996 Forest Stewardship Council

FSC is a non-profit international organisation established to promote the
responsible management of the world's forests. Products carrying the FSC
label are independently certified to assure consumers that they come
from forests that are managed to meet the social, economic and
ecological needs of present and future generations.

Find out more about HarperCollins and the environment at
www.harpercollins.co.uk/green

To my smiley little monkey

ACKNOWLEDGEMENTS

The Eleventh Plague would certainly not have been either possible or half as much fun to write, without the names listed below.

Consequently, I am duty bound to say thanks:

To Tracy, Aimee and Riley for the fun, love, laughter and amusement they provide me on a daily basis. To all the diligent folk at The Friday Project and HarperCollins, with special thanks to Scott Pack for his unwavering faith and editorial guidance. To Carol Anderson for some exceptionally fine editing support. To my stalwart friend, Karl Arlow (who hates spoilers, so won't let me discuss what I have planned anymore which is a bit of a shame). Lastly, I would like to thank a certain conjuror for introducing himself, giving me the inspiration and impetus to write some rollicking, thrilling and fun adventures, such as the one you hold in your hands.

There are many more tales of the Cornelius Quaint Chronicles to come in the near future. Some will shock, some will thrill, some will entertain and some will be downright despicable, but I do hope that you will come along for the ride because it wouldn't be the same without you.

You still have not seen the last of me.

Darren Craske, November 2009

THE STORY SO FAR . . .

WHEN A SERIES of grisly murders coincided with the arrival in London of Dr Marvello's Travelling Circus, the performers found themselves caught up in some rather sinister goings-on. Prometheus the strongman was named the chief suspect and it fell to Cornelius Quaint – master conjuror and the circus's proprietor – to clear his name. Ably assisted by his Eskimo valet, Butter, and his clairvoyant confidante, Madame Destine, Quaint set out to discover the identity of the true killer before it was too late.

What appeared to be random slayings were actually part of an elaborate plot by his arch-nemesis, the French mercenary Antoine Renard – a plot designed to keep Quaint's attention solely on his strongman's plight, and off the Frenchman's real objective. Renard was being employed by the Hades Consortium – a nefarious organisation that had crossed Cornelius Quaint's path before. They sought a legendary elixir believed buried in a London cemetery. Over the centuries it had mutated into a deadly poison, its potency augmented tenfold by its contact with water, which was not good news considering their target was the River Thames itself.

Not without considerable hardship to himself and his troupe, Quaint managed to stop the Hades Consortium's plans, and he watched Renard drown before his eyes. But the conjuror's trials were far from over. He soon learned that the Thames was just the rehearsal. The main act was the River Nile in Egypt, and Cornelius Quaint could not help but consider the possibility that he was too late to stop what was already in motion . . .

CHAPTER I

The Eager Pupil

FANTOMA, EGYPT, 1853

'I S IT TRUE, teacher? Is Antoine Renard dead?' The young woman stormed into the cavernous chamber. The meeting room was almost pitch-black save for a row of torches affixed to a far wall, and their flames snapped at her as she walked past.

The older man sitting at the oval-shaped table barely acknowledged her arrival. His grey eyes watched the olive-skinned woman scrape a wooden chair across the stone floor and slump herself into it before he spoke, a voice coated with a thick Italian accent. '*Si, la mia allieva*. It is true,' he said.

'Then my operation here in Egypt is sunk! If Renard is dead, then so is everything that we worked so hard to procure in London. That poison was essential for what I have planned for the Nile.' Spying the look of discontent on the man's face, the woman quickly lowered her guilt-ridden eyes to the floor. 'I have failed, teacher.'

'Almost,' growled the man. 'Prior to his premature death, Renard was able to dispatch the consignment of poison into another operative's hands. The Hades Consortium has more than one dog in our kennel.' Without warning, the Italian slammed his fists down onto the marble table, sending a glass carafe crashing to the floor. 'London was a mistake, Jocasta! I was against it from the start! You allowed Renard too much slack on his leash, and look what happened as a result. He derailed a delicate operation that took months to plan – and for what? A petty feud with a *circus magician* of all things!'

The woman's eyes flared. 'But surely you do not think that I had any power over *that*, teacher. Antoine Renard was always reckless!'

'As are you, Jocasta, but as my protégée I keep you tamed – at least, that is what I tell the Hades Consortium's inner stratum. I am quickly running out of favour with the council, and more rides on the success of your plot than just your own fortunes. You have a lot of ground to make up.' The Italian twisted his bulk awkwardly in his seat as if constricted by a straitjacket, and he washed his tongue over his pearly teeth. 'It was not just Renard that we lost in London, remember? The Hades Consortium had been planning Commissioner Dray's ascension within Scotland Yard for years! Sir George will not be best pleased to hear of his son's death.'

All colour drained from the woman's face. 'He . . . does not *know*?'

'Sir George is busy with Consortium affairs in India at present. I do not think the news has reached his ears. Perhaps you would like to be the one to tell him, *cara mia*. After all, it was your botched operation that was to blame for his son's death.'

'Surely you are more experienced in reporting failure to Sir George, teacher – or need I mention China?' said the woman, with a vague smile. 'It is not just me that has lost cultivated resources of late.'

The Italian fumed. 'That bloated Chinaman was a stubborn fool. There was no way that he would allow us to encroach upon his boundaries, especially after what happened in the old days. There is bad blood between Cho-zen Li and me, let us leave it there. If I were you, I would be more concerned with my *own* affairs.'

'I promise you, this project will be a success!' said the eager pupil, her smile now in full bloom. 'On New Year's Eve, the River Nile will be awash with the deadliest poison known to man. Egypt will be on its knees begging for mercy, and there are no circus magicians to get in the way this time.'

CHAPTER II

The Fond Farewell

'WHERE THE HECK is Mr Q?' the knife thrower asked the Chinese identical twins, as she coiled her hair nervously around her fingers. 'He should be here by now!'

Dressed in their matching leotards, decorated with the black and white symbols of their namesakes, Yin and Yang exchanged awkward glances and silent thoughts.

'He will be here soon, Ruby,' insisted Yang. 'The boss would not miss a party, especially one where he is the guest of honour. He is probably on his way here as we speak.'

'My brother is correct,' added Yin, also seeking to mellow Ruby's mood. 'The boss is a man of his word. When has he ever been late before?'

A sudden hush descended upon the trio. Poor Ruby, she had worked so hard to plan this party to be perfect. It was just a shame that she had not factored Cornelius Quaint's legendary unreliability into the equation. Although capable of great marvels whilst on stage, the conjuror's timekeeping was decidedly less than marvellous.

'Well . . . there was that one time in Spain,' said Yang. 'We had to perform the entire programme without him.'

'And Austria. Don't forget Austria,' added Yin, unhelpfully.

'Ah, yes. Quite right, brother,' nodded Yang. 'I had forgotten Austria.'

'He spent almost six hours being measured for a new suit and we missed getting our papers stamped, remember?' offered Yin. 'We had to wait three days at the border before they would let us in.'

'Now that you come to mention it . . . the boss is always late,' Yang said.

'Actually, he is renowned for it,' agreed Yin.

'Thanks, boys,' said Ruby through gritted teeth. 'You're just the tonic I needed. Remind me never to come to you if I'm feeling suicidal – which might be in about ten minutes if the boss doesn't show up!' The young woman threw her arms in the air and moved swiftly away from the acrobats, leaving them to practise their routine.

The platform at Grosvenor Park railway station was a crowded affair. Colourfully decorated banners, streamers and flags adorned the side of the circus steam train. A hand-painted sign reading 'Bon Voyage' hung from the iron girders of the roof, and all the company's performers and crew had flocked onto the platform awaiting the arrival of their employer. Clowns, jugglers and acrobats were decked out in all their glory in readiness to perform a proper send-off befitting the much-respected – albeit currently absent – circus proprietor.

Jeremiah the clown had painted himself up (reluctantly, if the look on his face was any indication) and stepped into his most garish outfit alongside his co-performer, Peregrine, who was dressed in a striped shirt and high trousers – high trousers, indeed, for the dwarf, who measured just shy of two and a half feet tall. Whilst Jeremiah gulped from a bottle of nondescript brown liquid, Peregrine seemed oddly transfixed by the cuffs of his shirt.

'Perry, you've got a face like a slapped arse,' said Jeremiah. 'Have a swig of this stuff – it'll cheer you up no end.' He offered the bottle to the dwarf, who pushed it away as if it were arsenic.

'Is that your homemade liquor?' squawked Peregrine. 'Christ, I ain't drinkin' that stuff again, Jerry. I'll be chuckin' me guts up all night like last time.' The dwarf took sniff of his cuffs, and retched. Standing on tiptoes, he presented his wrist to Jeremiah. 'Do us a favour and 'ave a sniff of this, will you?'

Jeremiah leaned down and took a brief sniff of Peregrine's cuff. He recoiled, clamping a hand over his mouth. 'What the hell's that stench?'

Peregrine scowled. 'It's that flippin' tiger, I swear! The bloody thing has been usin' me trunk as a bleedin' lav' again.'

'You want to have a word with Kipo, mate – that stuff stinks!'

'No wonder no one's botherin' to come over and chat!' grumbled Peregrine.

'Oh, I don't think that's got anythin' to do with it, mate.'

Peregrine looked up hopefully. 'You don't?'

'Course not. Tiger piss is a darn sight more fragrant than the stink you normally give off,' said Jeremiah with a toying grin.

As Ruby approached, the two clowns stood to attention and saluted.

'Officer on deck!' chimed Peregrine.

'Everything's ship-shape and ready for your inspection, ma'am,' added Jerry.

'It was funny the first twenty times, lads, but now it's wearing a bit thin,' said Ruby. 'I've come to ask if you've seen Mr Q – if it's not asking too much to get a straight answer for a change?'

'Straight answer?' chirped Peregrine, scratching his bushy beard. 'From us?'

Jeremiah leaned over to him. 'Maybe she's got us confused with someone else.'

'Could be,' said Peregrine, glancing at his colleague's baggy trousers, red-and-green-striped shirt and carrot-orange wig. 'We do get mistaken for the twins a lot.'

'We *heard* that,' chorused two Chinese voices from across the platform.

Ruby held up her hands. 'Never mind! I'll go somewhere else for some sense.'

'Good luck with that,' called Peregrine. 'Most people have had some of Jerry's grog so there ain't much sense left in many of 'em. If the boss doesn't show his face soon this party will be over without him!'

'Thanks for reminding me,' said Ruby as she turned away swiftly, bumping headlong into a diminutive Inuit dressed in a smart pinstripe suit, with an off-kilter bow tie at his neck.

'Sorry, Miss Ruby. I did not see you,' the Inuit said, doffing an invisible cap.

'Butter! At last, someone capable of normal conversation,' Ruby said, steering the Inuit away from the cackling clowns. 'If anyone knows where the boss is, it's going to be you.'

Butter beamed up at the pretty knife thrower with besotted eyes.

'Well?' Ruby asked, with a shrug.

'Yes, thank you, Miss Ruby. The party is all going swimming!'

'We've still got a way to go on your English lessons, I see,' said Ruby. 'I meant "Well?" as in "Well . . . have you *seen* him?"'

'Seen who?' Butter enquired.

'Who do you think?'

Butter laid his head on one side. 'You can give me a clue, yes?'

'I had better luck with the clowns,' Ruby said under her breath. 'A bossy six-foot-tall conjuror with a shock of silver curls. Ring any bells?'

Butter broke into fits of giggles. 'Oh, Miss Ruby, I have played this game. It is much fun! And now I must guess who you say, yes?'

Ruby was not quite at the end of her tether – but she was making extremely good progress towards it. 'This isn't a game, Butter! I'm asking if you've seen our illustrious leader anywhere.'

'Oh . . . you mean Mr Quaint?' the Inuit asked.

'Unless you know any other bossy six-foot-tall conjurors with shocks of silver curls?' enquired Ruby.

Butter carefully considered the question. 'No. I do not think that I do.'

'Never mind. I'll find Prometheus and ask him,' Ruby said, turning around.

'Prometheus, yes. I know where the strongman is!' said Butter.

'Yes?' asked Ruby expectantly.

'Yes!' announced Butter with pride.

'You know where Prometheus is?' asked Ruby again, just to be sure.

'Yes!' repeated Butter.

'You're absolutely sure?'

'Yes! Yes!'

'Okay then . . . so where is he?' Ruby asked.

'He is with Mr Quaint,' the Inuit replied.

Ruby waved goodbye to her tether as it vanished into the distance. She should have won some kind of award for keeping her composure, but as she bent down closer to the Inuit, it was clear that her fixed smile was obviously causing her some discomfort.

'And . . . why did you not *tell* me that when I asked?'

'But Miss Ruby, you ask if I have seen Mr Quaint, yes? For which the answer is no, but for where is our strongman, it is yes. Prometheus has a spotty business.'

Ruby waggled her finger in her ear. 'He's got a spotty what?'

'Prometheus says he is going with the boss for "a spotty business down by the docks",' the Inuit confirmed.

It was at times such as this that Ruby had often wished that she had listened to her mother, and learned skills more befitting a young lady than being able to catch a knife between her teeth from twenty yards.

'When did he tell you that?' she asked Butter.

'It has been more than two hours, Miss Ruby.'

'*Two hours?*' groaned Ruby.

'Something is wrong perhaps?' asked Butter.

'When the boss is involved it's pretty much guaranteed, isn't it?' said Ruby, darting off down the platform and leaving the Inuit in a state of bewilderment. 'I'll find Madame Destine. If anyone can tell me whether Mr Q is actually going to bother showing up to his own farewell party, it's her!'

Ruby pushed through the eclectic collection of circus performers towards a veiled woman kneeling near the front of the brightly decorated steam engine, seemingly immersed in deep conversation with a muscular tiger.

'You naughty pussycat, you should be ashamed of yourself,' the woman said to the tiger, her lilting French accent draping every syllable in silk. 'Peregrine is a dwarf, not one of your cubs.' The tiger growled back its discontent. '*Oui*, I am well aware that he is small and furry, but it is not acceptable. You will just have to find something else to snuggle up with at night!' Madame Destine looked up at the white turban-wearing, gangly Indian, holding the tiger's chain. 'I think Rajah has learned his lesson, Kipo. Hopefully Peregrine will no longer have cause for complaint.'

'Bad Rajah! No supper for you,' said Kipo, as he tugged on the tiger's chain and led him back onboard the steam train.

To anyone else this might have seemed a strange affair, but for Ruby Marstrand it was a common occurrence as part of Dr Marvello's Travelling Circus. Surrealism she could handle – it was reality that was sometimes difficult to grasp.

'Destine, thank God I've found you,' she said breathlessly.

The elderly fortune-teller lifted her white lace veil. She was in her seventies, but her complexion was smooth and her misty blue eyes sparkled with youthful vigour. 'Something that I can do for you, *ma chère fille?*'

'I hope so,' replied a flustered Ruby. 'Mr Q hasn't turned up and Butter says he's gone to the docks with Prometheus. How can this be a farewell party if the guest of honour is nowhere to be found?'

Madame Destine rested her hand upon Ruby's shoulder. 'Calm yourself, child. I can feel your apprehension.' Although her exceptional clairvoyant abilities had been noticeably infrequent of late, Destine was still possessed of her uncanny ability to perceive the emotions of those close to her – not that it was all that difficult on this occasion. 'Do not worry, my sweet. Cornelius has a habit of making a grand entrance. When he arrives I shall let him know how he has worried you so. In the meantime, please try to enjoy yourself. This is a party, *n'est-ce pas?*'

'It was *supposed* to be.' Ruby puffed her cheeks in submission and pushed up on her toes, flapping her arms at her sides. 'I'll say one thing: it's going to be awfully quiet around here without Mr Q. You've known him nearly all his life . . . how on earth are you going to cope whilst he's away in Egypt?'

The Frenchwoman's smile slipped, and she quickly pulled her veil down to cover her face. '*Pardonnez moi*, Ruby, I . . . I have something that I must attend to. Will you please excuse me?'

Ruby grabbed Destine's wrist and tugged her back. 'Destine? Are you . . . crying?' She brought the fortune-teller into her embrace. 'Oh, sweetheart, don't do that, you'll start me off. Listen, I'll miss him too. We *all* will. But he'll be back before you know it, you'll see. It'll be like he never even went away!' Ruby gently pushed against Destine's shoulders, hoping to see a smile blossom once more upon her delicate face, but the expression was as cheerless as before. 'What is it? What's wrong?'

Madame Destine looked at the crowd that bustled around them, before leading Ruby to a more secluded area of the platform.

'I am afraid that it is not just Cornelius whom the circus will miss, Ruby,' she said softly. 'You see . . . I have decided to accompany him.'

Ruby's face went ash-grey. 'Accompany him where? To Egypt, you mean?'

'*Oui*, that is so.'

'But . . . why?'

'Because he needs me,' the Frenchwoman replied.

'Rubbish! Mr Q doesn't need anyone!'

'He likes people to think that, true . . . but as you said, I have known him all his life. Far better than most. Better than he knows himself, in fact. Soon, he will be in most desperate need of a guiding light . . . and I must be there for him,' said Destine, with an audible lament to her soft tones.

'But . . . what about us? What about me? I need you too! You're the only person that I can have a decent conversation with around here without you breaking wind, talking in riddles or bouncing around the place like a rubber ball. Losing Mr Q is one thing, but losing you as well? How on earth am I supposed to cope without you?'

Destine smiled warmly, fresh tears in her eyes. 'You will cope just fine, Ruby.'

'But . . . I don't understand. After all we've been through recently . . . with what happened to Twinkle, and Prometheus being locked up. Why do you want to go?'

'That is just it, my child, I do not . . . but I must,' replied Destine. 'Before my clairvoyant gifts became clouded with inter-ference, they left me with a tantalising souvenir . . . a vision of something that is to occur in the near future. It is connected to the plot that Cornelius is hell-bent on preventing, I am certain. That is why I requested to accompany him on his voyage.'

'And it's bad news I take it?' asked Ruby.

'With Cornelius is it ever anything but?' smiled Destine. 'With my gifts absent, I cannot translate the true meaning behind what the vision was trying to show me, but even so the message was clear.'

Ruby could not resist asking, 'And . . . what was it?'

'Dark times are coming, my dear Ruby,' Destine replied. 'Dark times for Cornelius . . . and possibly for us all. The words in my vision still haunt me even now. "The past and the present shall entwine once more. Beware the dawn of the Eleventh Plague." I can only assume that it refers to Cornelius's impending quest. After all, was Egypt not visited by ten biblical plagues? The poisoning of the River Nile would certainly fit amongst their number. With my prophetic gifts playing hide and seek, it is like taking a leap of blind faith, and I must accept much. It is most disconcerting for a clairvoyant to be faced with an unknown future, Ruby. I only pray that the fog in my mind will clear once we arrive in Egypt.'

'But what if it clears too late?' asked Ruby.

'I do not know, but I have to try,' replied Madame Destine, taking Ruby's hands within her own. 'Cornelius is about to take the first step on a path that will be long and difficult, and the more that he progresses, the darker the path will get.' The Frenchwoman smeared her wrist underneath her eyes, wiping tears from her cheeks. 'I fear that if I am not there to guide him back to us . . . he will be lost for ever.'

CHAPTER III

The Unfriendly Negotiations

CHRISTMAS WAS LESS than a month away and scenes of revelry were not limited to the platform of Grosvenor Park station. In keeping with the season, all throughout London traders were busy selling roasted chestnuts in crowded market places, carol singers congregated on many a street corner, and the sound of brass instruments filled the air. Despite the onset of the season, however, there was one man severely lacking in any good will.

'This is getting rather monotonous, Ferret,' snarled Cornelius Quaint, sucking hard on his bruised knuckles. 'For the last time . . . what you know about the Hades Consortium's plans for the River Nile? Where is that damn poison?'

The owner of the neck that Quaint's other hand was wrapped around wheezed pathetically before collapsing onto the cold, wet cobbles of the fogbound alleyway.

'I already told you, Mr Q – I dunno what you're on about, I swear I don't!' Bob Ferris ('Ferret' to those unfortunate enough to know him) was a loathsome individual who had crossed Quaint's path before. Lacking in many redeeming qualities, his only speck of worth was that he was often party to insalubrious information. Few aberrant activities in London failed to reach his ears, and on a night such as this, Ferret's particular variety of information was vital to Cornelius Quaint's quest.

'Why don't ye let me have a go at loosenin' his tongue, boss?' growled the colossal Irishman at Quaint's side, his brush-bristle beard twitching as he spoke. 'I'm gettin' fidgety just stood 'ere twiddlin' me thumbs . . . especially when I'd much rather be breakin' *his*.'

'Keep it at the forefront of your mind, Prometheus,' said Quaint calmly. 'We'll try the nice approach first. If this worm still refuses to talk, we'll up the stakes.'

'Look, I swear, Mr Q, I don't know nuffin' about any poison,' Ferret spluttered, getting up and wiping his fingerless-gloved hand under his nose.

'If there's one thing I abhor, it's bad grammar, and double negatives stoke my coals something chronic,' said Quaint, sucking air between his clenched teeth. 'I don't have all night to play games, Ferret.'

Still Ferret protested. 'But I don't know nuffin' about none of it!'

'I *warned* you about that grammar!' Quaint punched him in the face, and a fine seam of blood trickled from Ferret's nostril. 'Let me make this easier for you, Ferret . . . I know that poison is headed for Egypt, and I know what the Hades Consortium plans on doing with it once it gets there. I just need to know where it is right now. A man in your line of work – and I use the word "work" loosely – is surely in receipt of such knowledge.'

'Please, Mr Q, I *can't* tell you,' Ferret whimpered.

'Can't?' said Quaint.

'This is the bloody Hades Consortium we're talkin' about, Mr Q – they'll do me in!' pleaded Ferret.

'One of their crimes that I will applaud,' said Quaint. 'Ferret, you are one of the most despicable little parasites in all of London. You feed off lies and deceit like a maggot feeds off dead flesh, and even Cheapside's rats take a bath after they've been in your company. You could die right here and now in this gutter, and not a single soul on the face of this earth would mourn you.'

'Look, Mr Q, I'd love to help you, surely I would, but if I spill me guts, I'll be dead by the end of the week!' spat Ferret.

'And if you *don't* you'll be dead by the end of this conversation,' parried Quaint.

Ferret's tear-stained eyes appealed to Quaint's better nature – which was a wasted effort, for the caustic conjuror was devoid of one. 'You . . . you wouldn't do me in . . . would you, Mr Q?'

'Me? Certainly not!' trumpeted Quaint.

'Thank you, sir! Thank the Lord!'

'But I didn't invite my gargantuan friend here along for his good looks,' said Quaint. He motioned over his shoulder to his Irish cohort, and Prometheus took a step closer to Ferret's quivering form. 'I'm beginning to tire of this. Prometheus, grab his hands. Break one of his fingers for every minute that he refuses to talk.'

'What happens when I run out of fingers, boss?' asked Prometheus.

'The human body has over two hundred bones in it, my friend.' Quaint leered as close to Ferret's stench as his tolerance would allow. 'We could be at this all night until we run out of things to break.'

Ferret's bottom lip trembled and he slid down the alley's brick wall, sniffing into his hands. 'All right, Mr Q! You made your point. Just . . . just call off your dog! Maybe I do know sumfin',' he said, with a deflated sigh. 'I was in the Blue Boar last night and there was this foreign bloke, pissed as a newt. He was on about shippin' sumfin' to Egypt, and I heard him say the name of the bloke he was takin' it to. Said his name was Al somebody or other. Al Fekesh, that's it!'

Quaint's black eyes narrowed. 'He said that name – are you absolutely sure?'

Ferret's glassy eyes blinked in earnest. 'I'd bet my life on it, Mr Q!'

'If you're wrong, Ferret . . . I'll be back to cash in that bet,' said Quaint.

CHAPTER IV

The Breadcrumbs

CORNELIUS QUAINT BLAZED out of the grimy alleyway with his boots scuffing against the cobbles and his long black cloak dragging in his wake – much like Prometheus.

'What the devil is *wrong* with this world?' Quaint snapped. 'What happened to the good old days when the threat of a good thrashing was enough to weaken the resolve of any lice-infested ne'er-do-well? Now I've got to get my *hands* dirty!'

'What did ye expect, considerin' where we are? This is the arse end of London! The place is full of Ferret's kind. Maybe ye're just gettin' old.'

'How dare you!' snapped Quaint, with a prominently raised finger. 'I am *not* getting old, Prometheus! I'm only fifty-five, damn it.'

'I love the way ye say "only",' said the Irishman, as Quaint shot him a look. '"We're just off fer a stroll along the docks," ye said. "Friendly negotiations," ye said. Surely ye didn't think this was going t'be *easy*.'

'Well, it would have made a nice change.' Quaint removed his top hat and swept his hand through his silver-white curls. 'I really don't need these distractions at the moment. I've got far too many other worries to contend with!'

'I noticed.' Stopping dead in the middle of the street, Prometheus cleared his throat loudly to gain Quaint's attention. 'Are ye even aware of what's goin' on at the station right now? The gang are holdin' a farewell party, wishin' ye well before ye take yer leave . . . and where would Cornelius Quaint rather be? Out in the pissin' cold roughin' up the local sewer life!'

Quaint said, 'Hardly by choice. Running into Ferret was just a coincidence.'

'Don't give me that rot, ye don't *believe* in coincidences!' Prometheus eyed Quaint's rugged face. The conjuror was foremost his friend before his employer, but of late there had been a chasm forming between Quaint and his circus, and it was growing wider by the day. Quaint was becoming more of the employer and less of the friend. 'I'm worried, man. More than usual, I mean. What's happened t'ye recently?'

'That is a *very* long conversation for another time, Prom. There are other topics that beg my attention at the moment,' Quaint said, recommencing his stride.

'And the cares of a friend ain't one of them?' asked Prometheus, rooted to the spot. 'For years I convinced myself that I was mute, remember? I was trapped inside a prison of my own makin' whilst I tried t'figure out what was goin' on in my head. I know all about keepin' things to myself, and I know all about how easy it is t'slip the mask on and forget it's there. After a time it replaces yer real face, so much so that ye forget what ye look like.'

'This is *different*, Prom,' called back Quaint, his pace not decreasing.

'Oh, is it now? Ye've been distancin' yerself from the circus, and at show-time that just ain't like ye.' Prometheus looked ahead of him into the enveloping shadows of the wharf, but the conjuror was nowhere to be seen. Cursing, he had no recourse but to follow. 'Ever since that episode in Whitehall, neither ye nor Madame Destine has been actin' right. What happened, Cornelius? Why won't ye tell me?' Prometheus jolted to a standstill as he bumped into Quaint, hidden within the shadows. 'Jesus! Ye nearly scared the life out of me!'

'I think I preferred it when you couldn't speak,' said Cornelius Quaint, a tired smile across his lined face. 'Prometheus, you're as stubborn as a mule!'

'Must be the company I keep,' said the strongman.

'All right! If only to cease your incessant interrogation, I'll tell you exactly what happened the other night. But you might not like what you hear,' Quaint began, stepping into a shard of moonlight. 'After I prevented the Hades Consortium's plot to poison the Thames, I thought that would be an end to it. I thought that we could all go back to our lives as if nothing had ever happened. I was wrong. As our resident fortune-teller is so keen to remind me: sometimes, Fate has other plans for us. Just before I killed Antoine Renard . . .' Quaint allowed a slight pause as his lips burned at the name, '. . . for the second time, as it goes . . . he let slip that the Thames was just the tip of the iceberg. There was more of that poison. How much, I don't rightly know, but I can't afford to take any risks. Egypt is in peril unless I can find that poison before the Hades Consortium can get its hands on it . . . and that is why I have to go.'

'Why?' asked Prometheus.

'Why? Why what? I just told you why,' clipped Quaint.

'No, I mean why is it that *ye* have to be the one to go? Why not just tell the police and let them handle it? It's their job, after all, not yours.'

'Prom, have you forgotten Commissioner Dray in Crawditch?

He was a Hades Consortium puppet, and for all I know Scotland Yard is rife with them! I don't know whom I can trust, and I can't just cross my fingers and hope this all blows over – there's just too much at stake. I have a breadcrumb to follow . . . and follow it I must.'

'All the way to Egypt? And I don't suppose there's any point in tryin' t'talk ye out of it?' asked Prometheus.

'Not this time,' replied Quaint. 'You know how pig-headed I can be.'

'I'm constantly surprised,' grimaced the strongman, sweeping his large hands over his bald pate.

'Anyway, it's too late. Our tickets are already booked. We set sail tomorrow morning aboard a steamship bound for Cairo,' added Quaint.

'And ye never thought t'tell me about any of this? We're supposed t'be mates. Ye can't just swan off whenever ye—' The sentence dried in the strongman's mouth, killing it dead. 'Did ye just say *our* tickets? *We* set sail tomorrow?'

'Destine is coming with me,' replied Quaint. 'In fact, she insisted upon it!'

'Ye're draggin' *her* halfway around the world after what *she's* just been through?' asked Prometheus. 'She was *poisoned* a matter of days ago, remember?'

'I don't need reminding of that, thank you very much!' Quaint snarled back. 'She was poisoned with the very stuff that I'm trying to stop getting to Egypt! And whose fault was it that she was poisoned, hmm? Prometheus, the Hades Consortium is like a puddle of oil leaking from a can. The stain will spread further by the second unless someone plugs it up. That someone is me.'

'But ye said that ye were done gallivantin' about the globe. Ye aren't gettin' any younger, y'know!' said the Irishman.

Quaint folded his arms across his chest. 'True, but neither am I getting any *older*.'

'And what's that supposed t'mean?' frowned Prometheus.

Cornelius Quaint forced himself to swallow the words resting on his lips.

Although he wanted (perhaps even *needed*) to talk to someone about what had happened, he was not sure he believed it himself. The conjuror was certainly no stranger to the sublime, but whenever his mind replayed the events of the past week (which was frequently and without mercy) it all seemed so absurd. Had anyone told him that alchemists of the Anglican Church had created an elixir of immortality and buried it within a dockland cemetery in London, he would have pointed them in the direction of the nearest sanatorium. But that was before the bodies began stacking up, and Quaint discovered the involvement of his deadly nemesis, Renard. With the Frenchman's hand implicated in the plot to unearth the elixir, Quaint had all the proof he required. Renard's employers – the secret cabal known in hushed tones as the Hades Consortium – were searching for the elixir not for its potency over life, but for its potency over death. After centuries buried underground, the elixir had mutated into a deadly poison. Quaint was all too familiar with the toxin's effects, for both he and his confidante Madame Destine had witnessed it firsthand. Against the odds, Quaint managed to obtain the antidote, and, just in time, he halted the deadly poison's attack. But just as the elixir had mutated, so too had the antidote.

Quaint and Destine were brought back from the brink of death, but not as they once were. A bizarre chemical reaction occurred within their bodies. The antidote triggered the elixir's original life-enhancing design, and from that moment Quaint and

Madame Destine would never age, never suffer disease, and their life expectancy was immeasurable.

Whilst Destine was full of wonder and awe about what had been bestowed upon them, Cornelius Quaint's mind was racked with doubt – even though the telltale signs had been plain to see. As his body accepted the chemical change within him, a gunshot wound to the shoulder miraculously healed within hours. Gashes, grazes, cuts and bruises disappeared completely, and old muscles and limbs discovered new vigour. But there was a downside, Quaint's once brown-grey hair had been bleached an embarrassingly premature silver-white.

Still not subscribing to the notion of immortality, Quaint took his newfound lease of life as a sign that he must bear the burden of defeating the Hades Consortium for ever more. But although he would not admit it (least of all to himself) even he had his limits. He had faced danger, duplicity and discord countless times in his life, but succeeding in such a daunting task would be far greater than any miracle he had ever performed onstage as a conjuror.

'Well?' asked Prometheus, snapping the conjuror from his thoughts. 'What's goin' on in that muddle of a mind of yers right now, Cornelius?'

'Once I unravel it myself, I'll let you know,' Quaint said numbly. 'But what I do know is how this plot to poison the Nile will end if left unchecked . . . and that is a nightmare that I dare not entertain. Now, thanks to Ferret, I know where Renard sent that poison.'

'Yeah, so that'll be an end to it. Maybe ye don't have to go to Egypt at all then, eh? We can just go and see this Al Fekesh bloke and rough him up a bit, make sure he hands over the poison and we're done!' grinned Prometheus, relishing the prospect of getting his hands dirty. 'Nothin' to worry about, right?'

From the expression on the conjuror's face, there was everything to worry about.

'I wish it were that simple, Prometheus,' replied Quaint, grinding his teeth. 'Al Fekesh isn't a *bloke* – it's a place! Al Fekesh is a port just outside Cairo, a haven for smugglers, thieves and scoundrels of all varieties. If the poison is headed to Al Fekesh, the sand is already spilling from the hourglass, my friend . . . and Egypt doesn't have much time left.'

CHAPTER V

𝕿𝖍𝖊 𝕿𝖜𝖔 𝕭𝖎𝖗𝖉𝖘 𝖆𝖓𝖉 𝖙𝖍𝖊 𝕾𝖙𝖔𝖓𝖊

A HANDFUL OF MILES from Cornelius Quaint's position, standing outside a ramshackle old tavern on the outskirts of Wapping, a stunted figure hugged the shadows of the terraced street. More of rodent descent than human, his glassy eyes twitched this way and that in search of something (or some*one*) in particular. He pulled a fob watch from the inside pocket of his overcoat and cursed under his breath. Behind him, the nearby Thames lapped against the docks, and the gentle tolling of bells on the waterfront drifted in the air. The night was in full pitch. Midnight had long since passed, and all the warehouses along the docks were settled under a blanket of quiet, the perfect atmosphere for subterfuge. Like a changing of the guard, when those who walked in daylight retired to their homes, those who dwelt in twilight embraced the comfort of shadows. Hearing a stifled wheeze nearby, the man embraced the shadows that much deeper, and soon an ungainly red-haired fellow limped along the silent street towards him.

'You are late, Herr Ferris,' he said, speaking raw English laden with an unmistakable Germanic twang as he stepped into the wan light of a lantern affixed above the tavern's entrance. His face was unimpressive, neither particularly handsome nor memorably ugly. Heinrich Nadir was as unobtrusive a fellow as any man could be. The sort that you would walk past in the street without giving him a second thought – exactly how he preferred it.

Ferret's bloodied face lit up, and he limped his way over to the man's side. 'Evenin', Mr Nadir. Sorry I'm late. I had a bit of bother, courtesy of one Cornelius flippin' Quaint,' he said, as he picked a clot of dried blood from his nose and wiped it upon his lapel.

'You will be suitably recompensed for your inconvenience, Herr Ferris. So, tell me: did Quaint take the bait?' asked Nadir.

'Good and proper! I did me old "I don't know nuffin'" routine, and then told him that name you said. You should've seen his eyes light up!' Ferret sniggered, rocking back and forth on the balls of his feet. 'I wish I could see the look on his face when he finds out what's comin'. But I've gotta say, mate . . . your lot are taking an awful risk, aren't they? Lettin' him get so close? Why not just do 'im in now before he can cause any more trouble?'

'Because I have my orders, Herr Ferris, that is why,' Heinrich Nadir replied, his leather gloves squeaking as he clasped his gloved hands together. 'My employer has had previous business with Cornelius Quaint. He knows the man is tenacious, and notoriously hard to kill, and he wishes him to be dealt with quietly. That is why I have been assigned to follow Herr Quaint's every move. When his vessel departs for Cairo tomorrow, she shall also have *me* as a passenger. Thanks to my colleague Renard, I will be transporting the consignment of poison to Egypt personally . . . but whereas the toxin will arrive safely, Herr Quaint will not.'

'So your lot get your poison, and Cornelius Quaint gets thrown into the bargain, eh? Talk about killin' two birds with one stone!' laughed Ferret.

Nadir smeared a grin over his thin mouth. 'Actually, Herr Ferris, the Hades Consortium prefers to set a cat amongst the birds . . . and let them kill each other.'

CHAPTER VI

The Parting Shot

BY THE TIME Cornelius Quaint and Prometheus returned to Grosvenor Park station, the party atmosphere had long since ceased. All that was left on the platform were some discarded banners and streamers – as well as Jeremiah, surrounded by empty bottles, snoring like a hibernating grizzly bear. The conjuror and the strongman retired to their bunks, with Quaint contemplating where the night's discovery had taken him, and how much further he would need to go before he saw its end.

The following morning, Quaint and Madame Destine were up before the lark, and were packing to be ready for the long voyage. Butterflies swarmed in Destine's stomach, and unremitting tears stained her soft cheeks as she said goodbye to her friends, flittering from one cabin to the next. Quaint was his usual insular self. The woes of his mind had yet to lift from the previous night's foray into London's backstreets.

Out on the station platform, the company of circus folk lined up alongside the steam train. Quaint spoke to them each of them in turn, striding down the line with his hands linked behind his back like a sergeant major inspecting his troops. He shared a wink with Jeremiah, a tug of Peregrine's beard and a warm smile with Yin and Yang. Quicker than he anticipated, he came to the final three performers in the line – the three he had dreaded bidding farewell to the most: Butter, Prometheus and Ruby. He spoke to them all at once, spreading his gaze between them, never letting his eyes linger long before switching to another, keeping one step ahead of his emotions.

'Well . . . this is it,' he said, tilting on the balls of his feet. 'Butter . . . I leave our family in your very capable hands. They can be a rowdy bunch, but I have no doubt that they will continue to function as exemplarily for you as they do for me.' Quaint cupped a hand to Butter's ear. 'If the clowns get out of hand, just threaten to set Rajah on them – that's what I do.' Butter sniggered into his hands as Quaint turned to Ruby. 'My dear child, it is with my sincerest apologies that I was forced to miss the send-off that you so thoughtfully organised on my behalf last night. An urgent situation arose that commanded my full attention, but know that if there were any way that I could have avoided it, I most certainly would have. You are a very special young woman, my dear. You make me, and your old mentor Viktor, most proud.' He leaned closer and pecked the knife thrower on the cheek, sending a crimson flush to Ruby's cheeks. Quaint took a deep breath as he gripped Prometheus's great hand. 'And as for you, my friend . . . it'll take some getting used to, you know, turning around expecting you to be watching my back and yet finding you absent. Fear not, though, the Madame has offered to step in and be my brawn should the need arise . . . of which there is a high probability, it must be said.' Quaint took a step back, raising his voice to address the entire troupe. 'Madame Destine and I will only be away for a couple of months at the most. In that time, I expect each and every one of you to pull together like the family you are, and continue to do what you do best – namely, put on the best damn circus that this country has ever seen, bar none!' Quaint lowered his head. 'You may disperse to your duties.'

As the rabble broke ranks and rushed to shake Quaint's hand and hug Madame Destine, the fortune-teller felt a great twinge inside her heart. The conjuror had made a vow that he would come back home to their family. She only hoped it would not become a vow that he was forced to break.

A short time later, Quaint was alone in his office onboard the circus locomotive, packing a large canvas bag. There was a gentle tapping against his door, almost too faint to be heard. The door opened slowly, Butter's wizened faced poking gingerly around it.

'Am I not intruding?' he asked.

Quaint smiled. If ever there were something to lift his spirits, it was Butter's cheerful demeanour. Although the cloud hanging over his head could not be ignored indefinitely, perhaps Butter might succeed in pushing it aside for a while.

'No, Butter,' replied Quaint, a trifle confused. 'I mean, yes, Butter. That is to say: no, you are *not* intruding. Come on in.'

Butter entered, seating himself upon the edge of Quaint's bunk. He pulled down the hood of his sealskin parka and fixed his dark eyes onto the conjuror's like a hound awaiting a scrap at his master's table.

'Something on your mind, Butter?' enquired Quaint.

'I wish to speak prior to your departure. Is that agreeable to you?' Butter asked, in his usual childlike fashion.

'My Inuit friend, it is *most* agreeable to me,' said Quaint, 'as long as you don't mind my continuing to pack as you talk. The Madame and I leave for Dover within the hour.'

'Indeed, and it is of your journey far that I wish to speak,' said Butter, toying with the fur trim of his sealskin parka, stoking his courage. 'You say I now take care of circus whilst you are gone away, yes? I wish to know how long please?'

'As long it takes,' replied Quaint gruffly. 'That poison could be halfway to Egypt by now, and my best bet is to try to stop it at the source. The Hades Consortium is a crafty pack of buggers, they'll have covered their tracks. Thankfully, I know the country well. I spent a lot of my time there back when I was with . . .' Quaint's eyes dimmed as an old reminiscence passed through his mind. 'Well . . . I mean, when I was a *younger* man.'

'And what am I to do whilst you are gone, boss?' the diminutive Inuit asked.

'You carry on as normal, of course. You're my deputy, Butter. I'm relying on you to hold the troops together in my absence.'

'But . . . what if I cannot live up to your example, boss?' asked Butter.

'I wouldn't expect you to,' smiled Quaint, with a pat on the Inuit's head. 'But you'll be perfectly fine. You won't be on your own. Ruby and Prometheus will be about if you need them, and there's always Yin, Yang and Kipo too. And then of course if you get really desperate you can always rely on the clowns . . . although for the life of me I can't imagine for what.'

Butter cocked his head. 'But why must Madame Destine go also?'

'To keep me from making a fool of myself, keep me on the right track, and to stop me from getting myself killed,' Quaint said, with a grin. 'Although, not necessarily in that order.'

Butter rose from the bunk and threw his arms around the

conjuror, his stature bringing him just past Quaint's waist. The tall man looked down in surprise at such an unexpected display of affection.

'I think that I will miss you much, boss,' Butter sniffed.

'As I will you, my Inuit friend,' replied Quaint softly. 'As I will you all.'

'You will promise me something, yes?' Butter asked, looking up at Quaint eagerly.

'Anything!'

Butter gripped his fists tight together. 'Numbers one, you come back alive.'

'And number two?' asked Quaint.

'Numbers two, you punish the Hades Consortium for their bad plot.'

'You have my word, Butter,' said Cornelius Quaint, 'on both counts.'

CHAPTER VII

𝔗𝔥𝔢 𝔗𝔢𝔯𝔪𝔦𝔫𝔞𝔩 𝔍𝔫𝔱𝔯𝔬𝔡𝔲𝔠𝔱𝔦𝔬𝔫

THE DECEMBER WEATHER pulled no punches as Madame Destine and Cornelius Quaint stepped out of the horse-drawn carriage onto the crowded concourse that ran parallel to Dover's docks. The chill wind whipped in from the English Channel and scratched at Destine's cheeks, forcing the Frenchwoman to tighten her white headscarf.

Quaint paid the cab driver and looked up at the ice-white SS *Silver Swan* moored to the wharf, one of the first passenger steamships in existence. The tickets had cost Quaint an arm and a leg, but he would have paid the price twice over if it secured a swift passage to Egypt. A sailing vessel would have taken far too long for his needs, whereas the *Silver Swan* boasted that she could do the trip in half the time. It was a proud boast, but one that Quaint was willing to place his faith in. After all, time was a commodity in very short supply. With the mention of Al Fekesh, Egypt's most notorious port, it meant that intercepting the poison was an even greater priority. Little did the conjuror know that at that very moment, the poison was nowhere near Al Fekesh, or even anywhere near Egypt. In fact, it was as far away from Egypt as Quaint was.

Almost exactly to the yard, as it goes.

Heinrich Nadir pushed roughly past Quaint, jogging his elbow intentionally, as he bustled into the terminal dragging a large wooden trunk on a trolley.

Quaint gave him a scathing look. 'Excuse *me*!' he snapped, feeling Madame Destine's grip tighten on his arm.

Nadir spun around and his beady eyes flicked up and down, measuring his broad-shouldered mark. 'So sorry, sir! My trolley has a life of its own. You are sailing today onboard the *Silver Swan* I take it?'

'*Oui*, that is so,' Madame Destine confirmed.

'*Ausgezeichnet*!' said Nadir, rubbing his hands. 'Then I shall at least be guaranteed scintillating company upon the long voyage.'

'She gets that from me, thanks all the same,' said Quaint, taking an instant dislike to the German – and rightly so.

Madame Destine, on the other hand, prided herself on her propriety, and duly curtseyed by way of an apology. 'Please ignore my companion's lack of manners, monsieur. We have had a long and uncomfortable journey from London, and his temper is most fraught.'

'Ah! Well, I am certain that the journey will calm your tempera-ment, sir,' said Nadir to Quaint. 'If there is one thing guaranteed to relax a body, it is sailing across the ocean. I wonder, Fräulein, perhaps we can meet for evening drinks after dinner? You and your fraught-tempered companion, of course.'

'We should be simply delighted, *monsieur*,' Destine replied, nudging the conjuror's ribs with her elbow. 'Would we not, my sweet?'

'Oh, yes . . . simply d*e*l*i*g*h*ted,' cooed Quaint.

'My name is Heinrich Nadir,' said the German, removing his hat.

'Destine,' Madame said, offering the back of her hand.

Nadir accepted, planting his lips upon it. '*Enchanté*, Madame Destine! Until tonight then.' He picked up his trolley and idled away towards the check-in desk.

'What a polite man,' said Destine. 'Most sweet.'

'Yes, in that he's liable to rot your teeth,' Quaint said.

'Cornelius, shame on you,' scolded the Frenchwoman. 'He was being charming, a concept that it would not kill you to acquaint yourself with once in a while.'

'Oh, come on, Destine, don't tell me that he took your fancy. The man was obsequious! Not to mention the fact that you're old enough to be his—'

Madame Destine brandished her finger accusingly. 'I may not be able to see the future any more, Cornelius, but if you complete that sentence I can accurately predict that you will be in a considerable amount of pain in your nether regions!'

Quaint held up his hands. 'I was going to say . . . slightly older sister.'

'And for the record, he did not take my fancy! I was merely commenting on how polite he was. Companioning you, good manners are a rare commodity.'

Quaint lifted their luggage, and they breezed on towards the administration desk inside the terminal building. Standing in the queue, the French fortune-teller struck up a conversation with an elderly couple and, in a heartbeat, they were discussing wine, the weather and whist. Madame Destine was soon thriving on sociality and conversation, happily chatting to anyone within earshot without the slightest thought. As her companion, Quaint was reluctantly dragged into the conversation, and he glanced to the heavens as a doddery old lady offered him a sticky boiled sweet. Something told him that surviving the trip with his sanity intact was going to be a far bigger challenge than defeating the Hades Consortium . . .

CHAPTER VIII

The Cruel Mistress

SEVERAL HOURS LATER, once night had fallen, the *Silver Swan* set sail, leaving the ragged white cliffs of Dover far behind her. The steamship rode effortlessly across the English Channel, the waves parting for her bows' blade.

In his single-berth cabin, Cornelius Quaint made a final sweep with his cut-throat razor. He examined his face in the mirror as if it were something borrowed from a complete stranger. It had the usual wear and tear for a man in his mid-fifties, but it did not look too bad. His rugged face was decorated with furrowed wrinkles around his mouth and nose; crow's feet spread like forked lightning from the corners of his black eyes, and his wavy, silver-white hair swept back from his forehead culminating in a nest of entwined curls at the nape of his neck. It was seemingly immune to any oil or creamed hair product, and Quaint had long since given up trying to tame it.

He dressed for dinner in a black, long-tailed jacket cropped tight to his waist, matching trousers, and a broad-knotted bow tie at his neck. Perhaps a good meal would remove the ache inside him, he thought. He heard the reverberations of song floating through the wall from the cabin next door and smiled, reminding himself that he was not alone.

Madame Destine struggled with a hairbrush through her long silver-white hair, her thoughts just as entangled as her tresses. Although it was not evident from her outer appearance, inside her head and inside her heart she was in mourning.

Before the elixir had touched her lips, she was in command of a startling array of extrasensory abilities, and chief among them was her clairvoyance. As a sideshow fortune-teller, Destine was gifted with the power to foresee certain events in the future. But as much as the wondrous elixir had given her, it had taken away so much more. She had come to rely upon her clairvoyance but now it had deserted her, purged from her system virtually overnight. Even with Cornelius by her side, Madame Destine felt strangely alone. She had emerged from the cocoon as a butterfly, only to lament the life of a caterpillar.

On the night that the antidote worked its magic, Destine's mind was bombarded with a barrage of mysterious prophecies, as though her gifts were eager to impart as much information as they could before abandoning her. Destine's gift had never been entirely reliable, but the lines of communication to the future were degraded, muffled somehow, and they swamped her with mismatched images and disjointed words. But as she had told Ruby Marstrand the night before they sailed, there was one residual vision that remained stubbornly present when all others faded away: 'The past and the present shall entwine once more. Beware the dawn of the Eleventh Plague.'

As far as she could gauge, 'the Eleventh Plague' surely referred to the dreaded poison that she and Cornelius were duty bound to destroy, yet how it entwined with the past was a mystery, one of many swimming around her head. Her premonitions were often irritatingly mystifying, yet there was no misinterpreting the foreboding that chilled her blood.

Formerly Cornelius Quaint's governess, he had fondly nick-named her his 'compass'. He relied on her to decipher the indecipherable. But he was not one for prophecies and riddles. He believed in the here and now, his feet fixed firmly in the present where he could see things, touch things – hit things. But in truth she was more akin to his conscience, seemingly the only person that he ever listened to (when it suited him, of course). Destine had resigned herself to a life by his side, for ever his guard, and despite having cause to regret her decision on more than one occasion (usually when the man's bullish bombast got him in trouble with authority in one form or another) she knew that her life would have been emptier without him.

'It's gone eight, Madame, are you done?' called the subject of Destine's thoughts from the corridor outside her cabin. 'We'll have to hurry if we want to make dinner before the galley closes.'

'*Ayez de la patience*, Cornelius,' Madame Destine replied, as she straightened the high collar of her long gown, smoothed down the billowing bustle at her rear and took as deep a breath as she could within the whalebone restraints of her corset. Trying to ignore the impatient tapping of Quaint's foot, she hurriedly arranged her hair into a loose bun at the back of her head, adding a string of pearls around her neck on the outside of her collar.

'Madame, please,' moaned Quaint, 'my stomach thinks my throat's been slit.'

'Do not tempt me!' Destine crackled back. 'Do you not realise that a true lady must shine like a lamp at all times?'

'Even if it attracts the moths?' asked Quaint.

Madame Destine's brow slowly cleared into understanding. 'You are referring to the German that we met in the terminal earlier. You cannot avoid bumping into him at some point, you know. There are only so many places that you can hide on a ship this size. I am ready now, are you happy?' She snatched open her cabin door and stepped into the corridor like an actress making her entrance onstage.

'You look divine,' complimented Quaint, stepping back to admire her. 'I honestly don't know why you spend so much time worrying, Madame. You'd still manage to look radiant were you to dress in nothing but a potato sack.'

'Your flattery is most welcome,' nodded Destine.

'And well deserved,' said Quaint. 'Is that a new dress for the journey I spy?'

'It is an old dress, my sweet . . . but perhaps a new *me*,' Madame Destine answered, as they began a brisk stroll towards the dining saloon.

After a few minutes, a comfortable hush had nestled itself between the conjuror and the fortune-teller as they walked along the carpeted corridors. Madame Destine teased her lips with the tip of her tongue. Even though her clairvoyance had deserted her, she was still in possession of her mysterious sensitivity to the feelings of those around her. At that moment she could read Quaint's emotions more easily than words on a page.

'There is something bothering you, Cornelius.' Destine always had a knack of phrasing each question as a statement of fact. Quaint found this a most frustrating habit – especially on this day, and especially as she was correct.

'It's that obvious?' Quaint asked.

'Your eyes always did betray you, even when you were a child. That is why you are a poor gambler,' replied Destine.

'Madame, I take offence!' Quaint snapped in retort, stopping dead in his tracks, forcing Destine to do the same. 'Did I not win the circus from those Prussians in that game of cards all those years ago? Surely that proves that I'm an *exceptional* gambler!'

'Cornelius, you are a conjuror! You have been making a deck of cards dance to your every whim since you were eight years old. Just because you are a master at outwitting people with your repertoire of card tricks, it does not make you an exceptional gambler – just an exceptional con artist that has never been caught.'

'Yes,' said Quaint, soberly. 'But I do wish you wouldn't use the term "tricks", Destine. You know how that frustrates me. It makes it sound as if any old Tom, Dick or Harry can do it. Stagecraft is within a showman's blood. It's an art form that takes years to perfect, not something that can be stumbled upon by chance!'

'I concede, Cornelius, you *are* an excellent conjuror. Your eyes are swifter than a falcon's, your hands blur with their speed, and your talent for misdirection is second-to-none – such as you are displaying right now, might I add,' Destine said. 'Enough diversions – are you going to tell me what is bothering you?'

Quaint sighed, relenting to the Frenchwoman's assault.

'I'm just thinking about what I've got myself into . . . and what I've got *you* into. The truth is . . . I can't stop thinking about it. It's plaguing my every thought. Everything is so complicated now compared to the old days whenever I would go on one of these capers. When I inherited the circus troupe all those years ago, I didn't expect them to become—'

'So much like a family?' Destine offered.

'Exactly,' confirmed Quaint. 'I know that Butter will do his best to hold the circus together, but I worry about those people after what happened in Crawditch. Leaving the circus behind was the hardest choice I have had to make in quite some time . . . now that I know what I have to lose – and especially what I have already *lost* . . . losses such as Twinkle.'

'*Oui, mon cher* . . . I miss little Twinkle's light also,' said Destine.

'I don't think there will ever be a day that goes by when I will *not* miss it,' agreed Quaint. His eyes lost their focus, blurring the ship's narrow corridor into a mire of white-grey formless shapes. 'God knows how Prometheus copes. He hides it well, but he's bleeding inside. His room on the train is just next to mine, don't forget. I can hear him at night. He weeps for her, Destine. Almost every night. I have to resist the urge to knock on the wall to see if he wants to talk. He'll come to me if he wants my ears. What could I say that would be of any comfort to him anyway?'

'Prometheus knows that we all cared deeply for Twinkle . . . I think that is comfort enough, my sweet,' Destine said, her delicate accent giving her words the ring of wisdom.

'When I saw her lying there on that mortuary slab it was like looking at a complete stranger,' continued Quaint. 'She looked nothing like the young woman I knew. She was always my little star. So full of life. So full of mischief. Of warmth, of love. When she died, it was if a vast abyss had formed inside our family. I just worry that with us gone the abyss might grow ever larger.' Quaint's eyes dropped. 'For that I feel nothing but guilt.'

'Guilt?' asked Destine. 'Do not speak to me of guilt, Cornelius, or have you forgotten that it was my devil of a son that was responsible for everything that transpired in Crawditch? You could not have foreseen his involvement, my sweet – not even I did until it was too late.'

'Instead of allowing my anger for him to consume me, I should have *been* there with the people who were in pain!' Quaint snapped, as a pair of passing passengers stared at him. He led Destine over to the large oval windows and lowered his voice to a hoarse whisper. 'Where was I when the circus needed me the most, Destine? Was I amongst them, sharing their grief, their pain? No. I was elsewhere. Otherwise engaged. Thundering blindly like a wounded bull headlong into trouble, just like I always do!'

'But that is the point, Cornelius – your involvement was crucial. That is why you need feel no guilt! Had you *not* become involved, there would have been no one to prevent the Hades Consortium from poisoning the Thames, and then neither you nor I would be here right at this moment risking all to save Egypt, would we? Cornelius, it was meant to be! We are all servants to our destinies, my sweet. You of all people should know that.'

Quaint tore his eyes away from her and rested his forehead against the cold glass of one of the windows. 'A servant of destiny, eh? That sums me up nicely. Well, let me tell you, Madame, sometimes Fate can be a cruel mistress.'

'And we could spend all night stood here in the corridor discussing what is fate, what is consequence and what is sheer blind luck, and it would not make the blindest bit of difference,' Destine said, motioning for them to continue their stroll. 'I thought you were supposed to be hungry.'

Quaint managed a weak smile. 'Melancholic thoughts tend to put me off my food.'

'If that were the case, you would be as thin as a rake,' said Destine.

'Sarcasm doesn't suit you, Madame,' said Quaint, as he held open the ornate glass doors of the dining saloon. 'Let's get a table away from other passengers. Our topic of conversation is one that I'd prefer remained a secret.'

CHAPTER IX

The First Attempt

CORNELIUS QUAINT DIRECTED Madame Destine to a table positioned next to a huge oval window etched with images of exotic swans dancing with water nymphs. The room was half-empty and Quaint relished the seclusion. A waiter appeared and assisted Destine with her chair, before hovering over Quaint's shoulder.

'May I recommend the veal, sir?' the waiter offered.

'You may not,' replied Quaint. 'What do you have in the way of game?'

'Well, we have a nice breast of partridge with rosemary and minted potatoes and a crème brûlée for dessert,' said the waiter, shifting uncomfortably under the scrutiny of Quaint's glare. 'It really is rather delicious, I must say.'

Quaint contemplated the choice. 'I'll take it. But just the main course, if you don't mind. My reputation will be in tatters if I am caught eating crème brûlée.'

'And for you, ma'am?' asked the waiter, gladly shifting his eyes to Destine.

'I will have the salmon in dill and cucumber sauce, with cheese and biscuits to follow, *merci*,' she replied.

'Of course,' said the waiter, who smiled over-sweetly and hurried off to the galley.

He wove through the white-tiled catacombs, past bustling irate chefs and impatient waiters, towards the rear of the galley, to the ice-box, seeking privacy – although not necessarily seclusion.

Heinrich Nadir was waiting for him. 'Well? What has he ordered?'

'He went for the game, sir,' replied the waiter.

Nadir grinned fiendishly. 'I knew it. See that his meal is swimming in this stuff,' he whispered, handing the waiter a small, brown-glass bottle with a cork stopper. 'The entire bottle, mind . . . I want this man deader than dead.'

The waiter inspected the bottle. The label was nondescript, but he could guess at its contents. 'Poison? You . . . you want me to poison him?' he asked Nadir.

'*Nein*, I want you to season his main course to suit his damn palette – of course I want you to poison him!' Nadir snapped.

'Right then, and . . . and you'll pay me what you said, right?' asked the waiter.

Nadir nodded. 'I am a man of my word.'

'Good, because I owe the ship's card table three months' wages. This'll really save my bacon. But won't it cause a bit of a commotion when the bloke falls down dead at the table? Chef will have bloody kittens!'

'Do not worry,' replied Nadir. 'This particular brand of poison is designed to have a potent but delayed effect. Herr Quaint will be long gone from the dining hall when the poison finishes him off. I will stick to him like glue . . . and when he is at his weakest I shall strike. I have an arrangement with one of the engineers to dispose of his body in the ship's incinerator.

Trust me, there is no way that man is going to survive the night.'

The waiter burst through the double doors into the dining hall just shy of ten minutes later. As he locked eyes with Quaint he could not help but curl his lip at him, which thankfully went unnoticed. The waiter laid the plates on the table and uncorked a bottle of red wine.

'Would you like to sample it, sir?' he asked Quaint.

'I would as it goes,' Quaint replied, eager for the man to leave him in peace. He snatched the bottle from the waiter's hand, and as the man looked on aghast, he held it to his mouth and glugged heartily, finishing a quarter of the contents with a satisfied belch. 'I'll take it.'

With a somewhat discomfited nod, the skinny waiter bowed briefly, before turning on his heel for the galley.

Quaint scowled at him all the way.

'I suppose you're going to tell me that *he* was sweet as well, are you?' he asked Madame Destine, who was despairing at his lack of manners.

'Cornelius! First the gentleman in the terminal and now the waiter? Is there anyone that you are not planning to offend on this journey?' she said.

'Can I help it if I have a low tolerance for dislikeable little invertebrates?' Quaint said, grinning like a cat. 'And speaking of which . . .'

Destine looked up, just as Heinrich Nadir approached the table.

'Ah! What a remarkable coincidence,' Nadir said cheerily. 'If it is not Madame Destine and Mister . . . um . . . I am terribly sorry, sir, I do not recall hearing you introduce yourself.'

'That's because I didn't,' Quaint replied, taking a great deal of pleasure watching the flicker of discontent blossom in the German's eyes.

'Monsieur Nadir, *do* forgive my companion once again,' said Destine, jumping to Nadir's aid. 'I am afraid that he has a somewhat unique sense of humour.'

Quaint grinned shamelessly as he loaded some partridge breast onto his fork.

Nadir shuffled his feet in quiet disgust. 'Well, Madame, should your companion not provide suitable stimulation later this evening, I shall be located in the Fountain Room on the floor below this one, starboard side. I do hope that you will consider gracing me with your pleasant company. Until then, I bid you *au revoir.*' Nadir made a point of sneering towards the conjuror. 'Enjoy your meal, sir.'

'I will . . . once the audience has gone,' muttered Quaint, his forkful of partridge heading towards his open mouth.

Madame Destine waited until Nadir had left the dining hall before kicking Quaint as hard as she could under the table.

'Ow! What was that for?' he hissed, clattering the fork against his plate.

'Honestly, Cornelius, you are behaving like a juvenile!' Destine raised her glass into the air, beckoning Quaint to join her. 'Come, let us enjoy our meal and try to put a smile back on that miserable old face of yours.'

'You do love a challenge, don't you?' said Quaint, chinking his glass against hers.

'Why do you think I have stayed with you all these years?' said Destine.

'My unique sense of humour?' teased Quaint.

'Hardly!' said Destine. 'I stay with you to keep you out of trouble!'

'You're wasting your time. Trouble seems to find me no matter where I go.'

Madame Destine smiled. 'The story of your life, *n'est-ce pas?*'

'It's a page-turner, Destine, what can I say?' Quaint said cockily. 'Although of late, I have to admit that the tale seems to have become a trifle far-fetched.'

'Even for you?' enquired Destine.

'Even for me,' confirmed Quaint.

Destine rested her elbows upon the table and focused her stare at him. 'And here I thought that I was supposed to be the cryptic one. Would you care to elaborate before our main course gets cold? What is it that plagues your mind? More guilt?'

'Not this time,' Quaint replied. He half considered a lie, but he knew Destine better than that. She was too used to his techniques to fall for any bluff. 'I just don't know what to believe any more. About what happened to us, I mean. Ever since I drank that elixir, I seem to have found myself with far more questions than answers. I can feel it trickling through my veins sometimes. Especially at night. I know it's there . . . that it's real . . . but I mean, think about it, Destine. Eternal life? Immortality? It's the stuff of a penny dreadful, surely. Can it really be true?'

Madame Destine took a brief sip of her wine before answering. 'Are you asking me if the concept of immortality can be true, or merely our recent exposure to it?'

'Both,' answered Quaint.

'Well, one answer cannot be true without the other. I am afraid that I am not the all-knowing oracle that you often paint me to be, my sweet. Since my clairvoyance left me, I can only give you my personal opinion rather than a resolution based upon fact. True, immortality is a subject that belongs in the realms of the fantastic . . . but that does not necessarily preclude it from being impossible.'

Quaint pushed the food around his plate, toying with the vegetables absentmindedly. 'So there's no way of knowing for sure if that's what really happened to us?'

Destine smiled. 'Only one, my sweet, but knowing how impatient you are, I do not think you will be content to wait until the end of time to see if we are still drawing breath.'

'Destine, I need to know *now*!' said Quaint. 'I don't know about you, but I'm not comfortable with the thought of unknown chemicals rushing around my veins. They could be doing anything to our insides. They turned my bloody hair white for starters!'

'And healed your bullet wound and repaired all your cuts and abrasions too. Cornelius, your point is?' enquired Destine.

'My point is that the stuff could be dangerous! What if we both dropped down dead tomorrow?' asked Quaint.

The Frenchwoman raised an eyebrow. 'Then you would have received your answer, *non*? And know that your fears were well founded. But what if we are not dead tomorrow? It is pointless to worry about something that you cannot influence, Cornelius.'

'That's easy for an optimist like you to say,' said Quaint, taking his frustrations out on the partridge, reloading his fork once more. 'I need more proof than that!'

'Ah! And perhaps therein lies your quandary, my sweet,' said Madame Destine, circling her fingertip around the rim of her glass. 'What is proof for one is not necessarily proof for another.' She cocked her head to the side. 'Let me put it to you this way: I can feel the change inside my body just as well as you can. I choose to accept that the elixir was genuine, and the antidote that we consumed somehow awakened the essence that had remained dormant for so long. But that is only what *I* choose to believe. You may choose to believe that it is nothing of the sort. You may choose to believe that the antidote was just that . . . an antidote that quelled the ravages of the poison just as it was intended to do. That is the simple answer. The one that requires no faith.'

'So I'm expected to have *faith* now?' quizzed Quaint, his fork halting in mid-air, inches from his mouth. 'Don't get all pious on me, Madame. That's your answer to everything. That everything has some sort of cosmic meaning, even if mere humans aren't supposed to know what it is. I'm not talking about a quest for faith . . . I'm talking about a quest for the truth!'

'Is that why you are running around the docks night after night? Seeking a fight with the truth? Or is that merely your way of trying to put the theory of immortality to the test?' asked Destine, a definite barb to her voice.

'I never even entertained the thought!' Quaint slammed his fists upon the table and partridge, vegetables and potatoes flew into the air as the plate flipped up, landing with a smash upon the floor. 'But even if I were, where's the risk if I can live for ever?'

Although she was positively incensed by his temper, and even more embarrassed by it, Destine reached across the table and took hold of Quaint's shaking hands.

'Be careful, my sweet,' she whispered. 'Immortality is a very dissimilar beast to invulnerability. You may not be able to die, but you can still be *killed* . . . and that is a very big difference – especially to one as reckless as you. Anger is never the answer to anything, Cornelius, have I not always taught you that? Together we shall find the answers; together we shall discover the truth . . . in time.'

'A coincidental choice of words for an immortal, Madame.'

'It was?' enquired Destine, innocently. 'I had not noticed.'

Quaint's eyes fell to the mess on the floor. As the waiter rushed over, he gave the conjuror a decidedly distasteful glower. It was not the mess he was worried about – it was the fact that he had tipped a whole bottle of poison onto Quaint's plate and the man had not even taken a mouthful.

'It just . . . slipped,' Quaint mumbled.

'Accidents happen; it's quite all right, sir,' the waiter said, his expression saying exactly the opposite, as he set to work mopping up the steaming mess. 'Perhaps I can fetch sir a replacement?'

Quaint waved the man away. 'I seem to have lost my appetite all of a sudden.'

'Oh, but really it's no trouble!'

'I said *no*!' snapped Quaint, to the astonishment of the waiter, who scooped the food onto a plate and hurried from the conjuror's table as quickly as his bony legs could carry him.

He pushed through the double doors into the galley and headed back through the enclosed white-tiled corridors. As he turned the corner, he nearly leapt out of his leathery skin as he bumped into Heinrich Nadir once again, taking root near the ship's ice-box.

'Has he finished the meal already?' Nadir asked.

'No, sir, I . . . I'm sorry but there was a problem,' said the waiter sheepishly. 'He appeared to get angry at something his companion said . . . he knocked the plate onto the floor.'

'Did he eat *any* of it?' Nadir demanded.

The waiter looked to the floor. 'No, sir. I don't believe he did.'

'That's a shame.'

'Yes, it is! Does that mean I don't get my money?' asked the waiter.

'I meant that's a shame . . . for you.'

Nadir slipped a knife from inside his pocket and thrust it into the waiter's heart. The man wheezed as a deep red stain seeped through his white clothes, and he fell limply to the floor. Looking around, Nadir unlocked the door to the large ice-box and clumsily steered the dead man into it, stuffing his body into the corner.

'At least the incinerator will feast on one soul tonight . . . even if it is not my intended target,' Nadir seethed, dusting off his suit. 'I can see that killing you is going to cause me some bother, Herr Quaint. Next time I will not fail.'

CHAPTER X

𝕿𝖍𝖊 𝕾𝖊𝖈𝖔𝖓𝖉 𝕾𝖍𝖔𝖙

A FEW DAYS FOLLOWING, the *Silver Swan* was far out to sea and making good time as her great steam-powered engines motored the ship through the ocean. Waking just after dawn, Cornelius Quaint decided to take a morning constitutional along the deserted deck. He had so far lapped the ship six times, a distance equivalent to a couple of miles.

Quaint strolled along, setting his eyes out to sea. Soon he came upon a gentle old man idly mopping the deck as best he could – only for a wall of water to rise from the side of the ship and soak the walkway. As Quaint approached him, he stowed his mop into his iron bucket against the railings.

'What is this now, Mr Quaint? Seven or eight times?' he asked.

'Six, Alf . . . only six,' Quaint replied.

'You'll wear out your shoe leather at this rate,' Alf said cheerily, wiping his forehead with a cloth from his overall pocket. 'So which is it?'

Quaint frowned. 'Pardon me?'

Alf chuckled to himself. 'In my experience, there're only two reasons why a man loses himself in a haze such as yours,

Mr Quaint. You're either walking to remember something . . . or walking to forget it. So which is it?'

'A bit of both, I suppose,' Quaint smiled. 'The walking helps.'

'Oh? And do you reckon whatever it is it'll shift any time soon?'

The conjuror shook his head. 'Not until we reach Egypt, at least.'

Alf nodded his head knowingly. 'Bit o' sunshine does wonders, Mr Quaint, you'll see,' he chirped, as he wrung out his mop and continued to swab the puddles of seawater from the deck. 'I'll see you on your next lap. That is, unless you manage to shift that cloud afore then, eh?'

Quaint walked past the old man, but spun around as a loud crash behind him set his nerves on fire. Two smartly dressed children thrust open the door from inside and rushed out onto the open deck. One was a boy of about five years old, dressed in a blue sailor suit, whilst the other was an older girl. All pigtails, gap teeth and pleated skirt. They were both squealing madly, running in circles around Alf's bucket playing tag. Slipping on the wet deck, the young girl careered into her brother, sending both the young boy and Alf's bucket flying.

'Bleedin' mongrels, what have I told you?' cursed Alf, shooing the children away with his mop. 'That's the third time them little buggers've knocked my bucket over this morning. Their parents need to keep 'em locked up!'

'Children will be children, Alf,' the conjuror said with a smile.

'Aye, mebbe,' Alf half-heartedly agreed, swabbing up the water. 'You got any of your own, Mr Quaint?'

'None.' Quaint held his smile, feeling the corners of his mouth twitch.

Children. Now there was a subject seldom spoken of. He was

fifty-five years old and it was far too late for him to even think about starting a family – even if he weren't blessed with immortality. But that did add another layer to the question of his 'condition'. How could he watch his kin grow up and grow old as he was captured in a perpetual state of eternity? How could he explain that? How could he expect them to live with that as he buried them one by one as he himself never aged a single day? He didn't think he could bear it. He didn't even dare think about it. No, it was better this way. *He* was better this way. With a wave of his hand he continued his stroll, his mind quickly regaining its clouded state.

He was so absorbed in his thoughts that he failed to notice the furtive form of Heinrich Nadir peering out onto the deck through the porthole set into the door behind him. The German turned to a man at his side clothed in the grease-stained garb of ship's engineer. His low brow overshadowed his simple features, and he slapped a heavy iron wrench into his open hand.

'That's the one there, is it?' he asked Nadir. 'The tall one?'

'*Ja*. Do you know what you are to do?'

'Yep. I'm going to wait for him to pass again, crack this tool onto his skull, and then watch his brains go splat all over the deck,' rattled the engineer, taking up his position behind the door.

'I do admire a man that takes pride in his work,' said Nadir.

Some minutes later, Cornelius Quaint had nearly completed yet another lap and he was beginning to tire, so he decided to make this his last. Destine would no doubt be waking by now. As he saw Alf in the distance, he steeled himself for the impending conversation. So far that morning, every time he had passed him, the deckhand had continued his conversation virtually from the last word without missing a beat. Quaint prayed that he would gloss over the subject of children. Perhaps if he were to trigger a conversation first, maybe it would throw Alf off the scent?

'Nasty storm coming in from the west there,' Quaint chimed.

'So, what would you have preferred then, a boy or a girl?' Alf asked.

Quaint could have spat.

'Me, I've got three boys and a girl,' continued Alf. 'They're all grown up now course, but when they were young? Strewth! The boys were no trouble, but my girl was a proper madam, by crikey! I swear she's to blame for this sorry state of affairs upstairs!' He whisked off his cloth cap to reveal a practically bald head, save for sporadic patches of white tufts of hair. 'I used to have a thick mop of chestnut up top, and now look at it! Old age happens to us all at some point, I suppose.'

'Hmm,' agreed Quaint. 'I suppose.'

'I think you might be right about that storm, Mr Quaint,' said Alf, looking out to sea. 'Looks like there's something nasty heading our way.'

Alf could not have realised just how right he was.

Behind him, the door to the deck silently swung open and through it stepped the engineer. He scoured the soft pink flesh at the back of Alf's skull and made a mental note to sort him out too once his target was taken care of – just for fun. Taking a couple of swift steps towards Quaint, he raised the wrench in the air . . .

Just then, the door behind the engineer was smashed open and its full weight slammed into his back. His boots skidded on the slippery deck, launching him at a rate of knots towards the ship's railings, flipping him upside down and over the side like a rag doll. The last thing the engineer saw was two small children on their backsides in a pool of water with an upturned bucket between them, their excited squeals masking his screams as his skull smashed against the ship's hull.

Quaint and Alf spun around.

'Sorry, mister!' exclaimed the boy with an impish grin, before he and his sister poked out their tongues and ran off.

'Bloody damn bastard kids,' mumbled Alf.

'Oh, it's just high spirits,' said Quaint merrily. 'It's not as if anyone was hurt.'

CHAPTER XI

The Third Crack

ANOTHER WEEK PASSED, and Cornelius Quaint wished for a far quicker way to get to Egypt. He often looked up at the sky, wishing that he had a pair of wings like the seagulls that flocked above the ship looking for scraps to eat. He had always known that getting to Egypt would mean a long and arduous journey, but Madame Destine had convinced him that he should learn to calm his mind, and focus on the job at hand when the time came. But he could not afford to let go. He was primed for action and Cornelius Quaint was not a man who liked waiting.

For anything.

It was late into the evening, and Quaint was sat at the long wooden bar in the tavern onboard the ship. It was small but comfortable, decorated to resemble the lounge of an English gentleman's club. Quaint had never felt particularly at home in those places – too much pipe smoke and bloated posturing – but Tanner's Tavern served a great pint of pale ale and the conjuror had been glued to his seat all evening, way past the landlord's bell calling time.

The conjuror's mind was characteristically patchwork, endlessly replaying recent events and, in particular, Madame Destine's words on their first night onboard. 'We are all servants to our destinies,' she had said.

And she was right, not that it made Quaint feel any better. Was it all really down to destiny? Could it be that cruel? If only he had sensed Renard's presence in London some weeks past he would not be in this situation. He would be stood over the Frenchman's grave, spitting into it. But would he be at the grave alone? Even though Renard had been Quaint's most hated foe for much of his life, the man was so much more to Madame Destine. His betrayal ran so much deeper – within her blood. Having a callous, cold-blooded murderer for a son was a heavy weight to bear on its own, but knowing that the child she had brought into the world was mortal enemy to the man that had become her surrogate son was heartbreaking. Even the conjuror had to admit there was a certain sense of painful irony about that, and, strangely, that made Quaint smile. Every now and then, he was forced to revisit his past failures – and in truth, allowing Renard to draw breath after the first time they had crossed swords was a mistake. But Renard was finally dead now. No longer could he torment him. A score had been settled, a lifetime of battles won. So why then did he still feel on edge? Why could he not allow his mind to wander free? Why was he plagued with such doubts, as if death were stalking him from around the nearest corner? Had the conjuror been gifted with eyes in the back of his head, he would have solved that mystery.

Heinrich Nadir watched Quaint through the glass of the tavern's door, knowing that this was the night that his prey would die. There had been two slip-ups already and Nadir knew that he could ill afford a third. The closer they got to Egypt, the more his time was running out. This attempt would have to go like clockwork.

The landlord smiled politely as the German approached the bar, but flicked his eyes to the large clock above the main entrance. 'I'm just about to close up, sir . . . but I can fix you a quick nightcap if you wish?'

'A small cognac, thank you,' Nadir said, battling with a twitch in his right eye as he took a stool next to Quaint. 'Not having trouble sleeping, I hope?'

Quaint did not look up at this newcomer immediately; it was only when the German spoke that the flames of recognition were lit.

'It's being awake that I sometimes have trouble with,' said Quaint, supping his ale. His sozzled eyes looked at Nadir's face, transfixed by the multiple features swirling around in a whirlpool.

'A rare complaint from a man on holiday,' noted Nadir.

'I never said I was on holiday,' said Quaint.

'Indeed?' questioned Nadir. 'You are an intriguing man, Herr Quaint.'

'I hear that a lot,' said Quaint, finishing his ale quickly.

'Can I buy you another?' Nadir asked.

'No, thanks. I need to let Charlie here get some sleep. I've been bending his ear for hours. Right, Charlie?' Quaint asked the landlord.

'Always a pleasure hearing your old stories, Mr Quaint.'

Quaint slapped a handful of coins onto the bar and, with a wink to Charlie, he slid himself off his stool and tottered in a crooked line from the tavern. Nadir watched him zigzagging across the deck, the onrushing wind doing its best to dislodge his footing – and doing a good job of it too. The German's face entertained a subtle smile, and had the landlord not been purposefully checking his pocket watch, he might have wondered about such a devious expression of delight.

'Now is the moment,' Heinrich Nadir told himself, feeling the knife nestled within his jacket. Its blade would taste blood before the night was through.

Cornelius Quaint steadied himself against the ship's railings. He was looking forward to getting back to his cabin – if only he could remember where he had left it.

He fought against the wind to open the door that led inside, tripping over the raised step. He found himself at the end of a long corridor with rows of identical doors on both sides. Feeling inside his trouser pocket, he pulled out his door key and squinted at it whilst his inebriated vision tried its best to decipher the numbers embossed upon the key's tag.

'Is that a five . . . or a six?' he mumbled to himself.

Those ales were stronger than he had thought – or perhaps it was merely the number of them that he had consumed. He thumbed his lips, bringing the tag closer to his beleaguered eyes. He decided to wait until his vision remembered what gravity looked like, and he propped himself against the corridor's wall.

The ship was quiet. It was the early hours and most of the passengers were tucked up nicely in their bunks, the rocking of the ship sending them quickly to sleep. Only a few crewmembers were drifting around the ship like ghosts, tidying their stations, locking doors, checking safety equipment. Away from the ball-room and dining saloon and a lot closer to the passengers' cabins, the occupation was scant – a fact that Heinrich Nadir clung to. He lurked in the shadows just beyond Quaint's sight. He could hear the conjuror mumbling to himself, drunkenly chastising the world for all its ills, promising to set them right in the morning.

The German smiled at how easy this was going to be.

After finding his sense of balance, Quaint then discovered that his key wouldn't work, but when he turned the handle, he was relieved to find that he had left it unlocked. He opened the door, bouncing off the doorframe and into the cabin.

Nadir rounded the corner just as the cabin door closed shut. He grinned. Now his target was caged, in a drunken haze with nowhere to run. It almost seemed unsporting to kill him in such a state – but then he was reminded of the reward he would receive from his employers and all pity went out the window. For some reason that he was not party to, the Hades Consortium had targeted Cornelius Quaint. The order to kill had come from very high up, possibly from the inner stratum itself. That spoke volumes to the German. Killing such a high profile target gave him a chance to make a name for himself, and he would not let this moment slip through his fingers. Cornelius Quaint was going to die this night – even if Nadir had to drag him to hell himself.

Arriving outside the cabin door, he pressed his ear to it, hearing the rumbling of heavy snoring from within. His target had already fallen asleep or, more accurately, passed out. Removing his knife from his jacket, Nadir silently turned the handle and pushed open the door. He hovered in the doorway for a moment, not wanting to broadcast his entry into the room. Not that it would have mattered. His arrival could have been announced by a trumpeting fanfare and still the snoring beast would not have woken. He pushed the door closed, wincing as the latch snapped noisily into place. Stepping towards his mark, he raised his knife into the air.

'*Guten Nacht*, Herr Quaint,' he said.

And then he launched himself.

The blade struck its target, closely followed by the German's bodyweight. Again and again he brought the knife down, feeling his quarry flinch beneath him. Nadir thrust a pillow over his target's head to smother the screams, and then stabbed the man's heart to finish him off. Soon, the room was silent and still.

Silent that was apart from Nadir's heavy panting, stringy spit clinging to his lips.

Still that was apart from the nervous twitching of the man beneath him.

Nadir lifted the pillow to take one final look at the man that would cement his name in the ranks of the Hades Consortium for ever.

Except . . .

The face that stared back at him was that of a stranger.

Horrified, Nadir rushed to light the oil lamp on the bedside cabinet, which was quite a task considering how much his hands were shaking. Holding the lamp closer to the bed, he could not believe his eyes. The dead man was of a broad build, with a bushy grey beard lining his chin, branching into mutton-chopped sideburns, and very definitely *not* Cornelius Quaint.

'This can't be!' Nadir gasped.

Just then, he was distracted by a woman's scream in the cabin directly next door, as a familiar deeply toned voice apologised profusely. Nadir swore and dived to the door, listening intently.

'This is E16, you lunatic! You want D16, one deck up!' the woman screamed. 'I'll have you thrown overboard for this outrage!'

'Dear madam,' hiccuped Cornelius Quaint, 'it is quite possible that my present orientation is a trifle *out of order*.'

'I'll say! Now get out of here before I call the guard!' the woman yelled, before slamming the door in Quaint's face.

Heinrich Nadir smeared the blood from his hands across the bed sheets. Yet another body for the incinerator, he supposed. Once more Cornelius Quaint had evaded death, and Nadir had run out of chances. Killing him was obviously not as easy as he had first thought. Quaint was a wily foe, and not to mention blessed. Nadir's options were decreasing, and a change in tactics was called for.

'You have the gods on your side, Herr Quaint,' he said. 'But I wonder if your luck extends to your travelling companion? If I cannot kill you . . . perhaps I can make you seek out your death willingly.'

CHAPTER XII

The Awkward Silence

THE REST OF the trip passed uneventfully.

If anything, Quaint was a little bored by the time the *Silver Swan* arrived in Egypt.

The amber-hued sun blazed low in the sky, caressing the flat rooftops of the buildings with elongated shadows. There was a tangible sense of excitement in the air. The gleaming sugar-white steamship was moored in the port, and the cacophony of dockside activity was in full swing. A succession of suitcases and cumbersome trunks were being carried from the cargo hold to the docks by a flurry of eager Egyptians. The infrequent visits from passenger ships always created a tingle of expectation among the dockland community. High-pitched whistles, wails and booming yells floated on the breeze as traders, workers, travellers and all those in between made their way around the port. It was rapidly approaching nine o'clock in the morning, and most of the *Silver Swan*'s passengers were bustling about trying to grab the last remains of the breakfast service before it closed.

Bucking the trend, one passenger was decorum personified.

Cornelius Quaint grabbed the thin net curtain and peered out of the open porthole of his cabin at the chaos on the docks below.

'Ah . . . there's nowhere quite like Egypt,' he said, taking a long sniff of the air.

He pulled on a dark grey pinstriped jacket over matching trousers, and ran a thumb down his braces before buttoning up a tan waistcoat. He rested a brown felt hat upon his nest of curls, and strode towards the door.

'Room service,' he called, knocking on Destine's cabin.

'I ordered a braised ox with a sour temperament and passing interest in bad manners,' sang a French voice through the door. 'I trust it is fresh?'

'You've been spending too much time with the clowns,' said Quaint. 'Their poor excuse for humour is starting to rub off on you, Madame.'

Destine smiled to herself, as she snatched up a parasol and a wide-brimmed hat. The Frenchwoman was no lover of the sunshine and her pale, marble-like skin was painfully sensitive to the light. Today was no exception, and she placed a white-lace scarf around her neck to shield herself from Egypt's harsh sun.

Pulling open her door, she looked Quaint up and down, giving him a satisfactory nod of approval. 'You took my advice about the suit, I see. It slims down your waist and accentuates your shoulders nicely,' she said, stifling a yawn.

'Bad night's sleep, Madame?' Quaint asked.

'Non, just a malaise that has set in over the past few weeks. Perhaps it is all this time at sea. Other than our brief stops en route, I have not set foot on dry land for a long time. Now that we are finally at our destination, I must admit a slight fatigue. The hours on ship seem to obey a different clock than on dry land.'

'I know what you mean,' nodded Quaint, offering the Madame

the crook of his arm. 'Can you believe it was Christmas a couple of days ago? We did well getting an invitation to Captain Adamson's table. All the best goose and the finest of wines! Do you know it's the first Christmas dinner that we've spent apart from the circus in years?'

'Oui, my sweet, I thought that also,' said Destine. 'Although, I admit that I certainly did not miss Jeremiah's brandy butter. I spilled some once and it almost burned a hole in the train's flooring.'

'Brandy butter? Is that what that stuff is supposed to be?' Quaint rocked his head onto Destine's and laughed along with her. 'Come on, we've got a big day ahead of us.'

And the conjuror was not to be proved wrong.

Quaint and Madame Destine took their favourite table by the oval window in the dining saloon, and soon a lavish breakfast had been delivered. Whilst Destine tucked into warm bread with lashings of butter and conserves, Quaint devoured a platter of eggs, sausages, grilled tomatoes and mushrooms, topped off with a hefty slice of black pudding. After twenty minutes, with the majority of his breakfast consumed, Quaint sat quietly waiting for the conversation to resume. He ran his hands through his silver-white hair, choosing to occupy his eyes around the dining hall – anywhere but in Destine's direction. During the long voyage, they had spoken little of their plans once they arrived in Egypt – partly because the conjuror was intentionally ignoring the subject. It was only on this, the day of their arrival, that time seemed to catch up with him.

'You have something that you wish to tell me, Cornelius,' said Destine when she had finished her breakfast.

'Me? No . . . no, *certainly* not,' Quaint lied.

'*Vraiment?*' Destine asked. She removed her gloves, placing them neatly on top of the wide-brimmed hat on the seat next to her. This was a signal that she was not about to let the conversation drop. 'You are thinking about what we are going to do once we go ashore.'

'What makes you say that?' asked Quaint.

'Merely a logical assumption, my sweet – unless you have devised a way to thwart this plot without leaving the confines of the ship.' Madame Destine blinked hard. 'You have something that you wish to discuss – or is it that you have something that you do *not* wish to discuss? Have our plans changed without my knowing?'

'No, they haven't changed,' said Quaint. 'We're still here to stop that poison, but by now we've surely missed its interception in Al Fekesh, and that means that we're on the back foot. We're still no nearer to knowing what the Hades Consortium plans to do with it, other than tip it into the Nile. According to Renard, their plot is set to conclude at New Year, which means that we have less than a week to put a stop to it. This country isn't like England, Destine. At the best of times Egypt is unfamiliar and undoubtedly *unfriendly* territory. We can't trust anyone.'

'Not even the local authorities?' asked Destine.

'*Especially* the local authorities,' said Quaint. 'They practically make up the law as they go along here. We can't risk involving them yet. Not until we've found out more. Plus they might be a teensy bit interested in a little something called evidence, of which we have none.' He tousled his silver curls nervously. 'So I've been thinking—'

'How very unlike you,' interjected Destine.

'. . . about how best to play this,' Quaint continued. 'I think it's wisest if I venture out on my own this morning, just so I can test the water. It's been years since I was last here, and things have no doubt changed. Egypt has a distinctly murky side to it, Madame. There are some places that I would prefer you did not have to see.'

'I am no child, monsieur!' Destine snapped, defensively. 'Do not forget that I was brought up in the backstreets of Toulouse. I have seen things that would make your hair stand on end.'

'This is a little different from bordellos and burlesques, Destine.' Quaint leaned back in his chair, forcing the wooden frame to complain against its joists. 'I'm sorry, but my mind is made up. It's just too dangerous.'

'And what am I supposed to do whilst you are out snooping – stay onboard ship and powder my nose?' enquired Destine.

'Not at all. I know this fantastic little place called Agra Bazaar a few miles from here. You can buy anything and everything there. I went there many years back when I first visited this country. You'll *adore* it, Madame, I know you will . . . in fact, so much so that I've already arranged an escort to take you there,' Quaint said, chancing a smile.

Madame Destine rapped her fingernails on the table in annoyance. 'If you did not wish to be saddled with my company on this trip, Cornelius, you should have told me before we left England!'

'Destine, it's not like that,' insisted Quaint. 'Let me put it this way . . . ' He reached across the table and picked up the silver saltcellar next to a tray of conserves. Placing it in his hand, he enclosed his fingers around it, hiding it from sight. 'I'm going to have to do a lot of stone-lifting today, and some of the things that crawl out might not be very friendly. If we got separated, you could turn down the wrong alley . . . and just *disappear*.'

He unfurled his fingers one by one, revealing a completely empty hand.

The saltcellar had vanished into thin air.

'*Très impressionnant*, Cornelius,' said Destine. 'So if I am to be kept busy in this bazaar that you mention, what is going to keep you busy?'

'I need information about the Hades Consortium's operations in Egypt. How they operate, who their spies are and where they're based,' replied Quaint. 'I thought that I might track down an old friend of mine.'

'Are you sure that is wise? You have fallen foul of your "old friends" before remember,' said Madame Destine, warily.

'Alex's father was an old college professor of mine before he moved out here many years ago. He's the one who first ignited my interest in Egyptian history, the reason for my coming here back in the forties.' Quaint loosened the tie at his neck. 'Alex is a tailor, and you'd be amazed at what talk a tailor overhears. If there is a word to be heard about the Consortium, it will have reached her ears for sure.'

Destine cocked her head to one side. '*Her* ears? Alex is a woman?'

'Oh, absolutely – of the kind it's taken me a long time to forget,' grinned Quaint. 'Her brother Joran is due to meet us down on the dockside in about an hour. I'll accompany you as far as Hosni where Alex's store is located, and then take my leave.'

'Well, just promise me you will be careful,' Madame Destine said, as she collected her belongings from the seat next to her. 'I know what you are like when—'

She gasped, her hands leaping to her cheeks in shock.

Underneath her hat was a silver saltcellar.

She glanced across the table at Quaint – who was wearing the smuggest of smug grins. '*Mon Dieu*, how on earth did you *do* that? I never even saw you move. You were in your seat the entire time!'

'A magician never reveals his secrets, Madame,' Quaint said with a wink. 'The mechanics involved with making a saltcellar disappear are surprisingly simple; it's defeating the Hades Consortium that will test my abilities to their maximum.'

CHAPTER XIII

The Deadly Delivery

AMIDST THE HUSTLE and bustle of the docks, Heinrich Nadir strode down the gangplank of the *Silver Swan* with determined haste. He scurried from the port exit and across the street, weaving in and out of pedestrians, horses and camels. His beige cotton suit was marred by sweat stains emanating from under the armpits and striping his back, and he wore a hat low on his furrowed brow as he clutched a large, sack-covered item tight against his chest. Hailing one of the many horse-drawn carts that were lined up outside the port exit, he handed a crumpled piece of notepaper to the driver.

'And be quick about it!' he added, and the cart was soon on its way.

Less than half an hour later, Nadir arrived in Al Fekesh. Approaching a tavern, he stared up at the flaky painted sign above the door. This was the place. With one last glance at the dusty street around him, he entered the tavern. The morning sunlight had taken its time to bleach through the slatted blinds at the windows, and a lone bartender stood in the shadows at the empty bar. The German raised his hand to catch the man's attention – a pointless effort, for Nadir had ensnared *that* the second he had entered the tavern.

'Good morning, sir,' greeted the bartender. 'And how are you this fine day?'

'Miserable! I have spent a long journey with fools,' said Nadir, scathingly.

'Perhaps a drink will ease your troubles, eh?' the Egyptian asked, wiping the towel he used to clean the glasses over his sweat-soaked forehead.

'*Ja* . . . a large rum,' Nadir muttered, nestling his buttocks firmly into a stool.

The bartender nodded. 'In my cellar I have many quality rums. I am sure you will find something down there that you seek, Mr . . . ?'

Nadir looked blank, as if his name were a closely guarded secret.

'Nadir . . . Heinrich Nadir,' he said, shifting his eyes around him, scouring the empty bar. 'And I would very much like to inspect your cellar, *danke*.'

The bartender's dark eyes glanced at the package that the German had placed upon the bar. 'It might be sensible to bring your belongings with you, sir. We do sometimes get an *undesirable* element in these parts.'

Lifting a trapdoor set into the wooden floor, he ushered Nadir down the steps into the enveloping darkness. Nadir hovered at the bottom, fear rooting his feet to the spot. He was just about to take a step forwards, when he heard a noise from the far end of the cellar.

'Hello? Is . . . is someone there?' Nadir called out.

'Come closer,' said a gruff voice.

The German shuffled forwards as if his shoelaces were tied together.

'Where are you? I . . . I cannot see you!' he said, more shakily than he had planned.

A match was struck, and Nadir gasped as a dark-skinned, greasy face peered out at him through the darkness. The face was long and muscular, with a firm jaw sporting an unkempt goatee beard. As the light of the match waned, the fingers that held it beckoned Nadir closer.

'Is that the delivery?' asked the Egyptian, his voice all gristle and brutality.

'*Ja,*' Nadir answered. 'But I have specific orders not to hand it over until I am satisfied that you are the correct recipient. Show me your identity.'

The Egyptian struck another match and Nadir's eyes darted to the tattoo of a scarab beetle etched onto the back of the man's right hand.

'My name is Aksak Faroud, leader of the Clan Scarabs,' said the owner of the tattoo, more as a statement of fact than an introduction. He snatched a lantern from the cellar wall and lit it. 'You will open the box now.'

'As you wish, Herr Faroud,' said Nadir, as he lifted the wooden casket from the sack, and placed it on the cellar floor.

Aksak Faroud crouched down to inspect it, and Nadir saw the entirety of the man for the first time. He was in his early forties, wearing a long, ragged robe from head to toe. Clothes of function, not fashion. The garb of a desert rider. His eyes were tainted by grey shadow, and his fingernails were dirty, as if the man had just crawled out of his own grave. Faroud held the lantern over the box and ran his fingers across the engraved pattern of a sideways-tilted figure of eight – the mathematical symbol for 'infinity'. Lifting the lid, he saw twelve inlaid grooves, nine of which contained cylindrical glass vials, whereas three pockets were empty. He reached inside the box and pulled out one of the vials. It was roughly the size of his index finger, with decorative, ascending ivy etched into the glass.

'Mr Joyce will be most pleased,' Faroud said.

'I am sure that he will. But if he is pleased by that, then he will be positively ecstatic when he hears what else I can offer him,' said Nadir.

Faroud raised an eyebrow. 'Explain.'

'There was a woman onboard the ship. A Frenchwoman by the name of Madame Destine. Now, I have proof that she is possessed of a fantastic gift . . . and one that would suit a man like Herr Joyce's needs most spectacularly,' explained Nadir.

Faroud's stony expression did not budge for a second. 'And what makes you believe that this woman would be of interest to Mr Joyce?'

'She is able to see the future!' Nadir saw the look of distrust flicker in the Egyptian's eyes and spoke quickly to seal his words. 'I am serious, Herr Faroud. She travelled here with an Englander . . . the very same man that I was ordered to kill, yet he evaded my best efforts to do so.'

'An Englander?' Faroud's dark eyes narrowed into slits. 'How frequently they have come to desecrate my country! I have killed many who have tried.'

'Good for you,' chirped Nadir. 'And would Mr Joyce not profit greatly from a woman who could predict the future at his merest whim?'

Faroud pondered for a moment. 'This was not part of my agreement. I am merely supposed to collect this casket and deliver it to the British Embassy. However, your words give me pause. I will take you to Mr Joyce. If you can convince him of this woman's worth, perhaps he will let you live.' Faroud offered a tentative smile towards the German. 'Perhaps.'

CHAPTER XIV

𝔗𝔥𝔢 𝔗𝔴𝔬-𝔉𝔞𝔠𝔢𝔡 𝔐𝔞𝔫

AT THE EMBASSY in Cairo, Godfrey Joyce was not a happy man. Far from joyous at the best of times, this morning he was possessed of a particularly foul distemper. He was facing pressure on all sides, and not all of it courtesy of the British government, for Mr Joyce was a duplicitous man. He had successfully juggled careers both as British attaché to Egypt and as a Hades Consortium spy for several years, feigning servitude to Her Majesty Queen Victoria whilst secretly plundering the Empire's secrets. It was Joyce's foremost desire to gain higher notoriety within the Hades Consortium's inner circle, and he was fully prepared to sell his soul to achieve it. However, the urgent communiqué that he had just received was not sitting well on his portly stomach. His employers had requested his delivery of a certain casket, and with the Hades Consortium, a request was always construed as an order.

A gentle knock on his office door disturbed his discomfort, and a plump young man entered. 'Good morning, Mr Joyce,' he said cheerfully. 'It seems you have two gentlemen to see you this morning. Aksak Faroud, of your previous acquaintance, and one other gentleman. A rather *unkempt* individual, if I may be so bold, sir. They aren't in the appointment book, so I thought I had better check with you.'

'Faroud, eh? Oh, don't you worry about that, Reginald. He's got something of interest for me I hope,' Joyce said. 'Send him on in, lad.'

Joyce twisted around a small mirror mounted on his desk, checking his appearance studiously. His russet-red hair was greased flat against his head, sweeping down his pale face into two mutton-chopped sideburns that formed a thin moustache resting on his top lip. He was in his late forties yet his hair had a youthful vitality to it, apart from bushy eyebrows that perched like two white doves on his prominent brow. Despite the youthfulness of his hair, Joyce's face did not lie as easily. It was wrinkled with heavy-set jowls under his chin, clearly displaying his age for what it truly was. Like the man himself, Mr Joyce's face was one of conflicting allegiances.

A cough alerted him to another's presence as Aksak Faroud entered the office.

'Good day, Mr Joyce. I have the consignment from England, as requested,' he said, placing the rough sack on Joyce's desk.

'Excellent work, Aksak,' Joyce said. 'I know a certain young woman most anxious to get her claws on this.' He pointed at Nadir. 'And who is this? I didn't realise the Clan Scarabs were in the habit of picking up strays.'

Nadir offered a polite, but brief, bow. 'Herr Joyce, my name is—'

'I wasn't talking to you,' snapped Joyce, steering his eyes to Faroud.

'Apparently he is called Nadir, the delivery man from the Hades Consortium, the one that transported that casket from England,' answered Aksak Faroud.

'I am a little more than a mere delivery man,' said Nadir. 'I come to you, Herr Joyce, to inform you of an important development.'

Joyce looked mildly interested. 'You're not here bringing yet more bad news from our mutual employers, I trust?'

'Thankfully not,' said Nadir. 'In fact, I bring news of the highest quality. I have travelled from England to deliver that consignment as arranged, but there was something of far greater interest aboard the ship.' His beady eyes floated around the office, never settling in one spot for long. 'On my journey I met a very charming Frenchwoman. She is part of a travelling circus, acting as a teller of fortunes, but unlike most in her trade, her clairvoyant gift is genuine.'

Joyce snorted in sudden annoyance. 'Have you been at the gin, man? A fortune-teller? Those charlatans are two a penny down any side street in Cairo, what makes you think this one is worth my notice?'

'Her gift has been confirmed by an impeccable source, Herr Joyce, and one that carries all the confidence of the Hades Consortium, let me assure you,' said Nadir.

'And I take it that Lady Jocasta wants this fortune-teller for herself, does she?' asked Joyce.

Nadir shook his head. 'The Hades Consortium is not yet aware of this woman, Herr Joyce, nor her abilities. I came to you first.'

'Did you indeed?' said Joyce. He pulled a cigar from an ornate tortoise-shell box on his desk, and took a deep inhalation, savouring the rich taste of the tobacco permeating around his mouth. When he decided to speak, he locked eyes with Faroud and spoke without any hint of emotion: 'Aksak, take this stunted simpleton out of my sight at once.'

'Wait, sir – you must not dismiss this so swiftly!' pleaded Nadir.

'Why not? It's utter nonsense, man! Even if I believed a word of it – which I don't, by the way – what possible value could she be?' barked Joyce.

'*Value*, Herr Joyce?' Nadir's tongue darted from his mouth to coat his lips. 'Surely you can see that she is of the utmost value! Foreknowledge of the future would give any man ultimate power!'

A fog of cigar smoke masked Joyce's expression from Nadir's sight, but if the German could have seen it, he would have noticed a glimmer of interest.

'Yes . . . yes, it would. That sort of power would be of great interest to many, Mr Nadir . . . myself included.' Joyce rolled the fat cigar between his lips, coating the tip with strings of saliva. 'If it is true . . . if this woman really *can* see the future as you claim . . . then she would be a very valuable acquisition.'

'I overheard her say she was headed to Agra Bazaar, Herr Joyce, not too far from Cairo's main streets,' Nadir added. 'I can head there right away and intercept her! All I require is some assistance for her capture, should her companion decide to be a problem.'

'I have two of the Consortium's best assassins at my disposal for just this kind of job, Nadir. Silent, swift, deadly. Their résumé is really quite impressive.' Joyce sat forwards in his chair, grasping his fists tight in front of him. 'Go to Agra at once, Nadir! You must find her . . . find her and bring her to me! I will decide what to do with her *after* I have proof of her abilities – but if you are wasting my time, Mr Nadir, then my assassins might just take my frustrations out on you.'

'Understood,' said Nadir.

Joyce waited for Heinrich Nadir to scuttle from his office before glancing up at Faroud. 'What do you make of it all, Aksak? A woman that can predict the future?'

'If what the German says is true, then this woman is certainly worthy of attention,' replied the Scarab. 'And this news . . . you will share it with your superiors?'

'Oh . . . I don't think we need concern *them* at this stage, do you?' said Godfrey Joyce, blowing a flume of smoke into the air. 'No . . . I think that I would prefer to keep this little titbit to myself for now.'

CHAPTER XV

The Astronomer's Timepiece

THE SMALL DISTRICT of Hosni was decidedly off the beaten track.

For all its bare bones, this was Cornelius Quaint's destination. The intense heat had bitten at him all the way from Cairo, and so he had altered his attire accordingly. Discarding his jacket, his waistcoat was buttoned over his open-necked shirt and he wore a loose-knotted neckerchief around his neck. He adjusted his felt hat and placed his hands on his hips, sizing up the town.

It was like stepping back in time – how many years? Aside from various trading stores, scattered domiciles and a ramshackle tavern, there was little to entice anyone there. The uneven road was compacted by the frequent tread of foot and hoof, small two-storey buildings blasted sugar-white by the sand-whipped wind were dotted randomly about and a hubbub of chatter emanated from around every corner.

'Thanks for the ride, Joran,' said Quaint to a young Egyptian sitting in front of the cart. He had an inane grin fixed upon his face, seemingly finding great joy from something in the air around him. Somehow, Cornelius Quaint suspected that it was at his expense. 'Is something amusing you, son?'

Joran wore a small fez perched upon his head at a jaunty angle, but as if that was not comical enough, when the young man spoke, his voice rose and fell sharply between high and low octaves. 'My sister is very glad you come back to Hosni, Mr Cornelius.'

Quaint beamed. 'She is?'

'Yes, she said you owe her lots of money,' Joran snickered.

Quaint offered him an affected smile. 'Alexandria's got a better memory for an outstanding account than a Glaswegian ledger-keeper.'

Madame Destine sat in the rear of the cart, twirling her parasol over her shoulder.

'Another gambling debt, Cornelius?' she asked.

'Not in the way you might think.' Quaint motioned towards the young Egyptian. 'You should be fine with Joran, Destine. Just don't give him any money until you get back to the ship, or you'll never see him again. Oh, and keep an eye on your valuables. He's a damn magpie – anything gold and shiny goes straight into his pocket. He was five years old the last time I saw him, and the tyke stole my watch!'

Joran produced a fob watch from his waistcoat pocket and swung it by its chain tauntingly. 'You mean this one? You listen to him, lady. He speaks the truth. Joran still has his watch, and very nice it is too. Tick-a-tick! Still works, Mr Quaint.'

'Well, fancy that,' marvelled Quaint. 'Mind if I take a look?'

Joran was reluctant to hand the watch over – even to its rightful owner – but he begrudgingly did as he was asked.

'Would you look at that!' Quaint exclaimed, as he inspected the fob watch with his eyes aglow. 'I haven't set eyes on this old thing for . . . Oh, it must be twelve, maybe thirteen years! Lord, has it really been that long? I've got to hand it to you, Joran, you've kept it in remarkable condition.'

'It is the *best* thing I own, Mr Quaint,' Joran beamed with pride. 'I know that it was very wrong to steal it from you. Now I am all grown up, I would never make the same mistake again.'

Quaint grinned up at him. 'I'm glad you've seen the error of your ways.'

'Now I would go straight for your wallet,' Joran chuckled.

Quaint shook his head contemptuously. 'Just like your sister,' he said, as he returned his attention to the fob watch. It had a battered brass casing, with a large, expressive fascia. He depressed a protruding button atop the timepiece, and the watch's face snapped open within his hand. Poking carefully around inside the watch with his little finger, he plucked something from its insides.

Joran's eyes grew wide with wonderment as they spied a shining, golden coin.

'It's still here!' said Quaint, as Joran looked on jealously. 'It's a French doubloon from the wreckage of Napoleon's flagship *L'Orient*. Sunk at the Battle of Aboukir in 1798. It spent forty years lying at the bottom of the ocean before I found it whilst diving off the coast of Alexandria – the very same place your sister is named after, as a matter of fact. It is very rare and quite, *quite* priceless to certain maritime antiquity traders.'

'Priceless?' mumbled Joran, transfixed. 'I like that word.'

'Tell you what, lad . . . I'll make a trade with you,' said Quaint, holding up the golden coin. 'If you give me back my watch, I'll let you keep that coin. What do you say?'

The word 'priceless' still buzzed around the young Egyptian's ears and he took no time with his reply. 'I agree! You are most kind.' Quaint tossed the coin to Joran, and he turned it over in his eager hands. 'I think my sister is wrong about you. She says: "Cornelius Quaint is an arrogant man who breaks women's hearts as indifferently as a cow breaks wind."'

'That sounds like Alex,' said a disgruntled Quaint, turning to Destine. 'He doesn't know it, but I would have gladly traded a whole chest of those coins to get this old trinket back,' he whispered into her ear. 'Seeing this again certainly makes me think . . . the past does have a way of sneaking up on you, doesn't it? Would you care for a look?'

Destine took the watch in her hand and inspected it more closely.

'It is very . . . nice, Cornelius,' she fibbed, 'and clearly quite an antique.'

It was certainly that, all right. The casing was dented, the glass scratched, and it was a miracle the thing still ticked. Inside, underneath the main fascia, was displayed an engraved illustration of a large oval, with four circular discs positioned at the four points of the compass. Destine could tell by the expression on Quaint's face that he was chomping at the bit to explain the watch's function.

'So . . . it is not solely a timepiece, I take it?' she asked.

'Indeed it is not,' declared Quaint proudly. 'Marvellous little toy! As well as a watch, it houses a device used by ancient astronomers for measuring the phases of the moon. Later, it became popular amongst mariners as the moon not only provided them with illumination, but its phases also impacted on the tides.' Quaint clearly enjoyed the opportunity to elucidate on a subject that he knew much about, but rarely got the chance to discuss. 'It's called a Luna-meter, named so after "Luna", the Latin for "moon" – or the ancient Roman goddess, of course.'

'*Of course*,' sang Destine, finding it difficult to maintain a keen level of interest. 'Cornelius, I am sorry, but I fail to be as impressed by a thing in such a poor state of repair. Could you not have replaced it from any market stall anywhere around the world? It is in dreadful condition, and surely not unique.'

'Unique? Madame, if only you knew!' laughed Quaint. 'It was a gift to the Italian astronomer Galileo from the Vatican in 1639 as a sideways apology for his treatment at their hands. You see, Galileo theorised that the Earth was not anchored in the night sky, as most theologians believed at the time – but along with the other planets in the Solar System, it moved upon an axis *around* the sun. The Catholic Church condemned his findings as heresy. He was ostracised from society even though his studies were based upon scientific fact. The Vatican at the time even locked him up for it!'

'And you mean . . . this is *his* watch? *Galileo's* watch?' asked Destine.

'The very same, Madame,' confirmed Quaint, with a broad smile.

'In that case, my sweet, I stand corrected – I am *tremendously* impressed. So how did such a prize fall into your hands? Something else that you swindled from unsuspecting Prussians, perhaps?'

Quaint's black eyes glanced away from her, an intense distraction burning within them, and he fought a falter to his voice. 'It was a gift from my father just before he died. Back when I was a young boy.'

'Oh, Cornelius, I am sorry for doubting what I thought was merely a boyish attraction,' said Destine.

'It means a lot to me. That's why I would have given anything to own it once more,' said Quaint. 'Thankfully, Joran was not willing to barter more tenaciously, or it could have slipped through my fingers once again.'

'*Oui*, on a second look, it does rather look like a gift that your father would give. And what is this inscription, my sweet?' asked Destine, pointing to a row of odd symbols finely engraved into the watch's fascia. 'This language is unknown to me.'

'Yes, to me also. It is supposedly an ancient Chinese dialect, never recorded by any lexicographers, unfortunately. I never got around to having it verified by today's scholars, but supposedly it says "Fortune and Family" . . . my father's favourite words. He knew that I'd be fascinated with it, and he was not wrong. I always had an interest in astronomy as a boy. Remember, my father erected a telescope on the flat roof at the rear of the manor, and the two of us would sit and watch the stars for hours upon end? I think you even took to bringing my supper up there.'

Madame Destine remembered. And she remembered Cornelius's father too. Augustus Quaint had entrusted her to take care of his greatest possession – the man stood by her side. Cornelius had inherited much of his father's charm, confidence and intelligence – and all of his stubbornness. When the Quaints had been tragically killed, young Cornelius's world had fallen apart. Thankfully, Destine had been there to help him pick up the pieces. She had adopted the role of guardian angel ever since, long into his adulthood, vowing never to leave the conjuror's side until she felt confident he could live without her. It had been almost fifty years, and still that day had yet to dawn. The old watch had stoked the embers of painful memory and the sting in the man's eyes was clear to see.

'Tender memories always linger longest in our thoughts,' she said, softly stroking Quaint's shoulder. 'They are always the hardest to forget.'

'And the easiest to recall,' Quaint said, threading the gold chain through his waistcoat buttonhole. He pushed the timepiece snugly into his pocket, giving it a reassuring pat. 'Now . . . Joran has strict instructions to escort you directly to Agra Bazaar. Try not to lose him, Madame. He's not worth much, but he's the only hope you have of getting back to the *Silver Swan* by nightfall.'

'I will not take my eyes off of him for a moment.' Leaning forwards in her seat, Destine kissed Quaint's forehead gently. '*Bonne chance, mon cher.*'

'Same to you,' the conjuror replied.

With a 'cluck-cluck' from Joran, and a flick of the reins, the cart trundled off down the main concourse towards Agra Bazaar. As the conjuror disappeared amidst a cloud of dust, for once Madame Destine was grateful for being without her powers of premonition; for she feared they might only confirm the dull ache within her heart – a feeling that this was the last time she would see Cornelius Quaint alive.

CHAPTER XVI

The Vulture and the Viper

T O THOSE THAT knew of its existence, the Hades Consortium was a secret cadre of powerful individuals populating all corners of the world. It delighted in causing – and then profiting from – global unrest of its own design. It had influenced practically every landmark conflict in history, rocking the foundations of the globe, shattering alliances and shifting the balance of power in its favour. Its members were positioned throughout all levels of society in offices of power and influence, like chess pieces waiting patiently for the game to begin.

Scattered around the globe were many so-called 'sancta sanctorum' – places where members of the Hades Consortium could scheme away to their dark hearts' content. Beneath the ancient ruins of the city of Fantoma, two senior members had recently taken up residence – a fact that did nothing to placate Godfrey Joyce's distemper. He sat in the rear of a horse-drawn cart with the sack-covered item by his side, cursing every bump in the road. The painful trip was seemingly endless, and his buttocks were as tenderised as a side of beef.

'Have you ever thought of fitting cushions in this damned contraption?' he barked at the driver, ignorant of the fact that the toothless Egyptian had no understanding of the English language.

It was approaching midday. The sun was high in the sky and its relentless heat was already biting the back of Joyce's neck, igniting his irritability even further. But then his driver muttered something incomprehensible, pointing to the horizon. A wondrous sight greeted Joyce's woeful eyes.

The crumbled stone walls of Fantoma rose up from the sand all around him. Towering obelisks, once-great columns, temples and stone monoliths ascended into the sky. Abandoned centuries before, inhabited only by the ghosts of the desert, the city had been left to die, covered in a shroud of sand and dust. This was Godfrey Joyce's destination, and as the cart drew ever closer, the itch that smarted his nerves increased tenfold.

After a claustrophobic trek through chokingly dry tunnels carved from the rock itself, a very sweaty Godfrey Joyce finally arrived at a pair of tarnished stone doors, easily twice his size in both height and width. They were inset with a lavish picture of a pyramid, decorated in its centre by a golden ankh with rays of light emanating outwards. Joyce smiled at their grandeur. How their majesty was wasted on the Hades Consortium. He pushed hard on the doors, their hinges grinding against each other. In a blink, two large-bodied guards carrying spears stepped out from the shadows of the cavern beyond. They wore dark red robes, draping their bodies from their hooded heads to their ankles, with armoured adornments covering their forearms. They lowered their spears to bar Joyce's entry.

'I've got a delivery for Lady Jocasta. She's expecting this!'

Joyce said, lifting the sack-covered box. 'So if I were you, I'd best not hold me up.'

The guards parted their spears.

As Joyce moved deeper into the cavern, wall-mounted torches gave him a better view of his surroundings. The underground cavern opened up before him with every step he took. He made his way cautiously up a series of stone steps to an oval-shaped marble table positioned directly underneath a stream of natural sunlight, breaching the darkness from ground level. Pulling a chair to one side, Joyce sat down in silence, placing the sack next to him. His face was pale and sweaty – a symptom not of the listless dry heat in the place, but of the presence of the two occupants seated at the table.

Baron Remus sat in stony silence with his elbows on the table. His grey eyes stared intently at Joyce as if he was attempting to read his mind. Remus's peers respected his tolerance of neither fools nor failure, and his presence in Egypt only heightened Godfrey Joyce's very palpable fear. Remus had been an inhabitant of the Hades Consortium's higher echelons for decades. In that time he had carved some sizeable and not to mention highly successful campaigns across most of Europe, and was regarded highly by the inner stratum.

Seated next to the Italian was his protégée, Lady Jocasta. Her jet-black hair was tied into a long ponytail, interwoven with golden strands of decoration – although she needed none, for her beauty was captivating enough. Her dark eyes sparkled intensely, and her complexion glowed, exquisite in its texture. Although still an apprentice, Lady Jocasta was a powerful architect of chaos in her own right. Born into an affluent and influential Greek family, she had grown bored with an abundance of wealth and sought to entertain herself with more challenging pursuits. One day on the streets of Athens, her recklessness brought her into a fateful encounter with the Baron when she had tried to pick his pocket. Seeing qualities within the young woman that he could make use of, he took her under his wing, indoctrinating her into the Hades Consortium. Both were cut from the same cloth – a brooding vulture and a calculating viper.

'I must apologise for my lateness,' Joyce said, his palpitating heart choking his words. 'My driver was unfamiliar with the territory in these parts.'

'*Buona mattina a voi,*' Baron Remus said, waving away Joyce's words with a swipe of his hand. 'My apprentice has been eagerly awaiting this delivery for some time, Signor Joyce. A few hours will not kill her.'

Lady Jocasta's eyelids fluttered. 'Is that it? Is that the consignment from Renard?'

Joyce lifted the sack and slid it along the table. 'Yes, my Lady.'

'Signor Joyce, well done,' commended the Baron, as he stroked his striped beard, tugging at chunks of grey bristle on his chin. 'Your lackey in the Clan Scarabs performed his duty well. We should enlist him for our own uses.'

'Those damned Scarab dogs!' Lady Jocasta hissed. 'I do not know why we must resort to employing such diseased thugs!'

'Now, Jocasta, you know very well *why*,' appeased the Italian, his deep, baritone voice booming off the dry cavern walls. 'Should the need arise, those "diseased thugs" will make ideal sacrificial lambs. As you will learn one day, *cara mia*, the secret of good business is making alliances with those who are expendable. And do not let it slip your mind that had your plot in London succeeded we would not need the Scarabs' aid at all.'

Lady Jocasta bit her tongue. Her teacher's words were like vinegar on a cut, but he was right. It was his way of exerting his superiority, and she had no choice but to take notice, for the alternative was not a pleasant one.

Godfrey Joyce's eyes flicked to ground. 'Baron? My Lady? Do you still require my services? It's just that I have other matters at the Embassy to attend to.'

'Of course, Signor Joyce . . . you may go,' said Baron Remus. 'But continue to monitor events in the Black Sea and report back when you have news. I am most anxious to hear when the British Empire is thinking of throwing her lot in with the Ottomans. I have spent months laying the foundations and the Hades Consortium has much to gain from such a conflict.'

'As you wish, Baron,' said Joyce as he turned on his heel. He walked down the stone steps as quickly as he could without breaking into a sprint, eager to be as far away from Remus and Jocasta as soon as possible.

Remus stood swiftly and glared at Lady Jocasta as if she were his most hated enemy. His large nostrils flared as he gripped the backrest of his chair until his knuckles turned almost as white as his bared teeth.

'Why must you continually question me in front of others?' he seethed. 'I have a reputation to uphold and I will not see it whittled away in front of the lowers! I am your teacher, and as *such* you need to mind your tongue, *cara mia* . . . lest I order it removed! The Clan Scarabs are essential to the Consortium's anonymity in Egypt. Should anyone decide to sniff around our movements, they will take the fall. Are we clear on this?'

'Yes, Baron, of course,' said Lady Jocasta.

'And be wary of Joyce,' continued the Italian, his rage abating.

'His lust for power has not gone unnoticed. He does not care over whom he tramples.'

'Agreed,' said Lady Jocasta. 'Joyce is an integral part of my plot, but when it is done he will cease to be of any use to us. My plan will be a success, I swear to you!'

The Baron scratched at the marble table with his fingernails, fighting an obvious irritation. 'So you say . . . but still I await assurances. It is time that you explained in detail this plot of yours. Why can we not just dump the poison in the Nile and forget about it? Why must we wait?'

'If it is assurances that you seek, teacher . . . then I shall give them to you.' Lady ,Jocasta reached across the table for a large roll of parchment and unfurled it, revealing a map. 'This represents the length of the Nile,' she said, tracing her finger along the river's course. 'Each year the Nile floods its banks, known locally as the spiritual awakening of the year. The flooding has signified the rebirth of this land for generations, and the ancient ones even built their calendar around it.'

'Spare me the history lesson, Jocasta,' growled Remus. 'Details.'

Lady Jocasta continued with haste, seeing the impatience within her teacher's eyes. 'Once the flooding subsides, it leaves behind large tracts of black silt all along the Nile's banks. The silt is rich in fertile moisture, and Egypt comes alive once more. On New Year's Eve, the poison will be dispersed where the Nile's current is strongest. It will not only lay waste to half the population of this country, it will lay dormant in the silt, polluting agriculture for years to come. What brings life to Egypt will eventually deliver its death . . . over and over and over again and *nothing* can turn back the tide now.'

CHAPTER XVII

𝕿𝖍𝖊 𝕱𝖆𝖒𝖎𝖑𝖎𝖆𝖗 𝕾𝖙𝖗𝖆𝖓𝖌𝖊𝖗𝖘

STOOD OUTSIDE THE small tailoring establishment in Hosni, Cornelius Quaint felt an unanticipated smile creep onto his lips. It was an odd feeling looking at the sand-whipped paint on the shop's door, as if a tiny piece of him was coming home. Above the rattling din of a pedal-powered sewing machine, a woman's voice could be heard singing away from the other side of the door. Quaint knocked his knuckles hard against the dry wood, and immediately the noise abated. A beautiful woman with a mass of wild dark hair and even wilder dark eyes swung open the door.

'What do you want?' she demanded, looking Quaint up and down as if he had arrived at her door purely for her personal inspection.

'A "hello" would be nice,' Quaint teased. 'Is that any way to greet your visitors?'

Unrestrained inside her blouse, the woman's ample bosoms sashayed back and forth and Quaint was unintentionally mesmerised. 'Are you going to tell me what you want, or do you intend to stand there all day gawping at my chest?'

'Can I give me a minute to decide?' smiled Quaint.

She slapped his face and he quickly made up his mind, redirecting his eyes.

'You are English, am I right?' the woman asked. 'All Englishmen think they are *so* charming, with their pleases and their thank yous. Well, do not think for one moment that I will fall for any of your mucking about. Charm does not work on me – only money! And I hope you are not going to ask for a discount, because I do not *do* discounts.'

'Alex, will you shut up for a moment and let me speak?' said Quaint.

'How do you know my name?' the Egyptian woman asked.

'Because it's me!' Quaint insisted.

The woman's face glowed with a spark of recognition.

'Cornelius? Cornelius Quaint?' She quickly bundled him inside her premises, slamming the door shut behind him. 'Come inside, I am so glad to see you!'

Quaint looked at her dubiously. 'You are?'

'Of course – you owe me money!' exclaimed the tailor. 'And it is Alexandria, not *Alex,* if you please . . . I am a grown woman now.'

Quaint's eyes were drawn back to the woman's breasts. 'It hadn't escaped my notice.'

Alexandria linked her arm through Quaint's, leading him to her workshop along a corridor cluttered with rolls of material, clothing rails and dusty mannequins.

'My word, Cornelius, what are you wearing?' Alexandria said. 'You would not have been seen *dead* in pinstripes when you and I were . . .' She forced herself to look away for a moment, '. . . in the old days, I mean. And tell me, what has happened to your hair? Not a hint of grey when we last met, and now you are . . . what is the English phrase . . . as white as a sheep?'

'It's sheet,' said Quaint.

'I know what I mean,' said Alexandria dryly. 'Please do not tell me that I have aged as poorly as *you*.'

'As sensitive to my feelings as ever, Alex,' said Quaint. 'The years are unkind to us all eventually. I like to think of myself as a vintage wine . . . I grow in value with each passing year.'

'In that case, you must be worth a fortune,' Alexandria said. 'Well, for all your chips and cracks, I am relieved to see you are still intact, Cornelius.'

'And let me take a good look at you, eh?' said Quaint, stepping back to avoid further inspection. She wore a white blouse under an embroidered waistcoat, a flowing crimson skirt, and from a wide belt around her slender waist hung an assortment of bobbins of yarn and reels of thread. 'There is no doubt about it . . . you are still the most ravishing woman in all of Egypt. Surely if you'd been born in the old days, you would be revered as a goddess.'

Alexandria slapped his broad chest playfully. 'The same old lines to make a lady's heart beat faster, Cornelius? Shame on you.'

'Actually, that's a brand new one just for you,' said Quaint

'I very much doubt it,' Alexandria said. 'As much as I would like it to be true, I do not believe that you came halfway around the world just to see me. So tell me, what brings you back to Egypt after all these years?'

'Just a little bit of business . . . of the *unfinished* variety,' Quaint replied, as he began a stroll around the workshop. 'You know me, Alex. Nothing changes.'

Alexandria watched him, unable to take her eyes off him for a moment.

'No . . . nothing changes,' she said.

Quaint brushed his hands over the array of tailored shirts, jackets, coats and dresses. The workshop was an organised mess, with reams of silks and cottons arranged how a lover of books might display their collection. A large overcoat adorning a headless mannequin caught his eye, and he beamed at it as though it were a familiar face. It was an indigo, three-quarter length, split-tailed long-coat, with wide lapels and thick cuffs. As he stepped closer to the garment, the colour seemed to dance before his eyes, changing from blue to black, like oil across water.

'One of yours I take it?' he asked.

Alexandria nodded. 'It meets with your approval?'

'It's a work of art, my dear. It belongs in a museum,' Quaint answered.

'Hmm, well . . . it was a special order for a Chinaman named Cho-zen Li over six months ago. If he does not send payment for it soon, it might as *well* hang in a museum for all the good it is doing here,' Alexandria said gloomily, casting her eyes around the workshop as if it were her prison cell, and she its captive.

Quaint spied the anxious look in her eyes, despite her utmost efforts to hide it.

'I take it business is a little slow at the moment?'

'Not just at the moment . . . all of the time,' Alexandria replied. 'This district is not exactly a place to notice finery and good workmanship. I rely on all my overseas clients, many of which I have you to thank for their continued custom over the years. But I get by.' She moved a large box of cotton reels and sat herself up on a bench, swinging her legs back and forth. 'You have probably noticed that there are more garments cluttering up this place than there should be. The times are hard. Despite what I said to you when you arrived, I *do* give discounts . . .

sometimes more than I can afford. Joran is growing fast, and his is a big mouth to fill.'

'It certainly is,' grinned Quaint. 'So this coat . . . it's a bit on the large side for a Chinese, isn't it?' he asked, running his hand inside the overcoat's lapel.

'It is not my place to question my clients' measurements, Cornelius,' Alexandria said, with a quick glance at Quaint's waist. 'You have filled out with a bit of ballast of your own, I see . . . and you have not purchased a suit from me in over a year! Do not tell me you have defected to Savile Row?'

'And pay those vultures' prices? Certainly not! Rest assured, Alex, that I shall be a loyal customer of yours until the day I die . . . which I have on very good authority will be a long way off yet.' Quaint smiled to himself.

'I am glad to hear it. So . . . when was it that you were last here?' Alexandria asked, changing the subject with a distracted jerk of her head.

Quaint ruffled his curls. 'Hmm, now you have me. I was trying to work it out earlier myself. Eighteen forty, maybe? Forty-one?'

'That long?' Alexandria asked. 'And the last time we conversed, were you not some sort of circus magician? A man that pulls rabbits from hats, saws women in half, and escapes from chains in vats of water?'

'I'm a conjuror, Alex, and rarely dabble in escapology – unless it's on a purely personal basis. I rely on misdirection and sleight of hand, not rigged props and pretty assistants. Would you care for a little demonstration?' Quaint reached into his trouser pocket and produced a pack of playing cards.

Alexandria stared at him. 'You carry a deck of cards with you?'

'Doesn't everyone?' Quaint replied offhandedly.

'And so what is this trick all about?' Alexandria asked.

Quaint greeted her question with a terse exhalation. 'Alex, I detest the term "trick". My craft is more than mere trickery! I usually do this blindfolded, but no matter, we shall suffice. Now . . . observe.' He took the deck of cards and split it exactly in half, laying the two equal piles on the workbench behind him. Taking a pile in each hand, he locked his eyes into Alexandria's and shuffled the cards. She tried her best to keep up with him, but he split, shuffled and cut the cards deftly with experienced fingers at a blinding speed. Quaint stacked the cards back into a full deck, fanned them out like a peacock's tail, and offered them to Alexandria. 'Madam, would you care to pick a card?'

A curious grin on her lips, Alexandria tentatively did as she was told.

'Good. Now memorise it, but don't let me see it,' instructed Quaint.

Alexandria held the card close to her face and looked at the seven of diamonds.

'Now, place your card back in the deck,' said the conjuror. 'You will agree that I have not seen the card you selected? There are no hidden mirrors hereabouts and your choice was your own, correct?' Quaint waited for Alexandria to confirm. He relished the opportunity to step back into the shoes of a showman – he had almost forgotten what it felt like. Splaying the cards face down onto the workbench behind him, he floated his fingertips above them as if feeling for a breeze. 'I want you to think of the card in your head. Think only of the card! I will attempt to reach into your mind and pluck it from your thoughts.' Quaint's eyelids flickered as he mouthed an incantation of some sort. He flicked his eyes open and stared accusingly at the row of playing cards. 'Something's not quite right.' He licked his thumb and began counting out the cards onto the workbench, one at a time. Alexandria, meanwhile, had lost much of her interest in the impromptu display, and began picking at her fingernails. 'Just as I thought. I'm a card down!' he snapped, huffily stowing the cards back into his trouser pocket. 'It's not supposed to do that!'

'That is comforting to know,' Alexandria said, hiding her smile behind a swathe of dark hair.

'Ha-ha,' said Quaint without one ounce of humour.

'Is that why you ran away to the circus? To learn how to do it properly?' asked Alexandria. 'Perhaps you would do better cleaning up after the elephants.'

'I didn't run away to *join* the circus, Alex! As well as being its resident conjuror, I happen to own the bloody thing – and for your information, we don't *have* any elephants. Besides a tiger, we've no wild animals at all . . . unless you include a pair of sour-tempered clowns.'

'You *own* a circus?' Alexandria smirked. 'You of all people?'

'And what's that supposed to mean?'

Alexandria bit her lip. 'Can I be frank?'

'Are you ever anything but?' squawked Quaint.

'You are not exactly famed for your sense of humour,' said Alexandria, watching Quaint's face fall. 'I cannot imagine that any circus run by an old grump like you would be very entertaining for the audience.'

'Madam, you offend me!' said Quaint brusquely – and he was telling the truth. 'My circus is fantastic! We take a great pride in our shows. We've got feats of strength and skill that would amaze you, marvellous acrobatic displays and hilarious clown escapades – what more could you want? "Dr Marvello's Travelling Circus is a cornucopia of the strange and the fanciful," they say. Even royalty loves us! Did you know that after the Great Exhibition in Hyde Park, I was personally contacted by Prince Albert himself, requesting me to perform for Queen Victoria's birthday?'

'Someone else not famed for her sense of humour,' chimed in Alexandria.

'Bah!' snapped Quaint, turning on his heel.

Alexandria laughed even more at that. 'I am sorry, Cornelius, I was just teasing you,' she said, pulling him back by the crook of his arm. 'The look on your face is irresistible! I am sure you do an admirable job running your circus, I really am, and I am sure your performers are highly skilled. Tell me, do you wear a long red coat?'

'That's a ringmaster . . . and no, I don't,' growled Quaint.

'Good, because you always looked awful in red,' Alexandria said, sliding off the bench. 'So . . . how long are you here for on this *business* of yours?'

'That depends.' Quaint's face turned a shade darker as his true motives for his visit drove back into focus. 'We on a bit of a tight schedule. We only have until New Year's Eve.'

'*We?*' enquired Alexandria.

Her face fell, and she did not attempt to conceal her disappointment.

'I'm here with Madame Destine,' Quaint explained. 'You remember her – the French governess that I used to speak of. The woman who practically raised me?'

'The one who pretended she could see the future?' asked Alexandria.

Quaint scowled. 'She *can* see the future!'

'Of course . . . and I can whistle underwater,' said Alexandria.

'It's true! Well, at least it *used* to be true . . . she seems to be having a little trouble in that department recently, but that's another story.'

'Cornelius, I cannot believe that you brought your governess all this way with you! Is that why you are dressed so staidly? Does she still pick out your clothes each day and lay them on your bed for you?' mocked Alexandria.

'Don't be ridiculous!' Quaint said, quickly occupying his eyes around the room. The woman was uncannily (and embarrassingly) accurate, but he was not about to admit that to her and face yet more ribbing. 'On the matter that has brought me to Egypt, I needed someone whose counsel I revere above all others . . . which is why Destine is here with me. But some things require another's perspective. That's why I came to see you. I need your help, Alex.'

'My help? Cornelius, it has been thirteen years and finally you return, yet not for the reason that I would have preferred,' said Alexandria, a hint of resentment buoying every word. 'Whatever it is, it must be of great importance.'

'It is,' Quaint said, taking a deep breath before ploughing ahead. 'You see, a diabolical organisation called the Hades Consortium plans to deposit a deadly poison into the River Nile sometime very soon. That's why I'm here – to stop it from happening! So now that you know . . . what do you think?'

The look on Alexandria's face did not bode well. '*What do I think?*' she screeched, her voice skirting dangerously close to hysterics. 'I think that the Egyptian sun has gone to your head! What utter madness is this? You stroll back into my shop – back into my *life* – and expect me to believe that someone is going to poison the Nile?'

'Alex, please keep your voice down.' Quaint pushed his finger against her lips.

Alexandria slapped it away, and then slapped him.

'Ow!' Quaint said, rubbing his jaw. 'I think you loosened one of my teeth.'

'That is not the only thing loose around here! You must think me a fool, Cornelius. Poisoning the Nile? I have never heard of anything so absurd! And I suppose you have proof of this?'

Sadly, Quaint could offer nothing but a charming smile.

'I knew it! Same old Cornelius Quaint!'

'Alex, I'm serious, listen to me. When have I ever—'

'Shush!' Alexandria interrupted, brandishing her finger like a weapon.

'What?' interjected Quaint.

'I know what you are about to say . . . so shush!'

'What, do you read minds now?'

'You were about to say "When have I ever lied to you?"'

'Ah.' Quaint winced. 'Well, it's true! When *have* I ever—?'

'Have you forgotten how you left things between us?' interrupted Alexandria. 'You left me without so much as a kiss. No letter of explanation, no warning – nothing! It was almost a month before you wrote to explain why you had to go.'

'Okay, I admit that one time . . . but this is totally different,' Quaint said, hoping to recapture Alexandria's trust – not that he had much of it to begin with. 'This plot is real, whether you believe me or not . . . and it is going to *continue* to be real unless I do something to stop it! I'm not making this up, Alex, I swear. You have my word.'

'And you think that is something I have come to trust?' asked Alexandria.

'Alex . . . don't make this about you and me. I know how we left things all those years ago. There was a lot that I should have said . . . and probably a lot more that I should not have said, but I am begging you . . . *help* me.'

'What help could I possibly give you?' Alexandria asked.

Quaint held his tongue for a second, cementing his focus.

'The Hades Consortium is well connected, but they couldn't pull off a plot this big alone. I know how this country operates. They'd need someone local, someone doing the legwork, pulling the strings – someone with no love of Egypt! Look, I'm guessing, all right? I'm out of my depth here, Alex, I admit that. But you . . . you *know* people. You *hear* things. Gossip . . . rumours . . . boasts. Maybe you overheard something and didn't know what it was. Anything could be important!'

Alexandria turned her back to him. He was devilishly charming, of course. He always was. If she was honest, she did not need any evidence of this dastardly plot. One look in those all-consuming, jet-black eyes of his was evidence enough.

'All right, Cornelius,' she said eventually, 'maybe there is someone that might be able to tell you something. You can tell me more about how exactly you got involved in this plot on the way.'

'Thank you,' Quaint said. 'Wait. On the way? On the way where?'

CHAPTER XVIII

The Pain in the Backside

SIMILAR IN THEIR own way to the Hades Consortium – albeit far more crude – the desert thieves known as the Clan Scarabs lived an embittered existence scattered throughout the outlying regions of Egypt, splintered into nine separate clans, each under the control of district leaders called 'Aksaks'. Each region reported to an Aksak, with a higher Council of Elders overseeing all decisions. Thievery, violence, intimidation and murder were the craft of the Scarabs, and they employed a variety of tools to get the job done. Wrapped in tattered rags from head to foot, the bindings sheltered them from the harsh desert winds. Like wild, demonic wraiths, they spread terror wherever they went.

In the flatlands surrounding the Hawass Mountains, Aksak Faroud lifted his hand to his forehead to check the sun's position. He had been waiting for some time, and if there was one thing he loathed, it was being kept waiting. By his side, sat astride horses just as he was, two of the Aksak's fellow Clan Scarabs waited with him.

Eventually, their wait was over.

A wisp of dust was growing on the horizon, and heading in their direction.

'Wait here, my brothers. I shall not be long,' Faroud said, dismounting his horse. The two Scarabs glanced nervously at each other, and their hands darted to the hilts of their swords. Faroud waved a calming hand. 'Stand down. But be on your guard . . . this man can be a little slippery.'

The Scarabs relaxed at their leader's words, and let their hands fall from their weapons. Even so, they kept their beady eyes pinpointed on the approaching horse-drawn cart carrying the figure of Godfrey Joyce.

'Stop here!' he commanded his driver. 'My arse will be red raw from all this bloody travelling today. Twice in one day, Aksak? People will start to talk.'

'You sent word for me?' asked Faroud.

'Indeed I did, Aksak,' said Joyce. 'Something important has arisen.'

'Can I hope that now your business with the Hades Consortium is complete, you have news of my brother?' asked Faroud.

'Straight to business, eh? I don't blame you, this damn heat will be the death of me!' said Joyce. 'Sorry, but I've heard nothing new. We must be patient, I told you that. I am doing what I can, but you must realise that securing your brother's freedom is not *easy*. He did attempt to rob the British Embassy of several expensive items, after all . . . not to mention almost killing two of the guards in the process. I will do all I can to spare his life, but until that day do not forget that you are indebted to *me*.'

Faroud ground his teeth. 'I do not . . . *cannot* . . . forget that. But I do not understand. If you did not ask me here to provide me with news of Rakmun's release, what do you want?'

Joyce clapped his hands together. 'I have another job for you.'

'Another? But I collected the delivery from Al Fekesh as you commanded! What next must I do to secure my brother's release? When will these little "jobs" of yours come to an end?'

'You must understand, Aksak – greasing the political wheels takes time. Whilst I'm doing everything I can, I'm afraid there are a few things that have cropped up to distract my attention . . . such as a female archaeologist digging in Umkaza. If left unchecked, that woman might well stir up a bit of a sandstorm out there in the desert.'

'What trouble could an archaeologist cause?' asked Faroud.

Joyce pursed his lips, battling to restrain a grin. 'I have a few *skeletons* in my closet, you might say . . . and I have no wish for them to be unearthed.'

'So who is this woman?'

'Professor Pollyanna North,' replied Joyce. 'She happens to be one of England's most eminent archaeologists, and a ruthless campaigner for the acquisition and restoration of Egyptian antiquities. She's carved a little niche for herself out here since discovering the fabled Sceptre of Osiris in '49, and she fought hard for it to remain on display in Cairo's Museum of Antiquities. Her devotion to her trade has attracted a fair amount of attention back home, most notably from Her Majesty Queen Victoria herself. The Queen does *adore* such women of substance!'

'Once again I ask . . . what harm can this woman cause?' asked Faroud.

'Professor North must not be allowed to draw unwanted attention to my business,' said Joyce. 'Not right now. Not when the Hades Consortium is camped out on my doorstep! I want you to take your band of Scarabs and pay her a visit.'

'That is a lot of men to kill one archaeologist,' Faroud noted.

'Christ, I don't want her *killed*, man!' Joyce laughed, rising up on tiptoes to grasp Faroud's bony shoulders with both hands.

'I just need her scared . . . scared enough to want to pack up her crew and get the hell out of Umkaza. She might be a pain in the backside, but she is a *very well connected* one. If she were to die out here, we'd have a British regiment arriving within the week!'

Faroud stroked his beard restlessly. 'Those who come to steal my country's past from under our very feet, they do not deserve the Scarabs' mercy!'

'Ah, but the trouble is, Aksak, your government *disagrees* with you!' Joyce snapped. 'The revenue that Egypt earns from Great Britain on these little archaeological shindigs pays for much of the splendour you see in the capital, not to mention the Pasha's many beautiful sailing crafts. This country of yours has got more than enough treasure to share around.'

'But we Egyptians are *proud* of our heritage!' Faroud snapped back, causing his two Scarab companions to tense their muscles. 'Proud of what we have achieved in the past, and proud of what we have become! Surely my government would not sit idly by as our lands are looted by outlanders?'

Godfrey Joyce chuckled to himself. 'You natives really have no idea as to how deep the roots go beneath the earth, do you? A country's borders are nothing any more. There was a time when the world was small. Everyone was fenced in, and everyone knew their place. Borders were respected. But now the world is a free for all. It's a marketplace of commerce, nothing more. So I wouldn't waste my energy being loyal towards this country of yours, Faroud – because it's certainly not loyal towards *you*!'

Faroud nodded submissively. 'For my brother's sake, I will do this one last thing that you ask. I will order my Scarabs to attack Umkaza at once . . . but not my entire band. I will take but a dozen men. That is my decision.'

'Accepted,' said Joyce. 'But remember . . . the Professor is *not* to be harmed. Not so much as a chipped fingernail. If she was to be hurt out here, as attaché, my government would ask questions of me, and that would serve neither yours nor your brother's best interests, understand?'

Faroud bowed low. 'I understand.'

CHAPTER XIX

The Bizarre Bazaar

MADAME DESTINE SAID goodbye to Alexandria's brother as he gently steered his cart down the road. It was only when she lifted her hand to wave that she noticed something was missing. She snatched at her wrist frantically. Her bracelet was gone. A piercing whistle caught her attention, and she looked up to see Joran jeering at her from the end of the road – with her jewellery in his hand.

'Magpie!' she fumed, squeezing the handle of her parasol in frustration.

She surveyed her location. A towering stone archway served as the main entranceway to Agra Bazaar. The noise beyond it was tremendous, as if the walls had imprisoned all the sights, sounds and smells of the bazaar within and they were bursting at the seams.

Destine was drawn irresistibly inside.

Agra Bazaar was a bustling jungle of scattered shops and stalls situated within a labyrinth of twisting alleyways and narrow lanes, culminating in one vast, sprawling marketplace in the centre of the city. The bazaar's reputation maintained that it sold everything and anything that a person could wish for, and it was a proud boast that the city did its best to live up to. Its origins as Egypt's centre point for trade began centuries past with caravans arriving from the Asian continent bringing spices, silks and other luxurious goods such as gemstones, precious metals and tapestries. Soon after, Europe began extending its seafaring conquests in search of warm water ports and they brought with them an increase in trade. Agra Bazaar's revenue blossomed, and despite the fact that it was positioned at least an hour's journey from the main port, it managed to thrive beyond all expectations. There were no homes left in Agra any more – it was a district populated solely by businesses small and large.

No wonder Cornelius recommended this place, thought Destine, it will keep me out of his hair for hours.

She walked along the main street and into an explosion of people. All the many and varied shops' doors were carved into the rock-faces, each one a tiny cave of wonder, their facades painted in bright colours to entice the passing consumer. Destine was sorely tempted more than once, but she resisted. She knew that it was unlikely she would see Cornelius before nightfall – perhaps longer if Joran decided not to show his thieving little face again – so for now, Destine was happy floating about from shop to shop and from one stall to the next.

The unfolding bazaar and its wonderfully eclectic people occupied her attention completely. The swarm of colourfully dressed people's myriad emotions were playing havoc with her increasing sensitivity to them. Proud boasting, desperate pleading, unyielding begging – the whole spectrum of emotions was open to her, and Destine had to consciously muffle the noise from her mind. Just by being off the ship and able to stretch her legs, she had forgotten all about losing her clairvoyant gifts. Usually they were her guide as she navigated through life, but here in Agra Bazaar, she felt very much at home, and very much at peace. It was understandable after all. In such a public place, what could possibly cause her harm?

Plenty – was the answer.

As Destine manoeuvred her way through the street, she was oblivious to the fact that she was being watched. Heinrich Nadir followed her every move from a small table outside a tearoom. He paid close attention to the elegant woman's ports of call, lest she strayed too far from view. His two very deadly aces up his sleeve were held in reserve on the bazaar's outskirts. The Hades Consortium assassins would stick out like sore thumbs in Agra, and he did not want to risk frightening the Frenchwoman away. Too much was resting on her capture – more even than Godfrey Joyce was aware.

Blind to the attention she had garnered, Destine meandered along the concourse until she reached the bazaar's central square. Colourful banners and flags from the buildings' flat rooftops blew in the breeze. There was a large stone spire set into the centre of the square; around it tall wooden masts were dotted randomly. Lanterns were affixed midway up the masts, and streamers and ribbons were tied around every one, fluttering in the light wind. The whole place was alight with an atmosphere of colour and vibrancy. From out of nowhere, a scent floated lightly upon the air and stirred Destine's senses. She was reminded of her youth in Toulouse as the smell of freshly baked goods wafted past her nose, and she tried to recall the scent.

Cinnamon bread – that was it!

It was unmistakably cinnamon bread. Destine was stunned. But surely she was mistaken. It could not *possibly* be coming from within Agra Bazaar, could it? She was surrounded by stalls selling smoked fish, marinated chickens and spiced-lamb skewers, and there seemed nowhere capable of producing such an extravagant and familiar smell. It tugged at her senses, and she was desperate to find it. Leaving the hustle and bustle of the central marketplace, Destine moved towards the alleyways that branched in every direction.

Down a nearby lane, a gaggle of women gossiped like starlings at dusk. As Destine passed, one of them darted out her hand and grabbed at her wrist. Destine was stopped in her tracks as the Egyptian woman stroked her long, flowing dress and flashed a mouthful of haphazard teeth at her. She spoke with a rasping, guttural hiss and Destine knew it was not a friendly invitation to join in the conversation. This woman wanted money. Destine tried to pull her arm free, but in a flash the woman's friends rounded upon her, enclosing her within a tight circle. Destine was shoved violently against the brick wall. She felt a hand snatch at her neck, at her wrists, and more hands grabbing at her – invading her, picking at her bones. Holding up her arms to defend herself, Destine begged the women to stop.

Although the assault seemed to last for ever, it was over within seconds.

With a sudden eruption of laughter, the women pushed Destine to the ground, towering over her with an assortment of jeers and sneers . . . and then they were gone. They darted down an alley and around a corner, disappearing into the maze of streets like fleeing rats.

Rising to her feet, Madame Destine steadied herself against the wall, trying to catch her breath. Her necklace of pearls was gone, as was her charm bracelet; even her earrings had been forcibly ripped from her ears.

'*Merde!*' she cursed, thumping her hand against the wall. 'You *foolish* old woman, what were you thinking . . . wandering off alone?'

She stared down the alley in the direction the women had fled. Potent adrenalin buzzed around her veins, and Destine allowed herself to become inflamed by it. With her fists clamped into tight balls of fury, she set off in swift pursuit.

Rounding the corner of the alleyway she looked all about, but the women were nowhere to be seen. She cocked her head, listening above the hubbub of the marketplace, above the rattle of horse and carts, above the shopkeepers' boasts. She heard a raucous laugh from somewhere down the labyrinth of alleyways. Recognising it as her attacker, she set off after the thief. She moved past a small corner store selling carpets and flattened her body against the sandstone wall of an alleyway, trying to pinpoint her foes' location. The laughter was louder now, and she visualised the gang of women picking through her possessions. Destine approached the corner of the wall as quietly as she could. She tensed herself, ready for the confrontation and leapt into the alley with her fists raised.

The alley was empty.

The women could have been anywhere within the maze of side streets, and Destine's adrenalin would no doubt subside long before she found them. She was just about to turn tail and head back into the main marketplace when once again her senses were inflamed. It was that luscious scent of cinnamon bread. She looked around, using her nose as a compass, desperate to track the source of the smell.

And then she found it.

The carpet store that she had just passed beckoned her towards it. The smell was emanating from the store's rear window. Destine moved across the street swiftly, as if the store might vanish at any moment. So determined was she that she failed to see a horse galloping towards her at speed.

'Look out!' a man's voice yelled.

Destine spun around as the large, black shape loomed upon her like a great dark cloak. Something slammed into her body, wrenching her neck back like a rag doll, pushing her from the horse's path. She landed on the pavement, her fall cushioned by several rolls of soft carpet. Her eyes rolled, waiting for gravity to resume control. Lifting her head, she made out a blurred image of a dark-skinned man astride a large black horse in the street. He was cursing madly at her, raising his fist in the air. Destine slumped back down onto the carpets, trying to summon the strength to move. Her scatter-shot mind was flooded with questions – not the least of which being: 'Who is this strange little bearded man looming above me?'

'That was quite a tumble!' the man said. 'Had I not pushed you out of the way, it might have been far worse, ah?' The stranger was short and stocky, with a thick white beard skirting the circumference of his round face. Tiny spectacles sat askew on the bridge of a once-proud nose, and tufts of downy hair sprouted from the sides of his bald head. Most intriguing of all; there was something about his large, brown eyes that captivated Destine.

Something almost . . . familiar.

'Are you all right?' the little man enquired. 'You are liable to get yourself killed, standing in the street around here. Did you not see that horse?'

'Horse? *Non*, I . . . I did not,' replied Destine, her breath shallow. 'But, *oui* . . . I am fine. Just a little shaken. You saved my life, sir. I am most relieved you were passing.'

'*Passing?*' squawked the man. 'My dear, I was not passing, or have you forgotten that this is my carpet store?'

'Forgotten?' asked Destine.

'Ah! I do not blame you. A lot has changed since you were last here – except you, of course! You look exactly as you did twenty years ago, Destine. I cannot wait for you to fill me in on what I have missed, ah?' the man grinned.

Madame Destine scowled at the chap, rubbing at her bruised ribs. Surely she must have also struck her head during the fall. Either that or this man was mad.

'Since I was last here? Twenty years ago, you say?' she asked.

The man chuckled as he helped Destine to her feet. 'I know! It makes me feel old too, ah? Come along inside the store. I will make us a nice pot of tea, and as luck would have it, I have just baked some cinnamon bread with fresh butter and jam – just the way you like it!'

'But, monsieur . . . how could you *know* how I like it?' asked Destine, with a frown.

'How else, Destine?' piped the stout fellow, as he scuttled through the curtain of beads that hung from the shop's doorway. 'You *told* me.'

'I . . . I did?' Destine began to follow the man, but halted in her tracks. 'Wait, monsieur . . . did you just call me "Destine"?'

'Yah,' replied the cheery little man. 'Twice!'

CHAPTER XX

𝕿𝖍𝖊 𝕾𝖎𝖑𝖊𝖓𝖙 𝕰𝖈𝖍𝖔

INSIDE THE CARPET store, Madame Destine sat upon a stool at a large, circular table and looked around. The decor was exactly how her mind felt at that particular moment – hotchpotch. Virtually every scrap of wall-space was covered with swatches of carpets and ornate rugs, all arranged in a bizarre kind of mosaic. Huge rolls of varying types of carpet were stacked up against one of the walls in a long line.

Destine occupied herself by scanning every square inch for anything that might give her some clue as to who this man was . . . and how he seemed to know her. She found nothing, and as she heard a gentle melodic hum emanating from the rear of the store, she prayed that a little illumination would be forthcoming.

Accompanied by a delicious smell, the man approached the table carrying a wooden tray laden with warm cinnamon bread, fresh butter and a jar of conserve. A dented metal teapot sat upon the table, and the man nudged it carefully to one side in order to put the food down. Destine had not spoken a single word, but the stranger had done enough talking for the both of them. He chattered away merrily, barely pausing to take a breath.

The permanent smile etched upon his bearded face never waned, and his stubby moustache seesawed when he spoke.

'How are you feeling now, Madame?' he asked.

'My neck is a little sore, but nothing appears to be broken,' Destine replied, 'apart from my memory, it seems. I must admit to being slightly confused.'

'That was a nasty scare, but nothing that some tea and a slice of cinnamon bread will not fix, ah?' the man said, nodding to the table. 'I had no idea you were coming, dear Destine, why did you not write?'

Destine gathered handfuls of her gown within her fists, squeezing them tightly, trying to wring out an answer to her confusion. The little Egyptian had buzzed around like a miniature whirlwind ever since she had set foot inside his store. So much so that she was barely able to concentrate on the muddle that was her memory.

'Monsieur, I am sorry to be so blunt. You have been very kind, but I must ask . . . do I *know* you?' She watched the man's kind expression waver. 'I think that you might have me confused with someone else. Or perhaps it is I that am confusing myself for someone else, I do not know! I have never seen you before in my life, yet you claim to know me. I ask myself how this can be.'

'You have been through a very frightening episode, ah? It is no wonder you are confused. Here!' The stranger offered Destine a plate of warm cinnamon bread, to which she nodded her thanks and helped herself to a slice, spreading a thick blanket of butter upon it. All the while, the Egyptian's smile never waned. 'I have missed that appetite of yours.'

'Missed? Again, monsieur – where have we met before?' asked Destine. 'Who are you, what is your name? Where am I?'

The man sighed in mock frustration. 'Okay, I will play along if it makes you happy! My name is Ahman Nadim.' Ahman straightened the bow tie at his plump neck. 'This is my carpet store . . . modest, though it is. And you, my dear lady, are Madame Destine Renard.'

His words made Destine's heart miss a beat.

'R-Renard?' she stuttered.

This man Ahman knew her, all right. The very fact that he was aware of the name 'Renard' was proof of that. She had not used that name in a long while. Not since her son had tainted it so darkly. That still left the question: who was this mysterious fellow? How could he know such a private detail about her? She had never set eyes upon him before. Had she?

'Pardonnez moi, monsieur,' Destine said, considering each word carefully. 'I am having difficulty recalling. Have you ever travelled to the European continent? Perhaps I have done a reading of your fortune?'

'No, not me,' Ahman replied. 'I am not one who cares to know what life has in store. I shall surely find out eventually. What is the hurry, ah?'

'But . . . if you have not seen me in the circus, then how do you *know* me?' asked Destine, her manners pushed to their limits by her impatience. 'Please . . . I have had a simply dreadful time in this country since I arrived here. I have been assaulted, I have been robbed – twice, if you include by my chauffeur – and I was almost killed by a runaway horse. Please tell me that I am not living a nightmare!'

Ahman slid his ample backside off his stool, and stood at her side, resting his hand upon hers. 'Is it true, then?' he asked fondly.

'You really do not remember? You do not recognise me? Then
. . . why are you here?'

'By accident,' replied Destine.

Ahman frowned deeply. 'But you once told me that there *are*
no accidents.'

'Well, apart from this one, obviously,' said Destine. 'I am sorry
to disappoint you, monsieur, but although you know me, I have
no recollection of you . . . although I pray you are a friend . . .
for I am in desperate need of one right now.' She took a bite of
the cinnamon bread and immediately a flush of colour returned
to her cheeks – as did a smile. '*Mon Dieu*, this bread is superb!
How ever did you come by this recipe?'

Ahman scratched at his bald head, almost guiltily saying, 'You
gave it to me.'

Destine was beginning to feel as if she had walked into this
conversation halfway through. 'You are mistaken, sir. You must
be! I arrived for the first time in Egypt just this morning!'

'I do not wish to distress you, my dear . . . but it is you that
are mistaken. Perhaps I need to contact Agra's medical man to
ensure you did not strike your head when you fell,' said Ahman,
his bewilderment now almost equalling Destine's. 'We *have* met
before . . . many times. When I saw you moments ago, to be quite
honest I was most relieved. I have waited so patiently for so very
long for you to come back. I hoped that I would finally learn
the answer to that old mystery of yours.'

'Mystery? What mystery?' Destine asked.

'I will show you,' chuckled Ahman.

With that, the carpet trader disappeared behind a curtain into
the backroom, only to return a few moments later carrying a
small wooden box in his stout fingers. 'If it is answers that you

seek, perhaps this contains the missing pieces, ah?' said Ahman, as he ruffled through the contents of the box. He beamed a wide smile as he produced an age-stained envelope, handing it to Destine. 'For you, I believe.'

Destine looked at the envelope as if it were an illusion the likes of which she had seen Cornelius perform a dozen times. It was incredibly old. The ink was faded, but still just about legible to her eyes, and upon inspecting the envelope closely, she came across three startling discoveries.

One: the letter was unopened.

Two: the letter was addressed to her.

And three:

'*This is my handwriting!*' she gasped. Not even Cornelius could have managed an illusion this good. 'What manner of trickery is this?'

'No trickery, my dear! The letter simply is what it *is*,' said Ahman. 'Why do you not open it up and read what lies within?'

Destine's hands were shaking, and her heart was beating out of time. As she slid her finger under the envelope's flap, she could almost feel the stability of her world shuddering slightly, like the rumble of distant thunder. She brushed her fingers over the letter – written in French – and gathering her strength, she translated aloud:

'23rd October, 1833

My dearest Destine,

If you are reading this note, then my visions were correct, and I have returned to Egypt to complete the task that I have been forced to abandon. Two nights past, I was witness to a terrible massacre, and I must leave word of what transpired. I fear that I am pursued, and have no choice but to lead you to the truth.

I have placed three markers along the path that will take you there.

'My employer, Aloysius Bedford, has been betrayed, and tricked into disturbing something in the desert – something that was not meant to be disturbed. I watched many men die as a result, and due to my connectivity to others' emotions, I felt every death as clearly as if it were my own. Such an abundance of misery has caused my mind to cloud the memory, and even as I inscribe these words to you, I can feel it slipping from my grasp. I fear that if I do not commit this task to paper all might be forgotten. My premonitions have warned me that dire things are to come unless you succeed in this quest, but I have faith in you, Destine, faith in the future . . . in my future.

'Yours, Destine.

XXX

'PS. If by some miracle my dear Cornelius is still alive, give him a kiss for me.'

Madame Destine's quivering fingers laid the letter upon the table. It was like reading a message from a complete stranger, but a stranger who was as close to her as a twin sister. The words – her *own* words – carried such a strong resonance within her mind, yet still they failed to fan the embers of memory.

'I *was* here . . . in Egypt, some twenty years ago . . . just as you claimed, Ahman? So why can I not recall it? This letter speaks of events I have no memory of. I cannot even remember *writing* it, let alone witnessing them. It speaks of a task . . . a path to the truth . . . truth about this man's betrayal. How can I possibly know where to begin if my memory draws a blank?'

If Destine were to accept the facts as presented, her younger self had been to this country before. Something had happened, something bad, and her memory of the event was clearly waning. Yet she had known that she would one day return to complete the task. As fantastic as it sounded, the letter was undeniable proof of that. But she had not returned to answer her younger self's call . . . she was in Egypt to defeat the Hades Consortium. The two were unconnected, surely. What were the chances of her coming to Egypt twenty years later, being lost in a labyrinth in the bazaar, stumbling into Ahman's carpet store to pick up the pieces of this puzzle?

The carpet trader let the silence get comfortable before he spoke.

'You really have no recollection of this? Nor when you came to me in distress, begging me to keep the letters safe?' Ahman asked. 'Then we must help you remember, my dear Destine, for if I understand its meaning correctly this letter is far more than just a letter . . . it is a warning.'

'A warning? A warning of what?' Destine asked.

'In your own words, Madame, of dire things to come,' said Ahman.

CHAPTER XXI

The Comfortable Prison

TROTTING ALONG A sandy track that led from Hosni town into the flatlands, Cornelius Quaint was sat astride a mule that was past its prime to say the least. He looked down at his beast of burden, sheer disgust evident on every inch of his face. Alexandria rode next to him on a dapple-grey horse, taking amusement from his discomfort. The dusty track presented a large pile of white rocks with a single palm tree growing between them, and it seemed an excellent place for them to rest. Alexandria dismounted first, and took a large blanket and a canteen of water from a pack on her horse's saddle.

Quaint glanced at her as the gentle breeze toyed with her pirouetting curls, and he was reminded of their time together in the past. What they had shared was fleeting, what some might call a whirlwind romance. Of course, the problem with whirlwinds is that often they tend to leave a lot of devastation in their wake.

Alexandria tapped Quaint's shoulder, offering him the canteen of water.

'You were miles away,' she said with a smile.

'Actually, I was right here,' replied Quaint, taking the canteen.

'Just not right now. So, what about you, Alex? I'm surprised to see you are still in Hosni. I would have thought someone would have come along and offered to take you away from it all by now.'

'Where would I go, Cornelius?' Alexandria asked. 'Egypt is my home. It is where my heart is . . . and once was. All my memories are here. Both good and bad.'

Quaint licked his lips, wondering how best to broach a thorny subject resting upon them. 'So . . . I take it that you've still had no word from your father? It's been so long. I'd hoped that he would have contacted you by now.'

'So had I . . . once. But like the Nile eel, hope is a difficult thing to hold onto when it wishes to be free of your grasp.' A coil of her hair fell down across Alexandria's eyes and she valued its concealment. 'I will never know what the hardest choice for my father was – deciding to *leave* . . . or deciding never to return.'

Quaint rubbed furiously at the back of his neck. 'But I just can't fathom the man! More than my old tutor – we were friends! Your father was an intelligent man who loved his family dearly. I can't believe he'd just simply up-sticks and vanish without so much as a word.'

'Why not?' Alexandria asked. 'You did.'

Quaint reeled with the blow. 'That's different.'

'Your memory of him seems to be at fault, Cornelius. My father was far too busy with his obsession to worry about anyone's feelings. He cared more for digging around old desert tombs than being with his own family. Evidently . . . that is fact.' Alexandria fought back the urge to cry. She could not dare let her anger falter, for then it would only be replaced by sadness and she would not allow that. 'Joran was but a year old when my father left. He has no memory of him. He carries no anger inside his heart and I envy him for that. But my own anger is not something that I can discard so easily.' Alexandria's tone may well have been cold, but the emotion was all the more evident by its absence. 'What is past is past. My father is gone. If he wanted to return, then he would have already done so.'

'Unless he was unable to,' offered Quaint, hoping that Alexandria had at least considered that fact. 'Did you know that he was the reason that I came to Egypt in the first place? At college, his teachings ignited a passion for this country's history that still burns within my heart to this day. He was the best tutor that I ever had. If not for him . . . I would never have met you.'

'So now I have *two* things to blame him for,' Alexandria said.

'Twenty years is a long time to hold a grudge, Alex, especially against someone you can't make amends with . . . and I don't mean me, I mean your father, by the way. If you offer hatred shelter inside your heart, it will only end up taking permanent residence there. It will eat you alive . . . one little piece at a time. Believe me, I happen to be somewhat of an expert in that field.'

'My *hatred* is the only thing I have left to remember him by, Cornelius, do you not see? It is my only protection,' said Alexandria.

Quaint reached over and brushed the underside of her chin, forcing her to catch his eye. All her anger towards him had subsided now that she had found a more suitable target. She looked so fragile. 'It's not your protection, Alex – it's your prison. You're incarcerated by your hatred every day that you permit it to shackle your thoughts.'

'And so let us turn this conversation to *your* shackles, Cornelius . . . namely your altruistic streak,' Alexandria said, thankful for a change of subject matter. 'This task to save Egypt . . . why must it fall on your shoulders? Surely there are others in a position to help. What about the consulate in Cairo, what did they say when you informed them about this plot?' Seeing the blank look in Quaint's eyes, she stood swiftly from the blanket and kicked at a tuft of sandy grass. 'You have not even *told* them? Why do you think you are the only one who can put things right in the world?'

'Because sometimes I am!' flashed Quaint.

'You have to fix every damn thing that is broken, letting what is important slip through your fingers!' Alexandria fumed. 'That is why you ran away all those years ago. Something came to sway your attention, something that you could not leave alone, and you just upped and ran.'

'This isn't like that, Alex . . . it's my responsibility!' said Quaint, rising to his feet.

'It is your belligerent nature, more like!'

'I did not get involved in this plot to buff my ego, Alex – someone involved *me*! All I'm trying to do is make sure that he doesn't succeed! I want to wipe his stain from my memory once and for all. Whether you believe me or not, it doesn't matter . . . it is what I believe, Alex, and I won't fail in it. I cannot fail and I cannot relent, for there is no one else to pick up the pieces! But I can't do it alone . . . that is why I came to you.'

Alexandria reached out a trembling hand for him. 'I . . . I am sorry, Cornelius. I am being selfish. You are right . . . this is not about us. Seeing you again just took me by surprise, it . . . it brought some old feelings back to the surface. Forgive me.'

Quaint ruffled his hair. 'No, it's all right, Alex . . . I deserved it. And it's not as if I've not fought this argument before. Destine feels much the same as you do about my belligerent nature . . . but she knows that I do these things because it's just something that's a part of me. I can't ignore it . . . and I can't ignore what brought me to Egypt.'

Alexandria unclenched her jaw, and gave Quaint a gallant smile.

'I said that I would help you find someone who might be able to tell you something and here we are, for I did not choose this location by accident.' Her eyes skirted across the horizon, down into the valley below their feet. 'If there is any talk of criminal activities taking place in Egypt, *they* will know. The only question is whether you are brave . . . or foolhardy enough . . . to ask them.'

CHAPTER XXII

The Valley of Death's Shadows

QUAINT FOLLOWED ALEXANDRIA to the cliff edge, peering cautiously over the side. The desert wasteland stretched as far as the eye could see. A barren, grey-brown wilderness populated by nothing except hills, rocks, dust and sand.

'Down there?' he asked.

Alexandria nodded. 'If you wish to get answers about this plot of yours, yes,' she said, pointing to the inhospitable landscape below. 'Down into the valley of death's shadows, to the place where the souls of the dead roam, and their ghosts walk freely in daylight.'

'Ghosts?' laughed Quaint. 'Don't tell me you think this place is haunted!'

'Pay heed, Cornelius, for as you will soon discover, evil has made its home here. The valley is haunted by something far, far worse than the ghosts of the dead,' said Alexandria.

Unconvinced, Quaint scanned the valley in closer detail, when he noticed something almost shrouded from view. Nestled in between two gigantic, red mountains was an encampment. It was shadowed in a dark swathe of night, despite it being just past two o'clock in the afternoon. Not one ray from the sun penetrated the valley, as if the encampment did not merit its light.

'Where is this place?' Quaint asked. 'It's not on any maps I've seen.'

'It is a settlement from the old days named Bara Mephista,' replied Alexandria, as she watched the flicker of interest in Quaint's dark eyes. 'It was once home to a group of Nubian settlers who called themselves "The Fleeing Free".'

Quaint rubbed his jaw. 'A literal moniker, I take it?'

Alexandria nodded. 'They were a tribe of nomads that originally fled here from the city of Khartoum . . . and they are a legacy from my country's past that we do not celebrate. The Fleeing Free worshipped gods of death, and practised their dark rituals right there in the place you see before you. To look across these plains now, save for the remains of their old settlement, you would never know they even existed. They were purged by the pharaoh of that time, their name was struck from all historical records, wiping them from the face of Egypt. That is why you will not find this settlement on any map.'

'When your lot hold a grudge, you don't muck about, do you? I don't suppose one of your ancestors was in charge back then?' joked Quaint.

'Bara Mephista has been tainted by that dark reputation ever since,' Alexandria continued, unperturbed by the conjuror's sarcasm. 'Nubian history was my father's life, and he surely taught you that the ancient Egyptians worshipped Amun-Ra, the Sun God. As the sun was born each day, the eastern sky signified the birth of life, yes? Similarly, as the sun set in the west at the end of each day, it became synonymous with death.' She caught Quaint's sceptical eyes. 'The Fleeing Free built their temple facing west in veneration to the underworld . . . in service to death itself, hence the superstitions.'

Quaint looked down at the settlement dubiously. For all the

beliefs he held, the supernatural was not one of them. 'But how can a long extinct bunch of nomads possibly help me?' he asked.

'They cannot,' replied Alexandria. 'But those who now reside here might.'

Something made Quaint shiver, and he turned around to Alexandria.

'Did you say this place is called "Bara Mephista"?' he asked.

Alexandria smiled. 'It took you long enough to work it out.'

'But, Alex . . . Bara Mephista is old Nubian for—'

'Land of the Devil, yes. And it is very aptly named,' said Alexandria. 'Bara Mephista is home to the largest criminal infection that Egypt has ever witnessed . . . a disease that has spread throughout this country for decades, polluting anything and everything in its path. Like packs of wild dogs they roam, foraging and scavenging the land.'

'*They?*' asked Quaint.

'The Clan Scarabs. Murderers and thieves, every one of them. Ruthless and cunning, they would slit your throat without giving it a second thought.'

'Unreceptive to visitors, I should imagine,' gulped Quaint.

'You will soon find out,' said Alexandria. 'If anyone knows anything about this plot of yours – it is the Scarabs. If you are not to be swayed, then down you must go, willingly into their nest. But if you take but one wrong step in that place, it may well turn out to be your last. You must be cautious.'

'My dear, I'm the living embodiment of cautious,' replied Quaint.

'Cornelius, have you heard nothing of what I just said?' Alexandria snapped. 'These men are murderers! You will be lucky if you live long enough to introduce yourself, let alone ask them any questions!' She turned from the cliff's edge and began gathering up their things, stowing them into the pack on her saddle. 'If you really are going down there then you will not find *me* by your side.'

'Where are you going?' asked Quaint.

'Where do you think? I am going back home. Back to Hosni,' replied Alexandria. 'I have done my part and led you here. How you decide to kill yourself is your business.'

'Just like that? Alex, you can't just leave!'

'On the contrary, Cornelius . . . I can.' Alexandria grabbed hold of her saddle and hoisted herself upon the horse's back.

'I'm miles away from anywhere! What if they refuse to help?' asked Quaint.

'Then a long walk back to your ship will be the least of your troubles,' Alexandria said. 'Unlike you, I have much to lose. I must do what you should have done from the start . . . I will leave the heroics to someone else.' With that, she steered her horse towards the track. 'If you somehow end up walking out of this valley alive, Cornelius – make sure you say goodbye this time.'

Quaint tried his best to smile, and just about managed to, but it was a fleeting one. 'Alex, wait! Before you go . . . take a look in your pocket.'

Alexandria halted her horse with a gentle tug on the reins. She reached into her waistcoat, and her expression flitted between aggravation, surprise and then utter confusion.

It was the seven of diamonds.

Quaint grinned up at her. 'Your card I believe?'

Alexandria chewed at the inside of her cheek to stop herself from smiling. She cast the playing card into the dust. 'I take it all back . . . you *are* a good magician, Cornelius. But know this: if you wish to walk back out of this place with your life, you will need to be better than just *good* . . . you will need to be absolutely spectacular!'

Quaint watched her fade into the distance, claimed by a cloud of dust. He slowly walked towards the card, picked it up, and slipped it into his trouser pocket. Glancing into the valley to his destination, he smiled at Alexandria's words.

Thankfully, being absolutely spectacular was well within his means . . .

CHAPTER XXIII

The Viper's Venom

LADY JOCASTA WAS alone in her quarters deep beneath the ruins of the ancient city of Fantoma. Sweeping velvet curtains hung from the ceiling to the floor, and a large bed stood in the centre of the room. Wearing a flowing white silk dress, Jocasta was easily the brightest thing in the room. Flickering candles on her table signalled the entrance of a visitor, and Jocasta's eyes greeted Baron Remus. His ice-white three-piece suit was blemish-free, and the man had an equally pristine white hat perched upon his head. But under its brim, a subdued expression hung on his tanned face.

'Is anything the matter, teacher?' Jocasta asked.

'I have received word from Miss Ivy at our headquarters in Rome. Events in the Crimean peninsula are escalating and I must leave Egypt immediately,' the Baron's booming voice resounded. 'The Russian navy has been flexing its muscles in the Black Sea for weeks. They have stationed troops en masse near Wallachia's borders, and are busying themselves with the Turks, but soon many other nations will have no choice but to intervene. If everything unfolds as I have conceived, the French and British will soon join the battle, and when that happens war will be inevitable.'

Lady Jocasta nodded. 'Forward planning *is* one of your strengths.'

'A most coincidental selection of words,' said Remus. 'Before I take my leave, I need to be sure that your plans proceed in alignment with your schedule.'

'Why so concerned, Baron?' teased Jocasta. 'Afraid that I will not succeed . . . or afraid that I *will* and it will outshine your little fracas in the Crimea?'

From out of nowhere, the Baron lunged towards her, sending the contents of the table flying into the air. His thick, hairy hands compressed around her neck, his nails digging deeply into her flesh. Jocasta tried to force air down her throat as the Baron's grip squeezed ever tighter.

'Do not test me, woman!' he snarled, his teeth bared like fangs. 'There is more at stake here than you realise!'

'You are . . . *hurting* me,' Jocasta gasped, trying to unlock the Italian's fingers from her throat. 'Please, I beg of you – you're . . . *killing* me!'

At her words, the Baron released his hold, staring at his hands as if they were dripping with blood. Jocasta steadied herself against the bedside table, clawing at her neck. Thick red marks were smeared like a scarf around her throat, and tears were in her eyes as she stared up at the Baron. He made a move to grab her hand, but the Greek woman snatched it away. She glanced at him nervously as he fought to master his rage, his broad shoulders quivering as he turned his face from hers.

'Jocasta, I apologise . . .' he said. 'This place . . . its confinement is affecting my condition. My campaign in the Crimea is at a critical stage . . . and I should not have taken my anxieties out on you. Please forgive me.'

'You sought only assurances of my plot's success, teacher,' said

Jocasta hoarsely. 'You need make no apology for that. But your concerns are unnecessary, Baron. Every eventuality of my plot has been catered for. Soon the banks of the Nile will burst, but this time the river will be overflowing with corpses.'

'I hope your plot matches your confidence,' growled the Baron, as he removed himself from her quarters, lingering at the door. 'If it does not, your corpse will be amongst that number . . . and everything that we have fought for will be for nothing. Remember my words, Jocasta . . . for one day soon, it might not be me that seeks assurances from you, and you need to be prepared.'

Lady Jocasta watched the Baron leave, wondering what on earth he could have meant.

CHAPTER XXIV

The Clouded Truth

MADAME DESTINE WAS uncomfortable – not just perched upon the wooden stool at the table in Ahman's carpet store, but generally uncomfortable from all that she had discovered from the stout Egyptian. Gradually, the clouded truth about her past was being revealed, and for one formerly practised in foretelling the future, it was an uncomfortable experience.

'But I don't remember it, Ahman. Any of it!' Destine exclaimed. 'I am forced to believe this letter is genuine, and yet what other truths am I then forced to accept? That I was here in Egypt twenty years ago in 1833, and I foresaw that one day I would return to complete a task that I could not? But what task? This letter speaks of everything and nothing! Who is this Aloysius Bedford character? The more questions I ask, the more confused I become.'

'I am sorry, Madame, but I can add nothing other than what I have already told you . . . and what you have already told *yourself*,' said Ahman, watching Destine's deflated expression waver. 'Back then you entrusted me with two letters and one very large mystery . . . but no answers. I have been waiting all this time for you to come back.' Ahman smiled, trying to coax one in reply from Destine – to no avail. 'This is as strange for me as it is for you.'

'I doubt that, monsieur, for you are an integral part of the enigma,' said Destine, as she slipped off the stool and began to pace around the carpet store. 'You bake my favourite cinnamon bread – a lot better than I do, I might add – you know my name, you know *me*. I have so many questions that I cannot speak them fast enough!'

'Then perhaps our journey will enlighten you in time,' Ahman said.

Destine stopped pacing. 'Journey? What journey?'

'The one the letter speaks of, Madame,' said Ahman. 'We are going to continue this trail for the markers, are we not?'

'We?' asked the Frenchwoman.

'Of course we!' replied Ahman cheerily. 'You do not expect me to let you carry this burden alone, do you? What kind of friend would I be then?'

'I wish I knew, Ahman. In fact, I wish I knew a lot of things.'

'We cannot dwell on our yesterdays, Madame . . . what is done is done. We must focus on the here and now and unlock this trove of mystery. Blind to the past or not, we will follow your younger self's trail to uncover the truth – together!'

'If only I could remember!' The Frenchwoman thumped her fist upon the table, sending the small wooden box flying through the air. Its contents spilled onto the floor, and as Destine stooped to pick them up, something caught her eye.

It was another letter, an exact replica of the previous. As she turned it over in her trembling hands, she noticed the words: '2 of 3' written on the envelope's reverse.

'What is this?' she asked.

Ahman scratched at his beard. 'Ah, well . . . I did say you gave me *two* letters.'

CHAPTER XXV

The Second Letter

THE FURTIVE FORM of Heinrich Nadir stood at the alley's corner in Agra Bazaar, staring intently at the doorway of Ahman's carpet store. His quarry had been inside for well over an hour and he was getting restless.

Perhaps he had been careless and she had spotted him, making her escape through a rear exit. No, he had been vigilant, he was sure of that. His plan would all be for nothing without the Frenchwoman. She was still inside; she had to be. Even if she *had* seen him and recognised him from the *Silver Swan*, what did it matter? He was just an innocent sightseer, the same as she was. But he could not expect Godfrey Joyce to wait for ever for his prize. He folded his newspaper into the inner pocket of his jacket, just as Madame Destine appeared at the shop's doorway, closely followed by a small bald Egyptian. Nadir was intoxicated by this intriguing development.

By his appearance, it was obvious that the bald man was a local, but there was an intense argument ensuing between the two. He was certainly desperate to sell her a carpet, whoever he was. Perhaps this might scupper Nadir's entire plan. He would lose more than just face if he were to report to his employer of his failure – his life itself was forfeit. Deciding it required further attention, he removed himself back around the corner of the alley and silently observed, listening intently to every terse word carried on the back of the breeze.

'Madame, please understand – I was only abiding by *your* wishes! You cannot just go off like this,' called Ahman, rushing after Destine as she sped determinedly from his shop. Her dress billowed like a flag on a pole, and she clutched up handfuls of it within her fists, lifting the delicate skirts from the ground to ease her flight.

'Do not try to stop me, monsieur,' she warned. 'Bigger men than you have tried and failed!'

'But where are you *going*?' Ahman asked.

'Away from under this cloud of confusion!' Destine replied. 'I wish that I could trust you, Ahman . . . yet I do not feel I can trust anyone or any*thing* any longer – least of all myself! Why did you not tell me about this other letter?'

'Back then, you told me not to!' Ahman protested. 'You told me that you had to read the letters in sequence . . . that one would not make sense without the other!'

'Well, I was wrong, for neither of them make any sense! The letters speak of a tragedy . . . but it is two decades old. Surely something so important would be the first thing you mentioned when chancing upon me in this bazaar – if indeed it *was* chance . . . for all I know, this is all part of some elaborate confidence trick and you are trying to take advantage of me just like those banshees in the marketplace!'

Ahman's face dropped as Destine's words stung at him. He looked at her, past her furious fortifications, trying to find a spark of the woman he once knew. It was not easy, for her anger was difficult to pierce. He only wished that she could remember who she was and see herself as he did. Although Destine had no memory of her time in Egypt, for Ahman the years had passed slowly. How he had missed her. How he had yearned for her. *His* Destine was in there somewhere; he knew that, and he was not about to give up searching for her just yet. He could not lose her again.

'I would never deceive you, Destine. Never!' he said. 'The envelopes were sealed! They were meant for your eyes only, and had I opened them, what good would it have done? They were written in *your* language . . . and I do not speak French, ah?'

Destine touched her hand to her forehead. She had to sit down somewhere and try to regain her sense of balance. She lowered herself onto a pile of stacked carpets outside the store.

Gingerly, Ahman joined her.

'Please believe me, Destine,' he said. 'I did not deceive you.'

'Ahman, I am so sorry . . . but please understand that I must place a lot of faith in your words, and faith in *you* – a total stranger. I thank you for your hospitality, but I have to return to my ship.' Destine tightened the knot at the rear of her head-scarf and stood swiftly, keen to resume her course. 'Cornelius will be waiting for me.'

Ahman reached after her. 'Cornelius? But, Destine, after what the other letter said . . . how can you go to him knowing what will happen?'

Destine lowered her eyes to the ground. 'Because I have nowhere else to go.'

'I am your friend, Destine – if only you would remember me as such,' said Ahman, earnestly. 'You may have tasked this mystery to yourself, but that does not mean you have to accomplish it alone. We shall discover the truth together!'

'I do not think I could *cope* with much more truth!' Destine adjusted her corset and regained her composure. 'If I listen to my heart, I *do* know you as a friend, Ahman . . . but if the revelations within this second letter are to be believed, the road ahead will be long and arduous, and I do not know if I have the strength to walk it.' She pulled the letter from inside the sleeve of her dress and unfolded it, holding it with trembling hands as she read aloud:

'My dear Destine,

'This letter is the second of my three markers to you. I have done what I can to point you towards the truth, and I have laid the clues that you must follow. You must go to a sacred place where the sun's rays touch just twice a year. Seek the temple of the Shaded God, one that was once lost, but has since been found. There, you will find the answers to this great mystery, and the knowledge of what you must do.

'The truth is hidden within the third marker.

<u>Of utmost importance is this</u>: My visions have warned me that you MUST NOT involve Cornelius in this task, for your reunion shall signal the beginning of the darkest chapter of his life, where everything he once believed will crumble before his eyes. He must not face this peril until the time is right. You must promise me on this, Destine. Cornelius must be allowed to discover his own destiny in due course, even though in truth, it is that which is my greatest regret of all.'

'Whatever does she mean by that?' Destine said. 'Cornelius might be in grave danger, just as I foresaw before my prophetic gifts deserted me, but if I were to run to him, it would spell his doom . . . perhaps even his demise. How could I have forgotten something such as that? What has guided me here to you, and brought me in contact with these secrets hidden from my memory . . . and why now?'

'What makes you think you were guided here at all?' asked Ahman. 'From what you say, it is sheer blind luck that has led you back to Egypt.'

'I doubt it,' Destine replied. 'As you said, I purport that accidents rarely happen. If my experience with premonitions has taught me anything, it is that all things happen for a reason, Ahman. As much as Cornelius hates to admit it . . . everything is connected. It seems that I must collect every missing piece of my past and put this jigsaw back together again. But where do we start looking, *mon ami*?'

Ahman scratched frantically at his bearded jaw, watching a brand new Destine rise from the pile of carpets. 'Well, the first clue would seem to be this temple that we are supposed to travel to, ah? This "temple of the Shaded God". The letter called it "a sacred place where the sun's rays touch just twice a year". Whatever can that mean?'

'I wish I knew,' said Destine, hungry now to accept her task. 'And what is this in the centre of the page? This strange symbol seems more than just a random doodle. What is it supposed to mean? Could it be a clue of some kind?'

Ahman's eyes lit up. 'What did you just say?'

'This triangular marking here,' said Destine. 'Perhaps my younger self means for us to seek a pyramid of some kind?'

'Symbol,' Ahman muttered, as though talking in his sleep. 'I wonder . . .'

'You wonder what?' asked Destine, vexed by Ahman's response as he buried his head in his hands, chuckling merrily to a silent joke. 'What is it? Do you know what this symbol means?'

'Can it be that easy?' mumbled Ahman. 'You thought that this pictogram might be a clue of some kind . . . and if I am right . . . I tend to agree with you. You see, if I recall it correctly from teachings in my youth, it is an ancient Nubian text. The triangle with the circle inside was the hieroglyph for "temple" . . . but if I am correct, it means a whole lot more than that.'

'You are speaking gibberish, Ahman,' said Destine.

'Bear with me, Destine . . . but what if we took the symbol literally? Using the clues from your letter . . . what if we translate "symbol" into "*Simbel*"?' asked Ahman.

Destine shrugged. 'I do not know . . . enlighten me.'

'Now this is merely a guess, you understand. There is a place I know . . . an old temple on the outskirts of the Wilderlands a little way south of here. Sekhet *Simbel* is its name! It was consumed by the desert, lost for all time until it was rediscovered. "Once lost, but has since been found." Sekhet Simbel would seem to match that description. Do you see? If the word "symbol" becomes *Simbel* . . . it all fits!'

'But this temple . . . if it is indeed the place mentioned in my letter – what about the sun? How can its rays only strike this temple twice a year?' asked Destine. 'These clues . . . they are so cryptic!'

Ahman laughed heavily. 'Destine, is that not the point? "The truth is hidden within the third marker" – remember your own words? And it is up to us to seek it out. This is it, I am certain of it, my dear! We can be in Sekhet Simbel in a matter of hours. Well? Are you coming?'

'I have little choice, my newfound old friend,' said Destine. 'To Sekhet Simbel we will go . . . and may we finally discover the truth when we get there.'

CHAPTER XXVI

𝕿𝔥𝔢 𝕾𝔠𝔞𝔯𝔞𝔟'𝔰 𝕹𝔢𝔰𝔱

DECIDING THAT HE would make better headway on foot, Cornelius Quaint discarded his mule and walked the rest of the way to Bara Mephista. He reached into his waistcoat pocket and pulled out his recently reacquired fob watch. It was late afternoon, day one in Egypt. At the rate he was going, he would be lucky to get to the Clan Scarab settlement by sundown, and if there was one thing that he knew would be suicidal, it was wandering around that camp after dark.

It was dangerous enough doing it in daylight.

Several stone buildings were peppered about in two split semicircles around a central, rectangular building. Bleached sugar-white by the wind-whipped sandblasting over the years, it was remarkable that it was still standing. There were no 'locals' as such to Bara Mephista. If the remote location this far out in the desert failed to put people off, then rumours that it was Scarab territory almost certainly would.

Arriving at the main building, Quaint noticed a row of horses, donkeys, and even a young camel, tied to a long wooden post outside. This was the place, he assumed – an assumption given weight by the hubbub of cheers, jeers and catcalls that filled the air.

By the time he reached the door of the building, the noise from inside was loud and raucous; an atmosphere that would no doubt be shattered the moment he entered the place. If Bara Mephista was to be likened to an uncivilised town on the frontiers of the Wild West of America, then Cornelius Quaint was about to set foot in the equivalent of a saloon bar at high noon.

He pulled the rope handle and opened the door to the smoke-filled building, sending streams of stilted daylight into the place. Momentarily blinded, his eyes were unable to adapt to the contrasting light, and he stood exposed.

One by one, the occupants inside the place quietened their row as every one of them stopped and gawped at the stranger in their midst. As Quaint entered the tavern, the only noise that he could hear was his boots striding across the uneven, creaking wooden floor like the ominous ticking of a grandfather clock. This place obviously served as the Scarabs' resident drinking establishment, with rows of benches and tables scattered about against the walls, each one populated by hunched, shadowed figures scowling in his direction. Feeling many sets of eyes follow his approach, Quaint walked confidently towards the long, wooden bar.

'Good afternoon, my good man!' he said in fluent Arabic, smiling broadly.

'What do you want?' asked the bartender in his native tongue.

'Wine, please. Red, if you have any. I don't know about you, but I simply can't stomach white wine. It's far too watery for my tastes. Give me a nice, earthy red any day of the week,' Quaint rambled.

The bartender glared back at him. 'You misunderstand me, stranger – I meant what do you want *in here*?' he sneered, his greasy brow glinting with sweat.

Removing his hat, Quaint placed it upon the bar next to him and scanned the dusty array of label-less bottles lined up on the shelves, searching for a clue as to their contents. 'No wine, eh? Goes without saying, I suppose. What do you recommend?' Quaint asked, ignoring the distemper in the bartender's eyes.

'I recommend that you turn around and get out whilst you still can,' said the bartender.

'Hmm. One before I go then?' said a disgruntled Quaint.

'Forget the drink,' shouted a voice from behind him. '*This* is what you will get!'

The blade of a large knife thudded into the solid wood of the bar just shy of Quaint's hand, spearing the brim of his hat. He turned slowly, searching for the knife's owner.

It did not take long to find him.

A mean-looking one-eyed Scarab sat at a table in the corner, his one good eye staring fixedly at the conjuror.

'You have a good aim, sir,' complimented Quaint.

'Hardly . . . I was aiming for your back!' sneered the one-eyed man.

'Well, in that case I suppose that I'm rather fortunate you seem to be deficient in the ocular department by fifty per cent,' Quaint chirped.

Ignoring the attention that he had gained from the one-eyed man, Quaint reached into his waistcoat pocket and pulled out his fob watch. Time was ticking on. He had not expected to win the big prize on his first day in Egypt, but he was at least hopeful that he would pick up on a nugget of information regarding the Hades Consortium. It was surely not too much to ask. His only hope was that these desert scavengers held the key that would set him on the right road. That, and surviving long enough to make good use of the information.

Angered at being ignored, the one-eyed man slammed a bottle of murky liquid onto his table and sidled up to the bar. He spied the watch in the conjuror's hand and washed his tongue across what few remaining teeth he possessed. He prodded his finger into Quaint's shoulder.

'I want that,' he sneered.

Quaint popped the watch back into his pocket, and turned his head to look at the one-eyed man. 'Just coming up to a quarter to four.'

'Not the time, fool – I want the watch!' growled the one-eyed man. 'Give it to me.'

Quaint laughed. 'I'd rather not, if it's all the same.'

'It was not a request.'

'Even so . . . my answer remains,' said Quaint.

The portly bartender swiftly removed all the glasses and bottles from the bar and waved his hands to gather attention. 'Now, Sebul – I do not want any trouble, not whilst the Aksak is gone! Take a fresh bottle and sit down!'

But Sebul had no intention of doing either.

Again, he prodded Quaint's shoulder with his grubby finger.

'In Bara Mephista, we have a tradition . . . if a Scarab wants something, a Scarab *takes* it.' The one-eyed man grabbed hold of his knife, still embedded in the bar, and wrenched it from the wood. Looking Quaint up and down, he brandished the blade inches from the conjuror's face. To his credit, Quaint did not even flinch. 'So I will ask only one more time, stranger . . . give me that watch or I will gut you where you stand and *take* it from you! Understand?'

'Perfectly,' said Quaint. 'But you see I have a little tradition of my own.' Beckoning the Scarab towards him, he grabbed the back of Sebul's head and slammed it into the bar, breaking his nose. He reeled as Quaint followed with a powerful open-handed punch to his jaw. For good measure, the conjuror kicked his legs out from underneath him and slammed his elbow onto the back of the Scarab's neck.

Sebul slumped onto the sawdust-covered floor – very bloodied and quite extremely unconscious.

A low growl from many throats sounded behind him, and Quaint was conscious of being surrounded by Scarabs. He turned to face the mob, all armed with threatening glares – as well as hooks, metal spikes and daggers. Dirty and dishevelled, and stinking like a pack of wild dogs, the men closed upon him.

A mental checklist of his options blazed across Quaint's mind – fleetingly, for he had none to consider. He measured the crowd gathering around him as an uneasy silence quickly settled. The air held the scent of violence and he was fully aware that it was at his expense.

'Don't tell me you all want the time,' he said. 'Don't any of you have a watch?'

There came no reply.

Staring down the crowd, Quaint held his ground, continuing his charade of confidence as best as his spent nerves could manage.

Eventually, the Clan Scarabs' anger subsided. They could not quite measure the stranger in their midst, and none of them were too eager to get a helping of what Sebul had just had. They soon returned to their business as if nothing had happened.

'You enjoy chancing your luck, stranger,' noted the bartender.

'Every day,' Quaint smirked.

'Well, I would not push it . . . luck does not last long in Bara Mephista.'

'I'll bear that in mind,' said Quaint. 'So . . . I presume you are the proprietor of this establishment?'

The bartender's double chin wobbled as he nodded. 'And I must say, you speak Arabic very well for an Englishman.'

'How do you know I'm English?' asked Quaint.

The bartender measured the conjuror from top to toe. 'Just a wild guess.'

The tavern full of Scarabs was still in shock after seeing Sebul so deftly quashed, and they listened intently to the unfolding conversation as the bartender slid a stained glass across the bar.

'The last of our red wine. Drink it and go,' he said. 'You are not welcome here.'

Quaint grinned shamelessly. 'Clearly. But I'm not here for trouble. I only want to see your leader.'

'Aksak!' snapped a Scarab behind him.

'Yes, that's the chap,' said Quaint, with misplaced cheer. 'Mr Aksak.'

'We call our leader Aksak!' yelled another.

'Aksak Faroud!' said yet another, with a defiant stomp of his foot on the floor – causing his friends to mirror him.

'That's what I said,' Quaint answered. 'We're old pals, you see. I was in the neighbourhood and just thought I'd pop in and see him. Good old Aksak Faroud . . . what a champ!'

'Friend of the Aksak's?' mumbled a chorus of Scarabs.

'How would someone like *you* know the Aksak, stranger?' asked a pockmarked, scab-infested man as he spat upon the floor – causing his friends to mirror *him*.

'Why . . . from our old robbing days in Cairo, of course,' answered Quaint, lies trickling from his tongue – a talent he held in great esteem. 'I'll bet he's not changed a bit. Still a grumpy old sourpuss, is he? The look of the Devil about him and rarely a smile unless a woman is in the room?'

The pack of Scarabs went silent. Strangely, this description of their leader seemed perfectly acceptable, and they required no further validation of Quaint's identity.

Cornelius Quaint was not one of the most beguiling conjurors in Europe for nothing. His bravado had talked him out of (and into) a lot of trouble over the years, and if there was one thing that he was supremely gifted at, it was being able to fool an audience. And bloody spectacular at it he was too.

'Aksak Faroud is not here,' the bartender said. 'He is away on urgent Scarab business in Umkaza.'

'I'll wait,' said Quaint, throwing a dried date into his mouth from a bowl at the bar. Finally he would have someone to ask questions of. This man, Aksak Faroud, surely he was a reasonable sort of chap. Quaint pulled out his deck of cards. 'Why don't we pass the time with a little illusion I like to call the Equivoque Principle?'

CHAPTER XXVII

The Footsteps of History

PROFESSOR POLLYANNA NORTH was an educated woman. In her late thirties, she had already made a name for herself as one of only a handful of female archaeologists working in service to Queen Victoria, and this fact alone made her the object of much attention. 'A rare gem of a woman' and 'One of the Empire's finest exported treasures' were just two of the niceties that her peers had bestowed upon her. Polly was under a great deal of pressure not to come back to England empty handed on this dig, especially as the Queen herself had seen fit to honour her at a forthcoming gala dinner. That would normally have sent tingles of excitement up and down the woman's spine, but she currently had nothing of worth to present.

The abandoned district of Umkaza was some miles away from Bara Mephista on the outskirts of the low-lying flatlands to the west of the River Nile. Abandoned years before, it had become home to a small group of archaeologists and historians. Polly's benefactor was convinced that Umkaza held a glorious treasure and he had invested a great deal of money in this venture to discover it. Polly was desperate not to let him down, but after digging with her small crew for some time yet finding little of value, she was rapidly running out of both hope and luck – in equal measure. Rebuilding, reconstructing and retracing History's footsteps were not tasks for the impatient, but even Polly's vaunted endurance was sorely waning of late.

The Professor was up to her armpits in sand and dust when she became distracted by several of her young crew running up to her, gathering her up in their excited swarm as they led her to one of the many deep pits dug at the far end of the marked site. She placed her hands on her hips and scowled at the two excited men in the pit, their filthy faces smudged with dust and dirt.

'What on earth is all the fuss about, Mal? Have you found something?' she asked.

'Yes, ma'am!' said the smaller of the two Egyptians. 'Something quite odd.'

'I'm sufficiently intrigued, Mal,' said Polly. A small crowd gathered around her, all eager to hear her assessment. She squatted down onto her knees and leaned into the pit, as Mal handed her what he had discovered in it. It was unmistakably a bone. Removing a magnifying glass from the top pocket of her blouse, Polly lifted the bone closer to her eyes and blew the remaining dust from it. 'Approximate length eighteen inches . . . width: just less than an inch.'

'There are lots of them down here, ma'am. The deeper we dig, the more we find. Perhaps as many as fifteen, maybe more,' said Mal. 'What animal do you think it might be? Horse? Camel?'

Polly North clenched her jaw. 'Human.' The word was like a crash of thunder to those crewmembers within earshot. 'It's a femur – a thigh bone, to those unfamiliar with anatomy. How many of these things did you say were down there?'

'At least fifteen, ma'am,' replied Mal. 'But there are lots of other bones too of all shapes and sized, piled one of top of the other. We will have to dig a little deeper to know how many for certain.'

'Don't,' said Polly. 'Leave them where they are, Mal. Fifteen bodies in a pit, piled on top of each other can only mean one thing. This is a mass grave, and it's never good news to go excavating a mass grave, trust me.'

'Why not, Professor? These bones . . . might they not be ancient Nubian in origin? There are so many in one place; if this is a sacrificial site . . . perhaps they might be a clue. Perhaps they might eventually help us find "The Pharaoh's Cradle?"'

'That's highly unlikely, Mal, especially if my instincts are spot on.' Professor North held her magnifying glass an inch from the bone, inspecting its length carefully. 'It can't be much older than twenty or thirty years at the most. Sorry to say, Mal, there is no place for them in the Cairo Museum of Antiquities . . . and no way could the Pharaoh's Cradle be buried here. We'll just have to keep on searching, chaps.'

The crowd chorused a disappointed sigh. But rising above it, Polly was distracted by a tumultuous noise echoing all around her.

Screams littered the air.

Aksak Faroud and a band of twelve Scarabs tore into the encampment astride horses. Wearing a dark red hood, the Scarab leader held his sword high in the air. Professor North's crew were caught between an intense desire to flee and the inability to do anything about it, their fear freezing them to the spot.

'Who are these men?' asked Polly of Mal, clutching at the younger man's clothes as he crawled from the trench.

'Clan Scarabs!' he gasped.

'Clan Scarabs?' cried Polly. 'What are they doing so far from their territory?'

'I am sorry, Professor . . . but I do not plan on waiting to find out.' With that, he climbed from the pit and ran at top speed across the dig site, his arms flailing in the air as if he were being pursued by a swarm of wasps.

Pretty soon many other workers followed his lead. Polly looked around at the ensuing chaos. Her excavation crew were running scared in all directions, the merest mention of the words 'Clan Scarabs' igniting a fire underneath their feet. Polly was dumbfounded, unable to move. What could she do? Where could she go? Polly had never heard of them attacking an archaeological site before.

It made no sense.

Aksak Faroud's quarry was an easy target to spot. The only pale-skinned female around – actually, one of the few people around full stop, for most of the others had fled. Polly gulped down her fear. The bestial pack headed towards her determinedly.

'But this is insane!' she said to herself. 'We have nothing worth taking!'

Apart from Professor Pollyanna North herself, it seemed . . .

CHAPTER XXVIII

The Kindred Spirits

THE AREA KNOWN as the Wilderlands was an inhospitable, hellish landscape. The flattening of feet, hooves and cart-wheels had formed an uneven road from the rough, chalky terrain. Travelling through these lands, you never knew what you were stepping on, or riding across or walking through. You could just as easily set foot in a scorpion's nest as drive your cart into a two-foot-deep trench obscured by the playful sand-storms. As Ahman gently whipped the reins of his small, two-seater cart, his horse whinnied indignantly at the roughness of the terrain. Sat next to the Egyptian, Destine's eyes were occupied elsewhere, not wanting to miss a thing. The stark beauty of the barren locale was unlike anything the Frenchwoman had seen before. Except that was not strictly true. She had seen it all before, she just could not remember. Still, there was something to be said for her umbrella of amnesia – at least she was able to experience such a beautiful sight with fresh eyes.

The final part of the journey from Agra to Sekhet Simbel was uneventful, and yet in the back of the cart, Destine was perched on the edge of her seat for the entire duration. Ahman continued to reassure her that they would not be able to simply pass the temple by and not notice it, and as the cart reached the top of the dunes, she understood why.

Sekhet Simbel was truly breathtaking – in a very literal sense. The façade of the temple seemed to materialise out of the shimmering horizon, and Destine's fingertips tingled with anticipation.

She was unaware of it, but she was near to tears. She had returned to Sekhet Simbel. Yet this was no joyous homecoming as she was forced to remind herself. This was a matter of life and death. Even so, the temple was an echo from the past – a subject that she so dearly wished to embrace. She climbed from the cart and walked closer, taking in the full splendour of the place. She sensed an unusual affinity spread through her veins, like two kindred spirits coming together. She beamed a huge smile at Ahman, who merely nodded along with her silent thoughts.

'It is beautiful, monsieur. Truly!' Destine exclaimed. 'The closer I get, the grander it becomes.'

Ahman stood back and looked up at the temple, marvelling at its majesty. 'Yah, I know what you mean. Even as an Egyptian, I find this place a marvel myself. Being so close to the Wilderlands, it is hardly first stop on the traveller's trail. We ignore it, we forget it . . . to our loss, I admit. It is sites like this that bathe the eye and warm the soul.'

'So I am not alone,' noted Destine. 'You are in awe as well, *mon ami?*'

'How can you not be, ah?' Ahman's pride presented itself as a sparkling twinkle in the corner of his dark brown eyes. 'I remember many folks in awe when the temple was unearthed. The rumours moved from settlement to settlement like the smell of freshly baked bread on the breeze. At that time we did not even know its name . . . we still do not, actually . . . its *true* name I mean, but Sekhet Simbel seems to fit.'

'True name? How do you mean, monsieur?' asked Destine.

'Local legend tells that a young Egyptian girl led two explorers to this area about thirty years ago. With no other documentation to rely on, the men decided to name the temple after her, and she was called Sekhet Simbel. Those explorers put the place on the map, and it was only after the entirety of the temple was revealed, after nearly four years of constant excavation, that the historians and archaeologists began to decipher its use . . . but they are still only halfway there, apparently. I like to think that its purpose is merely to astound the visitor by its sheer magnificence.'

'It is odd to think that such a thing of beauty lay undiscovered,' said Destine.

'The past has a way of hiding itself from view if it does not wish to be found,' said Ahman, wiping a fine seam of sweat from his neck with his handkerchief.

Destine raised an inquisitive eyebrow. 'An apt snippet of wisdom, Ahman, for my own past might be hiding within this temple and I aim to find it . . . whether it wishes me to or not.'

'Come then,' said Ahman, 'let us not keep it waiting.'

Ahman led Destine through the large entrance constructed of huge blocks of weathered stone and into the magnificent temple's interior.

In the hazy light beyond, they could see a series of halls going deeper into the distance. The brilliance of the sunlight at their backs shrouded everything in a misty fog, a perfect accompaniment to the grandiose spectacle. The visitors were in the presence of gods and pharaohs, after all. As Destine stood rooted to the spot, tiny flecks of dust rose into the air. She could feel the resonance of history in every stone, every carving and every inscription. It was as if the phantoms of her past had been waiting patiently for her arrival. They swarmed about her, welcoming her into their abode. An instinct made her shuffle a little closer to Ahman, the act masking the footfalls of another visitor to the temple.

'Can I help you?' he boomed.

Ahman and Destine leapt like startled cats as they spun around.

'I am sorry, but the temple is currently closed for scientific studies . . . as the sign clearly states,' said the new arrival, motioning towards a small painted sign just inside the entrance, virtually obscured by the darkness.

'We did not see it,' apologised Ahman.

'That may be the case, sir, but I must still ask you to leave. Immediately, if you would be so kind,' said the man in an authoritative tone that could not be ignored.

'Monsieur, if you wish to stop people entering this temple, might I suggest placing the signs *outside* the building?' said a defiant Destine.

'*Destine*,' Ahman said sharply, gripping her arm.

'I am sorry, Ahman, but we are doing no harm,' replied Destine.

'I agree, but—'

'And we have travelled a *great* distance to get here on a journey of the utmost importance!' supplemented Destine. 'All we want is to inspect the temple's beauty not plunder its treasures! We did not come so far to be barred entrance upon arrival, not when we are so close.'

'Destine!' glowered Ahman.

'Ahman, please do not try to silence me, you know how important this is!'

'I do, but—'

'We have earned a look, have we not? I mean, it is not as if we are—'

'*Destine!*' Ahman yelled abruptly – and so forceful was he that Destine's mouth clamped shut. 'Listen to me for a moment! This man . . . you . . . you heard what he said?'

'*Oui*, Ahman, of course I did, but we cannot simply turn around and—'

'No, I mean . . . you *understood* him?' asked Ahman firmly.

'Of course – why should I not have?'

Ahman's eyes went wide. 'Because he was speaking Arabic.'

Destine's senses were aflame. 'Nonsense! I heard every word as clearly as I am talking to you now. If he were speaking Arabic, how on earth could I have understood a word he said?'

'That is entirely my point, Madame,' said Ahman 'This man was definitely speaking Arabic. But importantly . . . so were you. Fluently, I might add.'

'Me? *Mon ami*, I do not think so,' laughed Destine. 'I cannot speak Arabic!'

'I am sorry, Destine,' said Ahman, 'but it seems that you can.'

Destine felt the corners of her mouth twitch, unsure whether to smile or cry.

The stranger cleared his throat. 'This is fascinating, but if I may be so bold as to interrupt? Now that we have proved that you understood what I asked, there are no more excuses! This temple is currently off limits, so I must kindly ask you to continue your discussion outside.'

Destine gave the man a once over as if she had only just realised he was there. He was dressed in a white cotton suit, with a broad-knotted tie at his neck. He held a lantern in one hand and a notebook in the other. His shiny bald head caught a halo of the sun's glare, offsetting the steely look within his eyes.

'And might I ask who you are, sir?' asked Destine.

'I am Feron Mouk, the curator of this site,' said the man, his bombast fading slightly as Destine took a step nearer to him. 'Perhaps I did not make myself clear: we are currently making some important renovations to some of our exhibits here. The desert storm sands are unrelenting, I am afraid, and every once in a while we must ensure the artefacts are cleaned. May I ask the purpose of your visit today?'

Ahman spoke: 'Mr Mouk, my companion has become bewitched by Sekhet Simbel's majesty, have you not, my dear?'

'*Mais oui* . . . yes,' agreed Destine, following Ahman's lead. 'I have been here before, you see. Way back in the early thirties, and I have longed to return to this place ever since.'

'Ah . . . the thirties, now those were glorious days, ma'am, *simply* glorious!' cheered Mouk, tapping a beat on the sand with his foot. 'Much has changed since then – in the world outside *and* within this temple. We have unearthed a great deal more of this place, including the smaller annexed temple to the east. You are most welcome to peruse that before you leave, but as I said . . . I am afraid this particular area is off limits.'

Ahman shuffled over and steered Mouk's arm.

'We understand, sir, but the last time my companion was here, she laid eyes on a most wonderful artefact and she was quite taken by it,' he said, consciously leading Mouk away from the entrance and deeper into temple. 'Yet it was so long ago now, and I am afraid that she has quite forgotten where it is. I am most intrigued, I must say. I just wish I had the knowledge and skill to decipher her meaning, but I am far from knowledgeable in such matters. Surely not even the most studious academic in all of Egypt would be able to locate it. Unless . . . I do not suppose someone as highly respected as *you* might be able to work out what she means would you, Mr Mouk?'

Ahman had said all the right things.

'Well . . . when you put it like that, sir, I can certainly *try*!' Mouk beamed pompously. 'I suppose that I might be willing to bend the rules a little. I do *so* love to meet people with an appreciation of the past.'

'Recently I have found the past *most* enlightening,' said Destine, with a wink at Ahman.

'Very good, then!' said Mouk. 'Tell me what you can of this piece that you admired so much, ma'am, and I shall do my best to locate it for you.'

Destine smiled sweetly, relishing the role of dotty old woman as she felt a little flurry of butterflies take flight in her stomach. 'It is like a dream, but all I can remember is that it was called "The Shaded God" . . . more than that I cannot say. I am afraid I am a bit forgetful at my age.'

'The Shaded God . . . hmm, let me see.' Mouk was one of those that liked to tap their fingernails against their teeth when they were concentrating. 'Well . . . I have worked on this site for many years and I can modestly say that I am the foremost expert on its inventory of treasures. However, I can definitely say with all sincerity that we have *no* exhibit here of that name.'

Ahman and Destine's hearts sank simultaneously.

'Unless . . . the only thing I can think of . . .'

'Yes?' asked Destine eagerly.

'This way!' Mouk announced, before darting off. 'But do try to keep pace. If you get lost down here it may take hours to find you.'

As Destine and Ahman quickly followed Feron Mouk's charge, his voice echoed off the enclosed walls all around them. He was giving a rapid commentary – not that his audience cared much for anything; their sights were set on but one target.

'These were amongst the first artefacts to be unearthed,' he said, pointing to two rows of magnificent statues as he continued through the temple. 'These two on the north side wear the White Crown of Upper Egypt, whereas these on the south wear the Double Crown of Lower Egypt. And as we move through into the next antechamber, these hieroglyphics here depict the great Battle of Kadesh, where Rameses the Great fought the Hittite warriors of King Muwatalli.'

Mouk's potted history lesson continued as he led Destine and Ahman ever forwards, into the belly of the temple. They soon entered a many-pillared hall with beautifully inscribed columns decorated with various pictorial images and hieroglyphics. The hall gradually gave way to a vestibule in the middle of a low-ceilinged room. There was no natural light at all in the room, but four lit torches were affixed at points on the brickwork.

'Here we are!' announced Mouk, as he approached the wall at the far end of the corridor. 'This might be what you are searching for.'

'Here?' asked Destine. She was looking at a wall no more than twenty feet in width, with four statues seated upon four stone thrones against it.

Mouk looked at her unchanged expression. 'This is not what you sought?'

Destine was uncertain what to say. 'Possibly . . . but I just need to familiarise myself with it a little. Where is this place?'

'This is the Innermost Shrine, ma'am – the heartbeat of the temple!' proclaimed Mouk. 'The entire reason for its being you might say. And might I add an enigma that has outfoxed the combined intellects of the world's greatest Egyptologists – including myself, if I might be so bold as to count myself amongst their number.' Mouk grinned broadly from ear to ear, and beckoned Destine forwards. 'Come, ma'am, take a closer look.'

'But, Monsieur Mouk . . . look at what? I see nothing but statues . . . the likes of which are all over this temple, are they not?' said Destine, understandably deflated.

'Ma'am, it is the symbolism behind these particular statues that is important,' explained Mouk. 'Each one has a history, and each one speaks volumes to those educated in all the subtle nuances of the Ancient's testaments.'

Destine inspected the statues, with her tongue frozen firmly at the back of her throat. 'Monsieur Mouk . . . you said these sculptures represent the "Shaded God"? Might I ask you to explain?'

'But, of course, ma'am! Behold . . . the mystery that lies deep within the heart of Sekhet Simbel.' Mouk said, as he pointed to the sculptured figures. 'As you no doubt are aware, our ancestors worshipped many gods and goddesses. Egypt is replete with temples, shrines and edifices venerating all sorts of deities from the sun to the moon to the wind that shakes the trees. Here we have the four deities to whom this particular temple is dedicated. We have Ra-Horakhty, the hawk-headed God of the Rising Sun. We have the deified Pharaoh Rameses the Great right here . . . and next to him we have Amun-Ra, the Sun God. And here . . . this is the fellow that you wish to reacquaint yourself with, I believe.' Mouk tapped upon the statue with his knuckles. 'This is the god called Ptah. One of the most maligned and misrepresented deities in ancient Egyptian history. Some academics would have us believe that Ptah was the god of death . . . but if we ignore our modern, nineteenth-century translation of him and view him with the eyes of the ancients things can take on a different slant.'

'How so?' asked Destine, hungry for more.

'Well, instead of death, Ptah was actually associated with the exact opposite – with creation, with life beginning anew,' replied Mouk, eager to feed his audience's curiosity. 'In fact, some scriptures tell that the world itself sprang forth from his dreams! Ptah was the creator of *everything*. Literally translated, his name means "the opener" – as in the opener of worlds, the opener of minds, the opener of mouths even – such is his misinterpreted symbolism with death.'

'The opener of mouths?' repeated Destine in a whisper.

'Yes, indeed, ma'am!' cried Feron Mouk. 'The act of an undertaker opening the deceased's mouth is still practised to this day, and stems back to the ancient times. Ptah believed that if the mouth were closed during the burial process, the soul would be trapped for ever within the mortal shell, denied its eternal life amongst the stars only to crumble to dust.' Destine and Ahman were quite uncertain what to say, and the curator seemed positively thrilled that he had provoked such a response.

'Marvellously macabre, is it not?' he chuckled.

'And what of the story I have heard that the sun only strikes this place twice a year?' asked Destine, hoping to cement the meaning within the words of her letter. 'How can that be so? We are right out in the middle of the desert – surely the sun will *always* strike this temple?'

Mouk clasped his palms together eagerly, enjoying another opportunity to show off. 'I am glad you asked, ma'am, for that is the reason for my bringing you to this place! It is what piqued my curiosity in your tale, in fact. Ptah's story is integral to the history – and indeed, the *mystery* – behind this very temple. Allow me to explain,' said Mouk, and Destine and Ahman gladly obliged. 'The sun does indeed strike the exterior of Sekhet Simbel all year round . . . but not the interior. You see, this temple was purposefully oriented in such a way that twice a year – in February and October – the light of the sun penetrates this very sanctuary from the main entrance behind us, illuminating the gods to which Sekhet Simbel pays homage.' Mouk proudly pointed to the four statues behind him and smiled, dropping an overlong pause. 'That is . . . all except one! Unlike the other gods deified here, Ptah's statue is *never* illuminated by the sun's rays . . . not once! But why not? I hear you ask. If the axis of the temple was of an intentional design, then why purposefully keep him shrouded?'

'Why?' Destine found herself asking.

'Why indeed, ma'am,' said Mouk. 'There are many theories as to why this is, of course, but we may never reveal the truth behind the mystery. Poor old Ptah . . . the god bathed eternally in the shadow of the sun, destined never to see its light again. Such is life . . . such is history. Sometimes the past refuses to give up its secrets.'

'I could not agree more,' said Destine.

'When you mentioned it earlier, there was only one piece in this temple that sprang to mind,' said Feron Mouk, clasping his hands. 'Am I correct, ma'am?'

'*Oui*, monsieur, it is all coming back to me now,' lied Destine. 'Such beauty. How could I have forgotten it? You have my sincere thanks, Monsieur Mouk.'

Mouk bowed. 'You are most welcome, ma'am. I have to attend to some other business in the archives. Why not stay awhile and admire Sekhet Simbel's majesty some more. If you do not mind seeing yourselves out, that is?'

Destine nearly bit his hand off. 'Of course! *Merci beaucoup!* Thank you.'

'Good day, ma'am . . . and sir,' Feron Mouk said cheerily, as he departed for a tunnel leading from the main hall. 'Do come again!'

'What a nice man,' said Destine. 'A trifle overzealous. But nice.'

Ahman snatched her hand and squeezed it tight. 'What next?'

'I have no idea, *mon ami*,' admitted Destine. 'We search for the third marker, I suppose – whatever and wherever it might be. We are not quite at the end of this riddle yet.'

Gathering her composure, still unsure exactly how the statue of Ptah might assist her, Destine caressed her hands over the stone. Her fingertips invaded every groove, every crack and every gap in the statue from its head down to its solid rock base. She froze like one of the temple's petrified exhibits as her fingertips touched against something embedded within the base of Ptah's sculpture. Something solid and thick wrapped in rough material. She quickly stowed it away within the folds of her bodice, not daring to even look at it.

'Destine?' Ahman asked, seeing the look on her face. 'What is it?'

Destine fought to gather her voice. 'Answers, *mon cher* . . . I hope.'

CHAPTER XXIX

The Pull of History

DESTINE MADE A hasty egress from the temple, with Ahman rushing behind her. Clutching the smuggled item close to her chest, her eyes darted around her. She was barely able to contain her excitement. The letter was correct. It had said that there was something to find in Sekhet Simbel, and she had found it. That confirmation proved much. It proved that everything in the letters was true. It was her legacy to find that cloth-wrapped parcel; perhaps even her destiny.

'Quickly, we must find somewhere safe to examine it,' she said to Ahman.

'Safe?' he asked, looking around. 'Are we not safe *here*? Who else do you think would be interested in whatever it is that you have there, ah?'

'I will not know until I open it, will I?' Destine said. The parcel seemed to pulse with its own heartbeat, radiating warmth as if it were alive. 'But I have no wish to do so right on Mr Mouk's doorstep. I am sure he takes a *very* dim view of people stealing from his temple!' Before Ahman had even finished untying his horse's reins, Destine was already sat in the rear of the cart.

'It is getting late in the afternoon and we should think about making camp for the night. I know a little place on a lake not far from here that is suitable,' said Ahman. 'It is not wise to be out in the open once darkness falls.'

'*Très bien*! Please . . . just let us be on our way.'

Although Madame Destine was clairvoyant no more, it seemed that she retained a slight semblance of her gift, for she was somewhat prescient in her earlier estimation that she was not safe.

As she and Ahman began their journey, a pair of furtive eyes watched their cart with interest from an overlooking hill. His eyes fixed upon the duo, a knife's edge of a smile sliced across Heinrich Nadir's face. He turned to the two men at his side – men swathed head to toe in dark red rags that climbed their bodies, coiling around their heads into an all concealing hood. Only their dark eyes peered through an inch-wide slit. These men were trained in the art of dealing death, and its stench clung to their clothes like must.

'There are your targets, *meine freunde*!' Nadir said. 'When the order is given, you may kill the male . . . but whatever you do, ensure that the female is unharmed or the Hades Consortium will have your heads. Whilst the Frenchwoman is certainly valuable, she is but the bait to snare an even greater prize.'

CHAPTER XXX

The Distressing Damsel

CORNELIUS QUAINT KNEW that walking boldly into Clan Scarab territory was always going to be a gamble, but he maintained a fondness for gambles – especially when the stakes were high. As things stood, for him (and for Egypt) the stakes were astronomical.

'So, Chullah,' said Quaint (now on first name terms with the bartender), 'what time can I expect your Aksak to arrive, anyway?'

'When he gets here,' replied Chullah. 'As I said . . . he is on Scarab business some miles away. He should be back before nightfall. Why did you wish to speak with him again?'

'I have a question that I hope he'll have the answer to,' replied Quaint.

At that moment, the tavern door was wrenched open, and a guttural voice spoke an inch from Quaint's ear:

'And what would that question *be*, stranger?'

Quaint turned around to face the grim-faced Clan Scarab leader standing in the open doorway of the Bara Mephista tavern.

'Aksak Faroud, I presume?' Quaint asked.

'You have me at a loss, Mister . . .?' asked Faroud, narrowing his gaze.

Quaint opened his mouth to speak. 'My name is—'

'Surely you remember your old friend Cornelius Quaint!' said Chullah.

'*Friend?*' asked Faroud.

Quaint could almost hear the ice cracking beneath his feet.

'Yes, from your old pickpocket days in Cairo! Your secret is out, boss – Cornelius here has been telling us some wild stories of your childhood together!'

'*Has* he now?' asked Faroud, eyeing the conjuror curiously. His voice was tempered and calm but his eyes bubbled away furiously, barely restrained.

'This man is a wonder, Aksak! He has been showing us miracles with a deck of cards – just do not play blackjack with him, eh? I have lost two bottles of gin already!' grinned Chullah.

Aksak Faroud ignored the bartender's cheer and leaned closer to Quaint.

'Whoever you *really* are, stranger, it seems that my men have warmly accepted you ... otherwise I would have had to step over your corpse on my way in. However, you will find that it takes more to appease me than fancy card tricks.'

Quaint winced. 'Well, they weren't exactly *tricks*. You see—'

'Silence!' yelled Faroud at the top of his voice. The atmosphere in the tavern became a static moment in between breaths as every pair of Scarab eyes surveyed the stand-off between Faroud and Quaint. 'You are in *my* world now ... and in *my* world, *I* make the rules.'

'Good policy,' said Quaint. 'Keeps any visitors in check.'

'We receive very few of them here,' said Faroud. 'Those who know of our presence steer well clear, and those who stumble across us by accident do not live to boast of the tale. You must either be very brave ... or very stupid. Which is it?'

'That depends on who you ask,' Quaint replied, pushing his luck.

'What do you want here?' demanded Faroud.

'I just need information . . . and it's a matter of life or death,' said Quaint.

'The Clan Scarabs are not an information service, stranger. I hope your journey here was worth it, for it will be the last you ever take.' Faroud drew a dagger from a scabbard at his waist, and thrust it against Quaint's neck. The blade grazed the conjuror's Adam's apple and he dared not swallow. 'If you thought you could just walk into my camp and request information, then you must have a lust for death . . . and I am only too willing to feed it! Now tell me, what information could a man like you possibly expect from a man like *me*?'

'The Hades Consortium,' Quaint wheezed.

The words had a remarkable effect on Aksak Faroud, and he released the blade at Quaint's neck. 'Did Joyce send you?'

Quaint shook his head. 'Never heard of him.'

'So what do you know of the Hades Consortium?' demanded the Aksak.

'A bit,' replied Quaint. 'I know what they're capable of, and I know what they're planning to do in Egypt very soon. The real question, Aksak Faroud, is: what do *you* know?'

'I can see that you are determined to pique my curiosity, Mr Quaint' said Faroud.

'I hear that a lot,' Quaint quipped.

'So speak on,' urged Faroud, tightening his grip on his knife once more.

'Righto,' sang Quaint. 'The Hades Consortium is planning to deposit a consignment of highly toxic poison into the River Nile at New Year.' He slid his finger inside his collar and touched gently at the thin wound on his neck, taking a brief look at the dab of blood on his fingertips. 'You wondered why I would come here knowing that I was risking my life? To see an end to their plot is why, so I need to know whose side you are on, Aksak: the Hades Consortium's . . . or Egypt's?'

Quaint was relieved to see Faroud's full interest flicker into life.

'My mother always said I was too curious for my own good,' said the Aksak, replacing his knife into its scabbard. 'You have just earned yourself a reprieve, Mr Quaint. We shall discuss this further once I have concluded my other business. But if I fail to be impressed by your explanation, you will be *begging* to die.' Faroud snapped his fingers and several of his men barged into the tavern obediently.

Quaint watched the procession of Scarabs with keen interest. As the last man entered the tavern and pushed past him, Quaint noticed that he was carrying someone kicking and screaming over his shoulder. By the shapely rear end, Quaint could tell it was a woman, and for one awful moment he thought it was Alexandria – until the woman cursed at her captors – a series of unmistakably unladylike oaths – and his heart relaxed. Alex would never use such colourful language – unless it was aimed in his direction. Whoever this woman was, Quaint had a nagging suspicion that she was about to disrupt all his best laid plans . . .

'Take her out back. I will join you in a moment,' Faroud said to his men, then spun on his heel back to Quaint. 'I must leave you for a time . . . time that you should spend thinking of a reason why I should not stake you to the ground and let the vultures peck at your carcass.'

Quaint grinned boldly. 'Well, for one I'm all gristle. Not good for the digestion.'

'Your wit is not endearing you to me, Mr Quaint,' said Faroud.

'I hear that a lot too,' said Quaint.

Aksak Faroud led Quaint to a small booth at the rear of the tavern, obscured by a ragged curtain. The Aksak ripped the curtain open and ushered Quaint to take one of the two chairs at the table. Two Scarab guards armed with curved swords approached and waited for their leader's commands.

'Watch this man,' said Faroud. 'If he becomes a nuisance, quieten him.'

As he slid himself into the confines of the chair, and as the curtain around him was drawn, Quaint heard Faroud's footsteps resound against the wooden floor. He heard a door directly next to him open, and then slam shut.

Chullah scuttled into the booth and placed a bottle on the table. As he removed the cork stopper, a sharp scent of anise flooded Quaint's senses.

'You like absinthe, Cornelius?' asked the bartender.

'I'm not sure "like" would be the correct measure of my appreciation, Chullah. The last time I had some, I felt as though I'd played ten rounds of croquet.'

'That sounds like fun!'

'As the ball?'

'Well . . . if you want my advice – enjoy the Aksak's hospitality whilst it lasts,' said Chullah, as he poured a glass of the pale green liquid. 'And I would think very carefully about how long you wish to live for.'

'It's crossed my mind, believe me,' said Quaint.

Once Chullah had gone, Quaint strained in his seat to hear the conversation in the room next door.

In that room, Professor Pollyanna North was bound to a wooden chair, her face covered with a rough sack. As Faroud strode over to her and ripped it off, Polly gasped for air, her eyes squinting madly. She looked around the room in a daze.

'Welcome to my camp, Professor,' said Faroud.

Polly spat in his face.

'I see you are not yet house-broken,' he said, wiping the spit from his cheek.

'You Scarab bastard! You wrecked my dig site! Your thieves have set my project back by six months!' Polly screamed, malice dripping from every word like hot candle wax. 'And you didn't even *take* anything!'

'On the contrary, Professor,' said Faroud. 'We took *you*.'

Listening as best he could on the other side of the wall, Quaint's attention was ensnared by this newcomer. So she was a professor – and a feisty one at that. But a professor of what? What could the Clan Scarabs possibly want with a professor?

'You're filth!' Polly snarled, her anger just about keeping her tears at bay. 'You scared off my entire crew! Do you know how long it took me to recruit that damn team?'

'The show of force was necessary to maintain your compliance,' said Aksak Faroud. 'My employer told me of your commitment, Professor . . . how you fight with honour to preserve the secrets of my country's past. For that you have my respect, but I know that you are an intelligent woman . . . and not to mention tenacious. No woman would come to Egypt without spirit, and no woman would dig so tirelessly in a place such as Umkaza unless they held a strong love for the land and its history. Your mother was Egyptian, was she not?'

'Did you bring me out here to discuss my family tree?' stormed

Polly. 'What are we going to do next, swap embarrassing childhood stories? What could a group of thieving murderers like you want from an archaeological site? We weren't causing any harm, and we've got the permission of the Egyptian government to dig there!'

'Permission is not my employer's concern, Professor . . . *you* are,' Faroud said. 'He wishes you to pack up your equipment from Umkaza and move on. The city of Anuk-Suresh has many treasures yet to be uncovered.'

'Anuk-Suresh is old news! Its people were smart. They made their treasures easy to find to keep the lazy diggers busy, distracting them from other more plentiful sites hidden elsewhere,' Polly said. 'That might work for the rest of my colleagues, but I don't follow the pack, and when someone tells me not to dig in Umkaza, it only makes me wonder *why*. My guess is that there *is* something worth finding there, after all . . . something I've yet to uncover, and I'll bet your "employer" is just trying to scare me off so he can get his hands on it! Who is it? Alberto San Marco, that slimy little snake? Or is it that hairy old bear Horace Arlow? He's been after the Pharaoh's Cradle almost as long as I have!'

'Those names mean nothing to me,' replied Faroud. 'You need not concern yourself with the whys and wherefores of your capture, Professor North.'

On the other side of the wall, Quaint's eyes widened. Professor North? *Polly* North? Quaint retained a healthy interest in Egyptology from his youth, and Pollyanna North's name was known to him. Her reputation was impressive, but not as impressive as her present display of bravery.

'If this is the part where you expect me to plead for my life, then you'll have a long wait! Just do what you have to do . . . kill me or let me go – either way, just get on with it,' yelled Polly.

'I have no wish to kill you, Professor. My services were hired merely to relay a warning – stay away from Umkaza. For good. Or next time I will not ask you so politely,' said Aksak Faroud.

'You could have warned me off in Umkaza. Why am I here?' asked Polly of her captor. 'Not that I even know where "here" is because some idiot stuck a bag on my head!'

'You are in Bara Mephista, Professor,' confirmed Faroud.

'The old Nubian settlement?' Polly asked. 'That's quite a trek from Umkaza. I must have been unconscious for some time.'

'For the sake of my eardrums, thankfully so,' said Faroud.

Polly replied with a sarcastic smile. 'So this employer you mentioned . . . I didn't realise you lot loaned your services out for hire. Since when did the Clan Scarabs become someone else's lapdogs?'

'The Scarabs are *nobody's* lapdogs, woman!' shouted Faroud. The back of his hand came from nowhere, striking Polly's left cheek. She crashed to the floor, still bound to the chair. Multicoloured flashes burst before her eyes. Faroud clenched his shaking fists tight, as if he held the entirety of his rage within them and he was desperate for it not to escape. He glared with furious venom at Polly, but then noticed a thin crease of blood at the corner of her mouth.

'No! I did not mean—'

He rushed over and righted the chair back onto its four legs. Grabbing the hem of his ragged robes, he dabbed at her mouth, wiping the blood as Polly struggled against him. 'Professor . . . I am truly sorry, I . . . I lost control of myself. Please forgive me.'

Quaint looked around quizzically. Was he hearing things? Had the Clan Scarab leader really just apologised? But that made no sense at all. It seemed that the rules of this game were changing by the second.

'Faroud, what the hell's going on in there?' he yelled.

'This is none of your concern, Cornelius Quaint,' snapped Faroud.

In an exact mirror of Quaint's expression, Professor North frowned deep grooves in her forehead as she tried to measure the voice of the newcomer next door. Who was he? Cornelius Quaint, the Scarab had said. It was certainly an odd name – ancient Roman in origin, if she was not mistaken. But was he to be a help or a hindrance? An enemy or an ally? Perhaps he was the Scarab's mysterious "employer", and the man that sought to steal the Pharaoh's Cradle out from under her nose?

'Sounds like the Professor touched a nerve, Faroud,' continued Quaint. 'Someone *is* pulling your strings! That Mr Joyce you mentioned? The Hades Consortium, perhaps?'

'You do not know of what you speak, Englishman – so silence your tongue before I rip it out!' yelled Faroud through the wall.

'What has the Consortium promised you, Aksak?' asked Quaint, with no intention of silencing his tongue. 'Do your lot get the spoils of war once the Nile is done with? Or perhaps they just appealed to your sense of fear. Is that it? They *scared* you into doing their dirty work for them?' Quaint knew that he was risking a beating by provoking the Egyptian's temper – but that was exactly his intent. If Faroud concentrated his anger upon *him*, it meant that he was no longer aiming it in Polly North's direction. 'Don't take it personally; the Hades Consortium has a thousand little thugs like you on their payroll. To them you are nothing!'

Faroud's displeasure exploded at Quaint's interjection, and he aimed his rage at the stone wall separating them. 'I am *warning* you for the last time, Mr Quaint! Shut your mouth or one of my guards will do it for you!'

'It's perfectly acceptable to hurt *me* then?' rattled Quaint unabated. 'But that isn't so for the Professor, is it? You've got orders not to damage the merchandise, am I right? So what do you think will happen when the Consortium discovers that you've been a bad boy? They won't be best pleased, you know.'

'I told you to shut up, Quaint! This does *not* concern you,' yelled Faroud, dusting down his vest to occupy his temper. 'Nasbek! Arus!'

Immediately, the two Scarabs guarding Quaint entered the room.

Faroud boomed with all his might, his eyes bulging in their sockets. 'Bring that loose-lipped Englishman in here. I want him where I can *see* him . . . and if he gives you any trouble, *please* hurt him.'

'Yes, Aksak,' agreed the first hulking Scarab.

'At once, Aksak,' agreed the other, a dour sort with a nasty scar bisecting his face.

Overhearing the command, Quaint's mind worked quickly. He looked around for a weapon of some sort and snatched the absinthe bottle from the table. Unnoticed by his two fat-handed foes as they arrived, he thrust it behind his back, tucking it into his trouser waistband. The Scarabs grabbed him by each shoulder, and steered him roughly into the small room. With a painful jolt between his shoulder blades, he was cast unceremoniously onto the floor at Polly North's feet.

'Who's this, someone else you're trying to scare?' asked Polly.

'We've not been formally introduced,' said Quaint, jovially. 'My name is Quaint . . . Cornelius Quaint, and I am quite an admirer of your work, Professor.'

She looked different to how he had imagined her – not quite pretty, but not ugly by any standard. He noticed her high cheekbones, firm lips and determined jaw. Younger than he had thought too. No wonder she had spent half her life in foreign countries. Quaint assumed that London's scientific community would hardly approve of such a distraction in their midst.

'Are you all right?' he asked her.

'Why is that any of your concern?' Polly yapped back, causing Quaint to flinch.

'I'm merely asking after your well-being, Professor,' he replied. 'We seem to have something in common.'

'You're an archaeologist too?' asked Polly.

'Actually I was referring to our present state of captivity. I'm no archaeologist, ma'am . . . merely a circus conjuror,' said Quaint.

'In a place like this?' asked Polly.

'I go where the work takes me,' Quaint said.

'From the looks of it, your show didn't go down too well,' Polly said, with a flick of her eyes towards Faroud and his two cohorts. 'A tough audience, eh?'

'I've had worse,' said Quaint. 'It seems that I'm an unwilling visitor just as you are, Professor.'

'Considering the fact that I'm tied to a chair and bleeding, I hardly think you're quite as unwilling as I am,' said Polly, as she stared at the well-built, middle-aged man at her feet with a shock of silver-white curls and charming glint in the corner of his dark eyes. Was he really all he claimed to be, or was it a ruse? If so, why was he antagonising the Scarab leader in such a reckless manner? Whatever the reason, he was doing a fantastic job of occupying the Scarab's attention, giving her time to work at the ropes binding her to the chair . . .

Quaint rose slowly to his feet as Faroud and his two Scarab guards watched his every move. 'Answer me this, Aksak – if you really *are* working for the Hades Consortium, why are they so interested in a British archaeologist? What's it got to do with their plot?'

'I do not know what you are talking about,' Faroud replied.

'Oh, really? I don't believe you,' snapped Quaint. 'Whatever deal they've offered you, it's not worth selling your soul for! Bargains with the Hades Consortium tend to be a little one-sided. Once they've finished poisoning the Nile, they'll simply divide whatever's left between them. You and your Scarabs will be fed to the lions!'

Faroud clearly found the very idea amusing, for his grin spread thinly and quickly across his mouth. 'Mr Quaint, I do not believe a word of what you say. The Hades Consortium has power, this is true . . . but how could they possibly poison a body of water the size of the Nile? They would need more poison than a hundred camels could carry! I am no fool. I know your plan. Did you honestly think you could just walk into my camp and rescue Miss North on your own? I think she would do better choosing her friends more carefully in future.'

'*Friends?*' asked Polly, scornfully.

'*Rescue?*' asked Quaint, with an equal amount of derision.

Polly and Quaint exchanged swift glances and then glared at Faroud.

'Wait, you don't think he's—'

'She's not my—'

'But I'm not with *him*!'

'I'm not with *her*!'

'We're not *together*!' Quaint and Polly chorused in unison.

Faroud smiled. 'Two troublesome Englanders in my camp at the same time . . . and you expect me to believe that it is just a *coincidence*?'

'That's *exactly* what it is!' snapped Quaint, pushing his intense disbelief in coincidences aside. 'Do you honestly think that I would risk my life to save *her*?'

Polly shot him a look of pure spite. 'What's that supposed to mean?'

'No offence, Professor,' Quaint said, with mock cheerfulness. 'I'm just trying to keep things light and upbeat. It's incredibly important in life-threatening situations to maintain a positive mental attitude. Would you not agree, Aksak?'

Faroud found himself nodding in agreement – and stopped it immediately. 'Mr Quaint, I am finding your frequent attempts at humour most tiresome,' he growled.

'For once we agree on something,' chimed in Polly.

'Enough of this!' said Faroud, slicing his hand through the air. 'Whether you admit it or not, it is of no consequence! I am Aksak here . . . I am in charge, and I will not permit this point-less discussion any longer. I was hired to procure you, Professor North, and that is exactly what I have done.' He turned to Quaint. 'But you, Mr Quaint, are an irritating distraction that I have no time for. I do not care why you came here. Whether you truly *do* seek information about this supposed plot or whether you have come in some vain attempt to save the Professor – I do not care! Your time here is at an end.' He clicked his fingers, and the two broad-built Clan Scarab guards approached Quaint menacingly.

The conjuror ached for the presence of Prometheus at his right arm. Not all the bravado in his arsenal could get him out of this one. 'Listen to me, Faroud, this is important!' he said, edging away from the advancing Scarabs. 'I just need to know all I can about the Consortium's plot before it's too late!'

Faroud raised an eyebrow. 'And what then? Let us suppose

that what you say is true . . . what could one man such as you possibly do to stop it?'

'Anything within my power,' replied the conjuror wilfully.

'Then it is a shame that no one will witness your courage,' said Faroud. 'Nasbek! Arus! Kill this English dog.'

Just then, Polly saw her chance and made her move.

It all happened so quickly – far too quickly for Aksak Faroud or anyone else to stop her. With the Scarabs' attention fixed firmly on Quaint, Polly slipped her slender wrists free from her ropes and, without a moment's hesitation, she leapt through the open window.

Faroud watched it happen, although he could not quite believe his eyes. It seemed to take an extraordinary amount of time for the sight to register before he turned slowly to Cornelius Quaint – who shrugged, innocently.

'Don't look at me,' he said.

'Scarabs, assemble outside!' Faroud yelled at the top of his lungs. 'The female has escaped! Hunt her down. She will not go far on foot. Go!' Hordes of heavy feet thundered from all directions at his command. 'And you, Quaint – what is your next move to be? Thinking of fleeing after your friend perhaps?'

'I wouldn't dream of it,' Quaint said. 'But considering that you're not allowed to actually *hurt* her, what are you going to do to when you catch up with her? Give her a stern telling off?'

'Perhaps that rule is no longer to be complied with,' Faroud said bluntly. He clamped his long sinewy arms onto Quaint's shoulders, squeezing so hard that the conjuror winced in pain. 'If I were you, I would worry for my own neck! Clan brothers, ensure this prisoner is made uncomfortable. Do not kill him until I return . . . but beyond that, you are free to do as your whim takes you. Just make sure that the dog can still talk . . . I have a lot of questions to ask him.'

With that, Faroud turned and exited the room, inflamed by the thrill of the hunt.

Within moments, Quaint heard a loud cacophony of neighing horses outside, and he turned to see Aksak Faroud and a gathering of Scarabs on horseback speeding past the open window. If he were to give chase (which, of course, he was considering) he would need to move fast. He turned as he heard a snigger behind him, and his heart began pumping a familiar blaze of energy around his body. He had no time for subtlety – ferocity was his weapon of choice.

'When diplomacy fails, it's time to fight dirty,' Prometheus had once told him.

It was good advice.

The biggest of the Scarabs, Arus, stepped towards Quaint, his fists raised. 'We shall grind your bones and feast on your entrails, Englishman!' he snarled.

Quaint smiled. 'Aren't you going to say "Fee-fi-fo-fum"?'

The hulking Scarab swung at him with his massive fists, surprisingly quickly for a man of his size. The showman was taken aback and the punch felled him. Sprawled on his back, Quaint kicked out like a mule and the Scarab wailed as his nose cracked.

'That's going to bruise in the morning,' Quaint quipped.

The other Scarab saw his chance and he leapt. The conjuror whipped the bottle of absinthe from his waistband and smashed it across Nasbek's face. Like a shot partridge, the Scarab fell to the ground on top of Arus, who was still nursing his bloodied nose.

Quaint wiped his mouth. The fight was done. Had it not been for most of the camp's Scarabs pursuing Polly, it might have been too big for him to handle.

'You are nothing but an old man,' said Arus, spitting blood.

'*What* did you just say?' Quaint asked, taken aback.

'He called you an old man!' said Nasbek. 'You cannot escape. Our clan brothers will kill you before you get twenty yards!'

'Oh, I doubt it,' Quaint said. 'They'll be far too busy putting out the fire.'

'Fire?' asked Nasbek.

'What fire?' asked Arus.

Quaint reached into his pocket and pulled out a silver tinderbox. Opening it, he struck the flint and a spark hopped from the box into the puddle of anise-smelling liquid spread on the floor. The flames followed the trail of alcohol, snaking across the room towards Arus and Nasbek as if they were seeking them out consciously. Arus howled as the fire caught hold of his robes. Soon, Nasbek joined him in the twisting, twirling dance as they tried to pat out the flames. The fire skipped to the walls, setting the door alight. Within seconds, the room was engulfed and the doorway out was searing with flames.

Quaint took the only exit available and followed the route used so successfully by the Professor. He leapt out of the window, landing uncomfortably on the veranda outside. He could hear yells and screams behind him as the tavern erupted in a crescendo of alarm, the fire spreading quickly to other parts of the building.

Heading to the makeshift stables, Quaint yanked the long pole that the Scarabs' horses were tethered to, and it fell free of its mooring. He clapped his hands and stomped his feet to frighten the horses, and they scattered in all directions, all except for a tan-coloured horse. Heaving himself onto the animal's back, he looked at the trail of dust rising on the horizon. Faroud was right. The Professor would not get far on foot.

Quaint recalled a word that seemed to induce a marvellous effect on horses, yelling '*Az-Toray*!' into the beast's ear.

CHAPTER XXXI

The Diversionary Tactic

CORNELIUS QUAINT STREAKED through the Bara Mephista valley in hot pursuit of Aksak Faroud's posse. Following the track that snaked its way between the towering, sand-covered mountains, he risked a glance over his shoulder. A gang of Scarabs tumbled out of the tavern, plumes of thick, dark smoke spewing from every window. One thing was for sure: he had blown any chance of getting information out of Faroud now. He followed the dust from the Scarabs' horses up a gentle incline until his eyes lost sight of it. The sky was darkening, and visibility was already poor. He could see the tips of a large mountain range in the near distance, framed against the burning purple-orange sunset, and he urged his horse on further, trying to beat the curve of the hill's rise. As the ground dipped sharply, Quaint saw something that made his stomach lurch.

Only fifty yards ahead of him was a herd of tethered horses, plus a group of four dismounted Scarabs standing on guard outside a large cave at the foot of the shadowy mountains. The incline of the hill had masked just how big the mountain range was and it fell deeply into the low-lying ground, spreading out across the landscape as far as the eye could see.

Quaint dismounted and quickly retreated down the incline to find a better vantage point to observe the Scarabs' movements. He would be of no use to the Professor if he got himself caught. Keeping as low to the cooling sand as his broad bulk would allow, he crawled along the ground on his elbows. Soon, he had circled around behind the men. It was then that he was faced with a conundrum – how was he to get past four armed Scarabs without being seen? He needed a diversionary tactic, something to thin out the odds, and as he noticed the gathering of horses tethered together nearby, a semblance of an idea struck him . . .

The four Clan Scarabs froze stock still as the frantic neighing of panicked horses filled the air all around them. A maddened herd – tethered together at the neck with their tails aflame – charged across the desert trailing plumes of stench-ridden smoke. The Scarabs stood open-mouthed. Despite their best efforts to translate the sight, an answer was not immediately forthcoming.

'What *was* that?'

'Demons!'

'Do not be stupid. It was not *demons*, Mukhtar!'

'But, Temis, they were creatures aflame like beasts from hell!'

'They were our horses, you fool!' said the more sensible of the Scarab quartet. 'If we do not get them back the Aksak will set *our* tails alight! You two stay here and keep your eyes keen.' The Scarab nudged the arm of a slight younger man on his right. 'Alifah, you can come with me!' The two men sprinted into the desert wasteland, following the golden glow that lit up the dusk in the distance.

From his position, Quaint grinned satisfactorily as he clipped shut the lid of his tinderbox. Now there were only two Scarabs left for him to deal with.

Much better odds.

He moved swiftly, rising from amongst the grasses, smashing his formidable mass into his foes. The dumbstruck Scarabs fell to the ground in a clumsy mess of sprawling limbs. As they dizzily tried to clamber to their feet, Quaint snatched up a discarded sword from the dust.

'You chaps have two choices,' he said, switching the sword from Mukhtar to Temis in time with his words. 'Either you can take a leaf out of your friends' books and run like mad . . . or you can stay here and tussle with me. But I warn you; I know how to use a sword, and whereas one of you might get lucky, the other one will surely taste the blade. Now, which one of you is going to be the lucky one?'

Mukhtar and Temis swapped nervous glances.

'Horses?' asked Mukhtar.

'Horses,' confirmed Temis.

They scrambled to their feet, and soon were just specks in the distance, their feet pummelling against the sand frenetically.

Quaint looked thoroughly pleased with himself. 'Not bad for an old man.'

In the cave behind him, he could hear whooping and jeering, and he was returned roughly to the here and now. The Clan Scarabs were on a hunt for their quarry and the chase had started without him . . .

CHAPTER XXXII

The Intriguing Development

A FEW MILES ALONG the road that followed the snaking bends of a lake, Ahman slowed his cart to a halt next to a small ring of trees. Helping Destine down, he laid a blanket onto the cool sand by the lapping waters of the lake. Along the banks, lush grasses and ferns flourished, reaching up to tease the breeze. The setting was an ideal stage upon which to discover the origins of the long-buried secret.

Ahmad made a small fire that battled against the wind to stay alight, and he rushed around busily, finding kindling to keep it burning. It was only when he was finally seated that Destine laid the parcel onto the blanket. Whatever it was, it was wrapped in rough sacking, fastened with a thin strip of leather tied into a thick knot. Savouring every moment, Destine unfurled each flap of rough, worn material.

Lying in the centre was a beaten, brown-leather book.

Destine looked up at Ahman, who greeted her silent questions with his usual aplomb.

'Well, my dear?' he said. 'Do not keep me on tenterhooks.'

Opening the cover, Destine cleared her throat and read aloud: 'Journal begun August 1833 – Aloysius Bedford, Archaeologist.'

She looked at Ahman, wide-eyed. 'From my letter! So he was an archaeologist!'

'Evidently so, Destine . . . now read on,' nudged Ahman.

Destine complied, turning the yellowed pages of the old journal carefully, as if it were an ancient manuscript found in a dusty old library. She skipped past illustrations of what appeared to be ancient artefacts. Various pieces of jewellery, figurines of cat-like deities and hawk-headed deities adorned every page. Once she had discovered the first entry in the journal, Destine began again:

'Soon I shall set forth to the dig site in Umkaza, and this journal shall assist me in keeping track of all that occurs upon this excavation. My sponsor speaks well of Umkaza, a place that he proclaims to hide a veritable feast of artefacts beneath the sand – but I have heard that before. Although I do not leave until tomorrow, there is still much to prepare. The Museum of Antiquities in Cairo has agreed to loan me a crew of diggers – however, they neglected to mention that the men did not speak English! I have consulted some of my colleagues, and they have managed to procure the services of a Frenchwoman to assist me, who is reportedly fluent in most languages, including Arabic. Madame Destine Renard is scheduled to arrive within the month.'

Destine looked up from the journal.

'A translator?' grinned Ahman. 'I suppose this solves the riddle of how you were able to understand Feron Mouk back at Sekhet Simbel. Please do go on, Madame . . . this is fascinating, ah?'

'This delay is a hard punch to my spirits!' continued Destine, as keen as Ahman to reveal elements of her own past.

'I only hope that once we begin digging I will have worthy results to show my benefactor. If he is right, Umkaza is one of three possible resting sites of the fabled Pharaoh's Cradle. That prize is a treasure of such magnificence! The very crib used by Rameses the Great – it is astounding to think that it might soon be within my hands! Should my hard work unearth such a wonder, my life would be changed for ever . . . for the better, I might add. I can hardly contain my enthusiasm.'

'I know just how you feel,' said Destine excitedly, stroking the inked words upon the page. 'This "Pharaoh's Cradle", Ahman . . . whatever it was, Aloysius was obviously quite enthralled by it. "A treasure of such magnificence," he says. Are you familiar with it?'

Ahman shook his head. 'Rameses the Great's crib? The very soul immortalised within Sekhet Simbel? No wonder this journal was placed there . . . but I have never heard of it, Destine, and I think the answer to that may be obvious considering that this is not just a treasure hunt . . . it is a hunt for the truth of what happened to Aloysius. He obviously was destined never to find his great prize.'

'You mean . . . because Aloysius never found the Pharaoh's Cradle?' asked Destine.

'Yah . . . the poor soul,' Ahman said. 'You can almost feel the sorrow in his words.'

'I *can* feel it, *mon ami*,' admitted Destine. 'Most clearly, in fact . . . from the page right into my head . . . almost as if this book were trying to speak to me. The more I read, the less distant the past feels somehow . . . as if this book is trying to repair my connection to my lost memories. Not all of them yet, and not with any clarity . . . but instead of a blank canvas, gradually I am beginning to see shape and form . . . and colour.' She turned the page, and read on.

'Madame Destine has arrived on the ship from England to begin her work as my translator and her first words to me were of her sleeping arrangements! No complaints about the long journey, or the banal conversation of my driver. Sleep was the foremost concern on her mind! If only all my employees were so easily pleased. Now my work can commence in earnest. The Madame seems a most remarkable woman, fluent in several languages including French, Italian, English and Arabic. She has such knowledge in her eyes – almost as if she is at peace with everything. My crew have quite taken to her, and have nick-named her "Madame Dusty" for she is always willing to crawl around in the sand alongside them. She is not one afraid to get her hands dirty, and that has ingratiated her much with the men – as it has done with me. She may just turn out to be the lucky rabbit's foot that my crew need to find our prize.'

A flourish of embarrassment painted Destine's cheeks, and she was forced to pause for breath. 'My!' she whispered. 'Aloysius speaks highly of me, and in great detail, yet I cannot recall him for a moment. How strange this is.'

'Not strange at all, my dear,' Ahman said, tugging at his beard, 'for he obviously remembers you just as I do.'

Destine turned the pages swiftly, eager to consume more. '*Sacré bleu*, Ahman – listen, just a few days later!

'It is astounding! Proof without doubt that somewhere beneath Umkaza's sands lays the Pharaoh's Cradle, and soon I shall unearth it. Yet, with my triumph comes great concern – I cannot shake the feeling that I am merely the horse pulling the plough and someone else will be picking at the furrows long before I get a chance. My foreign sponsor has put me in touch with the port administrator, a chap named Godfrey Joyce. He has recommended a local guide who claims to know Umkaza well. I would prefer not to share our glory with anyone – especially an outsider – but I am beholden to circumstance.'

Madame Destine's voice faded, and Ahman looked over at her.

'My dear, are you feeling all right?' he enquired.

But Destine ignored him. It was as if she were unable to hear him, or as if she had forgotten that he was even there. She rose to her feet, seemingly entranced. She began to pace around the sand, and Ahman experienced an emotion he thought never to feel in Destine's presence – fear.

'I am very *sensitive* to emotions, Aloysius, and the only emotion I sense from Joyce is deceit,' she snapped, her voice severe. 'I pray that I am wrong . . . but you must be mindful what you tell him about the Pharaoh's Cradle.'

'Pharaoh's Cradle?' repeated Ahman.

The words seemed to snap Destine from her trance and she raised a hand to her forehead. Ahman leapt to his feet, only just catching her as she wilted into his arms. Laying her gently down onto the blanket, he smoothed the hair from her face. He had no idea what sort of spectacle he had just witnessed. Destine was like a stranger, speaking words with an unrecognizable edge to them. The excitement of the day had obviously caught up with her,

Ahman suspected, combined with the heat and the journey from Agra. It had been a long day for them both.

Ahman looked around; it would make a suitable camp for the night, with the surrounding trees protecting them from the lake's chill. He rose to his feet and pulled a woven blanket from the rear of his cart, covering Destine's slumbering body.

'No more truth tonight, my dear,' he whispered. 'Your past will just have to wait until tomorrow, ah?'

CHAPTER XXXIII

𝔗𝔥𝔢 ℌ𝔲𝔫𝔱𝔢𝔡 𝔔𝔲𝔞𝔯𝔯𝔶

WITHIN THE BELLY of the mountain, Cornelius Quaint followed the sound of raised voices through the twisting, turning tunnel. It was just about large enough for him to walk through at a stoop, but every so often a protruding edge of rock forced him to navigate his broad shoulders through the tight gap. Moving faster than a slow walk was virtually impossible, not to mention downright painful. His shirt snagged on a jagged outcrop, slashing a six-inch wound to his forearm that bled profusely. Not nearly painful enough to deter him, he tied his neckerchief around the wound and continued his pursuit.

Seeing a massive burst of orange-white light up ahead, Quaint moved unerringly towards it. The tunnel opened up as he pressed on, and there ahead of him, standing in a large cavern, was Aksak Faroud, with his Clan Scarabs fanned out around him. Many held torches and the cavern was bathed in amber light as they listened intently as their leader's grinding, rasping voice echoed about them.

'Professor North?' Faroud called through cupped hands. 'It is useless to hide from us! We are many and you are but one . . . and a woman, at that. Enough of these pointless games, give yourself up!' He paused, giving Polly a moment to identify her location, but nothing came back. 'The night is almost upon us and even if you escape, where will you go? The desert stretches for miles in every direction; you will be dead before you reach the nearest settlement!' His fellow Scarabs whooped and hooted at this possibility; Faroud held up his hands to silence them. 'We are in no rush, Professor . . . if it takes us the entire night, we *will* flush you out.'

The Scarabs froze, awaiting a response. Nothing.

Quaint smiled. At least Polly was keeping her mouth shut for once. Responding to Faroud's taunting would quickly give away her position.

Faroud cursed under his breath. 'Scarabs, split into groups . . . scour everywhere,' he growled, stabbing his torch into the ground. 'I want every shadow lit and every stone lifted until that damn woman is found!'

Quaint watched from his hiding place as the pack dispersed. Soon the cavern was bathed in silence, and he cautiously moved from his spot. He tugged at his ripped shirt. Blood had seeped through his makeshift bandage and his sweat was making his wound sting like acid. He looked down at the injury, just as a drop of something struck his shoulder. He gently touched his fingertip to it and took a closer inspection.

It was a dab of red blood.

'You can come down now, Professor. They've gone,' he said.

High above his head, clinging to a series of stalactites, was Polly North. She dropped down onto the floor next to him. Her face was smudged with a mixture of dirt and sweat, and she was sporting fresh grazes on her cheek and arms – telltale signs that she had come the same way as the conjuror. She dusted off her khaki trousers and blouse, and stooped down to snatch up Faroud's discarded torch from the cavern floor.

'Thanks for not giving me away,' she said, and set off.

Quaint grabbed her arm. 'What the hell do you think you're doing? Don't go *that* way! There are twenty Scarabs waiting for you down there!'

Polly rounded on the conjuror, wrenching her arm free of him. 'Now you just listen to me, *Mister* Quaint! I'm an archaeologist. I've been in more catacombs than you've had hot dinners – I know where I'm going.'

'So do I,' said Quaint, 'the *wrong* way! We need to head back the way we came in.'

'Are you insane? They'll have posted guards at all the exits!' shrieked Polly.

'Not any more, I took care of them,' said Quaint. 'Look, it's the safest way for us to go, all right?'

'No, it's damn well not!' snapped Polly. 'That way still leads to their camp, and I have no intention of going back there. And what's all this "us" claptrap? You're a conjuror, right? So why don't you magic yourself out of here. Me – I'm going to take another way out!'

'What way?' asked Quaint.

'There are signposts all over this cave if you know where to look and what to look for.' Polly lifted the torch up towards the cave roof. 'Did you not spot those calcium carbonate deposits up there?'

'Do I look like a cave expert to you?' shrugged Quaint.

'Mr Quaint, you don't look like an expert on anything to me,' Polly said with a stony glare.

'There's no need to be rude,' said Quaint.

'Let me spell it out to you: the further north we go into these caves, the more limestone is present . . . and the more limestone is present, the more *moisture* there is filtering down through the earth from above. Those calcium carbonate deposits up there –

stalactites, to the layman – are formed by the build-up of sedi-
mentary minerals found in water.' She glared at Quaint's baffled
expression. 'Did you not pay *any* attention at school?'

'I must have been absent the day we did caves,' said Quaint
sarcastically.

'Well, if there are stalactites, that means there is water nearby!'
Polly said with a triumphant smirk. 'Faroud said that we're miles
away from the nearest settlement, and he probably wasn't bluffing,
but if this cave system is near water... and north of Bara
Mephista, then my best guess is that it must be the River Hepsut,
flowing through the lowlands until it reaches Nespa Point. So,
we follow the stalactites north, and we find a way out.'

'No one likes a show-off, Professor,' said Quaint.

'Look, I don't care what you do, but I'm getting out of this
place before those Scarabs catch up with me. Now, you can stay
here and wait to die, or you can come with me – as long as you
don't slow me down.'

'Slow *you* down?' Quaint spat ferociously. 'Look, I came here
to rescue you – at considerable risk to my own well-being, might
I add – the least you can do is show me a little gratitude!'

'I don't need rescuing by the likes of you, Mr Quaint,' Polly
stormed.

Quaint's temper rose swiftly. 'Those Scarabs are animals,
woman! No matter what their employer wanted from them, all
bets are off. They're going to *kill* you – and you say you don't
need rescuing?'

'You misheard me. I didn't say I didn't need *rescuing*,' replied
Polly. 'I said I didn't need rescuing by the likes of *you*! Look, if
you want to come, you'd best make up your mind.'

There was a low rumble behind them. The Clan Scarabs were
on the move.

Immediately, Quaint's priorities were back in order.

'You're the professor . . . *Professor*,' he said.

'And as long as you remember that, we'll get on just fine!' Polly snapped, heading into the darkness with her torch held above her head.

Muttering a silent prayer, Cornelius Quaint followed her . . .

A little way further, the walls of the cave closed sharply, forcing them to walk through in single file. Polly led from the front, her smaller build enabling her to slide easily through the gaps in the rocks. But Quaint was not so lucky. The rocks constantly snagged his bulky frame as if they had taken an instant dislike to him.

'What are you doing here anyway?' Polly asked, as she manoeuvred her way through the confines of the enclosed tunnel.

'Someone had to keep an eye on you,' Quaint said, knowing his arrogance would infuriate her – and he was quite right.

'I don't mean in these caves, man – I mean back in Bara Mephista!' Polly crackled back. 'What was your business with Aksak Faroud and his band of not so merry men? Nothing pleasant, I'll wager.'

Quaint asked, 'What do you mean by that?'

'Well, look at you! You're obviously some sort of a scoundrel,' was the reply.

'A scoundrel?' baulked Quaint, taking offence. 'A scoundrel would be miles away from here by now saving his own neck! A scoundrel would just leave—'

Polly spun around and jabbed her pointed finger into Quaint's chest. 'Don't you dare call me a helpless female, or then you really *will* be in trouble!'

'No, of course not. You are anything but . . . clearly. I was going to remark that a scoundrel would leave without giving you a second thought. I came to Bara Mephista seeking information – and I was doing all right in getting it until you poked your nose in! So right now you're my best bet of getting out of this place.'

'I agree . . . we need to get out of these caves as quickly as possible,' said Polly, 'that is if your constant blabbering doesn't give us away. Come with me if you must, Quaint, but just keep your mouth shut and watch my back,' she said curtly, as she crawled on her hands and knees, squeezing her ample backside through a tight gap in the rocks.

'Don't worry, Professor . . . I'll do that,' Quaint said, with a wolfish grin.

A little way further, Polly peered through the darkness as drips of water pelted her bare arms and face. 'It's cooler in here,' she said, taking a long sniff. 'And there's a lot of moisture in the air.' She stopped dead in her tracks, and Quaint nearly crashed into her. 'Listen . . . what is that? Do you hear that?'

Quaint could hear it all right.

Raised voices echoed in the stillness of the tunnel, emanating not just from behind them, but from seemingly all around. The pursuing Clan Scarabs were screaming obscenities and curses – quite distinctly too.

'They're close. And coming this way,' said Quaint.

'How many do you think?' Polly asked.

Quaint furrowed his brow. 'At a guess I'd say all of them.'

The raucous barks and yells of their pursuers rapidly increased in volume, building to a vicious crescendo. Both Quaint and Polly were fluent in Arabic, but even had they not been, the Scarabs' message was all too clear.

Quaint and Polly scrambled down the cave tunnel as fast as they could. The sharp rocks of the walls tore at their arms and legs as they went but they did not stop – they could not afford to. Trouble was coming, and it was coming very quickly. The Scarabs were close, only a matter of yards away.

Quaint pulled the Professor along by her wrist – much to her very vocal disgust. Cloaked in plumes of choking dust, they skidded down the steep incline of the tunnel as the uneven surface beneath their feet threatened to jar their bones from their sockets. Quaint's boots pounded at the ground, unable to gain purchase on anything. Polly was careering dangerously close to the tunnel wall, her momentum forcing her to twist and turn with every footstep.

Just ahead, Quaint could make out an orange glow. 'We're nearly there! Just hang on!'

He covered his eyes as the light blinded him. His foot made contact with a protruding rock and he only just managed to steady himself. All would probably have been well had Polly not stumbled over the same rock and smashed into him like a rutting stag. He fell a good three feet and then hit the rocky ground like a lead weight – then Polly crashed down on top of him. Caked in thick layers of coarse brown dust, they looked as though they had been dipped in cocoa powder.

Knuckling the dust from his eyes, Quaint noticed something.

It was the sharp end of a sword, and as the conjuror's eyes followed the length of the blade up to the hilt, he met Aksak Faroud and his band of ferocious Clan Scarabs.

'I thought we were dead,' spluttered Polly, wiping dust from her eyes.

Quaint's heart sank. 'Hold that thought, Professor.'

CHAPTER XXXIV

The Death Downstream

THE BAND OF Clan Scarabs dragged Quaint and Polly to a larger cavern within the vast cave system, and bound them together at the wrists either side of a massive column of rock that breached the ground. Wooden stakes were planted into the ground in a circle, and Aksak Faroud patrolled around the limestone column like a lion surveying its prey.

'I should have killed you the moment you set foot in my camp, Cornelius Quaint,' he said, and he punched his fist into the conjuror's ribs. 'But then I would not have discovered who you are . . . and what you want!' Faroud paced and he punched, he paced and he punched repeatedly – each one sending a lance of pain through Quaint's body. 'You have disrupted what was to be a night of celebration,' he sneered, as the veins on his sinewy neck squirmed, 'and for that alone, I shall kill you and make your woman watch!'

'For the last time . . . she's not *my* woman,' mumbled Quaint.

'And you make such a lovely couple.'

'Now you're just being unkind,' said Quaint. 'Just do whatever it is you plan on doing to us – and get it over with!'

'After all the trouble you have caused me? Oh, no, Mr Quaint, the least I can offer you is a death more *befitting* such a thorn in my side!' He snatched Polly by her ponytail and teased a dagger along it like a bow across the strings of a violin. 'The Sioux Indian tribesmen roaming the American plains have a tradition. They remove the scalps of their enemies to adorn their clothing as a mark of triumph in battle. It is a macabre tradition, I admit, but I can see its appeal. Perhaps seeing the Professor begging for her life will wipe the smugness from your face, Mr Quaint!'

'Don't mistake smugness for a considerable amount of pain,' said Quaint.

'And I will enjoy adding to that pain.' The Scarab's dark face flashed a broad smile as he released Polly. 'You are an interesting man, Mr Quaint. You seem to be affiliated with the Professor here, and yet you know of the Hades Consortium. For obvious reasons, those two worlds do not mix well. Who *are* you? Why are you here in my country?'

'I told you why! And I came to you hoping your Scarabs might know something . . . something that I could use *against* the Hades Consortium,' Quaint answered. 'Now . . . you can choose to do nothing and watch as your people slowly die around you, or you can help me put a stop to it!' He breathed awkwardly, the act obviously causing him discomfort. 'You say you don't believe me . . . but if there's a chance that I'm telling you the truth . . . even the *slightest* possibility that the Nile is going to be poisoned . . . can you really afford to risk ignoring it?'

'You still cling to this ridiculous idea that the Hades Consortium is out to poison the Nile?' asked Faroud. This Englishman was becoming more intriguing by the second. Even facing death, he was possessed of such conviction. 'And suppose I give your words credence . . . what would you want of me?'

'Our lives for one thing,' answered Quaint. 'Your help, for another.'

Polly strained against her bonds – causing the conjuror to scream as she nearly wrenched his arms from their sockets. 'Quaint, are you some sort of idiot? You don't need *his* type of help! He's a Clan Scarab – nothing but a damn animal, you said so yourself. And you want to *ally* yourself with a bunch of scavenging vultures like them?'

Faroud lifted his dagger and reflected torchlight into Polly's eyes, blinding her for a moment. 'Professor, need I remind you that you are still my prisoner? It would not be a wise idea to insult my men in such a fashion. And what of this plot, Mr Quaint? Why does it concern you – a foreigner to this land?'

'Not just me, Aksak . . . it concerns you too. Or at least, it should . . . as well as each and every other Egyptian!' replied Quaint. 'As I said . . . I only need information . . . information that you can provide.'

'Yes, but information about *what*, exactly?'

'You tell me – you work for the Hades Consortium!' blazed Quaint. Irrespective of his peril, his ire did not back down for anyone or anything. 'They ordered you to kidnap the Professor for some reason, and I want to know . . . how does that fit in with what they're planning for the Nile?'

'I was hoping you would tell me,' said the Aksak. 'I am sorry to say, Mr Quaint, but you are wrong.'

'About what?' asked Quaint.

'About who it was that ordered me to capture the Professor.' Faroud slapped his hands to his face, barely able to contain his glee. 'I am glad that I kept you alive, if only to see the smile wiped off your self-righteous face when you learn the truth!'

'So . . . you *do* know the truth then?' Quaint said. 'Then it looks as if you might be able to help me out after all.'

'And yet . . . you have not told me exactly *why* I should,' said Aksak Faroud. 'This plot you speak of . . . why should I get my clan involved in such a thing?'

Quaint spoke. 'Once the Hades Consortium unleashes its poison, the Nile will become a river of death. This country cannot function without it – you *know* that. You cut off the river, and it'll be like cutting off Egypt's blood supply!'

'But is such a thing within the Hades Consortium's grasp?' asked Faroud.

'Absolutely! The Consortium is more than capable of such havoc and so is that damned poison. I should know – I've seen it in action.' Quaint remembered only too well the ravaging effect that the poison had on his body in London – in truth, it was not something he would ever forget. It was as if someone had reinvented the definition of 'suffering' just for the occasion. 'Its potency is magnified tenfold by contact with water, which is why they chose the Nile. Just one damn vial of that poison is enough to do the job, polluting your lands, your cattle and your people – just one!'

'*Vial?*' Faroud asked numbly, as if he was talking in his sleep. 'This poison you speak of . . . it is held in a vial?'

'That's right!' confirmed Quaint. 'I managed to stop some of them in London, but God knows how many of them slipped through my fingers.'

'What does it look like?' asked Faroud.

'About six inches long with ivy etched into the glass,' said Quaint. 'Why?'

'That . . . was poison? I . . . I had no idea.'

Quaint's hardened expression slipped. 'You've seen them! Where, Faroud? Where did you see those vials and when?'

Faroud's eyes twitched left and right. He did not like being taken for a fool, for one thing, and he disliked even more being implicated in the plots and schemes of others. 'Godfrey Joyce instructed me to collect a delivery this morning that had come all the way from England . . . from an operative of the Hades Consortium in Al Fekesh. I saw those vials with my own eyes.'

'So who's this Godfrey Joyce fellow? What's his involvement?'

'He is the one who ordered me to apprehend the Professor. He is stationed at the British Embassy in Cairo as attaché to Egypt, but he is also employed as a Hades Consortium spy,' said Faroud, being suddenly quite helpful.

Polly's eyes went wide. She recognised the name Joyce. He had signed the papers admitting her expedition into the country. But if that were the case, why would he want her cleared out of Umkaza?

'Someone in the British government is a Hades Consortium spy, what a surprise,' Quaint growled. 'And earlier at the tavern when I mentioned it, you asked if Joyce had sent me. So that intimates that you have contact with him, yes?'

Faroud nodded. 'I have a bargain with him . . . of sorts. But my communication is solely with Joyce, not with his employers. I was a delivery man. That is all! Joyce told me to collect the package and ensure that it was delivered to him at the British Embassy.'

'Is it still there?' Quaint asked.

'I do not think so,' Faroud replied, as if in a trance. 'He was going to take it to his masters in Fantoma.'

'And you were *in* on the deal?'

'No! I knew *nothing* of what the Hades Consortium planned to do with it! If I had, I swear . . . I would never have delivered it into their hands!'

'Now they have the weapon they needed,' said Quaint. 'Thanks to you.'

Faroud's mind was fighting hard to accept what he had known all along, but had denied. As Aksak, he was used to riding roughshod over whomever and whatever he pleased, but he rarely looked over his shoulder to see the repercussions of his actions. Now the ripples threatened to consume him. He had delivered the vials of poison into the hands of those who wished to use them against Egypt.

He was as guilty as they were.

'I . . . I had no idea it was poison, I swear to you. How could I?' he mumbled, his eyes searching the ground at his feet for answers. 'All I was told was to collect the casket from Nadir in Al Fekesh – that is it! I did not need to know its contents. I did not want to know its contents!'

'*Nadir?* Heinrich Nadir?' Quaint recalled the bothersome passenger aboard the *Silver Swan*. 'That stunted little worm was the Consortium's delivery man? But . . . that means the blasted stuff was right under my nose the whole way here! I knew I should have chucked him overboard. So this Godfrey Joyce – why would someone like him want Polly cleared out of Umkaza? What has that place got to do with this plot? Was that on orders from the British government, or the Hades Consortium? And how would kidnapping an archaeologist benefit them? Especially one like *her*!'

Polly wrenched her wrists purposefully, yanking at Quaint's arm sockets.

'What's that supposed to mean?' she squawked.

'Polly, please . . . this is important,' said Quaint.

'Umkaza is the key,' said Faroud. 'Joyce was most insistent that the Professor was not to be harmed . . . merely frightened enough to vacate Umkaza.'

'Why?' Quaint demanded. 'Why is Umkaza important to the Hades Consortium?'

'I cannot say,' said Faroud. 'I do not know.'

Quaint nodded. 'So what's next, Aksak? For all your crimes, surely you aren't just going to stand idly by as thousands of your countrymen are needlessly slaughtered? Now that you know what is at stake – help me! Help me *stop* it.'

Faroud's heavy eyes were bathed in shadow. 'But what *can* I do? What can any of us do? How can we stop what is already in motion?'

'Leverage,' said Quaint. 'We need Joyce over a barrel, and the Professor's dig site is the key! That place is obviously of some importance to him – and by association, maybe to the Consortium as well.' The conjuror could feel his energy returning in leaps and bounds, like a caged beast fighting to be free. All he had to do was talk himself out of trouble, a feat he had accomplished many times in the past. 'So what is your next move to be, Aksak Faroud? Are you with me – or do you accept your part in Egypt's murder?'

The Aksak paced again, stroking his beard in rhythmic tugs, in time with his footsteps. There was much to consider. Taking on the likes of the Hades Consortium was akin to suicide. Not just for him, but for his entire clan. He would be signing the death warrant of every man under his charge, and that was a decision he would not – *could* not – make lightly. Yet Quaint was right – he had given the enemy a weapon with which to strike out at his own people. At the least, he was a traitor . . . and at the most, an accessory to genocide.

'You have given me much to think about, Cornelius Quaint,' he said. 'We must return to Bara Mephista. I will sleep on this dilemma and consult the Council of Elders first thing in the morning. They will guide my decision.'

CHAPTER XXXV

The Haunting Past

DESTINE HAD BEEN asleep for several hours, yet Ahman had not closed his eyes once. Few travellers used the roads by nightfall, so they would be safe – and yet still he could not relax his guard. The strange episode that had bewitched the Frenchwoman only a few hours before occupied his thoughts mercilessly. He sat against the tree like Destine's guardian angel, his eyes snapping to any sound around him. The lapping of the lake nearby, the gentle rise and fall of the wind across the cold sand, the digging of small rodents against the trees – every noise seemed to trigger his nerves. Ahman glanced over at Destine's peaceful form, the embers of the fire illuminating her soft features in a golden glow, and pulled his blanket up to his chest. Eventually, he let sleep embrace him.

As night took hold, Destine became restless. She rolled in her sleep, mumbling and whispering. Her eyes snapped open, searching for Ahman by her side – but he was not there. His blanket was lying crumpled and cast aside on the cold sand.

A sudden scream pierced the silence. Destine's first thought was of Ahman, and steeling her nerves, she threw off her blanket and rose to her uncertain feet. Taking gingerly steps, she pushed through the ring of trees, their sharp branches pricking her exposed face and hands. Her eyes and ears were aflame. She was being pulled. Pulled through the trees, pulled through the edge of the clearing . . . but pulled where? And towards what?

A cold rush enveloped her flesh as she stepped through the trees into an open space. It wrapped around her like a cocoon, restricting not just her physical body but her senses too. Her eyes were covered in a gossamer film and she was immobilised completely. As her breath hung in the air, she tried to blink sight back into her eyes and, gradually, her blurred vision dissipated. Destine knuckled the itching sensation from her eyes. But although her sight had returned, she was still not convinced that what she perceived was real.

What she was looking at was a desert encampment of some kind, lit by huge torches, flaming from pillars buried deep in the sand. Madame Destine's mouth fell open as she pinpointed the origin of the scream.

The encampment was besieged by a veritable army of men clad in pitch-black robes. Some were on foot, some were astride horses as black as their clothing. Tattered and torn, the material clung to the men's bones like the rags of hellish wraiths. Everywhere she looked Destine saw the flash of a blade as the demons attacked, scything at anyone in their path.

A nearby row of tents seemed to be the safest place to hide, and she quickly rushed to them. Keeping to the cloak of darkness, she was just about to furl back one of the tents' entrance and dart inside, when a dirty hand clamped itself around her mouth.

Destine could not scream even if she wanted to, the fear had paralysed her. She was viciously spun around – where she came face to face with a man. Not Ahman, or a face she recognised

– it was smudged with dirt, had a few days' growth of beard, and a neatly waxed moustache was perched precariously above his mouth. His oiled hair sparkled in the moonlight – and all at once, his features softened.

'*Destine?*' he hissed, releasing her, taking a step back. 'My God, woman, what the hell are you still doing here? Are you trying to get yourself killed?'

'But, I—' was all she managed before the man led her brusquely back into the cover of the trees.

'I told you to get away! What good can you do here against them?' he said, gesturing towards the pack of demonic hyenas rending flesh from bone, spilling blood in their wake. 'The Clan Scarabs are killing everyone in the camp – you've got to leave, Destine . . . now!'

A shaft of moonlight lighted the man's face and Destine gasped. '*Aloysius?*'

'What?' asked Aloysius Bedford.

'What . . . what are you *doing* here?' asked Destine, dumbstruck.

'I could ask you the same thing!' snapped Aloysius. 'You're as stubborn as an ass, Dusty! I told you to get out of the camp as soon as Nastasi's men arrived, didn't I? Umkaza is no longer a safe place to be!'

'*Umkaza?*' Destine asked.

Umkaza was the excavation site named in Aloysius Bedford's journal – the very same Aloysius Bedford who now stood beside her, seemingly very angry, very much alive . . . and very *real*. It was as if Destine was caught between two places at once – the past and the present, colliding together within her mind. Her senses told her that she was still near the lake, in the clearing where she and Ahman had settled for the night, and yet everything that she saw and felt contradicted that. Were her senses betraying her somehow? If so, which reality was the truth? Her mind was being fed tantalising sensations, similar to the rush of pins and needles whenever she experienced a premonition – which partly explained her confusion. She *had* no clairvoyant abilities any longer. They were gone, stolen from her weeks ago. Whatever this was, it was no message from the future.

'This place is Umkaza?' she asked, grasping Aloysius's forearms. 'But how . . . how can this be? How did I get here? Aloysius, what is happening here?'

'It's a damn massacre, woman!' said Aloysius. 'It seems your premonitions were right on the money. Joyce, the no-good lying snake, has betrayed us all.'

'Joyce,' mumbled Destine. 'The name from the journal? He stole the treasure?'

'He was never in it for the damn treasure!' hissed Aloysius. 'Neither him nor my damned benefactor! They just wanted to *use* me . . . just like you said. Only I didn't listen, did I? I was so blinded by my obsession. But I'm not blind any more, Destine . . . and that is why Nastasi and his band of Scarabs are here. They won't take no for an answer. So now I must take matters into my own hands.'

'But do what? What can you do?' asked Destine.

'Anything!' yelled Aloysius. 'Don't you see, woman? Your vision was right! About what would happen . . . about what *could* happen. You told me not to trust him, so this is my fault, my penance to pay . . . and pay it I shall – but I will never let them get their hands on the Cradle.'

'The Pharaoh's Cradle? So you *did* find it then, after all?' asked Destine, finally finding her footing in this remarkable dream; for that was what she had convinced herself it was – nothing but a dream. But how could that be? How could she be dreaming about past events with such clarity – and ones in which she was an active participant? Dreams stem from the subconscious, stray thoughts accumulated over time jumbled up into a semblance of reality. But Destine had no knowledge of her past time in Egypt. Was this real – or a subconscious distortion of reality? She was not sure, but she could feel the cold sand between her bare toes, the feel of the cold wind upon her cheeks, and the stench of blood on the air. And she could clearly see the look of fear within Aloysius Bedford's eyes. It was as real as real got and, gradually, Destine's mind became convinced of the most bizarre of all occurrences.

This was no dream.

'Oh, I found the Cradle, all right . . . but that's not all I uncovered,' continued Aloysius, wrenching Destine's thoughts back into the present – or was it the past? 'To hell with making a name for myself, this is too important. Joyce and his friends will never find the Pharaoh's Cradle whilst I draw breath.'

'But you will die!' blurted Destine uncontrollably, recalling the words from her letters. 'It . . . is unavoidable.'

'Maybe so,' said Aloysius, 'but maybe this time your clairvoyance has got things wrong, eh? Maybe I'll live to a ripe old age, watch my children grow up . . . bounce their own on my knee.' Aloysius smiled, one of a man in acceptance of his fate. 'Or maybe not. I know it will kill me, Destine . . . but better me than anyone else on *account* of me – and that includes you! For Christ's sake, woman, take a look around. You need to get away from this place . . . as far away as possible. Take my journal – it's all in there. Everything! Tell someone, Destine – tell *anyone* – about what happened here! *Tell* them . . . do you swear? Don't let this be forgotten . . . don't let it be repeated. Swear to me!'

'I . . . I swear,' Destine heard herself say.

'I have to go,' said Aloysius. 'I have to put things right.'

A sudden wall of flame burst free from the centre of the hellish encampment. Destine spun around, covering her face from the glare. Her ears were numbed by a dull sound, like the sound of many birds overhead. Something made the Frenchwoman look up. The moon was low, almost right above her. Its white light shone like a beacon. And when she looked down . . . once again the world rearranged itself.

'Aloysius!' Destine shrieked.

Gone were the sounds of men's screams, gone was the potent stench of death in the air. In an instant, she was transported back into the clearing – if indeed she had ever left it. She was laid upon the cold sand . . . clutching Aloysius's journal tight to her chest.

Ahman leapt awake, rushing to her side in a moment. 'Destine! What is it?'

The Frenchwoman was pale, her forehead speckled with beads of perspiration.

'I was there, Ahman,' she whispered. 'In Umkaza.'

'Yah, Destine, we know that. Twenty years ago,' said Ahman, knuckling his eyes.

'Not just twenty years ago, Ahman . . . just now.'

Ahman's face was a picture of bewilderment; he was convinced that Destine was confused. 'Can we not talk about this in the morning?'

'It is true, Ahman! I was just in Umkaza . . . with Aloysius Bedford stood right in front of me . . . as clearly as I am here right now,' Destine explained.

Ahman shook his head. 'But, Destine . . . you have not moved from this spot.'

'Maybe not my physical form . . . but my mind most definitely travelled,' whispered Destine. 'At last, my task is growing ever clearer! I know what happened . . . the massacre at Umkaza . . . and I know who was responsible!'

'You do?' asked Ahman. 'But . . . how?'

'Aloysius told me,' replied Destine.

'The Aloysius who is dead?' asked Ahman.

'Who else?' Destine said. 'Rather than a premonition, I am certain that what I sensed was the opposite . . . a vision *before* the now, as opposed to the *after*. An après-monition, if you will. I did not see the future, Ahman . . . but I saw the past – *my* past . . . as though my soul was transported from this body to inhabit that of my younger self! Ahman, it was so real – you must believe me!'

Ahman took hold of her shaking hands. 'I do believe you, Destine, I promise. Look at you . . . you look shattered, my dear. Try to go back to sleep, ah? We can discuss this newfound knowledge of yours in the morning.'

'*Oui, mon ami*,' Destine agreed. 'I do feel somewhat light-headed by all this excitement.'

'I know just how you feel,' grinned Ahman.

The morning came far too slowly for Madame Destine. She stretched her arms wide and cast her blanket onto the sand next to her. Rubbing the sleeping dust from her eyes, she looked around the small clearing by the side of the makeshift road through the desert. The clearing was still and Ahman's empty blanket lay discarded next to her. Destine's heart leapt, remembering the vision from the previous night. It had begun just as it was unfolding now, with her waking, searching for Ahman and finding him absent. Was she still trapped within that nightmarish vision?

The après-monition had shed a little more light on the task laid at her feet, but in true mystifying fashion, it had also conjured up yet more questions. She gripped Aloysius's journal so tightly that her knuckles threatened to burst through her skin. It had become a buoy for her to cling to – a lifeline to the ghosts of the past. Somehow, with Aloysius's journal close to her, she felt a connection to all the memories that she had lost. No matter how painful they might be. The link to Aloysius – his face now given form, given life – was clearing the fog from her head. What she had seen in Umkaza was so real. Similar to a memory, yet not one where it is viewed with hindsight – one in which she retained her own mind, her own fear. With Aloysius's words still resounding amidst her thoughts, Destine's hunger for the truth was even more intense.

Arranging her long, silver-white hair into a loose bun, she stepped barefoot onto the cold sand. She leaned against a tree and pulled on her ankle boots. With one last yawn, she searched around for clues as to Ahman's direction. She soon spotted his footprints. The wind had dragged the sand to obscure them, but not completely, and so Destine followed them. Slowly at first, but then something told her to make haste. Without her clairvoyance, she was learning to pay heed to her instincts.

Ahman was not far away. His horse was drinking thirstily from the lake near the tiny patch of trees, and the little man was sitting cross-legged on the sand.

'Good morning, Madame,' he said. 'How did you sleep?'

'*Bonjour, mon cher.*' Destine leaned down and kissed him on his soft-bristled cheek. 'I slept surprisingly well . . . apart from my *disturbance*. I am sorry for waking you.'

'Ah, think nothing of it, Destine,' said Ahman. 'I am just pleased that you came to no harm. That . . . what did you call it? That après-monition . . . it was startling in the extreme from what you say. I must admit that I am at a loss to explain it.'

'As am I,' said Destine, forcing a smile to ease the carpet trader's frown. 'You must excuse me, Ahman, for as a fortune-teller I am so used to being in time with my time. I know of my yesterdays, my todays and my tomorrows. They are all arranged in a neat and tidy collection in my mind. Having my yesterdays jumbled up with my todays is a most disconcerting thought.'

'I can well imagine, my dear. I only wish that I could be of more assistance, but those sorts of things are unknown to me.' Ahman held his hand to his brow, looking at the slow climbing sun in the sky above. 'So, where do we go from here?'

Destine smiled. 'Onward to the past, Ahman – where else?'

Ahman chuckled. 'That sleep did you good, ah?'

'I feel like a new woman, Ahman, one who is energised to carry on with our search. Yet I do not think it was the sleep – rather what I learned whilst I *slept*. I have ploughed the past and revealed the first seeds of what happened that night, and now I must learn it all. Aloysius said that I should warn people. But warn them of what exactly? It is still only a part of what I need to know. Where can I go to find the rest of it? The encampment that I was transported to last night . . . Umkaza . . . I am being drawn to that place. I wish to see it for myself . . . again.'

'But why, Destine? Surely you do not believe that any evidence of that night still remains?' asked Ahman. 'It was so long ago.'

'Not physical evidence perhaps,' replied Destine. 'But I am feeling a resonance from Aloysius's journal, giving my mind nuances of the truth. If what I am picking up from the book is giving me these tantalising snippets of the past, imagine what knowledge standing in Aloysius's footsteps might bring. I am sensitive to human emotions, remember? Even emotions buried within rocks and sand, two decades old. Some emotions leave a stain. Negative emotions most of all. Fear, pain, death . . . there seemed to be much of that in Umkaza, if my après-monition was any judge.'

Ahman scratched his bearded cheeks noisily. 'But to Umkaza? Destine, there is nothing there. It is a barren landscape! Surely whatever may have occurred all those years ago has long since faded away, swallowed by the desert winds, forgotten by time.'

'And not just by time, monsieur . . . by me!' declared Destine. 'When I was clairvoyant, I experienced many visions that mean nothing to me . . . just shards of the future. They were not real, not yet anyway. But in time they would occur, I knew this for a fact, and so I had time to take heed of my warnings. But with this mystery laid at my feet, I am blind. I know facts, dates, aspects . . . similar to my premonitions, but I *feel* none of it, Ahman! Not in here.' Destine tapped her forehead. 'Or in here,' she said, clamping her hands to her heart. 'Umkaza may hold the key to unlocking the spaces in between the truth. I can feel it drawing me there . . . and I cannot resist its pull.'

She was not of a mind to be swayed, Ahman could see that. 'Very well, Destine,' he sighed. 'To Umkaza it is, and may the heavens illuminate us once we get there.'

CHAPTER XXXVI

The Council of Elders

CORNELIUS QUAINT YAWNED like a foghorn, wincing as he nursed his bruised ribs. The night had not been restful. Partly due to his sleeping arrangements (a wooden bench in Bara Mephista), partly due to his sleeping companion (Polly had complained virtually the entire night about one thing or another), but mostly due to the many pairs of eyes that glared at him from every corner of the charred tavern.

'I hardly got a wink's sleep last night – I didn't dare close my eyes,' snapped Polly, wide awake and as vocal as ever. 'And *this* didn't help much either!' A thick coil of rope bound her and Quaint's wrists together – and like a marionette, the conjuror had no choice but to lift his own arm when Polly wrenched hers. 'I'd rather be tied to one of those Scarabs!'

'I'll have a word with Faroud, if you like . . . providing that he can find one of his men brave enough to volunteer,' said Quaint, ruffling his other hand through his curls.

'Sleep hasn't improved your sense of humour I see,' swiped Polly. 'I suppose I can't blame the Scarabs for not trusting you. After all, you nearly torched this place to the ground, and you left two of them with nasty burns. You certainly like to live dangerously, don't you?'

'Is there any other way?' Quaint replied.

'For you, I suspect not,' said Polly. 'Look at the way these uncivilised dogs are staring at us. They're itching for us to attempt an escape, so they can kill us where we stand!' She glared at the conjuror accusingly. 'And you want them as your allies?'

'It's not as if I have any choice, is it?' said Quaint. 'A lot is riding on the Council of Elders' decision.'

'Yes,' replied Polly, '. . . both our *lives*, for example.'

In a crowded room at the far end of the tavern, Aksak Faroud was in congress with the other senior clan leaders. The topic of discussion was Cornelius Quaint, and so far the wind was *not* blowing in his direction.

'Ally ourselves with an Englishman? Faroud, are you insane?' snapped a white-bearded old Egyptian, with straggles of hair matted down against his head by a golden headband. 'Or perhaps you have developed a yellow streak since Rakmun was captured?'

This was Nastasi, one of the Scarab Elders, and Faroud's predecessor as Aksak of Bara Mephista's clan. Nastasi had still to accept that his time as leader was done and, consequently, every one of his words was tainted with derision. Faroud did not rise to the old man's words, but his silence only served to fuel Nastasi's aggravation further.

'Lost your tongue, Aksak Faroud?' Nastasi asked, his rough old skin as dry as the desert itself. 'Surely you are not seriously proposing to the esteemed Elders present that you wish to assist this Englishman against the Hades Consortium?'

'And do not forget the woman, Elder Nastasi,' chipped in a gaunt Scarab at Nastasi's side, hunched on the table almost upon the older man's shoulder.

'Thank you for reminding me, Ellich,' said Nastasi with a nod. 'And a woman too! What on earth has addled your senses, Faroud?'

Faroud folded his arms stubbornly across his chest.

'I believe their cause to be just, Elder Nastasi,' he said firmly and confidently. 'The Hades Consortium seeks nothing less than total devastation of our country . . . we must stand against them!'

Elder Nastasi made a gargle of disgust in the back of his throat. 'And threaten our alliance with them? That would almost certainly spell extinction for our kind!'

'Have you not heard a word I have said, Elder? If we do nothing, our extinction will only be a matter of time anyway,' responded Faroud.

'On whose word, Faroud?' snapped Nastasi. 'Yours? This man Quaint's?'

Faroud leaned back in his chair and measured the council members' faces. What he was asking them to do was trust him with the sanctity of their clans, and that was not a small thing to ask he knew only too well. So far, Nastasi was the only Elder speaking – and it was a shame that it was *against* him.

'It is not as if the Hades Consortium is a benevolent care-taker of our clans! An alliance is not a stable one when it is so one-sided.' Faroud rose swiftly from his seat. His tattered linen robes swept past the other occupants of the room as he strode around the large, wooden table in its centre. 'Nastasi, I know it has been a long time since you were Aksak, but surely you have not forgotten that we Scarabs are supposed to be shapers of our *own* destiny, rather than allow others to dictate it for us?'

'I have forgotten nothing, Faroud,' replied Nastasi curtly.

'Cornelius Quaint risked his life to shine light upon the Consortium's plot! Need I remind you that he walked right into this very camp and requested an audience with me? That takes courage. A man who is prepared to gamble his own life to protect our country is someone we should hold in high regard!'

'If you believe *that*, then you are more easily fooled than I thought,' seethed Elder Nastasi, the lines on his face twisting into a cobweb of wrinkles.

'The world is not as it once was, Nastasi. It continues to spin regardless of how much you dig your heels in!' Faroud spread his arms wide to appeal to his fellow clan leaders. 'Elders . . . as Nastasi has rightly said: I wish to request the council's permission to aid Quaint in defeating the Hades Consortium and clearing them from Egypt for ever. We no longer have the luxury of time on our side. If this poison is as deadly as Quaint claims, our entire *country* could be decimated!'

'That is a very big "if", Faroud,' sneered Nastasi, much to the cackling delight of Ellich, shifting excitedly in his seat.

'Maybe so . . . but we have no choice,' said Faroud sternly. 'We Scarabs are not men of privilege; we are men of purpose! We cannot let this Englishman fight on our country's behalf whilst we sit around and do *nothing*.' He recommenced his pacing, ensuring his eyes met the eyes of the other council members in the room. He did not need their blessing for this venture – but he craved it nonetheless. 'The Hades Consortium has been holding our leash for far too long, giving us just enough freedom to make us believe that we truly *are* free . . . but we are only as free as they *wish* us to be.' Faroud gave an elongated pause to reinforce his words. 'That is not true freedom, my brothers – that is enslavement. Now I beg you this morning to make the right decision. We must band together as one united clan and stop this wholesale slaughter!'

Elder Nastasi chewed the inside of his mouth. 'You speak a very convincing argument, Aksak Faroud . . . but I am forced to ask how this outlander has managed to sway you so completely. I find my self questioning your judgement . . . your ability to lead,' the old man said.

'Neither of which is on trial here today, Elder,' snapped Faroud.

'What is to be this Englishman's first step on the path against the Consortium, Aksak?' asked a portly stomached Elder at the opposite end of the table to Nastasi.

'He believes that Godfrey Joyce's acquisition of the female is connected to something within her excavation site,' replied Faroud. 'Umkaza is to be our first stop.'

Elder Nastasi's hooded eyes flared. 'Umkaza? There is nothing there but sand and dust,' he said. 'He will find nothing of consequence in a wasteland such as that.'

'Maybe so, Elder, but Cornelius Quaint will uncover the intricacies of this plot, and I believe that he will defeat the Hades Consortium,' said Faroud. 'I only ask that each of you share a little bit of my faith.'

Nastasi made a slow sweep of the table, ensuring that he made eye contact with every Elder before he spoke. 'Well, my fellow Elders?' he asked. 'Do we give our consent?'

Time had crawled slowly for Cornelius Quaint and his eyes lit up as Aksak Faroud strolled in from the room at the end of the tavern. His face was expressionless, his eyes giving nothing away.

'Well?' Quaint asked.

Faroud said nothing. He reached for the scabbard at his waist and pulled out his dagger. Quaint's heart skipped a beat as Faroud advanced, his dagger raised.

'We need to talk,' he said, as he sliced the ropes binding Quaint's wrist to Polly's.

Quaint breathed an audible sigh of relief – mostly because it meant that Faroud had not been ordered to kill him, but also because it meant he was free of the Professor.

'Outside. Professor, you stay here.' Faroud glared at her. 'No arguments this time.'

'Perish the thought,' she said.

Faroud led Quaint out of the tavern and into the morning sunshine in the valley. Only the day before, they had been enemies. A lot had changed in the Aksak's mind since he had learned of his own part in the arming of the Hades Consortium. Today was a new day – a day for unification against their common enemy, and previous conflicts would have to be put aside if there was to be any hope of success. Not quite friends, not yet allies, there was a fragile sense of trust between them nonetheless.

'I want you to know that I believe in your cause, Cornelius . . . or else I would not have risked my standing within the council in such a reckless fashion,' Faroud began. 'I fought with all my voice, all my strength and all my authority for their understanding. I pleaded your case with the Elders until I was hoarse.'

Quaint nodded along to his words. 'And?'

'And I am sorry . . . I was unable to sway their decision. Elder Nastasi's voice is a loud and influential one, I am afraid. The

Aksak Elders must retain the integrity of the clan above all else. They do not see this danger as I do. They do not understand that we cannot let this atrocity unfold, no matter *who* our foes might be. In truth, they fear the Hades Consortium . . . and it is that which tipped the balance against you.'

'And so?' asked Quaint.

'And so I have decided to disobey them,' replied Faroud.

'Can you *do* that?' asked Quaint.

'We shall soon see.'

'Won't the council be angry?'

'Livid,' the Aksak replied. 'But I will have to deal with that another time. This is more important than the bruising of egos, my friend. I will aid you, Cornelius . . . my *clan* will aid you. As Aksak I have made that decision, be it for good or bad.'

Quaint shook Faroud's hand. 'That can't have been an easy choice to make.'

'For an Aksak there are no easy choices, but know this . . . I do not do this for you, I do it for Egypt.' The dark-eyed man clenched his jaw, a tiny muscle in his cheek flexing like a pulse. 'By working blindly for Joyce, I allowed my judgement to become impaired. I thought that I could loan out my men to him for his petty duties and there would be no repercussions. I was wrong, and so I must accept my part in what unfolds.'

'You are not to blame, Aksak . . . the Consortium is,' said Quaint.

Faroud laughed. 'Maybe so, but I am the type of Aksak that feels all the world's ills are his alone to bear.'

Quaint grinned. 'I know the feeling.'

At that moment, he would have traded his soul with the Devil to destroy the Hades Consortium. Alone, defeating them was impossible, but with the Clan Scarabs by his side to aid him, perhaps he stood a chance after all.

Was this the spark of good fortune that he was looking for? Was the wind finally blowing in his direction? Moreover, how long would it last?

Inside the Bara Mephista tavern, Elder Nastasi stared out of the window and watched the two men talking up on the rise. He looked to his side, to the almost skeletal Ellich, and his dried lips curled against his yellowed teeth.

'It is just as I predicted,' said Nastasi. 'Even now Faroud plots with Quaint.'

'What will the Aksak do, Elder?' asked Ellich. 'Do you think he will betray us?'

'Only if his heart is dominant over his common sense,' replied Nastasi. 'It has always been his Achilles heel, ever since he was a young man. He cares too deeply. Look at what havoc he has wrought trying to protect his fool of a brother. For that, he is as easy to predict as Egypt's weather.'

'And the Englishman's fate, Elder?' asked Ellich. 'Surely he must die!'

Nastasi waved the gaunt man's words away, as if he was a bothersome insect. 'Absolutely, he must . . . but not just yet. It seems the Hades Consortium has other plans for Mr Quaint. Ellich, see that your horse is ready. I want you to take a message for me to Cairo . . . to an old friend. I have a feeling that he will soon have some unexpected, and somewhat *unwelcome*, company.'

CHAPTER XXXVII

The Cold Shiver

LADY JOCASTA WAS bathing in the privacy of her quarters, soaking her soft, olive-toned skin in a marble bath of warm water and soapsuds. She dripped water from a natural sponge onto her breasts, relishing the feeling upon her naked skin. It was a welcome opportunity to wash away the humidity that had clung to her flesh ever since she had entered this underground cavern. She was smiling broadly from ear to ear, which for Jocasta was as rare an occurrence as pigs taking flight. For the first time in a long while she allowed herself to relax. Her plan was proceeding nicely, everything was in place, and it was now just a matter of waiting for her time to shine. Baron Remus had left Fantoma for Rome, and Lady Jocasta was secure in the knowledge that she was mistress of all she surveyed.

That, however, was about to change.

A rattling cough alerted her to another's presence in her bathroom, and she nearly leapt out of her skin. The bathwater slopped onto the dry stone floor, as she hid her nudity with her hands as best she could.

An old man stooped in the doorway, supporting his weight on a gnarled, wooden walking cane. A downy coating of white fluff covered the whole of the man's slightly misshapen head. He wore a blue three-quarter-length velvet jacket, with a crisp white shirt and silk cravat tucked into his collar. This man looked as if he was hundreds of years old, and yet his pale green eyes sparkled like finely polished emeralds.

'*Sir George?*' Jocasta gasped, reaching for her towel. She pulled it tight around her, and it clung to her sopping wet body. 'I . . . I did not know you were en route!'

'I was in the neighbourhood, so to speak,' said Sir George Dray, in rasping Scottish tones. His eyes pierced into Jocasta, as if burning through the towel itself to view her naked body. 'Didn't disturb you, I hope?'

'No, sir . . . you did not,' answered Jocasta, somewhat guardedly. 'I trust there is nothing wrong?'

'You tell me, lass,' said Sir George. A thin grin split a seam across his face, and the heavy wrinkles around his mouth parted like curtains of dead flesh. 'So, tell me . . . where is Adolfo hiding about this wretched place? I'd have thought he would've wanted to greet me himself.'

'You . . . you were not made aware?' asked Jocasta.

'Aware of what, lass?' asked the Scot.

'The Baron . . . he is not on site, sir. He is en route to Rome. Some issues arose that required his attention,' said Jocasta, unable to stop her teeth chattering because of the cold – or was it something else? Sir George's unexpected appearance sent a freezing sear up her spine. What was he doing here? And why now? What was Baron Remus playing at, deserting her at this time?

'He's gone to Rome?' asked Dray, flicking his dry tongue around his taut lips like a serpent tasting the air. 'Hmm. That's a pity. I've got some interesting news that I wanted to share with him. Get dressed and meet me in the audience chamber in five minutes, Jocasta. I want you to fill me in on this little project of yours, and I'm keen to learn if you really are as talented as the Baron says.'

Lady Jocasta hastily pulled on a long robe and fastened her dark waves of hair into a long ponytail that draped down her back to tickle the base of her spine. She glanced briefly at her fractious self in the tall, freestanding mirror.

If you do not wish Sir George to see right through you, you had best pull on your mask, Jocasta, she told herself.

A swarm of butterflies fluttered around her stomach as she contemplated facing the old man, one the most senior members of the Hades Consortium's inner stratum, a man but one shade darker than the Devil himself. She cursed Remus for not being there – and then a succession of thoughts struck her.

What if Dray had been informed of his son's death?

And what if he blamed her for the plot in London that led to it?

Had he come to Egypt seeking an explanation from her . . . or retribution?

There was only one thing she could do. She would hear what the old man had to say, maintain her resolve and deal with the consequences when they came along. Until then, she would remain confident of her plot. With her mind made up, Lady Jocasta rushed as fast as she could to the audience chamber.

Despite her best efforts, she arrived out of breath and anxiously pale. The frail old man was hunched in the comfort of a high-backed chair. His stooped frame melted into the seat's upholstery as if he were an invertebrate sack of skin and bones. Jocasta announced her presence with a cough, and as Sir George Dray craned his neck in her direction, she almost expected to hear a sound like the creaking of a tree's branches.

She lowered her head, and pulled out a chair from the table opposite him. 'I am sorry to keep you waiting, Sir George,' she said.

'I won't hear you all the way over there, lass. Come and sit next to me, I won't bite!' Dray said. His old face, cracked and flaking like brittle plaster, tried its best to entertain a smile. 'Don't look so worried, lass . . . I'm not here to check up on you! Well, not entirely. I'm just here to tie up a few loose ends. Seeing as I've missed the old wolf, I might as well learn more about this poison plot you've been cooking up . . . just so there are no surprises . . . such as the ones we experienced in London a few weeks back, hmm?' He grinned at Jocasta, a grin that sent ice-cold flames shooting through her veins.

As the old man's green eyes scoured her face, Lady Jocasta felt far more naked than she had done in the bathtub. She prayed that he could not see the nervousness in her demeanour, but it clung to her words nevertheless.

'I understand. I am sure that you will be pleased,' she said.

'We shall see, lass. I've been following your career for some time, ever since Adolfo brought you in,' Dray said, shifting gawkily in his seat. 'The Baron speaks very highly of you. You're confident, strong willed – if a mite too headstrong at times. Eager to please, sometimes at the expense of the bigger picture.' He stared into Jocasta's eyes, and seemed to take for ever to blink.

'But as much as I value the Baron's opinion . . . I like to make up my own mind. This poison of yours is the one that we obtained in London, I understand. I read your report on the way here, lass. Most thorough . . . in parts. And you have the stuff in your possession now, correct?'

'Yes, Sir George, and we are sched—'

'Good,' interjected Dray curtly. 'We can begin then. The longer we tarry, the more we open up ourselves to exposure!'

'Exposure, Sir George?' she asked. 'Exposure by what?'

'Don't you mean by whom?' asked the Scotsman. 'We can't afford to risk—'

'But, Sir George, there *is* no risk. My calculations—'

'Are *wrong*, Jocasta . . . trust me,' snapped Dray, waving a shrivelled finger.

'Sir, I can assure you that there is nothing to be concerned about,' Jocasta said.

'Oh, I seriously doubt that.' Sir George licked his dry lips, the sound like crushed autumn leaves underfoot. He leaned closer to Jocasta, close enough for her to smell the stench of alcohol on his breath. 'Our organisation went to a lot of effort to procure that poison and it was not without its losses, so this plan of yours had better pay off. Do I make myself clear, Lady Jocasta?'

Jocasta's nerves were at the point of shattering.

Losses? What did the old man mean by that? Was he referring to the death of his pet psychopath, Renard? Or his son, Oliver? Or was it just her paranoia tainting everything? She was seeing ghosts everywhere, hearing undertones of mistrust in every syllable. Every word was layered with an accusatory edge, as if the old man was trying to force a confession out of her.

'Sir George, this plan is not like London,' she said. 'Renard was unhinged! He refused to be reined in. My project is not reliant upon the fragile constraints of just one man.'

'Or woman?' said Sir George, eyeing her with a dull flicker in his eyes.

'Sir, my plan *will* be a success!' Jocasta insisted. 'I will make sure of it.'

'Aye, lass . . . I'm sure you will,' said Dray. 'You'll have to excuse me being jumpy. I'm a product of the old days, you see. More comfortable with the twist of a blade . . . the feel of a pistol in my hand . . . the smell of gunpowder.'

'With respect, sir . . . the old ways are gone,' said Jocasta. 'As I am constantly reminding the Baron, the Hades Consortium must learn to adapt if we are to retain our position of dominance.'

'The pupil becomes the teacher, eh?' sniggered Dray, as he pushed himself up awkwardly from his chair. 'Now I need to rest, lass. I've had a long journey from Rawalpindi and my back's giving me gip.' With a brief nod, he shuffled away from the table, back up the stone steps towards an archway into the shadowed caverns. At the top of the steps, he snapped his fingers. 'And make sure I am kept apprised of any problems that may arise whilst I sleep . . . especially any *unwanted* visitors that might show up at our door. A fly can drop into the ointment at any time . . . especially this particular fly.'

CHAPTER XXXVIII

The Unburied Secret

LIKE MADAME DESTINE, Cornelius Quaint also relied upon an element of prescient awareness, but his was nowhere near as refined as the Frenchwoman's gifts had been. He relied solely on instinct. He still had no idea where the poison was, nor from where the Hades Consortium planned to use it. Umkaza was miles away from the Nile, far too far for any effective demonstration of the poison's power. Yet, his gut feeling told him that the place was an essential part of the plot somehow – and Cornelius Quaint's gut feeling was seldom wrong.

Outside the Bara Mephista tavern, he and Aksak Faroud finished preparing for their journey to Umkaza. They fastened saddles to their horses, and stocked the panniers with enough food and water for the long ride. Faroud slotted his curved sword into the scabbard affixed to his horse's saddle. He glanced up as he caught Quaint looking at him.

'It is not for you,' he said, nodding towards the weapon. 'You have earned my trust, Cornelius . . . as I hope I have earned yours.'

Quaint nodded firmly at Faroud. He did trust him. He had to. He had no one else left *to* trust. The Aksak was risking his standing within the Council of Elders by throwing his lot in with him. That was firm proof of trust as far as Quaint was concerned.

'Your plan is foolhardy . . . but its recklessness suits you,' said Faroud. 'However, if we are to clash with the Hades Consortium, we had best make sure we have more than just courage in our hearts. We shall need a great deal of cunning and a lot of good luck! So, what of the Professor whilst we are gone?'

'She's coming,' answered Quaint.

Faroud stopped what he was doing.

'Why, is that a problem?' Quaint asked.

'Are you certain that you wish to be saddled with her on this journey? I much preferred her with a sack on her head,' grinned Faroud, raising one in turn from Quaint. 'I can ensure her safety here in Bara Mephista, if you fear for it. She will be treated like visiting royalty.'

'Which I'm sure she would just adore, but no one knows Umkaza like the Professor,' replied Quaint. 'Until we can figure out the Hades Consortium's connection to that dig site, I want her where I can keep an eye on her. I'm certain that Umkaza is crucial to working out the mechanisms of the Consortium's plot . . . then once we've figured it out, all we have to do is stop it!'

'You make me nervous,' said Faroud. 'I have no idea what you are thinking.'

'You'd be amazed how often I hear that,' said Quaint.

Just then, there was a sound of shuffling of feet behind them, and Polly North appeared from the rear exit of the tavern.

'Talking about me?' she asked of Quaint.

'Heavens, no!' he lied. 'We were just discussing our plan.'

'Plan?' Polly laughed mockingly. 'Oh, well, I'd love to hear it. What is it? Are you going to sell your soul to Satan and ask him if he wants to accompany us on this little jaunt *as well as* this Scarab dog?'

'I could always get that sack, Cornelius,' muttered Faroud.

'Keep it on standby just in case,' said Quaint from the corner of his mouth.

Faroud knew that he was only aggravating the situation, also he was reluctant to be in Polly's company for long. 'I have a few things to finalise with my men. I will leave you two to it,' he said, as he removed himself from the stable and re-entered the tavern.

The Professor eyed him devilishly all the way. 'Mongrel,' she hissed.

'I thought we'd been through all this,' said Quaint, as he tried to break through the brittle carapace of her anger. 'The Aksak's help is essential to—'

'To what? To torture me some more? To remind me what I've had to sacrifice?'

'Professor, I really don't think that—'

'Don't you "Professor" me, Cornelius Quaint!' seared Polly. She flopped herself down on an upturned wooden barrel and gazed disconsolately at the barren landscape around the encampment. 'I really don't understand you at all. One moment these Scarabs are nothing but scavenging animals picking at the carcass of life, and then you're prepared to fight alongside them as if they were your brothers! Does that not even *bother* you?'

'Bother me? Of course it bothers me! I don't relish throwing my lot in with the sort of people that on any other day I would probably be up against – but this is not any other day.'

'The enemy of my enemy is my friend?'

'Something like that,' said Quaint. 'The Hades Consortium is a big foe to fight, Polly, and I cannot do it alone. Allying myself with the Clan Scarabs was a hard choice to make . . . but it was also a *necessary* one.'

'And you're an expert in necessary choices, are you?' asked Polly.

'I don't expect you to understand, Polly,' Quaint replied, unsure if he really wanted to win this argument. 'I've learned a lot about human nature . . . particularly the darker side. I've travelled the world and I've seen much that turned my stomach – things that I could not just stand by and watch. So I interfered in matters that I knew little about. I intervened because I thought them to be wrong. But I wasn't qualified to make that judgement, don't you see? I judged them on *my* terms, by *my* ethics!'

'You're only proving my point for me. You're allowing your judgement to be impaired by circumstance, Cornelius. You talk about things like ethics, and yet where are they when you make a deal with the Devil?'

Quaint glanced down at the ground, kicking at a clod of dried dirt. 'Professor, this is a fight that neither of us can win unless we have walked in each other's shoes. I have experience with the Hades Consortium. Close up. I know what they're capable of, and the Clan Scarabs are insects compared to them! When you understand that, maybe you'll understand why I choose to lay down with dogs. Desperate times call for desperate measures.'

'And uneasy alliances,' said Polly.

'Sometimes,' said Quaint. 'But make no mistake, Professor – these are most desperate times indeed.'

Soon after, three streaks of dust cut a path through the desert sands towards Umkaza. The afternoon sunlight cast long shadows across the uneven territory as Cornelius Quaint, Aksak Faroud and Polly North rode side by side. The conjuror had been forced to change many of his opinions about the Clan Scarabs of late, and was now convinced the band of thieves at least had a semblance of civility about them. They had allowed him to change his ragged, bloodied clothing for some of their own garments. Clad in much more suitable attire for a desert trek, he wore a pair of loose-fitting khaki trousers and a plain white cotton collarless shirt, with a scarf wrapped around his head to shield himself from the unrelenting sun. Quaint did not ask where the clothes came from, guessing that the answer might sit uneasily on his mind.

Riding at his side, a disgruntled Polly North took every available opportunity to scowl at the hooded Scarab leader. She had an intense dislike of him – that much would have been obvious to a blind man, but she had been notably silent on the journey from Bara Mephista. Despite the fact that Faroud had joined Quaint on his mission, it did nothing to change her opinion of him.

Soon, Aksak Faroud raised his hand into the air, signalling the trio to stop.

'Umkaza, dead ahead,' he said to the conjuror.

They rode through a semblance of a wooden gate, wide enough for two carts side by side and twenty feet high. Quaint dismounted and took a slow look around.

'Dead ahead, indeed,' he said.

The ground was strewn with personal belongings of all kinds, an obvious sign that the inhabitants left in a hurry. A pair of spectacles lay bent and crushed in the sand, and notebooks, various pieces of ceramic pottery and a range of personal effects were discarded where they had fallen. A row of canvas tents up on the rise had been slashed into rags, the material flapping loosely from bamboo frames in the wind.

As his eyes gradually took in the sight before him, Quaint was numbed at how ghostly the place felt, how silent. It was hard to believe that just the day before it had been a thriving excavation site, buzzing with excitement. He looked cautiously at Polly, who had also dismounted, and he wondered how on earth she felt. She was uncharacteristically quiet, and now he understood why.

Polly was near to tears. She walked forwards slowly up the gentle incline, past several pits that had once been areas of excavation, now nothing but empty holes in the ground. She collapsed onto her knees at the edge of the pit. Her own notebook was lying in the dirt, the corners bent, the pages torn. After so many dead ends, so many fruitless searches, it had been her dream to uncover the resting place of the fabled Pharaoh's Cradle. Now, that dream was lying spreadeagled in the dust.

Quaint rubbed the back of his neck, uncertain what to say. 'Look . . . this doesn't have to be the end, you know. I'm sure you can put another crew together . . . start digging afresh.'

Polly's voice was upset. 'Not enough time.'

'Oh, come on! The treasures in this place have laid here for hundreds of years, what's a couple of weeks going to hurt? We can get you to Cairo, or Mos Nettair or somewhere to get a new crew,' offered Quaint. 'I know a few folk at the British Museum, surely they can—'

'No, Cornelius!' yelled the Professor. 'You don't know what you're talking about! It's too late, all right? I don't have the time to crew up. The paperwork alone takes weeks out here! It's over, don't you see?' She stood and kicked a crooked spade into the pit. 'The only thing I ever found even the remotest bit interesting in this place was a pile of bones anyway! And not even ancient ones . . . at least then I might have been able to salvage something from this trip. Stumbling across a mass grave only twenty or thirty years old is hardly a great historical find, Cornelius. No . . . it's far too late to repair the damage now.'

Quaint quietly approached her side. 'If it's a matter of cost—'

'Cost has nothing to do with it! Cost is the least of my troubles. It is *time* that is against me . . . and not even my sponsor's vast fortune can buy any more of that. It's almost laughable really,' Polly continued, rising to her feet, striding away from him. 'I can still recall him telling me about the wonders of this place. He was so confident, so driven. He said that I'd unearth the greatest find of my career . . . a find that would cement my name in the annals of archaeology for ever. How wrong he was . . . how wrong we *both* were. And now I've got no time left. I've got a ship bound for England to catch. I have to attend a celebration . . . in *my* honour, would you believe? A celebration? What do I have to celebrate? Now I've got no choice but to return to the Queen as a failure!'

'The Queen? As in . . . Queen *Victoria*?' asked Quaint.

'The one and only,' confirmed Polly.

'It sounds like your benefactor has quite a pull with aristocracy,' noted Quaint.

'Cho-zen Li is one of the richest men in the world,' Polly said. 'He has quite a pull with *everyone*. He was so sure that I'd find the Pharaoh's Cradle that he organised a celebratory gala dinner for me at Buckingham Palace. The fifth of February, just over a month's time. I'm supposed to present my *treasures* as a gift for the Queen. I'm in luck if she thinks that nothing but bones and dirt are treasure!'

'Cho-zen Li? Now, where have I heard that name before?' Quaint rubbed at his jaw, like an angler feeling for a bite on his line. Once he felt that familiar tug of curiosity, he would never give up without reeling in his prize. But this time, the truth seemed to slip free off his hook and it was gone. 'And this treasure, this Pharaoh's Cradle . . . I suppose it must be valuable.'

Polly stared at him as if he were a simpleton. 'Valuable? It's the very crib that held the infant Rameses II, dating back to the thirteenth century BC – of *course* it's valuable! It is supposedly made from solid gold, adorned with hundreds of precious stones – emeralds, rubies, sapphires, diamonds – the lot!'

'No wonder you were so keen to find it,' Quaint said.

'Cho-zen Li had such faith in my abilities. He spent a small fortune hiring the best archaeologists that the world has to offer. His confidence inspired me . . . no, it *fooled* me . . . into believing that I would uncover it. I've let so many people down,' Polly said, her eyes glazing. She believed every word of what she was saying. She believed that she had failed. For a scientist, that was a hard blow to recover from. 'Cho-zen has donated hundreds of exhibits to the Cairo Museum of Antiquities, the British Museum, and the Paris Archives. It was his love for the reconstruction of history that drew me to him, and I've been trying to do him proud since the very first day I disembarked in Alexandria's port.'

'That's it,' exclaimed Quaint, snapping his fingers. 'Alexandria!'

'What?' asked Polly.

'That's where I know that name from!'

'Alexandria? Well, it *is* a fairly well-known port.'

'Not *Alexandria* – Cho-zen Li!' barked Quaint. 'It all makes sense now.'

'Not to me, it doesn't,' said Polly dryly.

Quaint shook his head impatiently. He hated being interrupted when he was rambling. Finding coherence within incoherence was a gift he had cultivated since a child, and he was exceptionally good at it.

'Alexandria is a friend of mine. A seamstress from Hosni, and

I recall seeing this coat that she'd tailored for a client in her workshop,' he explained breathlessly, his black eyes twitching left and right as he sifted through recent memory. 'It was *his* order! His coat – Cho-zen Li's coat . . . right there in a backstreet tailor's shop . . . and now here we are . . . on an archaeological dig in the middle of nowhere with his name cropping up again.'

'Well, I have to admit . . . that *is* a bit of a coincidence,' muttered Polly.

'That's what worries me,' said Quaint, his face the picture of discontent. 'But surely it can have no connection to *this*. Let me think.' The conjuror plucked at his ear lobes impatiently, and then began to stroll around in circles, all the while drilling his stare into the ground, as if trying to sift the truth from the sand beneath his feet. 'Joyce wanted you gone from this place. Joyce works for the Consortium. But archaeology holds no interest to them . . . unless . . . unless they want to sell the Pharaoh's Cradle to the highest bidder – which could be this Cho-zen Li chap if he's as rich as you claim. Maybe they're trying to get their hands on the treasure first! But that's still out of character for them. They don't need *money*. There's more to it than that, there just has to be! Joyce went to a lot of trouble to scare you away, but if you'd been digging here for as long as you had, why all of a sudden take umbrage? Could it be that you were close to unearthing something . . . or perhaps already had done so?'

Polly coughed loudly into her hand. 'Sorry to disturb your mad ramblings, Cornelius, but I've already told you – I found nothing! The Pharaoh's Cradle could be anywhere underneath this desert, or it could be *nowhere* here!'

Quaint ground his teeth. 'I wasn't referring to the Pharaoh's Cradle, Professor.'

'Then . . . what else is there of value here?'

'Not value necessarily . . . but *importance*,' answered Quaint, with not a small degree of displeasure. All of his five senses were operating at a rate of knots and it was painfully exhilarating. He hated it when his gut feeling was right. 'Did you not say that you'd uncovered a mass grave full of bones? What if that's the link? What if that's why Joyce wanted you scared away from here?' Quaint called over to Faroud, silently astride his horse nearby. 'Aksak, you know Joyce better than any of us. What is his history in Egypt? Was he in the country twenty or so years ago?'

Faroud raised a cautious eyebrow. 'Why . . . yes, I believe so. He moved here in the late twenties as the port administrator in Alexandria prior to being assigned the role of British attaché to Egypt. If it helps . . . when Joyce ordered my Scarabs to apprehend the Professor, he did not claim that it was for the benefit of the Hades Consortium. I merely inferred that, knowing who his masters were. He just said that he had a few "skeletons in his closet" that he did not wish to be unearthed.'

Quaint's face lit up. 'By someone whose job it is to dig for secrets, perhaps?'

'Oh, nonsense,' said Polly. 'I'm still not convinced that Joyce is involved in any of this. We've only got this Scarab's word for it, remember? The man is the British attaché to Egypt, for crying out loud! He could have been speaking *figuratively*.'

'But what if he wasn't?' countered Quaint without missing a beat. 'That's why he wants you gone from this place, on account of those bones you found! No wonder he doesn't want that grave made common knowledge. People might start asking awkward questions of him, and then where would he be? He would expose not only himself but the Hades Consortium too!'

'Quaint, if you keep talking long enough no doubt you'll end up convincing yourself that you're right, but you're forgetting one thing – proof. Something you lack!' snapped Polly. 'This is all just some incredible story, and I'm not swayed by it for one moment.'

'Trust me on this, Professor . . . unravelling these sorts of webs is my speciality,' said Quaint. 'As a conjuror, I have an insatiable hunger to work out what makes things tick . . . why things are what they are. I wanted leverage to use against Joyce and this is it!'

'This is madness! Not to mention slander,' Polly stormed, throwing her hands up into the air. 'If you're so convinced that Godfrey Joyce is guilty, why don't you just trot on over to the British Embassy in Cairo and ask him?'

'I like the way you think,' said Quaint. 'We can make it by nightfall if we hurry.'

'What?' asked Polly, aghast. 'I was *joking*!'

'Aksak, what do you think?' Quaint asked him.

Aksak Faroud bunched his fingers into a fist and gnawed on his knuckles as though he was trying to force his words back down his throat.

'Joyce is a dangerous man,' he said eventually. He had only wished to help the conjuror discover a clue as to the Hades Consortium's plot. By going up against Godfrey Joyce, the Scarab leader was risking far more than just his own neck. 'If you set foot in that Embassy, you will be on *his* territory. If you really are going to face him, you will need an airtight plan.'

'Don't worry, Faroud.' Quaint gripped his horse's reins and pulled himself up into the saddle. 'Airtight plans are my speciality!'

'I thought you said that unravelling webs was your speciality?' asked Polly.

'I diversify in my specialities, Polly,' said Quaint. 'Come on, folks! Let's go and put our friend Mr Joyce in an awkward position that he can't wriggle out of.'

CHAPTER XXXIX

𝕿𝖍𝖊 𝕻𝖊𝖗𝖘𝖎𝖘𝖙𝖊𝖓𝖙 𝕻𝖆𝖘𝖙

THE POTHOLES AND loose debris on the road from the lake to Umkaza made travelling at high speeds a dangerous business, but Ahman was in no particular hurry. He was quite content to trot Moses along at a gentle pace. After all, Umkaza was going nowhere. There was no need to rush – quite the opposite to Madame Destine's thoughts, who was eager to arrive at their destination. After all, it was a place that she had put all her hopes in. Even so, the Frenchwoman was full of optimism as the cart trundled over the dips and troughs. She was far too wrapped up in the pages of the journal to notice any discomfort.

'Listen to this!' she called to Ahman.

'Godfrey Joyce appeared on site again this morning accompanied by his so-called "guide", a man named Nastasi – a scurrilous-looking fiend if ever I saw one. As hopeful as I am, I do not feel comfortable with this man taking such an interest in the site. He possesses no interest in archaeology, and seems to involve himself in many furtive conversations with Joyce. Whenever I approach, I am certain that they consciously change the subject. Whatever the content of their talks, I sense that it can only spell trouble.

'And this, Ahman, listen to this, just a few pages later. It is just as my après-monition detailed . . . why Aloysius had to get me away from Umkaza. Listen:

'A large group of armed men have come from the desert in the night – led by this man Nastasi. They have positioned themselves around the site at Joyce's command. We are effectively prisoners. Joyce tells me not to be concerned, but how can I not be so? He tells me the men are for my crew's protection. But protection from whom? All the dangerous folk seem to be right here in Umkaza.

'I am writing this to leave word. I have a nasty feeling that once the tomb of the Pharaoh's Cradle is opened I will be superfluous to requirements. I cannot let this happen. Madame Destine warned me about dealing with Joyce. She said that no good would come of our association, and I am starting to believe her. She senses that Joyce wants the treasure for himself, and all others are dispensable – myself included.'

Destine ran her hands down her face despairingly. 'My word, Ahman . . . this journal is a painful read, is it not? It is as if we can see this betrayal happening in front of us . . . through a misted window separated by time . . . and yet it is becoming clearer with every page we read. I just wish that I could help Aloysius somehow.'

Ahman rested the reins in his lap and sighed. 'It is all in the past. You can do nothing to prevent it now, ah? I do not know what you hope to find in Umkaza, but I pray it will be of comfort.' He looked over his shoulder to see Destine rubbing at her tired eyes and then looking down at the journal in her lap. It was as if the book were dragging her down, pulling at her to commit its will.

'Listen, my dear, why not take a break from that book, ah? I fear that it is draining you to the point where it is all you can think of. Let me take care of it for the remainder of our journey and you try to get some rest. I promise that I will tell you once we have arrived in Umkaza. It is not far now. I hope that there we shall find an end to this torment of yours.'

'I pray that you are right, dear Ahman,' Madame Destine smeared the backs of her hands over her pale blue eyes. 'It feels as if the past is desperate not to be forgotten, and unless I resolve this matter, I shall never be free until my dying day.'

Not far behind the meandering cart rode Heinrich Nadir, and next to him, his two silent assassins. As they galloped ever closer to the cart, the dark riders focused upon their prey. Like emotionless automatons, they simultaneously removed curve-bladed swords from scabbards affixed to their backs. With the occupants of the cart ahead oblivious to their peril, the two assassins moved their horses into position . . .

Ahman vaguely noticed something in the corner of his eye. He looked around, spying a man on horseback keeping pace with his cart. Ahman frowned, thinking his old eyes deceived him, until an odd twinge made him look over his other shoulder, where he discovered another man. With his cart masking the rider's approach, Destine was thankfully unaware of the impending threat – unlike Ahman. His cart was penned in on both sides, and there was nothing he could do to evade his pursuers. The nearest rider to him craned over in his saddle and pulled down his hood, showing his face.

His dark skin was pockmarked with swirling black tattoos around his cheeks and eyes, but the most ghastly thing of all was his gaping wide mouth. His tongue had been removed, and his black throat screeched an inaudible scream.

Ahman leapt in fright, startling Destine.

'Hold onto something, Madame!' he yelled, as he wrenched the reins furiously to one side, just as the rider slashed at him with his sword. 'We have company.'

'Who *are* they?' gasped Destine in horror.

'I do not know, but whoever they are, they are not friendly!' said Ahman, desperately whipping the reins harder. 'Go, Moses, go!'

Even if the carpet trader's horse was capable of picking up speed at the drop of a hat – which it was most assuredly not – there was no way it could attain the kind of velocity needed to escape its pursuers' muscular steeds.

As Ahman whipped harder on the reins with an enthusiastic '*Hyah!*' that bordered on the terrified, something flashed brightly. It was the glint of sunlight against metal as the other rider to his right swung at him with his sword.

Luckily, the potholed road was on Ahman's side, and the assassin's horse stumbled in a ditch. The blade missed its target – but only just. Standing upright in his saddle, the assassin attempted another pass – and this time his blade made contact.

Ahman wailed in pain as it sliced a deep gash into his right shoulder.

Destine screamed too, consumed by her panic.

Ahman clutched the reins as the buffeting craft leapt along the road, careering left and right wildly. Searing pain scorched his shoulder as blood seeped relentlessly.

'Give them to me!' Destine shouted, as she snatched the reins from Ahman's loose grip. 'We must stop!'

'No! Must . . . keep going,' Ahman replied, his eyes rolling.

He was losing concentration as well as blood, and both were retreating from him with haste. The cart struck something in the road and it lurched into the air. Destine watched helplessly as Ahman was lifted from his seat. She tried to reach him but it was too late. Ahman toppled over the side of the cart and struck the dusty track hard, tumbling in circles over and over, arms flailing, coming to a stop in a crumpled mess by the side of the road.

Ahman did not get up.

Ahman did not even move.

Soon, he was masked by a cloud of dust – and Destine's mind was a muddle. Still the men pursued her, drawing level with her on both sides. She wept, her flooded eyes no longer able to visualise anything clearly. In a final act of desperate surrender, she yanked hard on the horse's reins. With nowhere to go, and no hope of survival, she succumbed to her fate. She lowered her head, waiting to die . . .

CHAPTER XL

The Discarded Debris

QUAINT, NORTH AND Faroud travelled the road leading east away from Umkaza. Their plan to infiltrate the British Embassy and question Godfrey Joyce firsthand was certainly one fraught with risk, but Quaint was blissfully optimistic of its success. But as is always the way with best laid plans, they seldom run their course without incident – especially plans laid by Cornelius Quaint.

A mile outside the limits of Umkaza, his keen eyes spotted something by the side of the road that made his heart lurch in his chest.

It was the motionless body of an old man.

He was caked in dust and grit, with a nasty wound on his arm that spewed a puddle of blood onto the sand. He was quite still, just another piece of discarded debris on the road. Quaint and Polly were off their horses in a second. Polly lifted the fallen man's head and cradled it in her lap, as Quaint pulled his canteen from the pannier on his horse and splashed water over the man's face. The liquid washed away a fine layer of grime from his spectacles, and cleared specks of dirt from his thick moustache and beard. The old man coughed and spluttered as the water shook him back into consciousness.

'Sir? Can you hear me?' asked Polly. 'What is your name?'

'Ahman . . . but where am I?' he spluttered.

'You're about a mile from Umkaza. Who *did* this to you?' asked Quaint in Arabic, spying the deep gash to Ahman's shoulder.

'Desert riders . . . two of them,' mumbled Ahman, his face twisted in pain. Tears welled in his large brown eyes as he tried to roll onto his side.

'Lie still, sir,' Polly said, as she looked at Quaint. 'Cornelius, this wound is fresh, but it's deep and he's lost a lot of blood.' She looked appealingly towards Faroud. 'Scarab, you know these territories better than us, is there anywhere we can take him for medical treatment?'

'I hardly think he has enough time left,' Faroud replied, gripping his horse's reins tightly, eager to be on his way. 'Leave him. He is no concern of ours.'

'But he was attacked, you animal! Did you not hear what he said?' Polly shouted.

Faroud reluctantly bowed his head. This woman was going to be the death of him.

'Very well,' he said. 'In my camp . . . there is a man named Bephotsi who can assist him. He has many medical supplies.'

'Then we've got to get back there immediately!' Polly said looking at Quaint.

'Not a chance,' said the conjuror. 'Cairo is this way . . . Bara Mephista is in totally the opposite direction.'

Polly motioned to the injured man. 'But we can't just *leave* him here.'

'I know, but . . . what can we do for him? You said it yourself, he's lost a lot of blood. Who says he'll even make it as far as Bara Mephista. Polly, this thing with Joyce is a much larger affair. The whole of Egypt is at stake. We can't just derail now, not when we're so close to getting somewhere. We just don't have the time.'

'Neither does he!' snapped Polly.

'I'm sorry, Polly. The answer is no.'

'Fine! Then I shall take him back myself!'

'Then I shall pray for you both,' interrupted Faroud coldly. 'Tell Bephotsi that I sent you. He will give you any assistance that you require. That is the only solace I can offer this man.'

Quaint looked down at Ahman, searching his round face. 'Sir, can you hear me? The Professor here is going to take you somewhere . . . somewhere you can get some help, do you understand me?'

'Where . . . where is she? Can you see her?' Ahman wheezed.

'She is right here, sir,' answered Quaint.

'No! Not her . . .' Ahman said. 'Not . . . *her*.'

'The heat has already begun to addle his mind.' Polly looked at Quaint and then down at Ahman. 'You are here alone, sir. We have to get you out of this sun. Just hold onto me and we'll be all right.' She nodded to Quaint. 'Cornelius, give me your scarf, I need to patch his shoulder or he won't make it a mile.' Quaint did as he was instructed, and Polly began binding the large gash in Ahman's shoulder. She was putting on a brave face, but not brave enough that the conjuror could not see right through it.

'Are you going to be all right?' he asked her.

'I'll be fine!' she snapped. 'You two are off on your little boys' adventure, and I'd hardly be any use to you in a fight anyway . . . because you are going to have a fight. You realise that, don't you? If Godfrey Joyce really is involved in this plot, then he could have all manner of tricks up his sleeve!'

'No doubt, Polly,' said Cornelius Quaint, 'but I've got a few of my own.'

CHAPTER XLI

The Rat Trap

As thankful as she was that she was not yet dead, Madame Destine's situation was not all that improved. Blindfolded and flanked on either side by the two silent assassins that had attacked her, with Heinrich Nadir trailing behind, she was brusquely steered through the winding white corridors of the British Embassy.

The ride from the outskirts of Umkaza to Cairo had taken quite some time, and everything was a haze in her mind. The last thing she recalled with any certainty was seeing Ahman fall from the cart. How could she *not* recall it? Her mind replayed the moment repeatedly. She feared that Ahman was now almost certainly dead. Even if the assassins had not finished him off, the harsh desert heat surely would have.

As she was pushed roughly through the carpeted corridors, her next thought was of Cornelius Quaint, and how he must be going out of his mind with worry by now at her disappearance – and then she remembered her words in the letter. If her younger self's premonitions were correct, at that moment Cornelius was beset by a challenge of his own.

She prayed that he was having better luck than she was.

Hearing one of her captors knock loudly upon a heavy door in front of her, Destine was yanked to an abrupt stop. She had reached her destination, the end of the line – in perhaps more ways than one.

'Enter,' said Godfrey Joyce.

He watched the quartet file sombrely into his office. Ignoring the two assassins and oblivious to Nadir, it was Destine that he was most anxious to see. His quarry was older than he had imagined her to be, if he was honest, and she looked disappointingly lacking in spiritual prowess.

'I think we can dispense with the blindfold now, gentlemen,' Joyce said, greeting the Frenchwoman's blinking eyes with a wide grin. 'Madame Destine, I presume?'

'Who are you? How do you know my name?' she demanded. 'What do you want with me? Where am I?'

'Questions, questions!' said Joyce. 'But this is my party, so I get to go first. Mr Nadir, where did you find our guest?'

'Just outside Umkaza, travelling with a companion in a horse-drawn cart,' said Nadir.

The hazy fog that clouded Destine's mind cleared as she recognised the German's voice. 'The man from the *Silver Swan*? What are *you* doing here?'

'I am flattered you remember me, Fräulein,' Nadir said with a swift nod. 'And to answer your question . . . I work here.'

'Nadir, you mentioned a companion. Where is this man now?' asked Joyce.

'Dead, sir,' replied Nadir, 'to the best of my knowledge.'

Fresh tears filled Destine's eyes at the German's words. Her legs lost their strength and she collapsed onto the floor lifelessly. Godfrey Joyce snapped his fingers and pointed to a chair opposite his desk. The two hooded assassins lifted Destine like a doll and deposited her firmly into the seat. She slumped into the leather, her head in her hands.

'You made the right decision for once, Nadir . . . any more prisoners in this room and I would need to lay on extra chairs,' said Joyce, with a genial flutter to his voice. 'Although I must admit, I had expected this prize to be a little more lucid. By the looks of the bedraggled old witch, she'll be no use to anyone! And she's supposed to tell the future?' His grin was as thin as a sheet of paper. 'It obviously didn't do *her* much good, did it? Madame Fortune-Teller . . . I wish to see a demonstration of your clairvoyant gifts.'

Destine looked up through bleary eyes. 'Clairvoyant? How do you know that?'

Godfrey Joyce gave a cheery smile. 'Mr Nadir here has told me *such* wonderful tales about the little boat trip that the two of you shared together, and he's also told me all about your wonderful abilities, Madame. I must admit to being rather intrigued. I'm dying to know how you do it. What is it? Tea leaves? Rune stones? Voices in your head?'

'I once was clairvoyant, that much is correct,' replied Destine, as she untied her headscarf and wiped away her tears. 'But I am afraid that your little spy's information is woefully out of date. I no longer have the ability to see the future. I have not been able to for some weeks now. And were I in possession of such ability, do you honestly believe that I would demonstrate it for the likes of you, monsieur?'

'She lies, Herr Joyce,' spat Nadir. 'I have it from an impeccable source . . . someone who knows all about her little gift.'

'Whoever it was – they were wrong!' Destine said, throwing her headscarf down onto the floor angrily. 'My abilities were taken from me. I am clairvoyant no more.'

'*Nadir* . . . this had better not be a waste of my time,' said Joyce.

'She is lying!' insisted Nadir. 'You witch, I know all about you and what you can do, why do you not just admit it?'

'I should have listened to Cornelius and had you thrown overboard, you treacherous little worm!' Destine snapped.

'Cornelius?' Joyce's ears pricked up. 'Cornelius *Quaint*, by any chance?' Destine's awed expression confirmed his enquiry. 'Now isn't that a coincidence. Until a few moments ago I had never heard mention of that name in my entire life, and now I have heard it twice within an hour!'

'What do you know of Cornelius?' demanded Destine.

'Not much, other than he seems to be making quite a reputation for himself.'

That sounds like Cornelius, thought Destine.

Joyce cackled victoriously. 'Your friend is on his way as we speak – accompanied by the leader of the Clan Scarabs. Whoever this man Cornelius is, he certainly likes to mix in dangerous circles . . . dangerous for *him,* that is.' He tapped out a rhythm on his desk with the blade of a golden letter-opener. By its side lay a neatly opened envelope. He plucked the note from inside and displayed it proudly. 'My old friend Nastasi has warned me that Mr Quaint intends to cause me grief . . . so it seems only sporting of me to cause him some back.'

'Did you just say . . . *Nastasi*?' asked Destine, her mouth falling open. 'That name . . . surely it cannot be? But that must mean . . .' Her eyes caught sight of a plaque on Joyce's desk. 'You are Godfrey Joyce! You betrayed Aloysius Bedford!'

The smug grin disappeared from Joyce's face in a flash and he shifted his position uncomfortably. 'How do you know of my association with him?'

'You are the man from his journal!' Destine snapped. 'The traitor!'

Joyce grabbed hold of the letter-opener and plunged its blade deep into his desk in anger. He stared at Destine with the ferociousness of a wild animal. With the mention of Aloysius Bedford's name, it seemed that Madame Destine had just touched a raw nerve.

A very raw nerve indeed . . .

CHAPTER XLII

𝕿𝖍𝖊 𝕭𝖆𝖎𝖙𝖊𝖉 𝕳𝖔𝖔𝖐

IMPRISONED WITHIN A holding cell beneath the British Embassy, Destine was seated on a long wooden bench with her back to the wall, silent and brooding. A tray of food had been placed outside the bars of her cell, but she was in no mood to eat. Be it fate, or circumstance, or even coincidence, something had caused her path to cross Godfrey Joyce's. Hearing the scuffing of footsteps down the flight of stone stairs, she steeled her nerve as the large double doors at the far end of the cell block were wrenched open.

'Not hungry, Madame?' asked Godfrey Joyce, tapping his toe against the tray of untouched food on the floor. 'That'll do you no good, you know.'

'I am not making a petition for release, monsieur,' Destine said calmly. 'I simply find it difficult to stomach food in your presence.'

'Hoping your friend Quaint will come and save you?' asked Joyce.

'If Cornelius is on his way here, then he is not coming for me,' said Madame Destine. 'He is coming for you.'

'You're sure of that are you? You've certainly got a lot of faith in your companion. I must admit to being a little intrigued by this Quaint fellow myself. Nastasi was rather vague. What is this man doing in Egypt?'

'Hunting,' Destine replied.

'Hunting what, might I ask?' Joyce enquired.

Madame Destine's expression did not falter. 'People like you.'

'Well, I am afraid that he'll find me a tricky prey to catch,' Joyce said, smoothing his mutton-chop sideburns. 'Fortune-teller or not, you are still just as good a bargaining chip as the fellow in the cell next door to you. Is that not right, boy?' Joyce stepped back and slammed his hand against the metal bars of the cell next to Destine's. For the first time, the Frenchwoman realised that she was not alone in her incarceration. 'Your fate rests in your brother's hands, young Scarab, but fear not . . . your time will come. Once you have outlived your usefulness I will have no hesitation in ordering your death.' Joyce returned to Destine's view. 'So, Madame . . . what exactly is in that journal of Bedford's anyway? And how much does your friend Cornelius know about it?'

'He knows what I know, *ver*!' Destine lied. Cornelius Quaint had absolutely no idea at all who Aloysius Bedford was, of course, but at that moment it was the only weapon she had at her disposal. 'He knows all about your betrayal and he knows what happened in Umkaza!'

'Does he now?' mused Joyce. 'Well, that puts an interesting slant on things. Nastasi didn't tell me that. It seems my hard efforts for Umkaza to remain secret were for nothing. So what was Bedford to you anyway?'

'A friend,' Destine replied, lowering her head. 'You pretended to help him, introducing your accomplice Nastasi, promising assistance, yet all the while all you cared about was stealing the Pharaoh's Cradle from under his nose!'

'The Pharaoh's Cradle?' Joyce took a step closer to the bars of the holding cell. An inch of iron was the only thing separating him and Destine, but it might as well have been a mile. 'Now *there's* something I've not heard mention of for a long time. My, you're just full of surprising information, aren't you, my dear? I may have misjudged you, Madame. Why is it that it has taken you so long to find your voice? All this stuff happened two decades ago. It's ancient history!'

'Not to me,' said Destine, grinding her teeth on the words. 'I warned Aloysius not to trust you!' She felt an itch somewhere at the back of her mind, the *vaguest* of recollections, the merest hint of a memory – confirmed by Aloysius's words in his journal. 'I warned him what you were planning, how you sought to betray him!'

'You? So you can see the future, after all.'

'*Non*, my clairvoyance is no more . . . but twenty years ago it was functioning perfectly!' snapped Destine. 'I saw what you were planning, monsieur. I saw that you were merely using Aloysius . . . and because of my intervention you never got your hands on that treasure!'

'Whoever said it was the Cradle that I was after?' asked Joyce. 'But anyway, as I say, that was a long time ago now. It really doesn't matter what you know about Umkaza . . . or what your friend Cornelius knows. No one cares any more!'

'On the contrary, Monsieur Joyce,' said Destine. 'I am sure that the British government will not look upon you favourably once they learn the truth.'

'It's not the *British* that I'm fearful of, let me assure you,' said Joyce. 'And even if you *were* in a position to speak of it, who would believe an old crone like you over someone like me, hmm?' He stared numbly at Destine as she began to laugh. 'Am I missing something?'

'I see now what my task was all along,' Destine replied, a tranquil expression on her face. 'My destiny was not just to shed light upon Aloysius Bedford's betrayal . . . it was to expose *you* for the fiend you are! You think that you are safe here within the walls of your little castle, monsieur, but you are wrong. Soon it will all come crashing down.'

'I hardly think so!' Joyce protested. 'If you don't mind me saying, you do seem to have a slightly *discoloured* appreciation of your present predicament.' He leaned cockily against the bars of the holding cell, grinning widely as if a distant relative had just passed away and left him a small fortune. 'I am dispatching you to Fantoma, to my employers, and I wonder how long it will take the torturers of the Hades Consortium's jail to wipe that smile off your face.'

'The Hades Consortium?' asked Destine shaken.

'I must leave you for a time whilst I check on the whereabouts of your companion, but I will return soon.' Joyce turned swiftly towards the cell block's exit, his voice trailing as he walked back up the stairs. 'Sorry to disappoint you, my dear, but I think the walls of my little castle will be fortified for *quite* some time yet.'

As he slammed the heavy iron door, Destine felt an uncomfortable silence settle upon her. If Godfrey Joyce was employed by the Hades Consortium, it did not bear thinking about. Surely Aloysius was not mixed up with them back in 1833? Was that why Cornelius was en route? Had his line of enquiries led him right to Joyce's door? Did Cornelius know of her fate? Would he arrive in time to save her?

'Pondering your fate, Madame?' said a familiar voice, as Heinrich Nadir peeled himself from the shadows.

'I wondered what that bad smell was,' said Destine.

'I see you have picked up some of your English companion's

bad habits since our last meeting onboard the ship, Madame,' said Nadir slimily. 'Now, like Cornelius Quaint, you are just another victim of the Hades Consortium.'

'You also?' demanded Destine.

'But of course,' said Nadir, with a bow. 'Herr Joyce seems a most confident individual. Certainly not one of our more astute employees, but he has at least enabled me to arrange things according to my plan.'

'Your plan?' asked Destine. 'I thought Joyce was in charge.'

'So does Joyce,' grinned Nadir. 'But even though we share employers, I suppose you might say that I pay heed to a higher calling than he. Joyce is just like you – a means to an end . . . and that end is almost in sight.'

'So that is why you have come down here?' asked Destine. 'To boast of your employers' plot to poison the Nile?'

'Not at all,' Nadir said deftly. 'I just wanted to look at you one more time. Before your imminent death, I mean. He has your eyes, I think.'

Destine was taken aback. 'He? Of whom do you refer?'

'Why . . . your *son*, of course,' the German replied, watching the jolt of disbelief on Destine's face. 'Antoine's lust for death is virtually unsurpassed in the annals of the Hades Consortium. I have worked by his side and watched him excel these past few years, he really is something to behold.'

Destine's eyes narrowed. 'You . . . you knew my son?'

'Oh, *ja* . . . we are old friends,' Nadir replied.

'Do you not mean "were"?'

Nadir grinned shrewdly. '*Do* I?'

Destine's heart missed a beat. Attempting to get a measure of what thoughts were running throughout the German's mind, she ordered her sensitive feelings to examine this creature.

Her incredibly delicate senses detected numerous layers to him, many conflicting with each other.

'I can see why Antoine would have liked you,' she said, eventually. 'You have such coldness in your heart . . . you are bereft of any feeling.'

'You possess a marvellously sharp intellect, Frau Destine – yet you are not quite on the mark,' Nadir replied, taking pleasure with every clipped syllable. 'I do feel. Revenge, hatred, passion . . . I feel them all when I am in service to the Hades Consortium – and, soon, your companion Cornelius Quaint shall feel them too. If only you still retained your ability to see the future, Frau Destine, perhaps you could have warned him that he is about to walk into a trap.'

CHAPTER XLIII

The Cog in the Machine

MINUTES LATER, GODFREY Joyce returned and stood in front of Madame Destine's cell, his arms linked behind his back, glaring with a self-satisfied expression as his two silent assassins manhandled her to her feet and dragged her from it and out into the Embassy's stable yard. She squinted her eyes as the blast of daylight hit her. Heinrich Nadir stood by a horse-drawn cart with a covered roof, his tongue silent, but the cogs within his brain ever working. His employer would be pleased. So far everything had transpired just as he had foreseen.

For Nadir personally, this boded well.

To her credit, Destine fought against her brutish captors the whole way, and as she was flung into the back of the cart, she lashed out with her feet, catching one of the assassins in the face. His nose spat blood. He raised his arm to strike her, but Nadir intervened, grabbing the assassin's arm.

'She is no good to the Hades Consortium dead, fool!' he reprimanded.

'Defiant until your last breath, Madame?' taunted Joyce. 'At least you'll have some company on the journey to Fantoma.'

He nudged the Aksak's brother, bound and gagged next to Destine in the cart, and he stumbled onto the floor, his face littered with bloodied bruises. 'But enjoy it, because once you get there, you'll never see daylight again.'

'Gloat whilst you still have a breath in your body, Monsieur Joyce,' retorted Destine sharply. 'Soon Cornelius will come, and I only wish I was here to witness your downfall. You do not know him as I do. When he sets his mind to it he is capable of moving mountains.'

'We shall see,' said Joyce, as he signalled to his assassins. 'Take her away.'

Nadir shook Joyce's hand limply and clambered up onto the front seat of the cart next to the driver. 'I will send Lady Jocasta your regards,' he said.

The Hades Consortium assassins tied a blindfold around Destine's eyes and a gag around her mouth. The material tasted of paraffin and the Frenchwoman retched, swallowing the acrid taste back down her throat. With the blindfold obscuring her vision, she did not see Godfrey Joyce's gloating face as the cart moved along the gravel driveway towards the rear gates – nor did she catch a glimpse of Cornelius Quaint crouch down behind the low wall, out of sight.

Quaint watched the cart disappear into the distance, consumed by the fading light of the passing day.

'I hope that wasn't Joyce, or this plan is over before it's even begun,' he said.

'It was not,' said Faroud. 'It was Joyce's driver . . . and another man and a woman. I did not see them clearly, but neither was our target, which means that the man is still inside.'

'Well, what are we waiting for?' asked Quaint. 'Let's go and say hello.'

'It will not be an easy feat to sneak into this place, Cornelius.'

'Whoever said we were going to sneak in?' replied Quaint with a cocksure grin.

'Somehow I knew you were going to say that,' said Faroud. 'Just remember what I told you about Joyce. He might not look a formidable threat, but his mind is always ticking away behind his eyes. He is as slippery as an eel . . . a traitor not just to his own country, but to Egypt as well. Surely there can be nothing more despicable than that.'

'And when did you find out that Joyce was a rotten egg?' the conjuror enquired of a suddenly perplexed Faroud. 'You know . . . a bad seed,' rephrased Quaint, attempting to clarify his point. If the Egyptian's expression was anything to go by, he had failed miserably. 'For the leader of a band of underground criminals, you are *woefully* out of date with your slang! I mean, how did you find out about Joyce's connections to the Hades Consortium?'

'Through my brother,' Faroud replied softly. 'Rakmun was captured whilst stealing from the Embassy. He almost killed two of the guards and was apprehended at the scene, supposedly.'

Quaint raised an eyebrow. 'Supposedly?'

'Rakmun was no angel . . . he was a Scarab, after all . . . but he was loyal to me as a brother and as an Aksak,' explained Faroud. 'He had never expressed any interest in thieving from the Embassy; he knew it would have been a pointless venture. What we Scarabs do, we do for the good of the clan. We would never attempt such a foolhardy exploit so far from Bara Mephista – especially alone. The last I heard of Rakmun that night, he was out near the ruins of Fantoma sniffing around the Hades Consortium's affairs. He had been observing increased activity in the area and wished to investigate further.'

'And yet he managed to drag himself halfway across the country to rob the Embassy?' quizzed Quaint. 'That doesn't make much sense.'

'No, Cornelius . . . there is much of Rakmun's crime that failed to make sense.'

Quaint raised an eyebrow. 'Oh?'

'Joyce made it known in the local communities that one of the Clan Scarabs had been captured. He knew it would reach my ears,' Faroud began, the details still fresh in his mind. 'I contacted him to try to broker a deal between us. Even though I thought he was far too convenient in his guise as my brother's saviour, I had no choice. He told me that Rakmun was to be hanged but if I agreed to aid him, he would petition his release.' Faroud's eyes seemed to cloud over, as if spread with a layer of fine frost. 'Yet that was many weeks ago now. Joyce claimed that only his influence is keeping my brother alive. With no other recourse, I was forced to do as he commanded. I became a lapdog . . . just as Professor North rightly called me yesterday. Rakmun is all I have left of my family, Cornelius . . . I had to do whatever it took to keep him safe. But no more. I want to get inside that Embassy and beat the truth from Joyce . . . which is why I agreed to your hasty plan.'

'Hasty? I take offence, Faroud.' Quaint grinned like a truant child enjoying a day's freedom from school. 'My plan has been carefully devised – which is a hell of a lot more prepared than I usually am on these little affairs, let me tell you! When it comes to the Hades Consortium, it pays to be well organised. New Year's Eve is but two days away, and if Joyce is as slimy as you say, no doubt he'll want to earn himself a gold star and hand me over to his bosses, which is just fine by me. Once I get inside the Consortium's nest, he's all yours.'

'Yes, but what if he sees right through our plan?' asked Faroud.

'It doesn't matter. The end result is the same,' said Quaint. 'Joyce's actions are easy to predict – he'll betray us at the first opportunity. At its root, the Hades Consortium is merely a machine . . . and all machines rely on well-oiled cogs to power them. If we take one of those cogs out – in this case, Joyce – with any luck, the machine will fail.'

'You seem awfully familiar with the Hades Consortium,' said Faroud, a nagging thought buzzing around his head. 'The Clan Scarabs have been encamped deep within Egypt's heart for decades, and we have never set eyes upon any of them, save Godfrey Joyce – yet we know they are there. For a circus conjuror from England, how exactly do you know so much about them?'

'I wasn't born a conjuror, Faroud,' answered Quaint simply. 'In my past, the road of my life has verged with the Hades Consortium on more than one occasion. Although I've tried to steer well clear of them, it seems that Fate has other ideas.'

'I see,' said Faroud. 'I just assumed that they had wronged you in some way . . . that it was personal.'

'Oh, it's personal all right!' said Quaint, as if it should be obvious to even the most simple of minds.

Faroud pondered the reply. 'And may I ask what they did to hurt you?'

'Not me,' said Quaint.

'A lover, perhaps?' enquired Faroud.

'Not a lover . . . but people I loved.' The conjuror hissed a low, inaudible sigh through his teeth as he countered the discomfort of the memory. 'The Hades Consortium murdered my parents.'

CHAPTER XLIV

The Awkward Questions

THE MAIN DOORS to the British Embassy opened slowly to reveal a gaunt-faced butler with a thin, wispy moustache and black hair stretched across his scalp like oily bootlaces. His false smile faded quickly as glanced at the dust-clad forms of Cornelius Quaint and Aksak Faroud.

'How may I be of service to you, er . . . *gentlemen*?' the butler asked.

'I am here to see Mr Joyce. I have a gift for him!' growled Faroud, holding a knife to Quaint's throat. He played his part well – a mite *too* well, in the conjuror's honest opinion. 'And before you ask – yes, it is important, and no, it *cannot* wait!'

The butler stepped back, allowing the two men entry, and he led Faroud and Quaint through the corridors on the ground floor to Mr Joyce's assistant, Reginald, who was seated at a desk in an open foyer. As they approached, the young man looked them up and down objectionably.

'These two gentlemen are here to see Mr Joyce,' the butler said. 'Apparently, it's important.'

'Don't bother looking us up in your appointment book, son – we're not in it. Just hurry it up and take us to see Joyce,' said Quaint.

Reginald's lower lip floundered. 'Um . . . without an appointment, sir?'

'Yes, without an appointment!'

'But, sir, that's highly irregular,' complained the young man.

'Listen, son,' said Quaint, boring his steely black eyes into Reginald, 'we can stand here and debate irregularities, or you can announce us to Mr Joyce right away. It's your choice, but my knife-wielding friend here is keen for his blade to taste blood, so it's either going to be yours or mine. Obviously, I'd prefer it to be yours, and I think so would your maid, because blood has a tendency to stain the carpets . . . especially mine.'

'I'll announce you right away!' snapped an anxious Reginald.

'Good lad,' piped Quaint.

Reginald knocked upon the door and opened it a fraction, just enough for his chubby face to squeeze through. 'Mr Joyce, you have someone to see you, sir . . . the same chap as yesterday morning, with another fellow . . . and, um . . . they aren't in the appointment book again, sir,' Reginald said, as if the blame for such slack protocol lay fairly and squarely on his slumped shoulders. 'I told them it was most irregular!'

'Faroud is here? Right now?' Joyce asked, trying to feign surprise. 'All right, lad, show him in.'

Outside, Faroud whispered into Quaint's ear. 'Just keep quiet and let me to do the talking! We need to find out my brother's location before we go breaking things.'

'Am I not always the picture of restraint?' said Quaint.

'Do I really need to answer that?' Faroud said, pushing him into the office.

Joyce rose from his seat and beamed a wide smile. 'Well, this is an unexpected surprise! I was not aware we had an appointment today, Aksak.' Joyce could not resist a curious inspection of the conjuror. 'Why is it that every time you come to my office you bring a stray with you? Who is *this* one, might I ask?'

Faroud nudged Quaint in between the shoulder blades and the conjuror crashed down clumsily onto Joyce's desk. 'He was found wandering near Bara Mephista's caves by my men. He claimed to be lost, but when we took him back to our camp he began asking some awkward questions.'

'What *sort* of awkward questions?' Joyce enquired.

'About the Hades Consortium,' replied Faroud.

'Oh?' Joyce raised one of his white eyebrows. He relaxed himself into his chair, allowing the charade to play itself out until he could be surer of his footing. 'What have you to say for yourself, man?' he asked Quaint. 'Who are you and what were you doing sniffing around the Scarab camp?'

'Cornelius Quaint,' Quaint said, with a polite nod. 'This is all some dreadful misunderstanding, sir. You see, I hadn't realised the caves were off limits. There are no signs or anything to warn a passing scientist.'

'Scientist?' asked an increasingly curious Godfrey Joyce.

'Yes, sir,' confirmed Quaint. 'I am here in Egypt examining calcium carbonate deposits in the Bara Mephista region, it being so near to the River Hepsut and all. I was en route to Nespa Point, but got a little sidetracked. I merely stumbled into this nice gentleman's encampment seeking proper directions.' His response was calm and earnest, and it raised an interested glance from Faroud, who almost had to question the authenticity of Quaint's story, he was that convincing.

'And what of these questions you were asking about the Hades Consortium?' inquired Joyce. 'How would a scientist know of such an organisation?'

'I might ask that of the British attaché to Egypt, sir,' Quaint replied, mustering a whiter-than-white expression.

'I happen to have direct contact into Whitehall, sir!' said Joyce. 'The government is familiar with that group, although no one is quite convinced of their existence. So tell me, Mr Quaint, I don't recall seeing any official documents requesting your secondment here. Might I ask which universities or academies you represent?'

Quaint began to answer but then stopped. He was taken by something in the air, as if someone nearby had just called his name. Intense furrows upon his brow, he took a brief sniff of the air, sensing a flash of recognition. It was a familiar scent . . . but try as he might, he could not place it. It passed in an instant and he paid it further thought.

'*Mr Quaint?*' Joyce rasped. 'I asked what college you represent.'

'Oh . . . lots,' mumbled the conjuror. 'I'm what you might call an adviser.'

'Yet you were asking questions about the Hades Consortium,' said Joyce.

'Well, it was more of a passing comment than an actual question, really.'

'In the middle of a Clan Scarab encampment?'

'Like I said, I was lost.'

'And then you were found by the Aksak,' said Joyce, 'and brought here to me.'

'Lucky old me,' said Quaint.

'Perhaps,' Joyce said.

Each man delivered his words plainly and deftly, as if they were venturing out onto a frozen lake. The ice was cracking with every step they took, but still they kept on walking. Each knew more about the other than either was aware, waiting patiently for the final revelation.

'So where else has your work taken you, Mr Quaint?' Joyce asked.

'Oh, lots of places,' Quaint answered. 'I spent a bit of time in Umkaza recently. History is such a fascination of mine, Mr Joyce. Who lived in the area, who *died* in the area, that sort of thing. You'd be amazed what you can dig up if you know where to look.'

Joyce's discomfort was beginning to show. 'And did you . . . find anything of interest in Umkaza?' he seethed.

'Not really. It was a bit of a dead loss,' replied Quaint, finely balanced sarcasm a hair's breadth away. 'But not to worry. As you probably know only too well, Mr Joyce, the ghosts of the past rarely stay buried for ever.'

The ice had just cracked.

'Faroud – kill this man at once!' Joyce bellowed.

Yet Aksak Faroud did not move.

Joyce scowled at him. 'Well? What are you waiting for, man? Kill him!'

'Actually . . . I would rather not,' said Faroud, as he slashed at the ropes around Quaint's wrists with his knife, setting the conjuror free.

'I second that,' said Quaint, rubbing his wrists.

'Wh-what are you doing?' yelled Joyce.

Faroud aimed the blade at him and he shrunk back into his seat. 'You have lied to me, you have deceived me, and you have used my Scarabs as your own personal puppets – but no more! I know what you and your Consortium allies plan. We have come here for two things: my brother and the location of the poison . . . and we are not in any mood to wait for either!'

'So . . . you have allied yourself with him,' Joyce said, sneering at the Scarab leader. He gripped the hem of his waistcoat and smartened himself in a desperate attempt to reassert his authority. 'You have just sacrificed more than your life, Faroud – your brother will die because of your treachery!'

'I don't think it'll be all that easy for you to give orders any more, Godfrey,' said Quaint, watching the man squirm in his seat as Faroud edged the blade closer to his face. 'You see, we know all about you . . . and we know all about the Hades Consortium's plans for the River Nile. I know you're not the one pulling all the strings . . . I want to know the name of your puppeteer.'

'What, and you think I'll just roll over and tell you?' said Joyce, his cocky tone contradicting the uncertainty in his eyes. 'There is nothing you can do to me to force me to betray my masters!'

'Oh, I wouldn't bet on that,' said Quaint. 'I can be *very* persuasive. If I were you I'd want to—' He stopped again mid-sentence, as if he had forgotten what he was talking about. There was definitely something familiar in the air. It teased at his senses, distracting his attention. He scowled away the confusion and focused on the matter at hand.

'Where is Rakmun?' interrupted Faroud.

'Your brother's life is forfeit . . . just like your own!' Joyce yelled. 'I promised I'd help you get him free, didn't I? But now you've gone and brought this *man* here, it changes everything! Your threats mean nothing to me. You're just going to have to kill me.'

'That sounds like a fair offer,' said Quaint, as he grabbed hold of Joyce's tie and yanked his head down, making contact with the desk.

Joyce collapsed onto the floor, sending paperwork, his box of cigars and the large table lamp flying. Quaint was on him in a second. His strength was formidable at the best of times, but it was nothing compared to how strong he was when he was enraged – and at that moment, his rage was all-consuming.

'Tell me what you know about the Nile project or you die!' he shouted. Quaint pulled back his fist, but then froze – he could smell that smell, but this time it was not quite as elusive. It was the scent of lavender. It grew stronger the more he concentrated, strong enough for him to locate it.

On the carpet underneath Joyce's desk was a headscarf.

Spellbound, he snatched it up and buried his nose into it, instantly recognising its owner.

'Destine?' he gasped. 'Here?' He turned his attention back to Joyce and clamped his hands around his throat. 'Where *is* she? Where is Destine? If you've harmed her, I'll—'

'Get your hands off me or she dies!' Joyce wheezed.

Faroud grabbed at Quaint's clothing, trying to pull him off Joyce, but it was no easy feat. 'Cornelius! Stop this! Remember why we are here! This was not part of the plan. We need him alive, remember?'

'To hell with the plan, I need to know where she is!' barked Quaint.

'What are you talking about? Cornelius, we have to *leave*! If this worm knew anything before he is useless to us now. Look at him! Even if his life depended on it, he will not speak. His fear of the Consortium is too great!'

'I'm not going anywhere until I know where she is!' Quaint snatched up the letter-opener from Joyce's desk and held it an inch from his right eye. 'And unless you want to be called Cyclops from now on, I'd tell me if I were you.'

'You're bluffing!' spat Joyce.

'Am I?' Quaint jabbed the tip of the blade into Joyce's cheek-bone and a tiny dab of blood appeared. 'That was a warning shot.' The point of the letter-opener brushed against Joyce's eyelashes – proof enough that this was no bluff. 'I'm growing impatient, Joyce. Where is Destine?'

'Enough!' Joyce said. 'Just promise you'll let me live . . . and I'll tell you everything . . . I swear!' The man's rough, leathery skin glistened with sweat, and his hands quivered as he clutched at Quaint's wrist, trying frantically to steer the letter-opener's tip away from his eyeball. 'She's in the Embassy cells downstairs, along with the Aksak's brother!'

Quaint unfurled his fingers and the letter-opener fell to the floor.

'*Show* me . . .' he hissed.

CHAPTER XLV

The Calling of Destiny

MANY MILES FROM Cairo, Polly North had managed the long trek from Umkaza with the injured Ahman upon her horse, and they were now in a room at the far end of the Bara Mephista tavern. Ahman was laid out flat on a table, with a bundle of blankets serving as a makeshift pillow. He winced as Polly swabbed water over the wound to his shoulder. The mention of Aksak Faroud's name had done as the Scarab leader had claimed, and the Clan Scarabs had agreed to assist Polly with her wounded patient. One of them had arrived and offered Polly use of a large wooden crate of medical supplies. She was begrudgingly thankful, but as she rifled through the crate, she recognised the stamps upon the medicines' labels, and a cold frost of recognition burned into her mind. She had packed the very same first aid equipment for her dig. The Scarabs had obviously stolen it. Although she could not really complain – without the fresh bandages and liniment, fixing Ahman's wound would have been twice as hard.

'It hurts so *much*,' he groaned, his head twitching from side to side restlessly.

'I'm sorry, but I have to make sure the wound is clean,' Polly apologised. 'Once that Scarab returns to stitch you up, I can bandage your shoulder properly.'

'Thank you . . . you have been most kind,' said Ahman.

'My pleasure,' said Polly with a comforting smile.

'What bothers me more, is where Destine can be!' Ahman swallowed awkwardly, as if the act caused him great difficulty. 'That devil's blade struck me . . . and I fell from the cart . . . but he did not seem to be bothered with me at all. I think they were after her! But who were they? Why did they want her?'

'I'm sorry, Mr Ahman, but when we found you there was no trace of your friend at all,' said Polly. 'I wish there was.'

'So do I, Miss Polly . . . so do I.'

The door to the backroom swung open, and the moustachioed Bephotsi re-entered. His eyes met neither Polly's nor Ahman's, making it clear that he wished to be out of their company as quickly as possible. He carried a small wooden box, and from it produced a long piece of thread attached to a crooked silver needle.

Ahman caught sight of it and his eyes flared. 'What is *that* for?'

'What do you think?' Bephotsi grunted. 'It is to stitch you up.'

'With a needle like that? I am not a stuffed cushion!'

'You want me to mend you or not, eh? That is a nasty wound. Unless it gets stitched, it will not heal . . . you might even lose your arm altogether.'

'My *arm*?' asked Ahman, licking his lips nervously.

'Look, there's nothing to worry about. I'm sure he has done this lots of times,' Polly said, nudging Bephotsi's elbow. 'Right?'

'Of course!' Bephotsi replied. 'Although . . . my experience of this nature does begin and end with pigs, it is true.'

'*Pigs?*' squawked Ahman.

'Calm yourself,' said Bephotsi. 'I know what I am doing . . . in theory.'

'*In theory?*' screeched Ahman, right before he promptly fainted.

Ten minutes later, Bephotsi had completed stitching the wound and left the room. Polly wrapped fresh bandages around Ahman's right arm and shoulder. She covered him with a blanket and the man's rotund belly protruded like an erected circus tent. He slept soundly, his body's way of coping with the recent shock, and Polly found herself staring at him. He looked like a kind man, a good man, and at his age he was undeserving of such pain. She began to neatly fold his clothes into a tidy pile, when something caught her eye.

It was an old and beaten leather journal.

Curious, she flipped open the first page and read quietly aloud: 'Journal begun August 1833 – Aloysius Bedford, Archaeologist.' Polly read the words again as if she could not trust her eyes. 'Aloysius Bedford?' Licking her lips, she inspected the book in detail. The cover, the binding, the texture of the pages – everything about it, as if it were just as much an ancient treasure as those she was used to unearthing. 'But . . . I don't understand this at all. Bedford's name is legendary in the field of archaeology. He wrote most of the texts that I used in my foundation years. But then he disappeared . . . way back in . . . when was it, 1833? But that's the year this journal was written! What on earth is this thing? A lost journal by an equally lost archaeologist?'

Polly breathlessly thumbed through the pages of the book. Notes, diagrams and detailed illustrations, all with fine handwriting in the margins, decorated every single page. She recognised

– and corroborated – the information within. To her, it was every bit as priceless as the lost artefacts that it depicted.

'The Anklet of Bast discovered in Umkaza site D, although I cannot take credit for the find – my guide, Vincent, was the lucky soul who unearthed it. Now I can say for certain that Umkaza holds much, much more, and Cho-zen Li's estimations were correct – there is more to be found here, perhaps even the greatest find of my career.'

As Polly mouthed the words, she felt her knees go weak and she flopped down onto the wooden floorboards. As she did so, she failed to see a faded envelope slip from the book and slide underneath the table.

Sat with her legs crossed on the floor, Polly was breathless once more.

'Bedford dug in Umkaza? And Cho-zen Li . . . sponsored it? Since when? Why didn't Cho-zen mention it to me? Where the hell did this book come from?' She looked over at the slumbering Ahman; a million questions flooded her brain until it was fit to burst.

As she turned the page, she came across something that sent shockwaves through her blood. Staring back at her from the page was a drawing of an ornate child's crib decorated with a variety of gemstones, with detailed pictorial inscriptions of pyramids, winged beasts and a variety of Egyptian deities inscribed at the head and foot.

'The Pharaoh's Cradle!' Polly exclaimed, causing Ahman to stir slightly.

She had seen many artistic impressions of the Pharaoh's Cradle before, but this was different. The ink drawing was far too accurate, far too detailed to be mere conjecture on Bedford's part.

Dotted around the picture were notes on the artefact's dimensions, and to Polly that seemed to prove only one thing.

'Bedford found it!' she gasped. 'He found the Pharaoh's Cradle! But what does this mean? If Aloysius Bedford found it . . . where is it? Why did he not reveal it to the world? And why didn't Cho-zen tell me anything about any of this?'

The weight of the journal was too much, and it slipped from her shaking fingers onto the floor. It fell open on the last entry, and some unknown force bade Polly to read the text that would end up changing her fortunes for ever.

I must ensure the Pharaoh's Cradle does not fall into the hands of those who wish to do harm. Therefore, I have hidden it, and hidden it well. They say the best hiding place is not right under one's nose; therefore, I have returned the Cradle back to the sand where it belongs, in a fitting monument to my courageous crew who lost their lives. They shall sleep for ever now in the Cradle of their ancestors.
    Signed,
    Aloysius X. Bedford, 1833.

Polly closed the book and squeezed it as if trying to wring the truth out of its pages. This beaten old journal could be her salvation. No, far more than that . . . it could be her redemption. She could go back to England with the promise of such richness, such glory! If only she could find the Pharaoh's Cradle. If only she could decipher Bedford's cryptic clue . . .

'The mass grave!' she cried. 'The one where we found those old bones in Umkaza! Twenty years old? My God . . . they were part of Bedford's crew! Is that what happened to him? Did he . . . did he die there? Damn it, the treasure it *was* under my feet the whole time!'

This revelation quashed any guilt that she might have had. The journal had ensnared her and she was helpless in its grasp. She had to get to Umkaza right away. She could not let this chance slip away. What was she thinking? The book was not her property. It belonged to Ahman. As she stared down at the journal, something washed over her body. It was like a disease trying to overcome her, to infect her, and it was something she had never experienced before in her professional life.

It was greed.

It was pure, selfish greed.

CHAPTER XLVI

The Change in Luck

THE SHARP TIP of Aksak Faroud's knife was pressed into the small of Godfrey Joyce's back for the entire duration of the short journey to the holding cells in the basement of the British Embassy. Soon they came to a pair of iron doors with large iron rivets around the seams, almost like the vault of a bank. Quaint wondered why an embassy would have need of such a secure environment.

'In there you will find what you seek,' Joyce said, motioning towards the heavy doors. 'But you must do as you promised . . . you must let me live.'

'Rakmun was here all this time?' asked Faroud. 'I should slit your throat right here and now!'

'Then you will *never* get your brother out of this place alive!' squawked Joyce. 'We don't tend to get many knife-wielding Egyptians turning up on our doorstep with prisoners, you see – especially British citizens! The Embassy guards would have been on high alert from the moment you rang the doorbell. Only I can get you, *and* your companions, out of here in one piece.' Joyce removed a large, brass key and turned it in the door's lock with a snap. He buried his head in his hands, and slid his back down against the wall, his shoulders rising and falling. 'Just let me live, I beg of you.'

'Leave him, Faroud,' Quaint said. 'He's not worth it.'

He snatched open the doors and stepped inside. The room was almost completely dark, save for two small barred windows positioned up high within the wall, catching a sliver of moonlight from the darkening sky outside. Both cells were completely empty, and as Quaint and Faroud's eyes eventually adjusted to the light, they came to a startling realization.

In perfect symmetry, they turned their heads to look at each other.

'Trap,' said Faroud.

'I should say so,' replied Quaint.

The words had not even left his lips before he darted towards the open doors, but he was too late. Joyce was not as incapacitated as he had made out – and he was a lot closer to the doors than Quaint was. He slammed the cell block doors shut. The sound of the key being turned in the lock echoed around the basement before mocking laughter resonated through the thick iron.

'How trusting of you gentlemen,' cackled Joyce, 'and how stupid. Now you are my prisoners, just as your companions were before you. It's such a shame. You missed them by a matter of minutes. If you're lucky, the benches might still be warm.'

On the other side of the fortified doors, Quaint cursed.

He looked around the prison feverishly. Although he and the Aksak were not imprisoned within one of the cells, they might just as well have been. The room was bereft of anything. There was no trap door, nothing to use as a battering ram, no windows large enough. No way out.

'Now what?' asked Faroud.

'We wait for our luck to change, my friend,' answered Quaint.

An hour later, they were still waiting.

Sitting with his back against the wall, Quaint glanced up at Faroud, who had not stopped pacing back and forth ever since Joyce had turned the key in the lock.

'Are you attempting to burrow out of this place?' Quaint asked him.

'What else is there to do? I thought you were supposed to be a conjuror – can you not pick the lock, or make us disappear in a puff of smoke or something like that?' the Scarab asked.

'That only works on doves,' quipped Quaint. 'And that lock is far too fortified for my meagre knowledge of escapology. Don't worry, we won't be here long. Joyce is not just going to leave us to rot . . . not when he can hand us over to the Consortium. This is all part of my plan . . . although I admit, it is not without its complications.'

'And what happens if Joyce decides to kill us himself and deliver our corpses to his masters?' asked Faroud, finally ceasing his pacing.

'Ah . . . yes, that's one of those complications that I mentioned,' said Quaint.

Just then, the lock snapped in the door and it swung wide open, revealing Joyce's pet assassins, their dark red hoods shielding their faces in shadow like executioners of old. They produced lethal swords from scabbards at their backs and brandished them menacingly towards the Scarab and the conjuror.

Quaint looked at Faroud. 'Friends of yours?'

'They are Hades Consortium foot soldiers,' answered Faroud. 'I have seen them before. Do not expect much in the way of polite conversation, my friend. They have their tongues removed upon joining the Consortium's ranks . . . it helps keep them subordinate.'

'I know a couple of clowns who could do with that treatment,' said Quaint.

Joyce then stepped into view between the two assassins. 'Your time has come, gentlemen. Guards, bind their wrists together so they can't escape,' he said, tapping one of his silent guards on the shoulder. 'Bind them like the cattle they are.'

Quaint recalled a similar predicament from the previous night. 'Let's hope you don't talk as much as my last partner,' he said.

'Did you two really expect me to betray the Hades Consortium?' laughed Joyce, satisfied that he had Quaint right where he wanted him. 'I knew that you and Faroud were en route, my source within the Clan Scarabs informed me before you even left Bara Mephista.' Joyce was noticeably more confident now that he was flanked by two Hades Consortium assassins.

'Source? Within my camp?' Faroud yelled. 'Nonsense! None of my men would ever dare betray me.'

Joyce grinned. 'Oh, they would if they had something to gain, Aksak. In your absence, there is much in Bara Mephista for an ambitious sort to get his hands on, were he that way inclined.'

'Where is Madame Destine?' sought Quaint. 'What have you done with her?'

Joyce laughed a throaty chuckle. 'Your French companion, as charming as she was, is now in the hands of the Hades Consortium.'

'And my brother? Where is Rakmun?' asked Faroud.

'At a location of my choosing,' said Joyce. 'Until you get to

Fantoma, I need you compliant . . . and his life will be dramatically cut short should you or your friend Mr Quaint decide to make things difficult. If you abide by my commands, both of your companions will be set free. They are useless to the Hades Consortium. But if not, they will die – and not at all pleasantly.'

'You filthy—' Quaint lunged, just as one of the Consortium assassins stepped into his path and brought the handle of his sword down hard onto the back of the conjuror's neck. He crashed to the floor.

'What spirit you have, Mr Quaint . . . Lady Jocasta will no doubt enjoy breaking that for you,' said Joyce. 'Men, escort these two out to the stable yard. We ride to Fantoma!'

CHAPTER XLVII

The Shot in the Dark

QUAINT AND FAROUD were led outside into the Embassy's yard and seated upon a horse. Quaint was at the front with Faroud behind him, their bound wrists linking them to one another. They rode steadily through the desert land for some time, following the lantern from Joyce's horse-drawn cart ahead, with the Consortium guards at their backs. The opportunity for escape was not forthcoming and Quaint grew restless as his limbs went numb. Every impatient inch of him wanted to get to Fantoma as quickly as possible, and it was agonising in every sense – not assisted by Aksak Faroud falling asleep on him an hour and a half into the journey.

'Hold here!' said Godfrey Joyce, pulling his cart to a stop.

Quaint heard a groan from the Scarab leader behind him, and he craned his neck as far as he could. 'You can wake up now, Aksak.'

'Where are we?' asked Faroud, blinking life back into his eyes.

'In trouble,' said Quaint.

'Still?'

'It's normal for me, I'm afraid,' said Quaint.

Faroud peered through the darkness, assaying their position.

A large mountain range was silhouetted against the night sky less than a mile away. 'This is not Fantoma, Cornelius,' he whispered in Quaint's ear. 'Is that a good thing, or not?'

'Probably not,' said Quaint. 'But all we can do is watch how this unfolds and make our move when we can.'

'I've got to rendezvous with my contact,' said Joyce to the mute Consortium assassins. 'Get these two dogs off their mount and onto their knees where they can't cause you any bother.' With that, he whipped the reins and his cart rode off into the darkness.

Quaint and Faroud were pulled unceremoniously onto the hardened ground. The assassins drew their swords and towered over them.

'Any ideas how we can get out of this?' Faroud asked quietly.

'I don't exactly work at my best under pressure,' Quaint replied.

'What is Joyce waiting for? Why not just kill us now and be done with it?'

'Don't knock it, Aksak. Everything is working out just fine so far.'

'You are still clinging to your plan?'

'Absolutely!' confirmed Quaint.

'Our plan is sunk, my friend. Soon Joyce will return and we shall die on our knees . . . most undignified for an Aksak,' Faroud said grimly.

'And for a Quaint,' added the conjuror. 'And speaking of the good Mr Joyce . . .'

Accompanied by a cloaking trail of dust, Joyce emerged from the pitch darkness. He was not alone – there was a single passenger bound and gagged in the rear of the cart. Quaint and Faroud tried to battle the darkness to identify the passenger, and the cart was feet away when Faroud's heart rose. It was Rakmun. His brother's face was bloodied and bruised, and his swollen lips tried to speak through the gag taut between his teeth, but it was nothing but an inaudible garble.

'Rakmun?' said Faroud. 'My brother. He is safe, Cornelius!'

Quaint looked at their surroundings. 'This is your definition of safe?'

Faroud glared. 'He is alive, that is what is important!'

'I wouldn't cheer just yet,' said Quaint. 'Now Mr Joyce has got something to threaten us with.'

'How I *love* a nice family reunion!' said Joyce, his callous expression reinforcing Quaint's point. He reined the cart to a halt, and snatched Faroud's brother by his rope-bound wrists, dragging him onto the ground. 'You two seem intent on causing problems for me, so I thought that perhaps you'd respond to a little more *persuasive* pressure to keep you in line.' He pulled a pistol from his belt and held it to Rakmun's head. 'You have an obligation to safeguard this young man's well-being, Aksak. This doesn't have to get messy . . . so long as you do as you're instructed.'

'Again you use my kin against me,' snarled Faroud.

'A precautionary measure, I assure you,' said Joyce. 'Previously your brother was merely an insurance policy to make you susceptible to my requirements. You just needed the right level of motivation to keep your leash tight. But now I need you restrained and he fits the bill quite nicely.'

The Scarab leader ground his teeth. 'The Hades Consortium would even go so far as to sanction killing a boy?'

'They would, without a second thought,' said Quaint. 'Except I'll bet they have no idea what he's up to. Isn't that right, Joyce? You've been using the Scarabs for your own purposes . . . such as covering up your dirty little secret in Umkaza?' Quaint smiled as Joyce's expression wavered for a second. 'Don't look so shocked, Godfrey – or did you think we hadn't worked out why you were so keen for Professor North to pack her bags? She was getting too close, wasn't she? Too close to unearthing the skeletons in your closet . . . or should I say under the ground? I doubt the Hades Consortium would relish doing business with a man in such a volatile position. You didn't cover your tracks as well as you thought, Godfrey, and the Consortium doesn't like to leave footprints.'

Joyce's eyes flickered with irritation, confirming Quaint's assumption. 'So . . . your French companion was telling the truth . . . you *do* know what happened in Umkaza in 1833 . . . but so what? It changes nothing!'

Quaint cocked his head like a robin listening for a worm. 'Destine? What do you mean by that? What did Destine say?' he asked.

The look of spite on Joyce's face spoke volumes. 'Mr Quaint, my guards have orders to behead you at my slightest whim, so I would be *very* careful who you toy with if I were you,' he said, and it was sound advice. His two assassins were primed like hungry dogs at a dinner table. 'Think about this young man here . . . or your friend the Aksak, and not to mention your French companion. Do you value their lives as little as you obviously value your own? All you have to do is comply and this will all be over.'

'We're bound and on our knees, Joyce. How much more compliant can we get?'

'You know what I'm talking about, Quaint. Aloysius Bedford's journal – give it to me,' Joyce demanded. 'And I will consider sparing your life.'

'*Aloysius Bedford?*' asked Quaint. 'What the hell has he got to do with this?'

Joyce removed his gun from Rakmun, and repositioned it at Quaint's forehead. 'Don't feign ignorance,' he sneered. 'Your Madame told me *everything*! She told me of her friendship with Bedford, of her time in Umkaza twenty years ago . . . how she had read of my betrayal in his journal. A distasteful affair, to be sure, and not one I can allow to become public knowledge, hence my insistence that you hand it over right now!'

Quaint shook his head. 'I don't have a clue what you're talking about. Why would you mention Aloysius, the man's been missing for—'

'For twenty years, yes I know,' concluded Joyce. 'And as you know very well considering that you have read his journal . . . he is dead! And we both know why. The idiot cottoned onto what we were planning. Now, let me make this easy for you, Mr Quaint. Give me the book, and I'll give you your freedom.'

'You're insane!' snarled Quaint. Joyce was very convincing – he certainly seemed to believe every word that he was saying. But how could any of it be true? 'I've never even *seen* Aloysius's journal, and as for Destine knowing him, then that is absolute hogwash! I don't know what you're getting at, but you're wasting your time.'

'Cornelius, explain – who is this Aloysius?' said Faroud.

'He was an old tutor of mine,' snapped Quaint, more in reply to Joyce than to Faroud. 'Alexandria, the seamstress that I spoke of? Aloysius was her father. He disappeared back in the early thirties whilst he was . . .' Quaint's mouth went very dry. '. . . whilst he was working on an excavation site. Good lord! What happened, Joyce? What did you have to do with Aloysius's disappearance?'

'This is an interesting little game we're playing, isn't it?' taunted Joyce. 'Like a little clockwork mouse. I just wind you up and watch you chase your tail. So . . . do you still deny that you have Bedford's journal?'

Quaint's voice was like gravel crunching underfoot. 'I do.'

'Very well.' Joyce nodded at his guard and, immediately, the Hades Consortium assassin grasped a handful of Quaint's silver-white locks and wrenched his head backwards. 'I won't be fooled by this little act of yours, you know. Your companion already admitted that Bedford's diary was no longer in her possession, that she had given it to her companion for safekeeping . . . and we all know who that companion is, do we not?'

'Joyce, she is wrong! *You* are wrong,' insisted Quaint.

The conjuror's mind was reeling. How could Destine have been speaking of Aloysius? They had never met, and he had certainly not mentioned Bedford's name in her presence – the man had been missing for years. It was sheer lunacy. Destine had never been to Egypt before. The facts were set in stone, they disproved everything Joyce was saying and yet . . . just as so many facts failed to fit together, so many more made perfect sense. If it was some kind of bluff, then it was an absurd one. However, if it were not . . . then it was even more absurd. Quaint waved it away. It was all just a bizarre coincidence.

Then he remembered something: he didn't believe in coincidences.

'That book contains some particularly incriminating evidence against me, Mr Quaint,' continued Godfrey Joyce. 'You know Bedford's name and you know of his disappearance, and you could only have learned that from his journal, so why don't you stop these foolish games and tell me where it is.'

'I swear to you, Joyce, I haven't got what you're after!' yelled

Quaint. 'I only know what happened in Umkaza because I worked it out for myself.' Trying to wrench himself from his guard's grip, he made a dart forwards – just as he felt the cold edge of a sword brush the underside of his chin. He relaxed himself carefully.

'A fruitless waste of energy,' Joyce said, stepping towards Quaint's kneeling form. 'You will tell me what I want to know, curse you! Tell me or you die right here and now.'

'What happened to Aloysius, Joyce?' demanded Quaint, oblivious that his position was not one well suited for making demands. 'What did you do to him?'

'The events are all quite grippingly serialised within his journal, no doubt,' said Joyce. 'Why don't you tell me where it is and we can share a nice little story time?'

Quaint was desperate to learn more. 'Tell me what happened in Umkaza!'

'Umkaza was a long time ago . . . but my life will be shot to bits if that nasty episode ever gets out. The British government won't touch me . . . the Consortium will probably *kill* me . . .' Joyce cocked the pistol's trigger and sighted its barrel at Faroud's brother again. 'That's why I need Aloysius's diary . . . and you have until the count of three to tell me where it is, or this little Scarab thug's brains will decorate the desert.'

'He is but a boy! He has nothing to do with this!' yelled Faroud, straining at his bonds. 'Cornelius . . . just give him what he wants!'

'I wish I could, it sounds riveting,' muttered Quaint.

'One . . .' Joyce began.

'Cornelius . . . I beg you,' pleaded Faroud. 'He is my *brother*!'

'Faroud, I don't know what the hell he's on about, I swear!' protested Quaint.

'Two . . .' said Joyce, gruffly.

'Cornelius . . . you must be mistaken!' snapped Faroud.

'I'm not!' yelled Quaint.

'Quite a double act, you two. Perhaps I'm aiming the gun in the wrong direction,' said Joyce, as he moved over to Faroud and jabbed the barrel of the pistol into his forehead, hard enough for all the pigment to fade away from the Aksak's dark skin. 'If the boy's life means nothing to you, then maybe your tongue will loosen now that your *friend* is in peril.'

Quaint remained silent, his eyes ablaze with anger.

'Cornelius, he will do it, you *know* he will,' screamed Faroud. 'He'll *shoot* me.'

'You should listen to your friend, Mr Quaint . . . I'm not bluffing,' sneered Joyce.

'Neither am I,' growled Quaint. 'I don't have what you want!'

'Three,' said Joyce, tightening his finger on the pistol's trigger. 'Time's up!'

A shot rang out in the desert.

CHAPTER XLVIII

The Shifting Sands

THE HOODED ASSASSIN behind Quaint fell to the ground as claret blood seeped from a large hole in the centre of his forehead.

Godfrey Joyce looked at the dead man in a mix of fascination and confusion. He stared at the tip of his pistol, trying to piece together what had occurred. Another shot rang out and whizzed past Joyce's ear. The back of the other assassin's head exploded, spitting fragments of brain and skull all over the dry sand. His body folded limply in half. Dead before it even hit the ground.

Joyce's eyes flared at the chaos running amok around him.

'What just happened?' he asked numbly.

'I think they did,' said Quaint, nodding into the distance.

There was a sudden chorus of loud voices. Silhouetted against the moonlit desert sky, a dozen Clan Scarabs approached on horseback, their rifles trained on Godfrey Joyce.

'The cavalry,' said Faroud, as he pinched a piece of nondescript bloodied matter from his shoulder and discarded it on the sand. He leapt to his feet, snatched up a sword and sliced the ropes binding him to Quaint's wrist. 'Although a little later than we had agreed.'

'I told you my plan would work!' cried Quaint. 'Why doesn't anyone have any faith in me any more?'

'What . . . what are you d-doing?' Joyce stammered.

'This!' said Quaint, as he launched a cracking punch against Joyce's jaw, sending the man crashing to the ground. He snatched up his pistol and aimed it right between his eyes. 'And I won't even count to three.'

'Rakmun!' yelled Faroud, as he ran to his brother. Skidding to his knees, the Scarab leader embraced him, his hands trembling. Rakmun collapsed onto Faroud's shoulders, clinging there limply, his legs too weak to support his weight.

With their arrival heralded by much braying and cawing – not to mention joyous laughter as they spied Rakmun safe and well – twelve Clan Scarab riders quickly dismounted their steeds and formed a circle around Faroud, Rakmun, Quaint and Joyce.

'It is good to see you, my clan brothers!' commended Aksak Faroud, warmly slapping his hands on two Scarabs' shoulders. 'Let us hope that is the last of the eleventh hour rescues that we have to make for a long time.'

One of the Scarabs, a tall, portly fellow with a patchwork beard and long, straggly black hair, stepped over to Faroud and flung his massive arms around him. The air escaped noisily from Faroud's lungs.

'My Aksak!' he bellowed.

'It is . . . good to see you too . . . Sobek,' he wheezed.

'I wish it were under more . . . pleasant circumstances,' said Sobek.

The Aksak frowned. 'What do you mean?'

Sobek's joyous expression fell and he grasped Faroud's

forearm. 'I bring dire news, Aksak. We must sit and talk with haste.'

Aksak Faroud, Cornelius Quaint and the small band of Scarabs sat cross-legged in a huddle around a large fire. Several torches were staked into the sand and the wind teased at their flames, carrying streams of smoke into the night sky. Godfrey Joyce was tethered to his cart outside the circle of men.

Faroud raised his hands for calm.

'Aksak . . . in your absence, a revolt has taken place in Bara Mephista,' began Sobek, his eyes adding the required amount of pathos to the tale. 'Elder Nastasi arrived unannounced with a large band of heavily armed men. They were not of our clan . . . but dressed in garb similar to those men over there.' Sobek motioned towards the crimson-clad Consortium guards lying dead in the sand. 'They were many in number, and heavily armed. They looked as though they were torn from the darkness itself, but they followed Nastasi's word like day-old lambs. He branded all those loyal to you as traitors to the clan. He seized control of the camp and demanded we turn over full command to him.'

Faroud's eyes widened. 'He did *what?*'

'Nastasi claims your mind has been distracted. He said you are unfit to lead, and called upon the rest of the Council of Elders to back his plea to regain overall leadership of the region.' Sobek looked disdainfully down at the sand. 'You have lost all support. Not an Elder among them will speak out against Nastasi now that he has garnered such military might.'

'But where did he get it?' asked Faroud.

'We do not know for sure, Aksak,' said Sobek.

'If they were dressed like those two over there,' said Quaint, 'I think we can narrow down the suspects.'

'The Consortium?' gasped Faroud. 'The Hades Consortium is helping Nastasi take control of the clan? That is madness! We must not let this happen!'

Sobek reached over and placed his hand on his Aksak's shoulder. 'Faroud . . . it has *already* happened. With those men on his side, they easily outnumbered our clan four to one. Nastasi was victorious. We managed to flee, but others chose to stay in Bara Mephista . . . under Nastasi's rule. They had a choice: follow you and die, or follow Nastasi and live. Most chose the latter option.'

'*Most?*' asked Faroud. 'Well, that is not good. However, I should have known that not all our brothers would willingly betray me. They will fight with their lives to protect our clan! Tell me, Sobek . . . how many men can I rely upon?'

Sobek glanced around the circle of Scarabs and smiled weakly.

'You are looking at them,' he said.

Faroud's heart dropped. 'Only twelve of you?'

'We are all who remain loyal, Aksak . . . we will follow you until our dying breath.'

'If Nastasi has an entire army against us – a Hades Consortium army, no less – then that may come quicker than you think. This is a fight we cannot win, my friends.' Faroud clenched his fists and slammed them down into the cold sand. His Scarabs shared anxious glances with each other. Never had they seen their leader so defeated. 'What does Nastasi think he is doing? What on earth possessed him to make such a move? What does he have to gain; he is already a Council Elder. He already *has* power!'

'If you think that's enough, then you don't know Nastasi like I do,' interjected Godfrey Joyce from his position outside the circle. 'Let me spell this out to you. Nastasi has been offered ultimate power by the Hades Consortium, far more than your pitiful little *council* can offer him – enough power to unify all nine clans! Superior weaponry and everything he needs at the click of his fingers.' He beamed a veneer of a smile towards Faroud. 'Nastasi will hold Egypt within the palm of his hand . . . which is very bad news for you, Aksak.'

'How do you know so much of Elder Nastasi?' asked Faroud.

'Who do you think I got to do my dirty work in Umkaza back in '33? Except he was called *Aksak* Nastasi in those days,' said Joyce. 'He was the one that informed me of your journey to my embassy, Aksak, and he was the one that handed your little brother to me gift-wrapped. He was the traitor in your camp.'

Faroud seethed. 'If the council only knew—'

'What *could* they do now that he has might on his side?' Joyce laughed.

The Aksak looked to Quaint. 'Cornelius, help me make sense of this. You know the Hades Consortium better than me. What would compel them to aid Nastasi in such a manner?'

'The question is, Aksak: what lengths would the Hades Consortium go to, to ensure their plan to poison the Nile is a success? The answer: just about anything. I assume that they require Nastasi – and the remainder of your clan – for something connected to their plot . . . something that uses intimidation as its fuel,' Quaint explained. 'This is an odd play for them though, I agree. I would have thought unification of the Scarabs would be the last thing they wanted. They would surely have to oust him at some point if they wished to regain a semblance of control in Egypt. Giving arms to the Scarabs, giving them even *more* power . . . it's tantamount to suicide.'

'It's obvious that you're not a man of politics, Mr Quaint,' Joyce laughed. 'The perception of power is all relative to what you have power *over*. Whatever the Hades Consortium has given Nastasi in return for his services, it is nothing that cannot be taken away again whenever they feel like it! Lady Jocasta is a fiendishly calculating young bitch, but you can't deny her skill – she knows just what carrots to dangle in front of your nose!'

'Lady Jocasta?' asked Quaint. 'Who is she?'

'She's in charge of the show! Everything that has transpired has been according to *her* design. The poison, the plan for the Nile – even Nastasi's coup! Whilst she sits at the top of her tree, there's nothing you can do to stop her.' Joyce fixed his gaze directly upon Faroud. 'You have been reunited with your little brother, Aksak . . . but I would make the most of it if I were you. Do you really think that Nastasi will let his biggest detractor just walk away? His only opposition? Oh, no! He's scared stiff that you'll try to rally your troops into a counter-revolt. Now he's got the Hades Consortium at his side, he'll stop at nothing to wipe you off the face of this earth!'

'I have no interest in your words, Joyce. Keep your mouth shut or I will ask my men to show you how we Scarabs deal with traitors,' snapped Faroud.

Joyce snorted like a pig. 'Don't waste your time trying to frighten me, Faroud; we both know you can't kill me.'

'Oh? You sound very sure about that,' said Faroud.

'I am,' replied Joyce smugly. 'You *need* me.'

'A scurrilous slime such as you?' countered Faroud. 'For what reason?'

A devilish smile seeped onto Joyce's taut lips, and he delivered his answer slowly and deliberately. 'Because, my dear Faroud, only the Hades Consortium's base of operations in Fantoma holds the answers that you and your little band of thugs seek – and *I'm* the only one that can get you inside.'

CHAPTER XLIX

The Unstable Alliance

'**Y**OU EXPECT US to go walking into the Hades Consortium's den with only your word as protection?' asked Cornelius Quaint, as he towered over Joyce. 'You must think us fools!'

'Well, if you want to put an end to Lady Jocasta's plot, then you don't have much choice, do you?' retorted Joyce. 'The Consortium has guards posted in a three-mile radius of their sanctorum. They will cut you and your brave little band to pieces the moment you set foot on their territory . . . but not me. They know me . . . they *trust* me. I can get you past their defences, right into the lion's den.'

'Don't make me laugh!' snapped Quaint. 'If you had that kind of pull, you wouldn't be out here in the desert; you'd be holed up in their secret HQ in Bombay.'

'Rome, actually,' said Joyce.

Quaint smiled. 'Rome, eh? I shall have to remember that.'

'Whether you like it or not, right now I'm the only hope you've got of stopping this plot, not to mention getting your fortune-telling friend out of Fantoma alive.'

'So why the change of heart?' asked Quaint. 'Why are you in

such a hurry to betray the Hades Consortium all of a sudden? Back in your embassy you were dead against it.'

Joyce pushed his tongue into his cheek coyly. 'Well . . . you know how this game works, Quaint. I've been trying for years to gain a better standing in the Hades Consortium . . . all to no avail. They kept me on their leash as I fed them what I learned from the Embassy, and then a whole load of them turned up . . . in *my* territory! Before that harpy Jocasta arrived, I was top dog.'

Quaint stroked his jaw. 'So . . . by getting us into the Consortium's heart we can disrupt this Lady Jocasta's plans . . . which makes her look bad, and sets you up for bigger and better things, right? You shovel manure in her direction and manage to come out smelling of roses?'

'Vulgarly put, but yes,' said Joyce. 'I'm going nowhere in this backwater country, I know that. I'm no fool. If I want to make a name for myself, I won't do that sitting behind a desk in the bloody British Embassy!'

Aksak Faroud scoured the conjuror's face intently, trying to decipher what might be going on in his head. 'Cornelius, can I have a word with you . . . in private?'

'What's on your mind?' Quaint asked, once they were out of Joyce's earshot.

'Him! *He* is on my mind. He captured my brother and forced me to become his personal slave. Are you seriously thinking about allying our band with him? He is nothing but a lying, deceitful snake!'

Quaint smiled. 'I seem to remember Professor North saying the same about you.'

'And she had good reason – as do I,' said Faroud. 'I know

this man, remember? He will betray us at the soonest opportunity. It is too simple . . . it is a trap!'

'Of *course* it's a bloody trap! Frankly, I'd be offended if it weren't,' replied Quaint with an unyielding glare.

Faroud took a step back. 'And . . . you are going through with it anyway?'

'Remember the plan,' Quaint said, shifting his voice from a whisper to a clipped snarl. 'Right now we're running out of both time and options, Aksak. I want to get into the Consortium's base, and his way works just as well as mine.'

'As contagious as your bravado is, my friend, perhaps you should have second thoughts about such rashness?' advised Faroud.

'Heavens, no, man!' Quaint said, slapping Faroud on the back. 'I had second thoughts *ages* ago; I must be on at least double figures by now. Here's what I think we should do . . .'

Five minutes later, Faroud kicked a cloud of sand into the air and cursed madly.

'That is the most foolhardy plan I have *ever* heard in my entire life! Even coming from you!' he raged, walking away from the conjuror at a pace as Quaint followed in his wake. 'You wish us to disguise ourselves as Hades Consortium guards whilst two of my Scarabs pose as you and me – acting as Joyce's prisoners – and then we simply walk into the base through the front door?'

Quaint smiled. 'Brilliant, isn't it.'

'No, it is not,' disagreed Faroud. 'I will tell what it *is* – it is utter madness!'

'It has to be, don't you see? It's the only weapon we've got!'

Faroud looked moonward. 'Then we really *are* in trouble.'

CHAPTER L

The Measure of Evil

LADY JOCASTA BLAZED through the stone corridors of the Fantoma sanctorum with intentional haste. She reached Sir George Dray's quarters, and raised her hand to tear back the thin curtain dividing his room from the low-ceilinged tunnel — but then something made her halt. Anxiety was an emotion that she was feeling more and more often since her superior had arrived in Egypt, and it buzzed around her stomach like a swarm of hornets. She shook the apprehension away, and cleared her throat to announce her presence.

Sir George bade her to enter.

The old man was sitting at a writing bureau. The waning light from a paraffin lamp burrowed deep shadows into the wrinkles on his craggy face. He held up his hand, ordering Jocasta to wait, and continued scribbling away into a leather-bound journal.

'What is it?' he asked eventually, like the culmination of all Jocasta's childhood nightmares rolled into a grating snarl. 'Don't just stand there gawping like a startled doe, lass.'

Jocasta stepped forwards into the dimness of Dray's quarters. 'Sir George, I thought you would like to know . . . our people have delivered the consignment of poison to the Scarab. Nastasi has orders to distribute the vials in accordance with my plan.'

'That sounds like good news to me . . . so why are you here in my room when I quite clearly asked not to be disturbed?' said Dray.

Lady Jocasta's stomach somersaulted. The shrivelled old man seemed to have an uncanny understanding of her thoughts, and that chilled her – for she had much to hide. She shifted on the balls of her feet as if she were about to bolt for the door at any moment.

'Heinrich Nadir has returned . . . with the Frenchwoman in his custody as you ordered,' she said.

Dray raised his wiry eyebrows. 'I'm still waiting for the *bad* news, lass.'

Jocasta's eyes fell to the floor. 'Well, sir . . . Nadir has also supplied me with some information about the Englishman that you mentioned.'

Sir George's interest was aflame. 'What of him?'

'According to Nadir . . . he was believed to have been en route to the British Embassy, although our scouts have since confirmed that he is presently encamped several miles from the eastern perimeter, along with a handful of Clan Scarabs from Bara Mephista that fled under Nastasi's charge. Godfrey Joyce is with them.'

Sir George rubbed his hands together. 'Now that *is* good news!' he cried.

Jocasta took a sudden step forwards. 'It is?'

'Of course! It means that Cornelius is on his way!' chirped Dray.

Jocasta was finding the old man's response hard to fathom. 'Then . . . we must send our troops to apprehend him immediately. If this man is an enemy of the Hades Consortium then we must—'

'No, Jocasta, we must not do a damn thing,' said Dray. 'I have gone to great expense to orchestrate Quaint's arrival and I do *not* intend to risk that when he is right in my lap, is that understood?'

'But, Sir George . . . may I ask why you stay your hand? This Englishman might attempt to subvert my plans for the Nile,' said Jocasta.

'Oh, almost certainly he will, lass!' grinned Dray. 'But once you get a bite on your line, you have to give the fish a little slack. You make it think it has a chance of getting loose . . . and then reel it in once its defences are down.' He linked his bony fingers together and smiled, his wrinkles stretched tight around his mouth like the opening of a drawstring bag. 'Tell the guards to give Quaint's line a little slack. Allow him and his friends undeterred passage . . . right in through the front door. Just make sure once they get in . . . there is no way they can get out.'

'I will speak with the captain of the guard right away, sir,' said Jocasta, with a compliant nod. She turned swiftly and took a step to leave, but then lingered on her toes by the door.

The old man looked in her direction expectantly. 'Is there anything else, Jocasta?'

'I hope you do not think me too bold, sir,' she said, taking a swift breath as she turned to face him, 'but I must admit that I am finding it difficult to understand your actions. This man Quaint . . . you say that he is our enemy, and yet you do not seem to be concerned that Joyce has led him to our citadel.'

'Concerned, lass? Far from it. I was damn well *banking* on it!' chuckled Dray.

The pieces had still not fallen into place for Jocasta.

'But I am most perplexed, sir,' she mumbled, almost thinking aloud. 'You said that this is the same man that derailed my plot in London. Surely he must have learned of what we plan here in Egypt from Antoine Renard.'

'It does seem that way, doesn't it?' Sir George snatched up his walking cane and wrenched his frame out of his seat with unexpected vigour. 'Once I found out about his involvement in London, I knew Quaint'd be hell-bent on putting a stop to what you were cooking up out here! Leading him to Egypt was the only way I could be sure to keep an eye on him.' Dray laughed, a sound like water gushing down a drain. He inhaled sharply, his hand darting to his chest, and he faltered, groping for a handhold. Jocasta rushed to his side to support him but he waved her away abruptly. 'I am fine, Jocasta, leave me. If there is one thing that I have learned from my previous dealings with Cornelius Quaint, it's that you can't afford to take any risks.'

'Baron Remus made no mention of this man to me,' said Jocasta.

'No? I can't fathom why. He's got a bit of history with Quaint himself.' Just then, Dray's face darkened as a grim thought graced his mind. His eyes drifted away from the Greek woman's face, down to the floor. 'My God, is that it? Has Cornelius finally discovered the truth? I hadn't considered that.'

Lady Jocasta scowled at Dray's pained expression.

'Sir George? What has the Baron to do with this man Quaint?' she asked.

'A lot more than Quaint knows, with any luck!' Dray replied. 'Someone once told me that you could measure how evil a man is by the shade of his enemies. Well, if that's the case, then Baron Remus puts the Devil himself to shame . . . but if there is one foe that even he might have trouble with . . . it's Cornelius Quaint.'

'I take it this man is a dangerous sort?' asked Jocasta. 'And has he no weakness that we can exploit?'

'Just one . . . and thankfully she is now in our possession,' said Sir George. 'I knew that Quaint would be drawn to his beloved Madame Destine like a moth to a flame . . . and soon his wings will be singed!'

CHAPTER LI

𝔗𝔥𝔢 𝔆𝔶𝔤𝔫𝔢𝔱 𝔞𝔫𝔡 𝔱𝔥𝔢 𝔖𝔴𝔞𝔫

SITTING UPON AN iron bed-frame in an otherwise empty room below Sir George's quarters, Madame Destine's mind was an uneven patchwork of conflicting thoughts and emotions. She clenched handfuls of her dress in her fists, tugging them towards her. It was late and she was tired, yet she could not sleep – not with that incessant voice constantly calling her name.

Destine's heart stopped.

Her name?

She looked around, but she was still in the room within Fantoma's bowels, still confined. Perhaps the day had finally taken its toll on her, and sleep had crept in unannounced. It must have been the last vestiges of her conscious mind giving way to tiredness. She lay down on the bed. She could feel the coolness of the underground room making her eyes itch, and she could feel the tightness of her chest drawing air. Amongst these feelings, something else began tugging at her senses, but it was not sleep.

A sensation descended upon her, similar to the glimpse of the past that had manifested itself the previous night. Knowing this,

Destine accepted the feelings more readily, forcing her mind to relax. She could sense something approaching. It was like a dim candle in a darkened room, yet she could feel its warmth upon her skin. Consciously, she steered herself towards it.

Her location melted away, and just like the après-monition in the clearing by lake, she was somewhere else. She was in the same place, but not necessarily in the same time. The sand was cold beneath her toes.

Sand?

An amorphous carpet of mist clung to the damp sand that parted between her toes. Trails of warm breath floated from Destine's mouth, curling into the violet-black sky. She moved forward across raised dunes, with the mist parting as she strode through it. Up ahead, she could see a silhouette of a man upon the rise of the hill, and she approached unerringly, feeling not one jot of fear.

He was in his mid-fifties with a thin, waxed moustache adorning his top lip. He was wearing braces over a collarless shirt, with a broad belt around his waist and a variety of items hanging from it, such as a telescope, a canteen of water and a small pocket-knife. He seemed to be waiting for her, and as Destine stepped closer, he beamed a once-handsome smile in her direction.

Yet another après-monition from my past, she thought to herself.

'No, Madame . . . not this time,' said Aloysius Bedford. 'You look surprised to see me.'

'Actually . . . I am more surprised that *you* can see *me*.'

'Of course I can see you!' Bedford replied. 'I might be dead, but I'm not blind.'

Destine faltered in her approach. '*Dead?*'

'As a doornail,' replied Aloysius.

'If you are dead . . . then you are obviously not from the present . . . nor the future. Yet you say you are not an après-monition? So what are you? I have never been able to commune with spirits of the dead before.'

'Perhaps they just had nothing much to say.' Aloysius gave a deep-throated chuckle. 'Your gifts are still a mystery to you, aren't they? Even after all this time? You truly have no idea what wonders you can perform . . . what wonders you *will* perform.' His voice floated upon the air like spring blossom, lighter than the cool breeze that nipped at Destine's bare feet. 'Perhaps it is time that I enlightened you.'

Destine scowled at the spirit before her, its form fluctuating in and out of cohesiveness. 'If this is no après-monition . . . how can this be, Aloysius? If that is indeed who you are and not some trick of my mind.'

'What do you think? Do you believe that I am Aloysius?' the ghost asked.

Destine shook her head . . . which then seemed to evolve into a nod of its own accord. 'I *wish* you to be . . . I have so much to ask you!'

'And I have so much to tell,' Aloysius responded, with a playful smile.

'But how can any of this be true? How am I able to *see* you? To speak with you?' Destine asked. 'As attuned to the spiritual world as I am . . . I had thought there was supposed to be a barrier between the living and the dead?'

'And indeed there is . . . yet some wrongs are worth crossing barriers to right,' answered Aloysius, his answer not remedying the confusion in the Frenchwoman's head. 'You are presently on a course laid out by your younger self, a course that has already been long and arduous, yet there is far more to be done before you will see its end. Your bewilderment is causing you to drift from the road . . . and I am here to put you back on track.'

Destine took a sudden step forward at his words, hungry for more.

'You know? You know of the task that I set myself in those letters? The task to find your journal?' she asked.

Aloysius nodded. 'Of course I know, Dusty. It is my actions that have guided you thus far.'

'Then tell me why I could forget all that occurred in Umkaza all those years ago?' the Frenchwoman demanded. 'So many dead – murdered! How could I have ignored that . . . choosing instead to write a letter that I had no assurance I would ever get to read?'

'You had assurance enough, Destine,' said Aloysius. 'You had your premonitions to guide you . . . even if they are no longer your guide at this time. That was the only thread you had to cling to, my dear, the only hope. You knew that you were power-less to undo what had been done . . . and only by sealing that night within your words were you able to survive. As for how it has slipped from your recall . . . what occurred twenty years ago in Umkaza was horrific for anyone to witness. But for someone as gifted as you are, it was even more so. It almost cost you your life.'

Destine so wished to interrupt, but something held her tongue. As the ghost of Aloysius Bedford continued, finally she was on the verge of so many answers.

'Your connectivity to human emotion has been a great tool to you in the past, yet on that night in 1833, it was almost your undoing. Back then it was not as easy for you to control . . . to deafen your ears to the feelings of those around you. Unknown emotions and sensations would come at you unannounced, and often you were unsure which were your own feelings, and which were those belonging to others. On the night that those men died in Umkaza, your senses were wide open. You had no defence. You "felt" every death as though it was your own and the extrasensory feedback almost crippled you.'

'That does not explain why I would forget,' said Destine. 'If I experienced all that pain for myself, surely it is something that would stay with me for ever.'

'The human mind is a conscious beast, my dear,' replied Aloysius. 'And it's propensity for self-preservation goes far beyond your conscious levels. When it is threatened, it does what many beasts do – it runs away. It retreats into itself. Yet no matter how long it curls up and cowers, the danger will always be there. That is why you have no memory of that time. It was hidden away, deep within your subconscious . . . because your mind knew that should you ever discover it . . . you would relive all that pain and misery and death all over again.'

'And yet . . . since I arrived in Egypt . . . since learning of my warning and finding your journal . . . I have felt glimpses of my past coming back to me,' said Destine. 'So what does that mean, Aloysius?'

'It means that you are near to unearthing that which you secreted in your memory, Destine,' Aloysius replied, his voice stronger now, more forceful. 'You have strong mental defences, my dear – far stronger than you know, but your reawakening to your past began weeks ago when you decided to come back to Egypt. Back to a place that harboured so many painful memories. Once you had learned of the letters, the stronger the psychic connections to your past became, and with every step that you took, the more your mind was opened.

'It was difficult for me not to reveal myself to you before now, and spell out your task in detail. But it had to be done slowly. At your mind's pace. You had to piece it together bit by bit. Were you to have access to your memories in one fell swoop, the pain would have torn your mind to pieces, leaving you nothing but a mindless husk!'

'I must be imagining this,' whispered Destine.

'You are,' replied Aloysius merrily. 'But don't let that put you off. Soon this will all make sense. Soon you will understand why matters of the mind cannot be rushed. You are a cygnet right now . . . but soon you shall become a swan.'

'And what is that supposed to mean?' Destine asked.

'You have discovered my journal, you have experienced the atrocity in Umkaza firsthand, and your task is now fully illuminated before you. You know what you must do, and so, now that it is safe for me to relinquish my hold over your clairvoyant abilities, they will soon return . . . and stronger than ever.'

Destine's mouth fell open, sensing shock for the first time since meeting the spirit, and her lips quivered with fear. 'Your hold? What do you mean . . . your hold?'

'It was necessary, Destine. For your own good,' said Aloysius.

'My own good? What are you talking about?' demanded Destine. 'What was for my own good?'

Aloysius Bedford's form dissipated slightly, as if it was difficult maintaining coherence. His pale face glanced at the Frenchwoman, seeing her anger all too clearly. 'I had to act to protect you. I have been trapped in this formless limbo waiting for you to catch up with your past, and once it became clear that you were to return to Egypt, I had no recourse but to do what I did.'

'What?' Destine snapped. 'What did you *do* to me?'

'As an astral being, it is forbidden for me to intervene in affairs of the living. We have discarded our physical forms, and with them . . . all ties to our lives are cast off also,' explained the ghost. 'But what happened in Umkaza was something that I could not abandon, Destine! Even a spirit can be haunted . . . and that memory would never fade from my mind. And so, when Fate conspired to bring you back to Egypt, I had to protect you and ensure that the clarity of the message was not diluted.'

'I am waiting, Aloysius,' said Destine. 'Ghost or not, my tolerance for being toyed with is not one that you wish to measure.'

Aloysius held up his hands in submission. 'You assumed that it was the elixir of life that had stolen your clairvoyant gifts from you, but it is not so,' he admitted, dolefully. 'It was I that stole them from you.'

'*You?*'

'But only because I had to!' insisted Aloysius, and his expression quickly adjusted to one of grave concern. 'Your thoughts had to be clear of noise. You had to *believe* in the task laid at your feet. If you were to think it a stray thought from your past, you would never have paid it any heed! I could not take that chance, and so even though intervention is not permitted, it is within my power . . . and it was necessary if light was to be shed on the crimes that occurred in Umkaza. But as powerful as I am in this form, I could not hold the memories back for ever . . . not once you got closer to your goal. Shards of your past have been slipping through my fingers these past few days . . . giving you glimpses of your time in Egypt. The chains that bound your memory were weakening, and I was forced to exert all my energies to ensure that your past was fed to you carefully . . . lest you go insane.'

'You mean . . . my après-monitions?' Destine gasped.

'Yes,' Aloysius confirmed, his eyes twinkling like onyx.

Destine's legs buckled and she slumped onto the cold sand. The mist rose up to her shoulders only to turn tail and evaporate around her. She almost wished that she would become lost within it, transported back to reality.

'All of this . . . it is so much to take in,' she mumbled. 'You are a ghost. After all I have seen and done . . . this is so unbelievable.'

'If it helps, try not to think of me as a ghost,' said Aloysius. 'Think of me as a sort of *intermediary* between you and your subconscious. A translator, if you will . . . surely you can identify with that!' He beamed a translucent smile. 'You asked me a few minutes ago how you were able to speak to me. This is why. Now your mind is clear for the first time in your life. No little side distractions from the future to get in the way. You have learned much of what occurred in Umkaza on the night that my fate was sealed . . . but you do not know it all, you do not know *enough*.'

'Enough to do what?' asked Destine.

'Absolutely the right question, my girl,' Aloysius grinned. 'I speak for all the men that perished in Umkaza, Destine. All their tormented souls, locked within that moment. There is more to be told before the scales can be balanced . . . and they will be free.'

Destine rubbed her arms furiously as another trail of warm breath floated from her mouth. 'So tell me . . . what is so important that you would tear down the barriers between life and death to communicate with me? Godfrey Joyce is our enemy, yet he works for the British government! I can do nothing to expose him!'

'This is more important than *him*,' said Aloysius. 'Just as

I was, Godfrey Joyce is just a plaything of a much grander puppeteer.'

'Enough riddles, monsieur!' snapped Destine.

'I have spent twenty years as a ghost, and you're the impatient one?' laughed Aloysius. 'All right. I will tell you . . .' In actuality, the ghost did not need to breathe, yet there was still so much of it that was still a man, and Aloysius Bedford took a long, thoughtful breath before he continued. 'Back in 1833, I was hired by a Chinaman named Cho-zen Li to find one of Egypt's greatest treasures – the Pharaoh's Cradle. A treasure lost for centuries beneath the sand, with rumour and guesswork the only guide to its location. Cho-zen promised that he knew the whereabouts of the Cradle, and I leapt at the chance to uncover it.'

'Cho-zen Li . . . I read of his name in your journal,' said Destine.

'Yes . . . devil that he is,' snarled Aloysius. 'You see, Cho-zen was after a bigger prize than the Pharaoh's Cradle alone. He'd heard tell of a curse upon it: any man to disturb the treasure would die. Now, I'm no fool, Destine. I've heard a thousand curses over the years, and not a one of them has ever been grounded in any truth . . . except for this one.'

'The Pharaoh's Cradle was cursed?' gasped Destine. 'It was responsible for the massacre in Umkaza?'

'In a way . . .' replied Aloysius. 'Yet the curse was not born of sorcery or witchcraft – the Cradle was infected with a deadly bacterium that had festered within its tomb. The expedition was all a sham so that Cho-zen Li could get his hands on that bacterium . . . and use it.'

'Use it? Use it how?' asked Destine.

'Let me rephrase that . . . use *me*.'

'To do what?' enquired Destine, hooked on every word. 'Why would your benefactor hire you to find the Pharaoh's Cradle if he suspected it might be infected with this bacterium?'

'He wasn't after the treasure – he was after the bacterium! He'd been searching for it for years . . . and my dig site provided him with all the proof that he required. We didn't piece it together at first . . . but when several of my men fell sick after examining some of the wrappings inside the mouth of the tomb, I knew something was up. It took us close to a month to clear the tomb's entrance to excavate the Cradle, but in that time, the sick men grew worse. Their eyes became drawn, their noses bled profusely, they became little more than walking dead.' Aloysius's shimmering light seemed to fade, only to return twice as brightly. 'The bacterium fed off them like a parasite, and I watched them wither away before my eyes. All three of them died exactly a month after infection, on the same day, the same hour, practically the same minute. Like clockwork. I'd never seen anything so ghastly, and our best medical man had no idea what we were dealing with.'

'How ever did you discover the cause?' asked Destine.

Aloysius smiled, just a hint. 'You warned me. You came barging into my tent one night, telling tales of a vision that you had experienced. You told me that Godfrey Joyce was betraying me and was allied with Nastasi. They sought to take the Cradle from me by force – now that Cho-zen Li's little field test had been successful. You told me things that horrified me, Destine . . . things that would occur if the Pharaoh's Cradle ever saw daylight again. Your visions were remarkably accurate, telling that the bacterium was transferred by skin contact . . . passed on by the merest handshake.' Bedford's spectral eyes looked down at the sand, losing their focus, yet his mind was as sharp as a pin. 'Had your clairvoyant gifts not warned me, I would have done Cho-zen Li's bidding . . . becoming infected with the plague myself.

'Imagine, Destine: I would have been welcomed back to England and hailed a hero. The scientific community would have flocked to my side, desperate to be seen with the archaeologist that found the lost Pharaoh's Cradle. I would have infected them all . . . every one of them. The Empire's greatest minds – dead because of me! That is why I had to act . . . and I died for it.' All light disappeared from Aloysius's face, making him look ghostlier.

'What happened?' asked Destine, remembering that she was talking to a dead man.

'After your warning, I did the only thing that I could. I uncovered the Pharaoh's Cradle, exposing myself to the plague in the bargain, and then hid it as best I could so that Joyce and Nastasi would never find it,' explained Aloysius. 'Then I wrote down what I could as a warning to others . . . sealing my thoughts, inscribing them for the future . . . and I gave it to you for safekeeping.'

'Your journal!' gasped Destine.

'That diary is the key, Destine,' confirmed Aloysius. 'But I misjudged how traumatised you'd be following the massacre in Umkaza. Your grip on reality was slipping away by the second, weakened by all that you had suffered. I prayed that you would be strong enough to leave word of what happened . . . just as I had left word to you.'

'My letters!' Destine cried. 'I remember! I was weak . . . in pain . . . and I feared that Nastasi's men were pursuing me. And so I took the journal to a place far from Umkaza, to a wondrous place that you had once shown me . . . Sekhet Simbel. I had hoped to return and collect it once my mind was healed.' She snapped her fingers, grasping the splinters of memory. 'Not knowing where to turn, I relied on my clairvoyance to be my compass. It led me to Agra, to the only friend that I could trust . . . Ahman. I sensed a strong link to that place – to him – and before my mind was cleansed of the memory, I sat down to write those letters . . . knowing they were safe in Ahman's care.'

'And they were, Madame,' reminded Aloysius. 'For twenty years those letters remained unopened . . . the secret preserved – until it was time for your destiny to bring you back to Egypt and they called you to them.' He looked over his shoulder nervously, as though someone were pursuing him. As he gripped Destine's wrists, she felt a cold chill constrict around them, as if they were submerged in iced water. 'Destine, you have to put an end to this! My diary is the key, remember?'

'Aloysius, what do you mean?' Destine called to him.

'Warn others! Warn them of the Eleventh Plague,' said Aloysius Bedford, his voice fading along with his spectral form, gradually becoming one with the mist that hung in the air. 'Destine, my time is short and I must go. They have come for me.'

'Who?' asked Destine. 'Who has come for you?'

An almighty white blast of light bathed the sand dunes and a piercing wail like a thousand screams shattered the silence. Destine clamped her hands to ears and crouched into a ball on the ground. Moments later, the silence returned and Aloysius was gone from the desert . . . and so was Madame Destine.

She was back in the underground citadel in Fantoma. Alone in the room. Numbly, she glanced down at her bare feet, staring at the sand between her toes, and she remembered. She remembered *everything*. The past was back in place, pigeonholed within her memories. And they were not alone in her mind. Her clairvoyant gifts had returned, just as Aloysius had said they would.

A shower of elation soaked Destine's body as she felt the tingle of her ability's re-emergence.

Madame Destine was whole again.

She had become a swan.

Her mind was being flooded with messages, images and visions of the future, as though she had returned from a long holiday to greet a carpet of unopened letters. As the onslaught besieged her, one vision in particular was possessed of clarity – the last prophecy that she had experienced prior to her voyage to Egypt. Considering all that she had learned from Aloysius's spectre, the words seemed to make a strange sort of imperfect sense:

The past and the present shall entwine once more.
Beware the dawn of the Eleventh Plague.

'The journal is the key!' Destine gasped. 'That is why I wrote those letters to myself, that is what they were leading me to . . . and now I know why! I have to use it to make sure that the Eleventh Plague can never rise again.' She patted herself down, sifting through the folds of her gown for the book – just as a sudden realisation slammed so violently into her mind that it brought a tear to her eye. She recalled the moments before the hooded riders on the road to Umkaza attacked her, she recalled giving the book to her trusted friend for safekeeping, and she recalled exactly where Aloysius's journal was.

CHAPTER LII

The Day of Reckoning

THE FOLLOWING MORNING, the sun loomed low over the Egyptian desert, casting the ominous shadows of the Hawass Mountains over the tiny encampment positioned at its foot. Yawning loudly, Godfrey Joyce pawed clumsily at his eyes as the sight of two hooded Hades Consortium assassins startled him awake.

'Oh, thank God,' he blurted uncontrollably. 'You've come to rescue me!'

'Rescue you?' smiled Cornelius Quaint, pulling down his dark red hood. 'Not quite, Godfrey.'

'You? I thought you were one of *them*!' gasped Joyce.

'That's the general idea,' said Quaint. 'I told you it would work, Faroud.'

Standing at Quaint's side – also dressed head to foot in claret-coloured robes – Aksak Faroud threw off his hood and patted his assassin's ragged uniform about his torso. 'We fooled him, but we have still to test them on the sentries guarding Fantoma.'

'Have faith, Aksak!' said Quaint. 'This plan'll work.'

'It had better – it is the only one we have got,' reminded Faroud. He motioned to the grouped Scarabs, as everyone slowly roused themselves awake. 'Come, brothers, we must ready ourselves for the battle that lies ahead.'

CHAPTER LIII

The Unwelcome Visitors

SINCE HER ARRIVAL at the Hades Consortium's lair, Madame Destine had been in solitary confinement. That situation was about to be remedied, yet the company would not be pleasant.

She lifted her head to greet the newcomers, noticing the stooped old man first. Sir George Dray dragged his hunched form into the room, huffing and puffing with each expense of energy, with Lady Jocasta following at his heels.

'Madame Destine, isn't it,' Sir George said rather than asked. 'It's a pleasure to meet you and I mean that sincerely. I hope you don't mind the interruption, but I want to ask you a question about a mutual friend, if you don't mind.'

'You may ask me as many questions as you wish, monsieur, but that does not mean I will choose to answer them,' Destine replied defiantly.

'That's hardly polite behaviour towards your host,' Dray grinned.

'What makes you think that I would relish consorting with a vile monster like you?' Destine replied.

'But we've not even been formally introduced yet!' said Dray, with a laugh.

'I know who you are, monsieur . . . I know *what* you are,' said Destine.

'And I know you, my dear lady,' Sir George said, teasing his cracked lips with his tongue. 'And I would have thought that someone like *you* would be used to consorting with vile monsters . . . after all, you gave birth to one.' The old man watched the effect his words had upon Destine with keen interest. 'It was a real shame what happened to Antoine in London. You have my sympathies.'

'You may keep them!' Destine said. 'I have long since given up shedding tears for him – he chose his life, and he deserved his death. He was nothing but a cold-blooded murderer.'

'True . . . but one of the most gifted cold-blooded murderers I've ever met,' said Dray, flashing a glimpse of his yellowed teeth. 'No remorse, no conscience, and no limits to the lengths he would go to get the job done. The Hades Consortium can't take all the credit, of course. All we did was encourage his skills along a little. But your son is not why I am here, Madame. Like I said, I have a question about a mutual friend . . . the man responsible for your son's death . . . Cornelius Quaint.'

'My son was responsible for his *own* death!' replied Destine forthrightly.

Dray cackled. 'So you approved of Cornelius's actions, did you? Interesting. That takes rare strength of character, Madame. I doubt that I'd be so generous if someone did that to *my* son!'

Lady Jocasta felt her blood chill.

It was almost as if the old man was speaking one thing, but meaning something else, and something directed only at her. She tried to mask her shattered nerves, praying he could not sense her fear.

'Cornelius acted with honour, as he always does, monsieur!' Destine said.

'Maybe so. We shall soon see if he holds *you* in as much regard,' said Dray, as he leaned on his walking cane and pulled himself unsteadily to his feet. 'Our sentries tell us that Cornelius is camped on the outskirts of this very base. He is no doubt coming for you, but when he gets here he will have a very nasty surprise waiting for him.'

Destine looked up. 'Which is?'

Sir George Dray smiled a tight, crooked smile. 'Me.'

CHAPTER LIV

𝕿𝖍𝖊 𝕬𝖉𝖛𝖆𝖓𝖈𝖊 𝕲𝖚𝖆𝖗𝖉

CORNELIUS QUAINT AND Aksak Faroud held centre stage in front of the group of Clan Scarabs (plus Godfrey Joyce) gathered around the ashes of the campfire.

'Right then, does everyone know their part?' Quaint asked. 'Faroud and I will be disguised as Consortium guards at the rear. Joyce is the vanguard, and Kulfar and Nehmet here will be masquerading as his prisoners – namely Faroud and myself respectively. Once we get close, the Consortium guards will be watching us like hawks so you'll have to keep your nerve – not to mention your wits.' He clasped his hands behind his back and looked out across the Scarabs' apprehensive faces. 'The rest of you are to be our second wave. After we enter the sanctorum, Faroud and I will be causing a commotion and drawing a lot of attention to ourselves. The Consortium will be running around like headless chickens. Wait for the signal before you join the fray. You'll know it when you see it. It will be up to you to back us up. We may be outnumbered and outgunned – but they won't be expecting us to bring the fight to them. Once we get a foot in the door, we'll bottleneck them within the confines of the tunnels, but whatever we do, we can't let them use numbers against us.' Quaint smiled effusively. 'Now, we've assembled an array of weaponry that you lot thoughtfully managed to procure from Bara Mephista before you left. I suggest everyone fills their pockets. Any questions? No? In that case . . . good luck to us all.'

Just outside the city of Fantoma, the band split into two groups, with the conjuror's advance guard heading towards the ruins of the ancient city, whilst their backup team moved into position in the shadows of the imposing Mount Zahi. Cornelius Quaint rode steadily at Faroud's side whilst Kulfar and Nehmet rode ahead of them. Godfrey Joyce led the pack from the front in his horse-drawn cart. Faroud looked at Quaint as they cantered towards the high walls of Fantoma. Although the conjuror's hood obscured his features, the Scarab leader could see the look of disquiet upon his comrade's rough, lined face.

'Joyce reeks of suspicion. We were wise to suspect a trap,' Faroud hissed.

'Suspecting a trap is one thing . . . *expecting* one is something else,' Quaint replied.

'I take it you have a backup plan?' asked Faroud.

Quaint grinned unabashedly. 'Aksak, if there is one thing you should know about me by now, it's that I *always* have a backup plan.'

The ancient site at Fantoma was just one of the glittering gems within Egypt's crown. Construction had begun as far back as the sixteenth century BC and, as a consequence, the ravages of both time and the weather had left their scars. Even so, just one look at the deserted city's many towering columns and walls – each one engraved with grand inscriptions by the phantoms of the past – was all it took to raise a lump in the back of Cornelius Quaint's throat.

In his lifetime, he had visited many ancient cities and places of worship in the Orient, South America and India, but none had more of a vibrant connection with the ghosts of the past than Fantoma. Huge multistorey buildings, crumbling and fading more by the day, nestled next to ornate obelisks and columns of white stone that pricked the azure sky. A bleached white shroud of dust covered every building and every monument, as the centuries of harsh Egyptian weather eroded former works of art and colourful decorations. Now everything looked the same, as though a master artist had created the landscape but with just one colour to his palette. Skilfully detailed carvings, scriptures scored into stone, venerated deities etched into the rocks – proof that not all of Egypt's treasures were to be found buried under the sand.

The small band traversed down a slender corridor between two huge edifices, no wider than ten yards, with high sandstone walls on either side. Godfrey Joyce looked over his shoulder, held up his hand, and pulled his cart to a stop. As Quaint and Faroud trotted towards him, he spoke:

'This is the main entrance, next to this temple, chaps. The passageway descends underground from here, and grows very slender on the way so I doubt the horses will make it.'

On foot through the high-walled passage, they entered a large building decorated with an array of mythical-looking beasts around its parapets. At its base at ground level, former artistic glories were only visible as etched scoring and flaky pockmarked artwork. Quaint wondered how magnificent the city must have been in its prime, but he could not allow Fantoma's grandeur to blind him to the dangers that lurked beneath the sand.

They found themselves heading down a steep incline, into a darkened tunnel carved from the rocks beneath the foundations of the building above. This dim place was bereft of both light and air, and something sent a chill up Quaint's spine. In such a narrow place, were they to get trapped down there, they might never get out. Quaint had, indeed, filled his pockets with tools from the Scarabs' armoury, and out of Joyce's sight, he deposited several explosive sticks upon the ground where a breach in the rocks led to the outside.

He mouthed the words 'Backup plan' to the Scarab leader, who greeted the sight with a roll of his dark-rimmed eyes.

The small band ventured through the maze-like tunnels in silence. Eventually, at the end of one dimly lit by a succession of mounted torches on the walls, they reached the pair of carved stone doors that signalled entrance to the Hades Consortium's sanctorum.

'We're here,' said Godfrey Joyce.

Quaint readjusted the hood of his commandeered uniform.

'This is it,' he whispered to his band of men. 'Play your parts . . . and wait until we're in deep before revealing yourselves.' Then he took a step towards Joyce. 'Just remember I'm right behind you. If you so much as think about double-crossing us, you'll feel my sword between your shoulder blades quicker than you can blink.'

'You are quite the motivator, Mr Quaint,' sneered Joyce.

'I hear that a lot,' muttered Quaint.

Joyce pushed hard against the doors with both hands, and their hinges complained noisily against each other, announcing the group's arrival better than a doorbell. Joyce stood pensively in the doorway, expecting the guards at the entrance to announce themselves. To his apparent surprise, the other side of the vast stone doors was completely deserted.

Quaint stepped forward gingerly, listening for any signs of habitation. There was nothing. No sound at all.

'Where is everyone?' he asked his comrades in arms.

Faroud shrugged. 'I do not know . . . but we should make the best of our luck!'

The group were just about to move into the main cavernous lair, when their ears heard a trembling sound. It was difficult to pinpoint its exact location; it seemed to be echoing from every direction at once. Quaint's mind tried to evaluate the noise.

It was footfalls, and lots of them.

'I think our luck just ran out,' he said grimly.

CHAPTER LV

The Wedge

LINES OF DARK red robed Hades Consortium troops marched towards them from the rear, brandishing long-poled spears in their hands, swords at their backs or pistols at their belts.

Their retreat was blocked.

'What do we do, Aksak?' asked Nehmet of Faroud.

'We stand our ground, my brother Scarab!' Faroud bellowed, pulling the sword from his scabbard. 'Stand shoulder to shoulder. This brigade will not halt our progression!'

'That is good to know,' said Kulfar, 'but what about that one?'

On the other side of the vast stone doors, another troop of Hades Consortium guards appeared, blocking any advancement forwards. With the enclosed tunnels penning them in at each side there was nowhere to run. They were wedged between the two brigades.

'It did not take them very long to mobilise,' said Faroud to Quaint.

'Almost as if they knew we were coming, eh?' said Quaint to Faroud.

Gone was their element of surprise, and if they wanted to

salvage anything even remotely resembling the upper hand, they needed to act fast. The soldiers numbered over twenty in each platoon – so they were outnumbered at least eight to one. The guards were all garbed alike, wearing long, dark red robes from their hooded heads to their feet. Whereas the inner stratum functioned as the brains behind the Consortium's campaigns, they were not without a reliance on hands and eyes to perform their menial tasks, and should any interlopers stumble across one of their hideaways, it paid to have some lethal measures on hand to deal with the situation.

Back to back with Quaint, Faroud called over his shoulder, 'What shall we do?'

'There's only one course of action open to us if we want to live,' replied Quaint.

'You mean surrender? Never! A Clan Scarab never surrenders!'

Quaint spied the array of spears, knives, swords and guns trained at them.

'Might I recommend a rethink of that policy?'

Faroud grimaced, clenching his jaw tight. Quaint was right, infuriatingly so.

'Stand down,' he said to his men. Kulfar and Nehmet exchanged quizzical expressions, first with each other and then with Faroud. 'That is an order!'

The two Scarabs reluctantly complied and, eventually, Quaint's band was relieved of all their weaponry. It was at that moment that Godfrey Joyce showed his colours.

He raised his hand, like a schoolchild begging his teacher's attention.

'Um . . . excuse me!' he called, bobbing above the heads of the mass of guards. He took a step to the side in an attempt to distance himself from Quaint's group. 'I'm not with these people. My name is Godfrey Joyce. I'm one of you! Check with your superiors if you don't believe me. I work for Baron Remus!' One of the Consortium troops stepped forward and Joyce took him to be the man in charge. 'This is all some dreadful misunderstanding! If you would be so kind as to run along and tell the Baron of my arrival, we can sort this all out nice and peacefully, hmm?'

The head guard pulled back his dark red hood. Tattoos swirled from the sides of his face, across his cheeks and up to his eyes where the patterns merged in a pit of black ink. His eyeballs were buried somewhere within the darkness. From the grim look of distemper on his face, this man was not one to suffer fools gladly. He took another step nearer to Joyce, looking all around his face in uneasy close-up detail, and then took a brief sniff of the man.

'What is he doing?' asked Quaint, from the corner of his mouth.

'He looks to be . . . *smelling* him,' replied Faroud.

Quaint frowned. 'What the hell is he, a Labrador?'

Just then, the head guard clapped his hands three times. At this cue, his men grabbed Joyce roughly by the arms and steered him back into Quaint's pack.

'Didn't you hear what I just said? I'm not with *them*, I'm on *your* side!' he cried, as he was led roughly to stand next to Quaint and Faroud. 'This is intolerable. Do you know who I am?'

The head guard cuffed Joyce roughly across the face.

'I'd take that as a yes,' quipped Quaint.

Faroud exhaled, pondering their predicament. He was a leader of men, and not such a bad strategist himself if he was being honest, but this situation was impossible to escape from. With over twenty men at the front and more than twenty at their rear, the odds were definitely against them. It was lucky for Faroud that he was partnered with Cornelius Quaint – a man that paid no heed to the odds.

'Cover your ears,' said the conjuror.

'Cover my ears?' asked Faroud, with a glower. 'Why?'

'Because there's going to be a loud bang,' replied Quaint.

He broke free from his guards' grasp, and before anyone had a clue what he was doing – let alone tried to stop him from doing it – he lunged for one of the wall-mounted torches. He tore it from its housing on the wall and threw it down onto the ground directly behind him. With a cloud of black smoke, the torch sparked into a furious wall of fire six feet high.

All hell broke loose as the Consortium guards' tongueless mouths screamed silent cries of alarm. They pressed themselves against the tunnel's walls to avoid the ensuing inferno, watching mystified as the trail seemed to spring to life and sped off down the tunnel and into the distance.

'What now?' Faroud yelled.

'Now?' Quaint pulled out his timepiece and consulted it carefully. 'We duck.'

The explosion that followed took everyone by surprise – especially the large group of Consortium guards that were crowded into the tight space behind Quaint. The force ripped through the brigade and the guards were thrown in all directions, crushed against the walls, slammed up into the ceiling. A large, violent crack formed itself in the tunnel roof and clouds of choking dust rained down.

Using the confusion to his advantage, Quaint grabbed hold of Faroud's robes and wrenched him through the ensuing curtain of smoke, with the Aksak fumbling blindly for Kulfar and Nehmet. They stumbled forward, barging straight into Godfrey Joyce, who was standing dumbstruck watching the events unfold. The men tumbled into each other through the huge stone doors and into the main audience chamber. Once through, Quaint looked around and saw a huge wooden beam by the doors.

'Help me!' he yelled, pushing the doors closed, containing the smoke-filled tunnel on the other side. Kulfar and Nehmet lifted the beam and fitted it in place, barring the doors.

With the entire brigade of guards trapped on the other side, Quaint afforded himself a brief respite, and he slid his bulk down the wall onto his backside, coughing violently. Faroud and the rest were also panting heavily as they tried to empty their lungs of the acrid smoke. Their faces were covered in a thick layer of red, chalky dust. Through the heavy stone doors they heard the stomach-churning screams of men as the fire consumed them. With nowhere to run, they were helpless. If the fire did not speed their deaths, the acrid, choking smoke that swamped the tunnel surely would.

'What in Ra's name was that?' demanded Faroud, wiping dust from his eyes.

'Backup plan,' said Quaint, coughing a sticky brown mess into the palm of his hand. 'I thought there was a risk of the tunnel being used against us . . . so I left a trail of gunpowder as we entered . . . leading right back to a stack of explosive sticks that I'd stashed by the main entrance.'

'Quaint, you lunatic!' squawked Godfrey Joyce, joining the fray. 'You almost brought the whole bloody city down on our heads!'

'Almost . . . but then I would've missed the pleasure of doing this.' Quaint punched Joyce hard in the face and a trickle of dust-clad blood seeped from the man's nose.

Aksak Faroud glared at Quaint. 'Do you feel better now?'

'Much,' grinned Quaint, blowing on his sore knuckles.

'But he has a point,' said Faroud. 'You are a lunatic. By now the whole base will know we are here.'

'Quite so,' agreed Quaint. 'But at least we're free to start some *serious* trouble.'

An icy expression graced Aksak Faroud's face and he grasped at Quaint's robes.

'I would not exactly class our situation as "free", my friend.'

Quaint looked in the direction of Faroud's fixated eyes, and what he saw was not to his liking.

Standing upon a large, stone plinth behind them, with a fresh brigade of at least fifty armed Consortium troops surrounding her, was Lady Jocasta.

'I do hate it when guests turn up uninvited,' she said.

CHAPTER LVI

The Rekindled Flame

FEELING THE SHOCKWAVE of the explosion at the opposite end of the sanctorum, Madame Destine stood swiftly from her bed and then smiled.

'Cornelius,' she said.

Since Sir George had left her quarters, she had spent her time contemplating her renewed gifts of clairvoyance, wondering what she was going to do now that all the pieces of herself were back together. Everything was so much clearer – none more so than her present predicament. How was she supposed to ensure that her task was complete if she were imprisoned?

A mute Hades Consortium guard stood motionless at the doorway, although every now and again he would glare at her as if daring her to try to escape. She was a prisoner, unable to affect the winds that blew in her direction. She prayed that Cornelius would come for her, but the man was obviously busy causing his particular brand of trouble at that moment. He would sort everything out and restore order to the world. Cornelius always said that she could notice a single ray of sunshine in a rainstorm. Nevertheless, she looked over at the imposing figure of her guard, clad in his dark red robes, and surveyed her options:

she could sit and wait for Cornelius to arrive, or she could grasp Fate with both hands and bend it to her will.

If only I could bend the will of my silent guard, she thought.

And then, as the words graced her mind, they triggered something of interest. She knew that she possessed a fine-tuned perception of the emotions of others, a one-way link that gave her access to their private thoughts and feelings . . . but what if that link was not solely one-way? Aloysius Bedford had said that she had no idea what she was capable of. If she were not to try, how would she know her limits?

At her age, that thought intrigued her.

She glanced across the room at the guard. Wave after wave of her prying sensitivity drifted out from her mind. Her guard's state of mind was an open book to her . . . and she decided to thumb through the pages.

Madame Destine could sense his hatred towards her, but it was misplaced. The guard had no idea just *why* he hated her – just that he did. His hatred had little foundation, he hated her merely because it was expected of him – or ordered of him. That worked in Destine's favour. Hatred with no emotional grounding can be easily shaken. All she needed to do was tap into it and replace it with an emotion a little more hospitable . . .

Destine began to slowly push his thoughts to one side, diluting every speck of hatred within his heart, purifying him, instilling a sense of peace within his mind. It took mere moments and, when she had finished, the guard was visibly changed. He tottered slightly on his feet, more asleep than awake, drifting between the two. As Destine approached him, the guard did not even flinch.

'That is right,' Destine said softly. 'Just relax . . . I mean you no harm.'

Her gentle, melodic accent lifted and fell poetically, captivating the young guard's senses. He faltered a little, as if stirring from a deep sleep, but as he heard Destine's songlike voice continue to massage his mind, he relaxed totally.

'I just want to borrow these,' she said, reaching for a large ring of keys affixed to the guard's belt. 'And I wonder, would you be able to escort me from this dreadful place? You see, I have a friend that has just arrived and I would love to meet him. You would? Oh, what a dear boy you are.'

CHAPTER LVII

The Scales Unbalanced

'WELL, GODFREY?' LADY Jocasta put her bejewelled hands to her hips and glared into Joyce's eyes. 'I am *waiting* for an explanation. Perhaps you wouldn't mind telling me why you have led these men here?'

Joyce's lower lip wobbled. 'Well, I . . . I thought—'

'Did you? Did you really?' snapped Jocasta. 'You mean to tell me that you actually put *thought* into betraying us?'

'N-no, my Lady, no! I did not betray you,' swore Joyce, the only one of the group not restrained. 'This man here plots against you! He destroyed the tunnels and killed your men! He . . . he knows of your plan to poison the Nile! He said he would stop at nothing to put an end to it. I . . . I intended to deliver him here to you . . . I was only pretending to be on their side to gain their trust! It was all a part of my plan.'

'More slithering, Joyce?' asked Quaint, bound in ropes by the swarm of guards surrounding Faroud, Kulfar, Nehmet and him.

'You must be Cornelius Quaint,' Lady Jocasta said with a smile. 'Do you not know it is impolite to interrupt a lady?'

'Oh? Are there any about?' smiled Quaint in reply.

Lady Jocasta fumed. 'Guard, teach this man some manners.' The guard at Quaint's side smashed his iron gauntlet across the conjuror's face. 'So which of these men is the Aksak from Bara Mephista?' Jocasta asked.

Joyce thrust out his finger and pointed at Faroud. 'That one!'

'You snivelling rat! You set us up!' Faroud screamed, spitting a glob of saliva in Joyce's direction. One of the guards chopped his hand upon the back of the Aksak's neck and he flopped limply in his captor's grip.

'Lady Jocasta, the longer we wait, the more of a threat these men are,' Godfrey Joyce yelled. 'They have more friends positioned in the eastern hills! We must send a detachment of our troops to counter them immediately!'

'How dare you bark orders at me!' Lady Jocasta's voice rose in volume, echoing off the dry walls of the vast cavern like an operatic singer delivering the greatest performance of her career. She nodded to two guards at her side. 'This man has ceased to be a viable asset to the Hades Consortium. His employment is to be terminated immediately.'

'*Terminated?*' questioned Joyce. 'B-but please, my Lady . . . you're not . . . you're not going to k-kill me . . . are you?'

Lady Jocasta feigned surprise. 'Kill you, Mr Joyce? No, of course not, whatever gave you that idea?' she said, watching the colour flush back into Joyce's face. 'That would be far too compassionate. No, Mr Joyce . . . I am going to hurt you until you beg with me to kill you . . . and then *watch* it happen.'

The colour withdrew once again from Joyce's face. 'But . . . I brought Quaint here . . . to *you* . . . so that our forces could detain him, so he could no longer be a threat!'

Lady Jocasta said, 'And we thank you for that. You have at least done one thing of value . . . that is why you are not already dead.' She turned her back on him and walked to the top of the stone stairs. 'You have your orders, guards. Disarm him.'

Joyce wept openly. 'But, Lady Jocasta . . . I don't have any weapons!'

Jocasta smiled. 'Figure of speech.'

From the contingent of dark red-clad Consortium guards stepped two wraith-like men. Flanking Joyce, they grabbed each of his arms and spread them wide like a scarecrow. Joyce's head twisted back and forth, pointlessly trying to break free. The guards pulled him from both sides as if trying to wrench his arms from their sockets.

Sweat ran profusely from Joyce's forehead.

Struggling against the guards restraining him, Aksak Faroud fought to catch the conjuror's attention. 'Do you not think we should—'

'Intervene? Certainly not!' scoffed Quaint. 'Joyce deserves everything he gets.'

'How can you be so callous?'

'Not callous . . . *calculating*. I just know how to turn a situation to my advantage when I've got dozens of swords pointed at me,' said Quaint.

'You will forgive me if I seem pessimistic,' said Faroud. 'But at least then I will not be disappointed.'

'Look, if it makes you feel better, I doubt there's anything that we could say that would make any difference anyway. Once that cow is done with Joyce, we're up next in the queue to die. So best we just sit tight and hope for a miracle, eh?'

'Oh . . . as long as there is nothing to worry about,' said Faroud despondently.

'Don't blame me,' said Quaint. 'You wanted the pessimistic version.'

'I think I preferred the optimistic one.'

'That's the spirit!' cheered Quaint.

Lady Jocasta smiled seductively in Quaint's direction and pointed her bejewelled finger at him. 'Do not think that you have escaped my wrath, Mr Quaint. Oh, yes! I know exactly who you are! I have organised something *special* for your arrival.'

'You shouldn't have gone to any trouble on my account,' said Quaint.

'Oh, it will be no trouble . . . in fact, it will be my pleasure,' Lady Jocasta purred.

She signalled two more guards, who detached themselves from the mass of robed figures and took position in front of Joyce. He was a quivering mess of jellified flesh and bone. The two guards facing him unsheathed their swords from their scabbards, and by the sudden hush that descended upon the cavern, it quickly became evident what was about to occur. With a nod of Lady Jocasta's head, both the guards sliced their raised swords through the air in a synchronised arc and Joyce's arms were severed at the elbow, falling to the ground with a dull, wet thud. His gut-wrenching howl echoed around the cavern, filling every crack and crease in the rocks.

'God . . . no,' he mumbled through saliva-coated lips.

'God . . . *yes*!' screeched Lady Jocasta, her feral eyes wide with delight.

With her long white gown trailing behind her like a phantom, she walked down the steps and stood over him, dominating his blurred vision. She wanted to watch him die, she wanted to be the last thing he ever saw. She stared down at his severed arms, the fingers still grasping the air manically.

'Pick them up!' she whispered, pushing her heel into his chest until he toppled over onto his back, his stumps still seeping blood. 'Your arms, Mr Joyce . . . I want you to pick them up.'

'You twisted bitch, can't you see he's had enough?' shouted Quaint, his outburst surprising all in the cavernous audience chamber – including himself.

Lady Jocasta gave Joyce's ribs a dig with her toe. 'You wait your turn!'

'He's half dead anyway!' yelled Quaint. 'Leave him be!'

'Cornelius is right, lass,' said a gruff Scottish voice from the shadows. An immediate silence fell as all eyes looked to Sir George Dray, standing at the far entrance to the chamber. 'You've made your point.'

Quaint scowled through the darkness of the cavern at the owner of the strangely familiar voice. Then, as the old man stepped into the flickering torchlight, Quaint was struck by a blistering shock of recognition. The man's craggy face had grown considerably craggier since Quaint had seen it last, but there was no doubt as to its owner's identity.

'*You?*' Quaint gasped.

'I'm flattered you remember me, Cornelius . . . it's been a long time,' said Dray, as he forced a smile from his rigid mouth.

'Not long enough.'

'Careful, lad . . . you'll hurt my feelings.'

'I hope so.'

'Still practising a sense of humour I see,' muttered Dray.

'What are you doing here, George?' Quaint asked.

'I could ask you the same question, Cornelius . . . but then I already know the answer,' Dray said, manoeuvring his hunched form down the stone steps on his walking cane. 'I see by the look on your face that you weren't expecting me . . . but I've been expecting *you*. Oh, yes.'

'Cornelius, I am confused. Who is this man?' Faroud asked.

'You don't want to know,' replied Quaint bleakly.

Aksak Faroud looked at the old man, and then looked back at the cold abyss within Quaint's black eyes. 'So did things just get better . . . or worse?'

Quaint smiled, but not the smile of a man amused – the smile of a man who knew once again that Fate was toying with him. 'That depends on whether you want the optimistic version or the pessimistic one.'

'Surprise me,' said Faroud.

'If we might have ever had the slightest hope in hell of getting out of this mess with our lives then it just went up in smoke,' Cornelius Quaint replied.

'I see.' Faroud gulped. 'And what is the optimistic version?'

Quaint grinned. 'That *was* the optimistic version.'

CHAPTER LVIII

The Face of the Enemy

SIR GEORGE DRAY walked past the still-convulsing form of Godfrey Joyce, towards the small band of men at the far end of the audience chamber. He ignored Faroud and his two Scarabs – there was but one target for his attention.

'So here we are, eh?' he said. 'Once again we find ourselves on opposite sides, Cornelius . . . and once again the odds are stacked against you. I should have put a bullet in your head back in Peru and saved myself a lot of trouble.'

'Why are you here, George?' asked Quaint. There was a noticeable edge to the conjuror's voice, as if all he wanted to do was rip the old man apart one limb at a time. Had the guards not restrained him, he probably would have given it some serious consideration.

'I just wanted to say hello to an old friend, what's wrong with that?' Dray mocked.

'You don't *have* any friends, George – old or otherwise – you stabbed them all in the back years ago,' said Quaint. 'So you're the brains behind this plot, are you? I should have known. Poisoning the Nile is a bit dramatic for you, isn't it?'

Dray gave a grin that scarred his face. 'Actually, lad, this one's not my doing. Lady Jocasta here has a wonderful imagination when it comes to death . . . just take one look at that bleeding sack of guts over there.' He pointed at Joyce, twitching on the ground in a pool of blood. 'She will be greatly rewarded by the Hades Consortium.'

'How very like you, George. You're still surrounding yourself with pretty things lacking in intelligence, I see,' Quaint said dryly, his eyes nodding towards Lady Jocasta.

Dray laughed. 'And you are still surrounding yourself with inferiors to make yourself look better, I see.'

'I am no inferior, *old man*, I am Aksak of the Clan Scarabs!' snapped Faroud, struggling against his captors. 'And who are you, may I ask?'

'This is Sir George Dray, Scarab dog!' snarled Lady Jocasta, striding towards Faroud. She gripped his dark face between her fingernails and squeezed tight, drawing blood from his cheeks. 'And you will bow down before him!'

'I would sooner die,' snarled Faroud.

Sir George Dray blinked slowly, a granite expression on his face. 'I would be glad to accommodate that request, lad . . . as Cornelius knows only too well . . . so if you've finished with your interruptions, maybe I can finish my little chat with your friend, hmm? So you know all about Jocasta's wee project then, Cornelius? Renard told you, did he? With his dying breath and all that? And, of course, righteous Cornelius Quaint couldn't let such a terrible catastrophe occur, and so you came halfway around the world to try to stop us?'

'My social calendar was dry this month,' said Quaint. 'This plot is nothing short of mass murder, George. Surely you must know that? This is on a larger scale than anything the Consortium has attempted before. Killing so many people, it's inhuman! You're an evil old bastard, true – but this isn't your usual fun and games. I *know* you. You like to see the whites of your victims' eyes.' Quaint switched his verbal attack towards Lady Jocasta. 'Poison is the weapon of cowards. This plot is no better than a knife in Egypt's back!'

'How dare you?' Lady Jocasta stepped forward and slapped her hand across Quaint's cheek. 'It is far more civilised than *that*! Do you have any idea of the amount of planning necessary to engineer such slaughter? Can you possibly comprehend the complexity of it all? Of course not! You are an ant.' Lady Jocasta flicked her ponytail, preening herself, watching the spite in Quaint's eyes ignite. 'From what I hear about you, Mr Quaint, you like to muddy your hands in other people's business. You may have had luck in the past, but it has now run out.'

Quaint glared at Lady Jocasta. 'I don't know who you are, woman, but I wouldn't stick my neck out if I were you. You haven't won yet and I'm full of surprises.'

'Typical Englishman. All swagger and boast,' said Lady Jocasta. 'Is that not right, Sir George?'

'Oh, yes, dear. Quite so,' confirmed Dray. 'You're in for a bit of a shock, Cornelius, because you see, I knew you were coming. I led you here, for God's sake! So did you really think that I would just allow the schedule for our plot to continue, knowing the risk that you possess?'

'What's that supposed to mean?' asked Quaint.

'You put up a valiant effort getting this far, but really you never stood a chance,' said Sir George. 'I've just been waiting for you to catch up.'

Quaint shook his head. 'Your overconfidence will be your undoing, George.'

'Did I not tell you that he's an arrogant bastard, Jocasta?' Dray put on a sympathetic face, like a parent about to tell their child that Father Christmas doesn't exist. 'Cornelius, you really have no idea, do you? I hate to break it to you, son, but this battle was fought and won before you arrived, and unfortunately . . . you lost. Dear, oh, dear . . . how deluded you are,' he said, folding his tongue into his cheek. 'Stopping what's in motion is way beyond your grasp now . . . unless you are a better magician than I give you credit for. Jocasta, my dear, what is the latest status report for our plot? And you might want to pay attention to this, Cornelius.'

Lady Jocasta licked her lips. Watching Quaint's bluster deflate, her face could not express any more satisfaction if it tried. 'We had intended to implement the plan at midnight tomorrow, on New Year's Eve. However, due to your unwanted involvement, Mr Quaint, it was felt that the longer we waited, the greater the possibility of you upsetting things. You do, after all, come with a reputation for poking your nose in where it does not belong. So to that end, Elder Nastasi of the Clan Scarabs will begin facilitating the dispersal of the toxin *tonight* . . . in but a few hours, one day ahead of schedule.'

'*Tonight?*' Quaint cursed the word.

'Nastasi?' asked Faroud.

Sir George looked over at Lady Jocasta and waved her to continue.

'Nastasi is not the man he once was. He has seen his former glory slip through his fingers, and so when we offered him a chance to reclaim what was rightfully his, the old fool practically bit our hands off!' she said. 'The Hades Consortium has given Nastasi the necessary support to gain control of all the nine regions . . . in exchange for his conformity to my plan. Tonight, on the stroke of midnight, those Scarabs unified under his reign will deploy the poison into the River Nile.'

Sir George smiled thinly. 'And their fate once this deed is done, Jocasta?'

'Purged, Sir George, just like the contagion they are,' Lady Jocasta answered. A tiny, sadistic giggle escaped the corner of her mouth. 'Every . . . single . . . one of them!'

'You forced my hand, Cornelius,' said Dray. 'All you have done is cement Egypt's fate that much quicker. I've been waiting all week just to see that look on your face!'

'All week? How did you know I was in Egypt?' asked Quaint.

'Because I *organised* the whole thing – why else do you think you failed?' snorted Sir George, shaking his head as if it were glaringly obvious. 'When I heard that you were sniffing around London asking questions about our organisation, I arranged for one of my contacts to find himself in your company and give you some very specific information.' Dray let this knowledge permeate for a moment. 'Mr Ferris is a loathsome individual, to be sure . . . but give him a few quid and he's as loyal as a terrier.'

Quaint's eyes narrowed. '*Ferret?*'

'You followed my little trail of breadcrumbs so willingly. How else was I to make sure you came to Egypt? I knew that I couldn't prevent you from getting involved, so if you were going to come, I wanted it on my terms.' Dray grinned at the effect his words were having, and he turned the screw one more rotation. 'Since I knew that you were sailing on the *Silver Swan* it was simplicity itself to arrange for my man Nadir to join you onboard, the same gent that babysat our little consignment of poison. His attempts to kill you failed . . . clearly . . . so he engineered events so that dear old Madame would come to Mr Joyce's attention. I knew that you would go to the ends of the earth for her – it was your predictability that I was relying on, laddie . . . and you didn't let me down!'

'You toyed with me,' said Quaint, with not a tinge of surprise in his voice.

'And you were fantastic!' replied Dray, inching himself forward on his cane. 'I may look like a foolish old man, but we both know I am anything but.'

'That's true,' said Quaint. 'You are Satan himself clothed in the ragged old shell of a crippled body!'

Dray curled his lips. 'That's mildly insulting at best, Cornelius – you can do better than that.'

'You used me! You used Joyce . . . and you're using Nastasi too? Is that all people are to you? Currency to barter with?' yelled Quaint.

'Joyce's ambition brought about his fate, not me. He thought he was a big spider in the middle of his web, catching flies left, right and centre. But little did he know that he was just another fly . . . in a web much larger than he could possibly imagine. And look where it got him.'

'Ever the puppeteer . . . just like you were with Oliver, always in *control*, your word above everyone else's – even to your own flesh and blood! Your filthy Consortium was pulling *his* strings for years!'

'My son has nothing to do with this!' barked Dray. He caught the eyes of the head guard gripping Quaint's arms. 'Take him and his Aksak friend to Jailer Agnafar! Secure them . . . and do it properly or I'll have your head on my mantelpiece! Break them . . . make them bleed, but do not kill them . . . not just yet.'

Faroud's eyes flicked to Kulfar and Nehmet at his side. 'What about my men here? I am their Aksak and they are merely following my orders. They mean nothing to you!'

'That is very true,' said Dray. 'Guards, release the Aksak's men.'

'So you do have *some* dignity, after all,' said Faroud.

'You interrupted me, Aksak,' said Dray. 'I was going to say release them . . . of their lives.'

Faroud watched helplessly as the guards holding Kulfar and Nehmet removed their blades from their scabbards in unison and thrust them into the Scarabs' bodies. Once more, wailing screams echoed around the cavern – and then promptly ceased.

'Remove these two from my sight!' said Sir George to his guards.

'George, wait!' shouted Quaint as he was dragged away. 'Think about what you're doing. Think about Oliver! Would *he* have wanted you to go this far?'

Sir George watched Quaint and Faroud disappear from his sight into the belly of the Consortium's sanctum sanctorum. He turned his head slowly to Lady Jocasta.

'You see what I mean, lass? Like a lit torch in a haystack!'

'But an intriguing foe, nonetheless,' replied Lady Jocasta.

'Oh, he's intriguing all right,' Dray muttered, nodding his agreement. 'I wonder what he meant.'

'By what, sir?'

'His parting shot about my son. He said: "Would he have wanted you to go this far?"' replied Dray. 'Seems an odd choice of last words, don't you think?' He pondered this, tugging at his large earlobes thoughtfully. 'Before Mr Quaint is executed, I think that perhaps he and I should have one last chat.'

Lady Jocasta felt her nerves constrict inside her stomach. If Cornelius Quaint was implicated in the failure of her plot in London, she could not possibly allow him to speak to Sir George.

She watched the old man drag his racked body from the chamber. When she was certain he had left, and she could no longer hear his grunting groans, she slowly set off towards the detention block. Cornelius Quaint would be dead long before he had a chance to open his mouth.

CHAPTER LIX

The Beacon of Hope

MADAME DESTINE MADE her way along the carved stone corridors. She was barefoot and the many skirts of her long dress trailed snakelike behind her. The Hades Consortium guard had thought it perfectly reasonable to lead her directly to the holding cells, and had even unlocked the main gate for her before returning to his duties with a vague scratch of his head, as if enchanted by a spell. Entering through the main gate, she heard muffled voices close by. The corridor was populated with an array of cells – some large enough to hold many men, and some no bigger than a wardrobe. Every so often she would freeze as the voices rose in anguish, her nerves on a knife's edge. Finding Cornelius was Destine's primary objective, and her sensitivity to emotions gave her an advantage. All she had to do was close her eyes and focus on the soul in the most torment and her gifts would surely lead her right to him.

But in the Hades Consortium detention block, torment was a common emotion.

She heard a man cry out in pain.

Moving unerringly towards the sound, the closer that she got, the more obvious it was that someone was at the receiving end of a vicious beating. Her sensory gifts were working overtime trying to compensate for such raw emotion – fear, pain, anger, misery. They were everywhere within the jail, but none more so than in a cell less than ten feet away from her. With her curiosity driving her onwards, Destine slipped into the empty cell next door and pressed her ear against the wall.

'Scream for me, Scarab pig!' yelled a man's voice, followed by another man's forced exhalation. The victim wheezed, desperate to catch a breath. 'Jailer Mullah, this will take some time!' he called to his colleague in the adjoining cell.

'My one is not talking either, Jailer Veriz,' snarled the Consortium jailer. 'Come on, dog – plead for your miserable life . . . what is left of it! Lady Jocasta has ordered you to die quickly – and I am more than happy to accommodate!'

This other prisoner was struck. Destine heard the victim gasp for breath, before retching. She heard three whispered words, more than enough to recognise the speaker.

'*Go to hell*,' snarled Cornelius Quaint.

Destine rested her head against the cell wall and muttered a silent prayer. Now came the hard part . . . how was she to get him out of that place? Charming a guard was one thing – but charming a whole platoon of them? A faint, melodic whistle wafted down the corridor behind her. Someone was coming! She squashed herself against the wall behind the cell's iron door, hearing the jangle of keys and heavy footsteps. Moments later, a broad-shouldered guard strode down the hallway and into the cell next door to hers.

'Sir George has sent an urgent command!' said the booming voice of the head jailer. 'He wants the white-haired one to be taken to the audience chamber immediately! Hang on . . . what is this?' He stopped and Destine's heart missed a beat. 'Look at him! The man is half dead!'

'We . . . we were merely following Lady Jocasta's orders, Jailer Agnafar. She wishes this Englishman killed for his treachery to the Hades Consortium.'

'That order has since been countermanded by Sir George! You are lucky, Jailer Mullah. Had this man died, it would not have been long until you would have *joined* him!' snarled the burly Agnafar. 'Do what you will to the Scarab, but take the Englishman to the audience chamber right now, or these dogs will not be the only ones at the receiving end of a beating!'

'Yes, Jailer Agnafar.'

'Sorry, Jailer Agnafar.'

There was a sudden sound of jangling keys and unlocking locks.

Destine's heart sank into the pit of her stomach as she witnessed Cornelius's unmistakable shock of curly hair dragged past her hiding place by his guard. He was soon out of her sight, and out of her grasp.

'Right, you piece of camel dung, now it is just you and me,' yelled the voice of Jailer Veriz. 'You are the leader of those Scarabs, yes? Aksak Faroud, they call you? Well, Aksak . . . let us see if you are still as high and mighty once I have finished with you!'

The chains binding Faroud to the wall shook and rattled, followed by the sickening dull thud of knuckles against flesh. Destine winced as Faroud's pain jolted through her. If she was going to make a move she had better do it soon. The man in the next cell did not have long to live, and her instincts told her that if she and Cornelius were to escape the Hades Consortium's lair, they would need Aksak Faroud's help . . .

CHAPTER LX

The One Little Thing

SIR GEORGE DRAY looked up from the table as a badly beaten Cornelius Quaint entered the audience chamber flanked by two Hades Consortium guards. The old man flashed a brief smile to himself at the sight. His enemy was broken and he had waited so very long to witness it. Without a word, Quaint took a seat at the large marble table opposite Dray. He sat bolt upright, his elbows on the table. His eyes were defiant and his spirit was not nearly as beaten as his body.

'Guards, you can leave us,' the Scotsman said, causing the two guards behind Quaint to exchange glances, as if they had both heard incorrectly. 'Don't worry, I've got a tight grip on his leash. He'll not be a bother if he wishes to see his Madame Destine alive again. Send in the maid on your way out too. It's so damn dry down here, I need a bloody drink!'

Cornelius Quaint sat in silence, staring into Dray's hooded eyes. The man had grown old. Like an exhumed corpse, his thin flesh hung from his fragile bones limply, as if it were dripping from them. But quite aside from his physical degradation, Dray's soul had decayed into something that went beyond misguided,

beyond spiteful – beyond evil. The man was now the embodiment of festering contempt, lacking in any redeeming qualities
whatsoever.

An Egyptian servant girl arrived from the tunnels carrying a
metal tray containing a large carafe of dark, full-bodied Burgundy
and two glass goblets. Dray silently observed the girl as she placed
the goblets on the table and nervously filled them, her hands
shaking with obvious anxiety. A single droplet of red wine escaped
the neck and fell onto the marble tabletop. The servant gasped.

'Master, I—' she began.

Sir George waved her away with a decrepit hand. 'Think
nothing of it, lass. Accidents happen, eh? Now off with you, this
is grown-up talk.' He watched her swift exit with a twisted sense
of satisfaction. 'You see, Cornelius . . . *that* is something that
you'll never command,' he said, swallowing down a mouthful of
wine. 'Respect!'

'Is that what you think that was?' Quaint asked. 'That wasn't
respect, George – that was fear. Pure and simple *fear*.'

Sir George wriggled in his seat as if he was trying to get
comfortable on a pincushion. 'You should try your wine,' he
said.

'It's a little bitter all of a sudden,' Quaint replied. 'So why am
I here, George? Why did you not just let your guards finish me
off? They were just getting in their stride.'

'So I see,' Dray said, spying the many cuts, abrasions and bruises
littering Quaint's face. 'I just wanted to set eyes on you one last
time . . . to see if I can finally figure out what makes you tick. You
intrigue me, Cornelius. You always have. Why would you knowingly risk your life to interfere with the Hades Consortium's plans
yet again? Was the last time you and I tussled not enough of a
warning? When we first met, you were an arrogant little snot

sitting in such self-righteous judgement . . . if it hadn't been for my son standing up for you, you'd be dead.'

Quaint said, 'The last intelligent thing Oliver did.'

'You leave him out of this!' Dray yelled.

'You brought him up,' said Quaint. 'But you're wrong. I don't seek to judge you, George . . . a higher authority than I will do that.'

'Are you really so blind? Look around you . . . things have changed since the old days. The world has changed!' Sir George's eyes glazed over with an opaque, glassy sheen as his rage thundered forth from his mouth. 'No one needs *heroes* any more. They're a dying breed . . . the Hades Consortium has seen to that. You are finished, Cornelius, your job is done. Just like me, you're a man waiting to die.'

'Die? You?' Quaint laughed. 'Now that I'd like to see! The hourglass may be running low, but you're one of those types that have a nasty habit of surviving. Oliver was lucky that he never lived to see what a wraith you've become!'

Dray squinted, uncertain what he was hearing, as if the conjuror was speaking gibberish. 'What do you mean by that?'

'He was a *victim*, George!' Quaint snapped. 'His soul was poisoned the minute you indoctrinated him into this damned club of yours! His blood is on your hands, just like so many others.'

'His blood?' Dray replied in a whispering wheeze. 'What . . . are you saying?'

'Are you that detached from reality?' snapped Quaint, his physical body like a stone statue, his wrath peppering every syllable. 'George, don't tell me you don't even know!'

'Cornelius, you're not making sense,' said Dray. 'If this is supposed to be some sort of threat it is absurd.'

'Threat?' squawked Quaint. 'George, this is no threat! Has no one told you what *happened* in Crawditch?' He pushed his chair from the table, and it screamed an obscenity against the stone ground as he rose swiftly to his feet. 'Don't you know what happened to your son?' He searched Dray's face, trying to read the old man's expression but there were so many grooves, wrinkles and liver spots that it was hard ascertaining any sense of emotion whatsoever.

Dray looked at Quaint with equal curiosity. He knew Cornelius Quaint well, but he had never seen that look in his dark eyes before. It was not just anger. It was pity. The old Scot tempered his breath. 'You're enjoying this, aren't you? Getting your own back . . . playing me at my own game? Honestly, lad, I'm surprised that you'd stoop down to *my* level?'

'Damn it all, George!' yelled Quaint. 'No matter what you might be you need to know the truth . . . if only to awaken the embers of a conscience in you.' He strolled around the table, closer to the old man. Amazingly, his voice exhibited genuine grief, despite what a treacherous and evil creature he was facing. 'Your son is dead.'

Sir George looked at Quaint. He knew that parlour tricks were not part of Quaint's arsenal. In a duel such as this, his weapon of choice would be the truth, for it would wound far more deeply.

'Oliver is . . . dead?' he mumbled. 'But . . . he *can't* be!'

'It's true, George,' confirmed Quaint.

'What . . . what happened to my son?'

'*You* did,' Quaint replied.

Oliver Dray had been no saint, and responsible for many a crime of his own, most notably throwing his lot in with Quaint's enemy, Renard. Perhaps he deserved his fate. As Police Commissioner in the dockland district of Crawditch, Oliver had used his position to flout the very laws that he was sworn to protect.

'Cornelius, *tell* me what happened, I beg of you!' Dray pleaded.

Quaint whispered through a sharp intake of breath. '*You* beg of *me*?' The conjuror took pleasure from Dray's pain. He was looking weaker and paler by the second as he tried to consume the information. Quaint wanted to prolong it. He resented giving the old man any sense of peace. He did not deserve it. But as Quaint looked into the eyes of the monster for the briefest of moments, he did not see a devil, no demon clad in human flesh – he simply saw a father, in mourning for his son. 'George, are you that detached from your conscience that you thought your machinations would never come back and bite you in the arse?'

Dray clawed madly at the downy hair on top of his balding scalp, drawing blood. 'I know what life I gave Oliver! I'm not *that* detached from my conscience . . . but he was a grown man . . . he could have walked away at any time. But I don't understand . . . how did it happen? How did my boy die?'

Quaint submitted to his own conscience. 'I can tell you the how, where and when he died . . . but you already know the *why*, don't you? The how: Oliver was murdered by a psychotic killer named Tom Hawkspear on Renard's orders. The where: Crawditch in London, in the yard of his own station. The when: around the end of November.'

'And no one even *told* me? How is it that I don't know? How is that it takes you – you of all people – to tell me of this?'

Silence manifested itself between Dray and the conjuror. They sat in a kind of restrained, unspoken conversation, as if waiting for something to happen.

'November, you say. And Oliver died . . . as a result of a Consortium plot in London? But that can only mean—' Sir George Dray sat back in his chair, as if an elusive equation had plagued him all day and he had just deciphered the answer.

'Tell me this is all part of your plan, Cornelius, please. Tell me this is you!'

Quaint shook his head vehemently. 'Once I'd found out just how deeply Oliver had been pulled into the plot, I went to him. I wanted to *save* him. But I was too late . . . too late to keep him from the rot that had set in . . . too late to save him from himself. He wasn't just killed, George – he was mutilated horrifically. He was hung by his entrails from his station, his blood painting the pavement, naked apart from his regulation jacket. Was that the sort of death that you wanted for him?'

George Dray snatched up his walking cane and hoisted himself to his feet, his green eyes aflame. He was remarkably agile, imbued with the potent medicine of vengeance.

'Where are you off to?' asked Quaint.

'To vent some anger!' snapped back Dray. 'I know who was running the plot in London in November . . . the one who was supposed to be holding Renard's leash . . . and I aim to find out exactly what she's got to say about it!'

'George, wait!' yelled Quaint, snatching hold of the old man's arm.

'I'll have plenty of time for *waiting* later. Right now it's *answers* that I want . . . that and a little revenge,' Dray seethed, the veins in his head pulsating under his flesh. 'Crawditch was Jocasta's project and I want her head on a pissing plate for this! She has to be brought to bear!'

'You want to settle a score, that's fine! I don't blame you . . . but you can do a whole lot more than just make her pay her penance. You can right a wrong . . . reset the balance of Oliver's death.'

Dray turned, his eyes almost looking through the conjuror. When he spoke, his words were sharp enough to cut diamonds.

'If you're trying to appeal to my conscience, you're wasting your breath. I'm detached from it, remember? But my vengeance, now that's another thing entirely . . . that I am very much in concert with. I'm sick, Cornelius. Dying to be exact. I don't know how much time I have left, but I promise you this . . . before I draw my last breath that bitch is going to pay!'

'George, listen to me . . . all I want is an end to this!' snapped Quaint. 'It's within your power, you know it is! If you're dying, then go out with some dignity . . . go out with some humanity, for God's sake, man!'

Dray shuffled on the spot anxiously. 'You could've let me squirm, twisted the knife in my guts even more. Lesser men certainly would have . . . I would have.'

'I didn't do it for you, George,' said Quaint.

'Aye . . . I know that,' muttered the old man. 'Whatever it was that poisoned Oliver, you and he were still friends once. Let's say I could even the score between us – and only *this* score, mind . . . we still have others to occupy ourselves with – what would you ask of me?'

Cornelius Quaint did not ponder long. 'Well, there is this one little thing . . .'

CHAPTER LXI

The Embrace of Death

A THIN TRICKLE OF blood seeped from the corner of Aksak Faroud's swollen mouth as he spat in the face of the brawny Hades Consortium jailer in front of him. The jailer cackled remorselessly and punched him in the gut. Faroud's head snapped back, striking the base of his skull against the solid rock wall, and his eyes rolled listlessly in his head. Blood-soaked bile spewed from his mouth, dribbling down onto his bare chest.

'You Clan Scarabs are not like us. You are filth, picking off any carrion weaker than you. Thieving . . . intimidating . . . killing. But no more,' said Jailer Veriz, wiping his hand over his mouth as he savoured his attack. He leaned closer, his eyes scouring every inch of Faroud's face in detail, as if he despised every speck of his being. 'This is how the Hades Consortium treats animals like you.'

'You . . . think yourself so different . . . to me?' protested Faroud weakly, barely able to vocalise the words. 'We do what we do . . . to survive. What is *your* excuse?'

Faroud was silenced by a blow to the ribs and the breath was purged from his lungs. His Scarab brothers, Kulfar and Nehmet, had been the lucky ones. Death had claimed them quickly. Faroud knew that soon he would join them. He did not have the strength within him to fight any longer and falling into death's embrace seemed more appealing by the second. As Jailer Veriz clenched his fists once again, Faroud closed his eyes tight, knowing this was the end. There was no one to save him now.

Or so he believed.

Faroud heard a sudden noise . . . a dull clang of metal striking against something solid. He opened his eyes slowly.

Standing over the unconscious body of his jailer was an elderly woman clad in an elegant mud-splattered dress, with a pair of heavy iron manacles swaying in her hands. Faroud blinked hard to remove the delusion, but to his surprise, it did not dissipate.

'Who . . . are you?' asked Faroud dazedly.

'Escape first, introductions later,' replied Madame Destine. 'We have to find Cornelius!'

CHAPTER LXII

The Turning of the Tide

LADY JOCASTA ENTERED the audience chamber clutching a large, cylindrical roll of parchment under her arm. Sir George Dray sat alone at the chamber's table with an expectant look on his wrinkled face.

'Sir George, I have brought the map as you requested,' Lady Jocasta beamed. Not waiting for an invitation, she delicately placed the parchment upon the table and rolled it out, placing small brass weights at each corner, smoothing the creases. 'In but a few hours, Nastasi and his Scarabs will deposit the vials of poison in the positions marked. Egypt will soon be crippled, and by then . . . it will be far, far too late to turn the tide.' She looked to Dray for approval.

He offered Lady Jocasta a broad smile – in contrast, the cold glare in his green eyes told an altogether different story. Grasping his walking cane, he pulled himself to his feet. Without a word, he slid the four brass weights from each corner of the map. The parchment curled its edges up like a snail retreating into its shell. The Greek woman watched, pleasantly enthralled by Dray's actions, but her expression faded as she saw Cornelius Quaint step from the shadows.

Lady Jocasta looked at the two men's faces, matching their nondescript expressions with one of her own. Dray held the parchment in his skeletal fingers and silently passed it into Quaint's hands.

There was no word of thanks during the exchange.

That was not part of the deal.

'Sir George?' Lady Jocasta enquired, seeking an explanation.

Dray ignored her. 'Consider our debt repaid, Cornelius. Take it and leave this place whilst you still can. You've got ten minutes, no more.' Quaint opened his mouth to speak. 'Don't bother thanking me . . . just pray our paths never cross again. This changes nothing between us.'

With an accepting nod, Quaint retreated back into the shadows as if he had never been there at all.

Lady Jocasta scowled incredulously as her whole world ground to a sudden halt.

'That was the map!' she said, unable to hide the ire in her voice.

'I'm aware of that, lass,' replied Dray.

'Then . . . may I ask why you gave it to Quaint, sir?' Lady Jocasta asked.

Dray replied, 'As I said . . . I was repaying a debt.'

'To him? What debt can you possibly owe that it is worth risking *everything* I have worked to achieve?' demanded Lady Jocasta. She had either forgotten her position, or was in full acknowledgement of it, it was difficult to judge. Whatever the answer, her rage was unrestrained. 'Now he has the means to destroy us – surely you must know that?'

'I know only that I have made this game a wee bit more interesting.' Sir George grinned maliciously. 'It's midnight in only a few hours. Even if he knows where the poison is being deposited, he is still just one man . . . he cannot be in nine places at once. It would take a miracle to stop what's in motion.'

Lady Jocasta's bile did not recede. 'But why take that risk?'

'Because if any man alive can do it, it's him!' Dray shuffled his form around the table to stand behind her. 'You have disappointed me, Lady Jocasta . . . and you have brought shame upon Baron Remus's tutelage. This will serve as a reminder of what happens when every eventuality is not catered for.'

'You have risked the success of my plot merely to reprimand me?' Lady Jocasta lowered her head upon her chest and closed her eyes. 'So . . . failure is to be my punishment.'

'No, Lady Jocasta.' Dray took his walking cane within both hands and pulled swiftly at the handle – removing a slender sword from within. With surprising ferocity, he slashed the blade's keen edge into Lady Jocasta's exposed, olive neck. Her head was cleaved from her shoulders. It rolled around directionless on the table, spilling a fine fountain of rich red blood as it went, coming to rest in the centre of the table with her big brown dead eyes staring at the ceiling.

'That was your punishment,' said Sir George. He consulted his pocket watch.

Cornelius Quaint had eight minutes.

Not enough time for a miracle, but still plenty of time to die . . .

CHAPTER LXIII

The Fleeing Free

CORNELIUS QUAINT COULDN'T believe his eyes as he pelted his bulk through the dusty labyrinthine corridors towards the Hades Consortium's prison cells.

Madame Destine walked slowly towards him, supporting Faroud. The Scarab winced in excruciating pain with each step, clutching at his tender ribs with his free hand.

'You always did have an eye for a charity case, Madame,' Quaint said.

He ran as fast as he could towards her. Destine braced for impact as the locomotive of a man thundered into her. He lifted her into his arms and swung her around in circles like a carousel. They needed no words, these two. It was enough that they were in each other's arms once again.

Aksak Faroud cleared his throat, forcing apart their embrace.

'Do not think me unfeeling . . . but can this wait? It is not exactly safe here!'

'I can't argue with that,' said Quaint. 'We've got about five minutes to get as far away from this place as we can.' He slapped the map into his palm. '*This* is what we needed! The locations along the Nile where Nastasi's men are going to deploy the poison. *This* is what we need to put an end to this plot!'

'You did it!' gasped Faroud. 'But I do not understand . . . you were done for . . . only death waited for us . . . how did you get hold of such a thing?'

'I gave the Devil his due,' Quaint said.

'You are truly a marvel, Cornelius Quaint,' grinned Faroud.

'I'm more than that, my friend,' grinned Quaint right back at him. 'I'm bloody spectacular. So, how about you, Aksak? You look terrible.'

'I have had better days, it is true.'

'Can you walk unaided?'

'Slowly . . . but yes, I think so,' replied Faroud.

'Good, then let's be going. Madame, you're with me!' trumpeted Quaint, as he snatched Destine's wrist and ran off down the tunnel, with a limping Faroud trailing behind.

Quaint was his usual self – thundering on until his bones snapped, until his muscles tore. But Aksak Faroud was not at all himself. The beating that he had suffered at the hands of his jailer had dislodged something inside him – a fact confirmed when he coughed a sticky wet clot of blood into the palm of his hand.

Retracing his steps, Quaint led Faroud and Destine through the deserted main audience chamber. They froze as they saw the headless body of Lady Jocasta, still sat in the same position at the table.

'I warned her not to stick her neck out,' said Quaint.

They continued through the chamber towards the main doors. Destine screamed as she stumbled over another lifeless corpse –

that of Godfrey Joyce. His stumps still wept the last of his body's blood, and his two severed limbs lay on the floor like discarded cigar butts. He had suffered until his last breath if the contorted expression on his face was anything to go by.

Quaint grinned. 'You know, Faroud, you said we couldn't trust him, but deep down, I always knew Joyce was ar—'

'Hush, Cornelius!' reprimanded Destine, pushing her finger against his lips. 'One glib comment is sufficient amusement; we have more important matters at hand!'

Quaint nodded like an admonished pupil. 'Quite right, Madame, come on!'

With Faroud still bringing up the rear, they quickly reached the huge wooden beam that barred the two stone doors.

'Faroud, help me with this!' Quaint yelled.

Groaning madly as the pain scorched his guts, Faroud aided Quaint and they parted the massive doors that reached from floor to ceiling.

A thick curtain of dust dropped down before their eyes, and a gust of smoke evacuated the confined tunnel past them into the cavern. As it cleared, the sight before his eyes brought a lump to Cornelius Quaint's throat. Just inside the tunnel, littering the ground everywhere, were the charred and scorched corpses of the brigade of Consortium guards. Huge chunks of rock from the stone ceiling were strewn amongst (and crushing) the bodies. Quaint looked down at them, remembering how they had come to lose their lives and his part in it.

'You obviously came this way,' said Destine.

Quaint clamped his eyes shut. He prayed that she could not

see the shame carved onto his face, but it was ever so difficult to hide anything from a woman who could sense his emotions as easily as if she shared half his heart.

'Cornelius, listen!' snapped Faroud, breaking the conjuror's thoughts.

It was the unmistakable sound of many footsteps mobilising in their direction, emanating from deep within the adjoining tunnels.

Quaint checked his fob watch. 'George was true to his word for once. The guards are on the move, people. We don't have much time!'

They set off as fast as they could, stepping over corpses and rocks, following the scarred crack in the tunnel roof towards the exit.

However, as they rounded the final corner towards freedom, Quaint's heart sank – the way out was completely barred by fallen rocks.

'A trifle overzealous with the explosive perhaps?' said Faroud sarcastically, as he brushed his hands over the rocks that blocked the entire tunnel. 'Now what? We're trapped!'

Reinforcing his statement, the heavy footsteps grew louder. The guards were catching up. Quaint and company were facing a dead end – in more ways than one.

A grinding, scraping sound came from the other side of the rocks behind them. Cracks in the boulders appeared as they shifted position and thin seams of bright white light appeared like incandescent veins.

Sobek's unmistakable voice reverberated through the rocks: 'Put your backs into it, Scarabs! I want these rocks cleared!'

'Sobek?' Faroud's face lit up. 'At last – we are free! We are safe.'

'Don't count your chickens, Aksak,' said Quaint, cupping a hand to his ear.

Faroud heard the sounds of their pursuers growing ever louder too and wished that he had kept his mouth shut. 'Sobek! It is me, Aksak!' he shouted towards a thin crack in the rocks. 'Hurry, we do not have much time!'

Destine tugged on Quaint's robes. 'Who *are* these men?'

'The cavalry, Madame!' Quaint replied. 'And for once their timing is impeccable!'

At that moment, a contingent of Consortium guards burst onto the scene. Crammed into the confines of the catacombs, they halted twenty feet away from Quaint, Faroud and Destine, blocking the tunnel completely. Each one brandished a weapon, each face twisted into a malevolent sneer.

Quaint considered his situation and the outlook was bleak. Just then, the huge boulders came tumbling down from the barred exit and great spears of illumination breached into the tunnel, flooding everywhere in a blast of raw sunlight. Quaint and his band were lucky, their backs were turned to the rocks, but it was the brigade of soldiers, who had all been glaring with wide, enraged eyes, that bore the full brunt of the explosion of brightness.

They were blinded, but it would not last long.

Sobek's face peered through the gap in the rocks. Spotting Quaint and Faroud, he beamed a relieved smile at them as he thrust his huge, fat arm through the hole.

'Come!' he boomed.

Quaint knew they had seconds to act before the guards would regain their sight.

He looked at Destine. 'You first, Madame!'

As Quaint grabbed her corseted waist, Destine could tell that there was no room for discussion. She looked up with uncertain eyes as Sobek's hairy arms grabbed her wrists and lifted her up into the light.

Several of the Consortium guards' sight had returned and they began to advance.

Quaint and Faroud had precious seconds to act.

'You're next!' Quaint yelled, grasping the Aksak by his hand.

Faroud shook his head violently. 'No, Cornelius, leave me! I can go no further.' He coughed, spitting congealed blood into his hands, a dark, maroon red, almost black, dredged from the very depths of his stomach. He was bleeding internally, his lungs punctured by broken ribs. 'I am done for, my friend . . . a gift from my jailer.'

'Faroud, we're getting out of here right now!' Quaint yelled. '*Together!* Now hold on tight, I'm going to—'

'No!' snarled Faroud fiercely.

'But we can *make* it!' pleaded Quaint. 'It's right there! Just a stretch away!'

'Leave me, I say!' growled Faroud. 'Someone . . . has to watch your back.'

Quaint he knew he was right. Faroud was in no condition to go anywhere and the guards were inches away. The conjuror reached into the folds of his commandeered robes and pulled out a stick of explosive.

'I held one back . . . just in case,' he said, pushing it into Faroud's fingers. 'Consider it a parting gift.'

'Just what I always wanted,' Faroud grinned. 'Now go . . . whilst I still . . . have the strength to do any good.'

Quaint grasped Faroud firmly around the back of his neck and bent him towards him, touching the Scarab's forehead to his own. 'I'm sorry I got you into this mess.'

Faroud managed a weak grin. 'For an Aksak . . . there are no easy choices, remember? Tell Sobek to take care of Rakmun . . . and make sure that my men make Nastasi pay.'

With a firm nod, Faroud gripped the explosive in his shaking hands and bit the fuse off with his teeth. Once lit, the explosives would explode practically instantly. Quaint tore a torch from the wall and offered it to the Scarab.

'Aksak Faroud, I have been proud to call you my friend,' he said.

'As have I . . . Cornelius Quaint.'

With a last nod of respect, Quaint reached for Sobek's grasp.

Reaching solid ground, he fell to his knees as Destine rushed to support him.

'Clear the entrance!' he bellowed.

Sobek looked at the breach in the rocks. 'But, the Aksak . . .?'

'It's too late, Sobek. Everyone to cover!'

The band of Scarabs scattered in every direction as a great explosion rocked the land. The deafening roar filled the ears of thieves, conjuror and fortune-teller alike. Ancient obelisks that had stood in Fantoma for thousands of years shook and toppled, crashing into each other, in turn striking others, pummelling the buildings at their feet. Thick walls of dust rose into the air as columns of ancient stone crumbled like chalk, collapsing onto the entrance to the lair of the Hades Consortium.

In a moment, all was still.

A fitting monument, thought Quaint, as he looked at the devastation around him. The area was cloaked in a wall of impenetrable dust. Surely all inside the sanctum sanctorum would have perished. If there was any justice in the world, not even Hell would take their souls.

'I have been away from you too long, my sweet,' Destine said by the conjuror's side, brushing flecks of masonry from his curls like a doting mother. 'I'd forgotten how much mess you can make.'

'How are you?' the conjuror asked her.

'Exhausted, my sweet. You?'

'Absolutely worn out,' Quaint replied. 'Which is a shame.'

'A shame, Cornelius. How so?'

'Because this battle is only half won and getting out of there alive was the easy part!' Quaint snapped.

CHAPTER LXIV

𝔗𝔥𝔢 𝔏𝔞𝔰𝔱 𝔥𝔲𝔯𝔯𝔞𝔥

A SHORT TIME LATER, with Madame Destine and Sobek and his adopted pack of Clan Scarabs riding at his side, Cornelius Quaint pulled his horse to a stop. He dismounted and removed the parchment map from the satchel at his waist, spreading it out flat on the ground. Using rocks to keep the edges from curling, he traced his finger down the line of the Nile's path. The sun was already falling in the sky. Time was in short supply. Motioning for Sobek to join him, the two men became embroiled in a deep discussion, with much waving of hands, confident nodding and pointing towards the horizon.

Nearby, Madame Destine was growing impatient.

Now that their escape from the Hades Consortium base was behind them, her mind had free rein to wander. Her worry for Ahman had returned and increased, and a hungry pain crawled restlessly around her body. Seeing Quaint occupied with other concerns, she sat upon the sand in contemplation. The Scarabs were doing much the same and were scattered in tiny groups, all of them silent and mournful. Their leader was dead and each of them grieved in their own way. Destine glanced at their dark, weathered faces, wondering how Cornelius had found himself in their company. But that hardly seemed important now; it was a tale for the long journey home to England – one of many, if she knew him. Destine strained her ears to hear Quaint's discussion. She liked hearing him boss people around – the man had a natural talent for it.

'We have nine entry points detailed here, Sobek,' said Quaint to the bulky Scarab overshadowing the parchment map. 'These are where Nastasi's men will be depositing the poison. Now that he has complete control over all the nine clans, it'll be a simple feat for him to mobilise everyone into position, and now . . .' Quaint consulted his fob watch, '. . . we only have four hours to stop him!' He snapped his watch shut to reinforce the urgency. 'We'll need to split up, head our separate ways, and with any luck we'll reach the spots before Nastasi's men do any harm!'

'Some of these locations are a long way from here, Cornelius,' offered Sobek.

'Then we'd better pull our fingers out! Not one vial of poison can enter the Nile.' He gripped the large Scarab's shoulder tightly. 'Understand? Not a single one!'

Sobek nodded, and his dark eyes fell to the ground.

'Cornelius . . . at first, I thought the Aksak was wrong to aid you . . . to risk our clan's stability for an outlander . . . but I then discovered that it was me that was wrong. Now I understand what Faroud saw in you. I only wish that I knew where you get such faith, my friend . . . for with this task ahead of us, I am in dire need of some!'

Quaint smiled. 'Sobek, my friend, I have long been a believer that faith can be found wherever you seek it. If we are without faith in ourselves, what do we have left?'

A shadow fell on the two men and the map and they both looked up to see Madame Destine standing over them.

'Cornelius? A word, *s'il vous plaît*?'

'You want to do *what*?' snapped Quaint.

'He is my friend!' snapped Destine in reply.

'Just like Aloysius Bedford was a friend, you mean?' stormed Quaint. 'What you've just told me is unbelievable! Godfrey Joyce was right! About Aloysius's diary, about you being in Egypt twenty years ago mixed up in that nasty business in Umkaza – and I knew nothing about any of it!'

'Do not blame me, my sweet. Neither did I.'

'You know how I despise coincidence, Madame, but the fact that our journeys mirrored each other . . . it's fantastic!' Quaint exclaimed. 'We were both following the exact same path . . . but from different sides! It's just too ridiculously coincidental to be believed!'

'I happen to think that it is all very Quaint, my sweet,' said Destine. 'Now, you shall misdirect my intentions no longer. Ahman is my friend, as Aloysius was, and I owe him just as much. He needs me. When we were attacked he was seriously wounded, but he is not dead!'

'Oh, and how can you be so sure?'

'My gifts have foreseen that he lives.'

Quaint scowled. 'They're back?'

'The ghosts of the past opened my eyes, my sweet.'

'That's marvellous news, Madame. Hang on – did you just say "Ahman"?' asked Quaint, with a determined point of his finger. Destine nodded. 'Your friend . . . you say he was hurt near

Umkaza? A short little chap about so high?' Quaint held his hand halfway up his chest. 'Round face and tiny spectacles?'

'*Oui? Pourquoi . . .?*' asked Destine, a subtle smile on her lips.

'I know where he is!' exclaimed Quaint. 'We came across him lying in a ditch by the side of the road just yesterday!'

Destine's smile grew even wider, her blue eyes even brighter.

'You mean to say that *he* is your friend Ahman? So the woman that he was searching for . . . that was you?' asked Quaint. 'My word, Destine, the coincidences in this caper just keep stacking up!'

'I trust you are a believer now, my sweet,' said Destine.

Quaint rubbed his jaw. 'I didn't say *that*.'

'And so . . .? What of Ahman? Is he all right?'

'Well . . . he was injured quite severely. A deep wound to his shoulder. We sent him back to Bara Mephista for medical treatment in the care of a woman from our crew. She promised to make sure his wound was tended to.'

Destine grabbed at his shirt. '*Oui? Est-ce que c'est vrai?*'

'Madame, I'm sure that he's been well cared for.'

'I must go to him! I must see for myself,' insisted Destine.

'Absolutely not!' Quaint spat. 'Nastasi has taken over Bara Mephista's camp for himself. That place is going to be swarming with Scarabs!'

'Nastasi? You mean Godfrey Joyce's accomplice?' Destine said.

Quaint took a step back. 'Stop that!'

'Stop what?'

'Stop knowing as much about this as I do!' said Quaint. 'If I can't show off now and again, what's the world coming to? Bara Mephista isn't on the cards, Destine. It's too dangerous!'

'Even more reason why I must *go* there!' Destine snapped. 'I shall travel there on my own if need be, but I must make sure he is safe.'

'Madame, you will do no such thing! Have you not heard a word I just said?'

'You do not understand, Cornelius! You may have walked your own path these past few days, but I have also walked mine. If not for Ahman I would not have been able to set forth on my journey. He held my head up and kept me travelling in the right direction. I will *not* abandon him when he needs me!'

Sobek interrupted: 'Cornelius, if I may? I could not help but overhear . . . I remember seeing this man you mentioned, if only briefly. He was resting in the tavern. Our medical man Bephotsi was tending his wounds.'

'And when Nastasi attacked did he know that Ahman was there?' asked Quaint.

'No, I do not think so,' said Sobek emphatically. 'He was too preoccupied with making his grand speech of conquest, and your friend was secreted within the rear of the tavern. Even if Nastasi had seen him, the old man's presence would certainly not have concerned him. He had visions of victory dancing before his eyes; he was quite blind to detail.'

'And Polly North? What of her?'

Sobek shook his head. 'Who?'

'The Professor! She was tending to Ahman. She was the one who brought him to the camp,' said Quaint. 'Surely you saw her at Bara Mephista.'

'Sorry, Cornelius, no. The old man was alone.'

'Well, Polly's the resilient type, I'm sure she's fine.' Quaint rubbed his hands down his face and looked over at Destine's rigid expression. His former governess could still teach him a thing or two about pig-headedness. 'So . . . what do we do?'

'I have a suggestion,' Sobek said. 'Let my men and me deal with the Nile and the poison. We still have enough of us to complete the task. You return to Bara Mephista with your lady here. She is worried for her companion's life. Would you not feel the same?'

'I can't go anywhere, Sobek. I have to see this through to the end,' said Quaint.

'You have done enough, my friend,' said Sobek, as his imposing bulk towered a few inches above Quaint. 'We are more grateful than you can possibly imagine for what you have done this day, Cornelius . . . but as our Aksak often spoke: we Clan Scarabs are shapers of our own destiny.' Sobek reached down and picked up the map from the sand. 'This is what we needed to defeat these devils . . . and it was *you* who gave it to us. For that, you will have our thanks for ever. Now it is time to care for your own.' He gestured with his eyes towards Destine. 'You have to heed the lady's request. That is what you need to do now.'

'But the battle is far from won!' protested Quaint.

'Cornelius . . . not all wars are won on the battlefield.'

'But I can't just—'

'Yes . . . you *can*,' insisted Sobek. 'We shall make Faroud proud of us. We shall shed light upon the shadow of the Hades Consortium and dispel it from Egypt's lands once and for all.'

Quaint shook Sobek's hand firmly. 'Looks to me like you just talked yourself into a job . . . Aksak,' he said with a grin.

Sobek frowned, as a barrage of cheers erupted behind him. He turned to face his men, who had all risen to their feet. He raised his arms to meet their cheers.

Quaint pulled himself up into his horse's saddle and looked at Destine, already mounted upon hers. 'Well . . . you got your own way again.'

'Was there ever any doubt?' Destine replied with a triumphant smile.

CHAPTER LXV

The Mask of Guilt

DARKNESS HAD FALLEN abruptly during Cornelius Quaint and Madame Destine's journey to Bara Mephista. There was no dusk, no subtle degradation in light as the amber sky gave way to the night. There was just blackness. Quaint looked at the shadows of the Bara Mephista encampment before him. It was hard to believe that it had only been a matter of days since he had arrived in Egypt. He remembered the first time that he had seen this camp, striding resolutely towards the tavern, ready to take on the world – such was his belligerent nature (as Alexandria had called it).

'This is Bara Mephista?' Madame Destine said, looking around the settlement.

'Yes, this is it,' Quaint confirmed, dismounting his horse. 'The Scarab camp . . . but I can't tell if there's anyone at home.'

He strolled towards the fire-damaged tavern, refusing to take his eyes from it in case Nastasi and his fellow Scarabs tumbled through the door at any moment. But he supposed that was unlikely. It was fast approaching midnight and those Scarabs loyal to Nastasi would have been in position along the Nile some time ago – as would Sobek's band of renegade Scarabs, with any luck. As he listened to the stillness inside the building, he was perfectly aware that Madame Destine's eyes were upon him.

As she watched his broad shoulders rise and fall, she wondered what was passing through his mind. She could usually sense his emotions quite clearly, yet a part of him was shrouded from her sight, a part that she could not quite make sense of. He was consciously trying his best to hide it from her, whatever it was. He was fearful, yet not fear born of their situation – fearful that she might see what he had been forced to become in this struggle, how easily he had taken lives.

Quaint was desperate to mask it from her. He could not bear to see the look of disgust in her eyes. He could imagine it already and that was torture enough. Without his *compass* by his side, without her to question him, to guide him, he had been almost lost. He had made some questionable choices, yet he was sure that he was justified in what he was doing – but what if his judgement been impaired without her to guide his mind?

Destine approached him and stroked his shoulder gently, steering him back into the real world. She smiled at him. A smile that told him what he wanted to know. A smile that told him enough.

'Shall we go and find your friend, Madame?' he asked, offering her the crook of his arm.

Destine accepted and they approached the door of the unlit tavern. As Quaint pushed it open, it creaked like a cat's meow. The place was deserted and, by the looks of it, it had been abandoned in a hurry.

Quaint took the lead. He walked past the bar, past the table where he had first sat and spoken to Aksak Faroud, and past the door to the room where he had first met Polly North. A slight palpitation took flight inside his stomach as he pressed onwards, pushing open a door at the far end of the tavern, seeking Ahman.

Shafts of pearl moonlight illuminated a sheet-clad shape laid out on a table in the furthest room of the building. Destine pushed past Quaint's shoulder, her heart quickening in pace.

Ahman was so serene, so silent.

Tears flooded Destine's eyes. 'Is he . . .?' she said, her hands running themselves over his motionless body. 'Ahman, can you hear me?' She cupped his bristled cheeks and planted a kiss full on the man's lips. 'Ahman, please . . .'

Ahman slowly opened both his eyes, as if a spell had been broken.

'D-Destine?' he murmured. 'Is . . . is that really *you*?'

Destine beamed a smile back at him and the room seemed to get a little brighter.

'*Oui, mon cher,*' she said, each word a caress. 'I feared you were dead.'

Ahman squinted. 'I was only sleeping.' He yawned, rubbing his thumbs into his eyes. 'What is all the fuss about, ah?'

'I am so happy you are alive!' Destine cried, with another kiss.

'As am I,' agreed Ahman, 'especially if this is to become a regular side-effect!'

'When you fell, I thought I would never see you again,' said Destine. 'How are you feeling?'

'Better, now that I have had a day to rest. My shoulder still aches though . . . and I am thirsty,' Ahman said.

Quaint reached into his satchel for a canteen of water and offered it to the elderly carpet trader. Ahman drank heartily, slurping mouthful after mouthful as if he would never stop.

'So who is this, Destine?' he asked eventually, water dribbling down his beard.

'How rude of me!' Destine scolded herself. 'Ahman, this is Cornelius . . . Cornelius, this is my good friend Ahman.'

'We've met.' Quaint shook Ahman's hand and the carpet trader winced in pain, his hand shooting to his shoulder. 'I'm glad to see you well, sir. It was my band that found you by the road in Umkaza's outskirts, do you remember?'

'So I have *you* to thank for saving my life, ah?' said Ahman. 'Without your aid, I would not be here. Destine has told me much about you, Cornelius.'

'I wish I could say the same,' Quaint said. 'I'm glad the Professor took good care of you. So where is she anyway? Don't tell me the Scarabs put a sack on her head.'

Ahman pulled at his bearded chin. 'Hmm. I have not seen her today. I have been very tired, you see, and have hardly spent more than a few hours awake at a time. I do not blame her for occupying herself in more stimulating company! Perhaps you should check with one of the Scarabs located herein, ah?'

'I would, but the place is deserted,' said Quaint. 'They've all left.'

'Without saying goodbye? Just like a Scarab. No manners!'

Destine rubbed at Ahman's bearded cheeks. 'I am glad to see your smile once again, *mon cher*. There was a time when I thought that I would never see it again.'

'Maybe I'll give you two some time to catch up,' Quaint said, with a wink to Destine. 'I need to check this place out more thoroughly. Polly's got to be around here somewhere.' The conjuror started towards the door, when something caught his attention on the floor.

It was a solitary envelope.

Something willed him to pick it up. He turned the letter over and his eyes darted left and right across the address on the front.

'Here, Madame . . . you must have dropped this,' he said.

Destine snatched the letter from his hands, recognising her handwriting immediately.

'Madame Destine Renard – Letter 3 of 3."

Quaint looked over at her. 'You look surprised to see it, Destine.'

'Indeed I am, my sweet,' the Frenchwoman muttered. 'Where did it come from?'

'It was just down here on the floor,' said Quaint perplexed. 'It's addressed to you, right? So . . . did you not drop it?'

'*Non*,' Destine said simply, sensing a fiery tingle at the back of her mind.

'So what's it doing here?' Quaint asked.

When he received no reply, he looked first at Destine and then at Ahman.

'I will explain later, my sweet . . . but if this letter runs true to the form of the others then I must read it at once!' Destine snapped, as she opened the envelope hastily and snatched out the letter inside.

Her heart pounded as she read aloud:

'Dear Destine,

If you are reading this letter, then you have found the third of my markers, and now your task is almost complete. Aloysius sacrificed his life so that the Pharaoh's Cradle would never be unearthed. His journal contains the only record of its location, and so if you are to prevent the unthinkable, the book must be destroyed.

We cannot allow this secret to be discovered.

The past and the present shall entwine once more. Beware the dawn of the Eleventh Plague.

May God bless you.

All my love,

Destine.'

CHAPTER LXVI

The Eleventh Plague

'MADAME, WHAT DOES that note mean?' asked Quaint, staring at the fortune-teller's wide eyes.

'This was the third marker . . . this letter!' Destine exclaimed.

'You've had more than one of these?' Quaint asked.

'*Oui*! This latest is but one of three. The others I stumbled across in Agra Bazaar when I was reunited with Ahman. We set forth from Agra desperately trying to piece together the legacy that my younger self had left for me. I had to discover what Aloysius was trying to tell me.'

'Yes, but this note talks about Aloysius's journal,' said Quaint. 'The same journal that Godfrey Joyce was going on about last night. He seemed awfully keen on getting his hands on it. He was convinced that I had it, for some unknown reason.'

'No, it is all right, Cornelius,' said Ahman, happy to join the conversation. 'I took the journal from Destine. It must be right here with my things.'

'The book!' Destine snapped impatiently. 'We must destroy it if the Pharaoh's Cradle is never to be found.'

'The Pharaoh's Cradle?' asked Quaint. 'But that's the artefact that Polly was after. Why would you not want it to be found? What does this letter mean?'

'It is my last warning,' said Destine.

'Yes, but a warning about what?' snapped Quaint. 'Is anyone going to explain any of this to me?'

Madame Destine huffed at his impetuousness. 'Cornelius, on our journey here, I explained to you that I was in Umkaza in 1833 when Joyce and Nastasi attacked, remember? They wanted to get hold of the Pharaoh's Cradle, but I learned that it was a most dangerous treasure, and one that if it saw the light of day again would trigger a catastrophic event.'

'Define "catastrophic event",' said Quaint warily.

'Back then, my premonitions warned me that the tomb was not all it seemed. It was infected with a bacterium that could be passed on by the merest touch of flesh upon flesh. It was deadly within one month of infection,' explained Destine. 'Once Aloysius learned of his benefactor's plot, he dug up the Pharaoh's Cradle and hid it away so that the Eleventh Plague would be contained . . . killing himself in the process.'

Quaint scratched his curls, lost in confusion, but then he clamped his hand onto Destine's shoulder. 'What did you just say?'

Destine began, 'Killing himself in the—'

'Not that bit!' yelled Quaint, startling the fortune-teller. 'What did you mean about his benefactor's plot? Which plot?'

'The plot to use Aloysius as a means to transport the bacterium to England, where he would unknowingly infect the greatest minds of the Empire . . . not to mention anyone else whom he came in contact with,' said Destine, lowering her head. 'Aloysius was tricked and betrayed by so many. Godfrey Joyce, Nastasi . . . and finally by his benefactor, a Chinaman named—'

'*Cho-zen Li*,' Quaint gasped. 'Professor North's benefactor.'

'Professor North . . . your companion?' asked Destine.

'The very same,' said Quaint grimly. 'Cho-zen Li sponsored her dig . . . her dig to Umkaza . . . to find the—'

'*Pharaoh's Cradle?*' Destine gasped. 'Just like he did in 1833. When was this?'

'Recently . . .' mumbled Quaint, pacing the floor.

Madame Destine's hand darted to her mouth. 'How recently?'

'As in right now!' Quaint snapped. 'That's why she was in Umkaza! To find the bloody thing – and on Cho-zen Li's instructions, to boot. He promised her that it was there . . .'

'That is what he told poor Aloysius also,' said Destine.

Quaint snatched at the air in frustration. It was as if the truth was playing hide and seek within him. 'But this is utterly preposterous! Why would Cho-zen Li hire the Professor?'

'To finish what he began?' suggested Destine. 'As preposterous as it sounds, is it any less so than the other coincidences that have befallen us, Cornelius.' She folded her arms and presented Quaint with a cold glare. 'Think about it, my sweet: I arrive in Egypt to discover an unknown past from twenty years ago, when I was a friend to Aloysius – a man who just *happened* to be your old school tutor and father of your old flame! Meanwhile, you have allied yourself with a professor who just *happened* to be searching for the exact same artefact that Aloysius was seeking in 1833 – and just *happened* to be sponsored by the very same man.'

'All just happenings, Destine,' said Quaint.

'These are twists of fate, my sweet – they are not just happenings! Aloysius told me last night that his journal pointed the way, but I just assumed that he meant his account of Joyce's betrayal. He told me that I must warn others of the danger that sleeps beneath the sand. He said that I must warn them of the danger of the Eleventh Plague.'

Quaint scowled. 'Now I'm even more confused. You just said that Aloysius told you this last night. I thought he was supposed to be dead.'

'He is,' confirmed Destine. 'His ghost told me.'

'His *what*?' asked Quaint.

'His ghost,' Destine repeated.

'His *ghost*?' asked Quaint.

Destine stamped her foot resolutely. '*Merde*, this is insufferable! This letter must have been hidden in the journal all along. Curse me for not spotting it! I could have saved us a long journey and a heap of trouble, Ahman.'

Quaint turned to Ahman; he had forgotten he was in the room. 'Bedford's journal, can I see it?'

'Yah, it is right here,' said Ahman, pushing himself unsteadily onto his elbows. He searched amongst his pile of clothes, frowning intensely. 'At least it . . . it *was* right here.' He produced a folded piece of paper and handed it to Destine. 'Look! You have written another letter! Perhaps this explains things in more detail, ah?'

Destine's heart missed a beat as she darted to pick up the letter, but her anxiety quickly subsided. '*Non, mon cher*, this appears to be a note from someone called "Pollyanna". It is not one of mine and I am thankful for that!'

'Pollyanna?' asked Quaint, as he snatched the note from Destine's hand.

The moments that it took him to read the words seemed to hang in the air for ever, and his face grew steadily darker by the second.

'Oh, Polly . . . what have you done?' he whispered, before reading aloud:

'30th December 1853.

Mr Ahman, I pray that when you wake you can forgive me.

Please know that I only have the truest intentions. As an archaeologist, just as Aloysius Bedford was, I have a zest to see the truth unburied. When he disappeared all those years ago, all his findings vanished with him, as well as his fantastic journal. There is enough in this book alone to spend a lifetime decoding. Now, at last I have a chance to complete the work that he began in Umkaza.

Pollyanna.'

Destine grabbed for Quaint's arm as he concluded the note.

'But, Cornelius . . . if this woman has Aloysius's journal . . . then she knows where he buried the Pharaoh's Cradle! If she is going to Umkaza, then all my efforts to avert a tragedy will be undone!'

'*Was* going to Umkaza, you mean,' corrected Ahman. 'Look at the date at the top of that letter. Today is New Year's Eve, ah?' The room fell silent as realization dawned. 'This letter was written *yesterday*.'

'*C'est mauvais!*' said Destine.

'It's worse than that, Madame,' said Quaint, chewing his lip. 'The Professor told me that she's got to get back to England in time for a function in her honour at Buckingham Palace . . . in the presence of Queen Victoria herself.'

'But . . . if she has opened that tomb—' started Destine.

'Then she'll be giving the Queen a hell of a lot more than just treasure,' Quaint said, completing the sentence. 'Just when I thought this thing was at an end . . .'

CHAPTER LXVII

𝕿𝖍𝖊 𝖀𝖓𝖍𝖆𝖕𝖕𝖞 𝕹𝖊𝖜 𝖄𝖊𝖆𝖗

A SHORT TIME LATER, the atmosphere in Bara Mephista was the exact opposite of how Cornelius Quaint was feeling. The tavern erupted in a riotous uproar, with much singing and dancing and revelry, as Sobek and his Scarabs returned. Quaint's insides were churning and his mind was doing much the same, beset by thoughts of Polly.

Sobek came over, clamping his hand onto Quaint's shoulder.

'Well, my friend, we did it!' he cheered. 'My men and I dispersed to every location. We found Nastasi's Scarabs and defeated them soundly. They never knew what hit them! Many of them had questioned Nastasi's ploy and turned away from him, so blood did not always need to be spilled. Once the balance shifted in our favour, we managed to defeat the Hades Consortium troops as a united clan.'

'And the poison?' asked Quaint.

'All the vials were destroyed,' said Sobek. He gave Quaint's ribs a nudge. 'Not bad for a bunch of thieves, eh?'

Quaint smiled. 'And what of Nastasi? I can't imagine the council will be too thrilled at his failure.'

'The Council of Elders knew nothing about it!' replied Sobek.

'It was all a ruse on Nastasi's part. He claimed to have the council's backing when he rode into Bara Mephista . . . but when I contacted them, they had no knowledge of such an order. They will deal with Nastasi in their own way . . . and it will neither be pleasant nor painless – of that you can be sure.'

'So what next? Do I call you Aksak Sobek?' smiled Quaint.

'I await the council's decision . . . but Rakmun appealed for me and as the former Aksak's kin, that goes a long way,' Sobek said, staring out into the desert flatlands. 'Maybe we Clan Scarabs have outgrown the old ways. None of us are young men any more . . . and few of us have families or loved ones to speak of. Perhaps it is time that we considered the future. Your influence no doubt, eh?' he said with a heavy slap on Quaint's back.

Rakmun strolled out of the scorched tavern and joined them. The young Scarab caught Sobek's eye and the larger man understood, making his way back into the tavern with a nod. Quaint turned to Rakmun, an expectant smile on his face.

'My brother, Cornelius . . . he sacrificed so much to save me from Godfrey Joyce's prison . . . and I never even got the chance to say thank you,' began the young Scarab. 'Many times I thought that help would not come. That I would die down there in that stinking cell and no one would even know. And then I would think of Faroud and I knew he would come for me. He should have known that he was risking everything by trying to free me. Yet it did not stop him.'

'Your brother was one of the most courageous men I have ever known, Rakmun. It was an honour to fight by his side,' said Quaint.

'I shall miss him, Cornelius.'

'As will I, Rakmun . . . as will I.'

'And now what of you?' asked Rakmun. 'I hear you are leaving.'

Quaint nodded. 'For Cairo, straight away.'

'I cannot convince you to stay and enjoy the revelry?'

'Not this time. Something has come up and I need to return to England immediately. I just have to make a little stop in Hosni first,' replied Quaint.

'Hosni?' Rakmun asked. 'What takes you to that place?'

'A tricky situation of the female variety,' smiled Quaint.

'Well, I wish you luck, Cornelius. If ever you are passing Bara Mephista again, our tavern door will always be open for you. And before I forget . . . Happy New Year!' Rakmun said, grasping Quaint's hand.

CHAPTER LXVIII

The Parting of the Ways

THE SUN WAS rising and the red mountains that dwarfed the settlement bathed everything in shadow. Up on the incline, Madame Destine and Ahman walked.

'Your mind is made up then? I cannot change it?' asked Ahman, his right arm in a makeshift sling.

Destine shook her head. 'I am sorry.'

'But . . . I do not understand, Destine. The danger has passed! Cornelius said the Hades Consortium was defeated . . . their base wrecked. There is no one left to fight. You belong here in Egypt, Madame . . . you belong here with me.'

'*Non, mon cher*. . . I do not,' Destine said gently. 'If Professor North is not intercepted, she will succeed in delivering death to Queen Victoria's door. Cornelius will need me and my rightful place is by his side. That is where I truly belong.'

'At what sacrifice to yourself?' Ahman clamped his eyes shut to deny the tears, but it was too little too late. They leaked from the corners, down his face, consumed by his bearded cheeks. 'Cornelius is a grown man . . . he does not *need* you any more!'

'My dear, sweet Ahman . . . I do not expect you to understand, but I have my gifts of clairvoyance fully restored now. I can see what the future holds.' Destine paused, taking a slight breath. 'You are wrong about Cornelius. I have seen what is to come in his future and his trials are far from over. When he learns the truth, he will need me more than ever.'

'The truth?' Ahman asked. 'The truth about what?'

'The truth about his parents,' she said simply. 'Cornelius will pursue his enemy to the ends of the earth, muddying his soul until he becomes one with the darkness . . . and I fear it will destroy him.'

Ahman watched the flicker of sadness in her eyes. 'And you will tell him?'

'*Non, monsieur*, it is not a revelation that Cornelius can be told . . . it is something that he must *learn* . . . no matter how painful it will be.'

The carpet trader looked at the fortune-teller and mouthed dry, barely heard words.

'I know . . . and that is why I must say goodbye,' Madame Destine replied.

CHAPTER LXIX

The Lucky Conjuror

SOME HOURS LATER, Cornelius Quaint stepped out of Rakmun's horse-drawn cart, leaving Madame Destine sat in the rear. He placed his hands on his hips and looked at the door to Alexandria Bedford's workshop, just as he had done only a few days before. He had opted for a change of clothing en route from Bara Mephista. A grey cotton shirt was tucked neatly into a pair of overlong khaki trousers, with thick braces stretched tight against his chest. Alexandria would surely approve. Despite his change in attire, his face displayed every inch of his recent adventure. Dust engrained itself into his wrinkled face, and the lines around his eyes spread out like dirty cobwebs. It was hard to believe that only three days before he had stood in the exact same spot nervously waiting to knock upon Alex's door, except then he was asking for aid – this time he had something to offer *her*.

'I won't be long,' he said, reaching for Destine's hand.

She offered him a brief smile, but she could not look him in the eyes – not just yet, her separation from Ahman was still so raw. She wore a white lace veil over her face and a band of golden trinkets was tied around her forehead. She looked every inch a fortune-teller once more.

Quaint placed his hand flat upon the seamstress's door. He could feel the gentle vibrations of machinery inside and he knew that Alexandria was home. His heart rose and fell at the same time as he knocked upon the wood.

'It's me . . . Cornelius,' he called.

The sewing machine's row abated.

Quaint hovered on his toes, waiting for the door to open, and for Alexandria to leap with joy into his arms, elated at his safe return. But he might have waited there all day and that would never have occurred.

'You are still alive then?' Alexandria shouted from inside.

'Just about,' replied Quaint.

'What do you want, Cornelius?'

'I promised to say goodbye, Alex . . . and I would much rather do it in person than from the other side of this bloody door!' Quaint responded, careful not to provoke the woman's temper. This conversation would be hard enough as it was, without a fight.

After a long wait, Quaint heard the door's latch being lifted and Alexandria's brown eyes peered around the small gap at him.

'Goodbye then,' she said, attempting to close the door, but Quaint jammed his toe in the frame before she had a chance. 'You might as well come in.'

After an awkward pause, Alexandria finally accepted Quaint's company and he was offered refreshment, with her dropping 'You certainly look as if you need it' into the proposal. She brought a carafe of fresh orange juice and they soon retired to her rooftop garden.

'I suppose I should congratulate you,' Alexandria said, seating herself.

'For defeating the Hades Consortium?' asked Quaint.

'No . . . for not getting yourself lynched by the Clan Scarabs,' Alexandria replied in clipped tones.

'Ah, they're a bunch of puppy dogs once you get to know them!' said Quaint, with a wave of his hand. He had not expected a warm welcome – which was advantageous, as he certainly did not receive one – nevertheless, he had learned much of Aloysius Bedford's disappearance and Alexandria had a right to know what had happened to her father.

'Sit, if you like. You are making the place look untidy,' offered Alexandria, sipping orange juice from her glass tumbler.

'I'd rather stand, Alex . . . I don't have much time.'

'I know you hate long goodbyes, but you have only just arrived,' laughed Alexandria, her dark eyes floating across Quaint's strait-laced expression. 'Let me guess . . . more obligations? Well, I suppose that I should feel honoured that you can spare me the time to say goodbye . . . it is more than I got the last time.'

'Alex, I'm tired and I could really do without this, if it's all the same,' Quaint said. 'A lot has happened over the past few days.'

'I have no wish to hear you boldly recount the tale of your adventure.'

'Perhaps not . . . but you *need* to hear it anyway,' Quaint said firmly. 'It's important . . . it's about your father.'

Alexandria remained silent. She sat on the edge of her seat and waited for Quaint to continue. And continue he did . . .

'I've learned much of late . . . about myself, about the Clan Scarabs, about Egypt . . . and much about your father.' He paused, expecting an interruption, but none came. 'What I have to tell you will shake you, Alex. It will shake you to the core of your being . . . but I think it may just help to heal a few old wounds.'

Ten minutes later, Cornelius Quaint had completed his tale, and he and Alexandria stood at the edge of her flat rooftop, their hands entwined.

'My father . . . did not leave us of his own volition?' Alexandria said, her eyes sore with tears. They flowed effortlessly, twenty years' worth of pain. 'He sacrificed himself, you say . . . so that others might live?'

Quaint held Alexandria's hand ever tighter, as if she was in danger of floating away from him. 'His last act was one of heroism, Alex, not of cowardice. Aloysius had to run away . . . but he was not running away from those he loved – he was running *for* them. He was infected with the disease. His death was inevitable. The only thing that he could do was get himself as far away from people as he could.'

Alexandria felt herself falter and she stepped away from the roof's edge, almost falling into Quaint's embrace. 'That is good to find out, Cornelius. But how can you know that?' she asked.

Quaint bit his lip. Your father's ghost visited a friend of mine and told her, sprang into his mind, but he thought better of it. 'Destine stumbled across Aloysius's old journal. It was all in there . . . word for word. Unfortunately, it was lost,' he said, happy with his discretion.

'So I have wronged him all these years then? He *was* capable of compassion . . . of love . . . of courage.' Alexandria looked desperately into the conjuror's black eyes trying to find an explanation within them.

'He was,' Quaint said, the words cooling on his lips. 'If he hadn't discovered what Cho-zen Li planned to do to the most intelligent minds in England, we could all be stuck in the dark ages by now! Your father gave his life so that others would live.'

'I have carried anger for him in my heart for so long,' Alexandria said, and the tears fell relentlessly. She had long since given up wiping them away. 'How could I have wronged him so badly?'

'You felt betrayed, Alex . . . no one can blame you for that,' said Quaint.

'*I* can blame me!' she yelled, her eyes ignited with a raging inferno of self-loathing. 'I do not weep for *him*, Cornelius – I weep for myself. All these wasted years . . . the years of hating him and yet loving him at the same time. How can I bear to look at myself in the mirror? How can *you* bear to look at me?'

Alexandria's body seemed to have trebled in weight and she could no longer support it. Shattered by guilt, she slumped herself deeper into Quaint's arms. How many people had she hurt over the years because she could never allow anyone to get close . . . never allow herself to trust? How long had she wrapped herself in a cocoon of such bitterness? How many men had she allowed herself to love? The answer to that was just the one . . . and he was stood by her side.

Here he was, close enough to touch, close enough to hold – but still a world away.

'When do you have to leave?' she asked through trembling lips.

'Right away.' Quaint steeled himself, swallowing back the emotion. 'I have to get to Cairo as fast as I can and try to cobble passage on the quickest vessel out of this country.'

Tiny formations of anxious saliva congregated at the corners of Alexandria's mouth as she tried to speak. 'Will you not stay with me, Cornelius?'

Quaint broke from their embrace abruptly. 'Alex . . . please don't ask that of me.'

'But why not?'

'Because I might just say yes,' Quaint said. 'Alex, in another world . . . another lifetime . . . another *me*, perhaps . . . I would stay in a heartbeat. But I have responsibilities that must take precedence. I cannot ignore them. I wish that I could.' His face flashed a brief smile, but his eyes stayed as dark as pitch. 'It seems that once again, Fate has selected me as its plaything . . . and once again, I find myself being drawn back to England's shores just when I—'

Alexandria cocked an anxious eyebrow at him. 'Just when you what?'

Quaint stopped himself from answering.

'Time is always our enemy, Cornelius,' Alexandria said. 'You and I never seem to find enough of it. Even if we could live for ever . . . there would still not be enough.'

'You cannot *possibly* appreciate how ironic that statement is to me, Alex,' said Quaint. 'Maybe I'll come back and tell you one day.'

'I would like that,' the Egyptian woman said, gathering up her courage, wiping away her tears. 'You want swift passage to England, you say? Well, I may just be able to help you out with that.' Alexandria pushed past him through the door to her inner quarters and darted down the whitewashed staircase into her shop.

Typical Alex, Quaint thought, one minute she's begging me to stay and the next she's practically booting me out the door!

Downstairs in her workshop, Alexandria began sorting through pile after pile of material covering a large desk that Quaint had not even noticed.

'I have a friend who owns a spice clipper,' she said. 'Captain Madinah's craft is blindingly fast, superior to all other vessels in the port. From what you have said, I imagine that you will be going after Cho-zen Li as well?'

'Once I disrupt his plans for the Queen . . .' replied Quaint.

'Well, I have something here you might be able to make use of,' Alexandria said, as she finally produced a dusty old ledger from under a roll of silk, which she discarded absentmindedly onto a nearby chair. 'He placed an order with me, remember? That coat over there that you loved so much? I have his home address, if you want it.'

Quaint's mouth fell open at the serendipitous development, and he tapped upon his teeth with his fingernails. Perhaps some coincidences were not that bad, after all.

'And I suppose you might as well keep this.' Alexandria lifted a dark indigo, almost black, long-coat from the rail at her side. 'I presume that you will have to kill Cho-zen Li, and finery like this is simply *wasted* upon the dead,' she said, throwing the coat towards Quaint. 'It must be your lucky day!'

'Alex, I sailed halfway around the world to save Egypt from destruction,' he said, with a reflective, melodic tone. 'I have been tied up, beaten, tortured, blown up and almost damn near *killed* on a number of occasions. I rescued a hot-headed professor from a gang of vile thieves that I was then forced to *ally* myself with. I defeated an old enemy's plot, only to discover a brand new one waiting in the wings . . . and now I must race steamship across the ocean to save the life of a queen who is under threat from something that she cannot see, cannot hear and cannot touch.' Cornelius Quaint offered Alexandria a defeatist grin. 'Oh, yes . . . I have simply *fabulous* luck.'

The End

Cornelius Quaint's destiny unfolds in:

The Lazarus Curse

We hope you enjoyed *The Eleventh Plague* by Darren Craske. We think that it is as good as the *Flashman* novels but if you don't agree please send the book back to the address below complete with a till receipt or proof of purchase and we will refund the cost plus 75p postage.

The Friday Project
HarperCollins*Publishers*
77–85 Fulham Palace Road
London W6 8JB